Catching Feelings

Catching Feelings

La Jill Hunt

www.urbanbooks.net

Urban Books, LLC
300 Farmingdale Road, N.Y.-Route 109
Farmingdale, NY 11735

ISBN 13: 978-1-64556-714-1
EBOOK ISBN: 978-1-64556-715-8

First Trade Paperback Printing February 2025
Printed in the United States of America

10 9 8 7 6 5 4 3 2 1

Distributed by Kensington Publishing Corp.
Submit Orders to:
Customer Service
400 Hahn Road
Westminster, MD 21157-4627
Phone: 1-800-733-3000
Fax: 1-800-659-2436

Prologue

"I think you're overreacting, Mason."

"Guess what? Right about now, I don't give a damn what you think."

Sabrina's eyes widened as she stared at her fiancé. She knew he was upset, but she didn't appreciate the way he was talking to her. She hadn't even done anything and was attempting to point that out to him, but his anger was preventing him from being rational.

Be nice, she told herself. *Remember, you're at work, not at the crib. Remain calm.*

She placed the cup of coffee she was holding on her desk, then walked over and closed the door to her small but cozy office before saying anything else. The morning was not going at all like she planned. It was Friday, her favorite day of the week. The only thing she was supposed to be dealing with today was taking care of some last-minute paperwork and chilling until noon, when she planned on taking off to enjoy the long weekend.

When Sabrina had arrived at the Bright Haven Hospital Pediatric Speech and Hearing Clinic, her dream workplace for the past four years, the usually bustling waiting room was eerily quiet. Typically, this space would be alive with the sounds of children's laughter and chatter as they enjoyed toys and activities under the watchful eyes of their parents. Today, however, the room was nearly empty. The large TV mounted on the wall, usually the favorite spot that kept the kids engrossed in the latest animated film, remained silent. It was the week after Christmas, and with most of the staff on vacation and only a handful of clients scheduled, the place felt abandoned. Even the coffee machine was cold and untouched, reflecting the lull in activity. Unable to function without her daily dose of "liquid crack," as her mother called it, Sabrina had run downstairs to grab a quick cup. She was pleasantly surprised to see Mason standing in her office when she returned. She was even more surprised to see him holding a crystal vase containing a beautiful arrangement of red roses and white chrysanthemums.

"Oh, my God, baby, they're gorgeous!" she gasped. "Thank you so much."

Just as she was about to rush over and hug him, she paused, noticing the frown on Mason's face. "What's wrong?" she asked.

"I'm not the one you should be thanking," he said.

"Oh, really? And just who should I be thanking?"

"Well," Mason said, removing the card and reading, "'Sabrina, you mean more to me than you'll ever know. Thanks for always being there. Love, K-Boogie.'"

Oh, shit, she thought, staring at the flowers. *K-Boogie. Thanks a lot, Khalil.*

"Mason . . ."

"What?" Mason's voice escalated. He was breathing so hard that she could see his chest rising and falling in the charcoal gray suit he wore.

"You know Khalil and I are just friends. Don't start tripping." Sabrina made sure her voice was soft and reassuring, knowing that she was going to have to point out why his reaction to the situation was clearly ridiculous.

"Oh, I ain't started tripping yet," Mason said and dropped the flowers into the trash can beside her desk. A few of the rose petals landed on the floor beside it.

"That was rude," she told him, folding her arms. "You need to calm down, for real. I can't believe you're acting this way over some flowers."

"And I can't believe you're playing me like I'm Boo Boo the Fool."

"How? For God's sake." She shook her head. "It's Khalil. He's engaged. Hell, Mason, we've double-dated with them, or have you forgotten that? As a matter of fact, have you forgotten the fact that *we're* engaged?"

When she and Mason started dating, she had made a point of mentioning her platonic male best friend early on. Introducing Khalil to Mason was one of her first priorities, hoping it would put Mason at ease and perhaps spark a friendship between them. Although Khalil was open and accommodating, Mason never seemed to warm up to him. While her family and other friends enjoyed the inside jokes and shared memories they often talked about, Mason found their interactions more tolerable than genuinely engaging. Sensing his slight discomfort, Sabrina eased back from Khalil, limiting their phone conversations to when Mason wasn't around. But every now and then, Khalil forgot about the boundaries she'd put in place, hence why she was once again having this conversation.

"No, I haven't forgotten that, Sabrina. But maybe you need to remind Khalil, or K-Boogie, as you call him, that his ass is engaged and so are you. Obviously, he forgot that little fact, especially when his ass called you at three thirty in the morning."

"Mason, he drunk dialed me. You know how Khalil is when he gets drunk."

"What I know is that Khalil wants to fuck you."

Sabrina stared at Mason like he was crazy. Clearly, he had lost his mind. "Are you smoking? I can't believe you even said that, Mason."

"I can't believe a lot of things, Sabrina. This shit with you and Khalil is getting real old, and I'm tired of—"

"What shit, Mason? We're friends and we work together. Other than that, there's nothing going on between Khalil and me."

She stared at him. He actually looked hurt, and she didn't understand why. She had been friends with Khalil Coleman since freshman year of college, when they were both 18. He was cute, athletic, smart, flirtatious, and funny. He held all the basic qualities that attracted women. But because he was overtly aware that he held those qualities, it made him arrogant and, most of the time, an all-around asshole in her opinion.

Sabrina realized this the moment they met and believed that because she failed to swoon over him unlike all the other females he encountered, she earned a certain level of respect from him. They had always been and always would be cool. They were 30 and still the best of friends, and despite Khalil being older, successful, and genuinely kind, he was still an arrogant asshole.

"I think the problem is that you don't realize there's something going on between you and Khalil."

"Mason, I know you have some trust issues, and because of that, I can see how you could possibly be misreading some things." Sabrina reached over and touched his chest. "But, baby, I promise we are just friends."

"Naw, you used to be friends." Mason shrugged.

Confused, Sabrina took a step back. "What?"

"Your friendship with Khalil is over as of right now."

"So, now you're telling me who I can and can't be friends with? I don't think so. I told you there's nothing going on between us, and if you can't deal with that, that's your issue, Mason."

In that moment, Sabrina looked down at the ring on her left finger. Nine months ago, she met Mason, and for the past three, they'd been engaged. She loved him deeply, but his insecurities were becoming increasingly burdensome and starting to get to her. At first, she thought the way he constantly called to check on her and make sure she was okay was cute. But she soon realized his concern wasn't from a place of love but stemmed from a fear of infidelity. He wanted to make sure she wasn't cheating, or thinking about cheating, or anywhere with someone who may tempt her to cheat. Mason's past was littered with tastes of betrayal—his mother, sister-in-law, best friend's wife, even his next-door neighbor all betrayed men they claimed to love. He was haunted by mistrust.

Knowing this, Sabrina reassured him that she was happy and would never betray him. She went out of her way to accommodate his anxieties, keeping him updated on her whereabouts, checking in if she was running late or had a change of plans. Still, Mason's trust remained elusive.

A moment of clarity came over her, and Sabrina realized that his lack of trust wasn't about her. It was deeply ingrained in him. She understood that even if it weren't Khalil, Mason would always find someone to doubt. There was no getting over this, no moving past this, no working through this. It was too much, too exhausting, too frustrating, too demanding, and not what she wanted in life or in love. Their relationship was unsustainable, weighed down by the exhausting cycle of suspicion and mistrust often leading up to their previous breakups.

Sabrina closed her eyes and heard her mother's voice in her ear, reminding her of what real love meant, how real love felt, and why, if love is real, it can overcome, overshadow, and overpower everything that comes against it. Despite her affection for Mason, she knew their love lacked the strength to withstand his insecurities. And even though it was painful, she understood that love shouldn't be suffocated by doubt and suspicion. True love wouldn't make her feel suffocated or controlled.

"What the fuck are you doing?" Mason frowned at her as she slipped the ring off her finger and held it out to him.

"I'm doing what needs to be done," she sighed.

For the last time, I'm doing what needs to be done.

"So you're ending what we have over this nigga, and yet you swear ain't nothing going on between you two. Ain't this a—"

Sabrina shook her head. "It is what it is, Mason. I can't do this anymore. I've told you over and over again that I'm not that chick. I'm not her!"

"What? What chick?" He continued to stare at the ring without taking it.

"I'm not the type of woman who sneaks off behind your back and disrespects either you or what we have. I'm not the one who is always looking for the next best thing or checking to see if the grass is greener. If I'm with you, I'm with you. I have tried and tried to explain it to you over and over again, but I get it now." She reached and grabbed his hand, forcing it open and pushing the ring into his sweating palm.

Please, God, let me be doing the right thing, because right now, the fact that I'm standing before this fine-ass, gainfully employed, intelligent, charismatic specimen of a man who loves me and giving him this ring back seems crazy as hell.

"What needs to be done is you need to leave Khalil's ass alone, Sabrina. That's all I'm asking you to do," he pleaded with her. "He wants you. You can't see what I see. A man knows."

"And a woman knows, Mason." She shrugged.

She had told Mason early on in their relationship that she didn't believe in arguing in a relationship, and it was something she just didn't do. Sabrina hated tension and refused to feed into situations that she knew would possibly lead to an argument. She didn't get the whole yelling and screaming, back-and-forth thing while trying to prove a point. Sabrina would simply listen, reply, and move on, simple as that.

Mason's forehead wrinkled, and he took a step back and stared at her. She looked into his eyes and searched for some sort of clue, some sign that would send a signal to her heart that maybe it could work. But there was nothing but peace. Peace and a sense of sadness that she knew would eventually pass.

"So, what, this is it? It's just over? Just like that?"

Sabrina just nodded and again reached out for him.

"Fine then, Sabrina, if this is the way you want it." Mason brushed past her and paused before opening the door. "The sad part about this is that I really thought you were the one."

"I am the one, Mason," Sabrina replied. "I'm just not the one for you."

Chapter 1

Sabrina

"Happy New Year, fam!"

"Hey, baby. Happy New Year." Her father stood and gave her a hug. Sabrina couldn't help feeling like a 4-year-old as she squeezed her arms around him. She had always been and always would be a daddy's girl.

"Hey, Daddy. Happy New Year," she said, then leaned down and gave her mother a kiss on the cheek. "Hi, Mommy. Happy New Year."

"Same to you, baby." Her mother grinned. The scent of Oscar de la Renta filled Sabrina's nostrils. Frances Chambers had worn the same perfume for years and refused to change. Her husband and children realized this after several years of buying her other scents. Frances had been grateful, but she still had yet to wear anything other than her infamous Oscar de la Renta.

All three of her children had inherited Frances's good looks. Tenille and Sabrina both had her high cheekbones, dark, piercing eyes, and dimpled smile. But where Tenille and her mother shared the same deep copper complexion, Nicholas and Sabrina were the smooth, chestnut brown color of their father.

"And happy anniversary to you both." Sabrina smiled, pulling a card out of her Coach purse and handing it to her father.

"Awwww, Brina, thank you." Her father pulled her into his arms again and squeezed her.

"What's up, Aunt Brina?"

"Boy, you better get up and give me a kiss." Sabrina pulled Marquise, her adorable 11-year-old nephew, out of his chair and kissed his dimpled cheeks. He was the spitting image of her sister, and her heart melted every time she saw him. "Mook Mook!"

Marquise frowned and tried to escape her grasp. "Aunt Brina, come on, this is not cool."

"I remember a time not so long ago when you weren't too cool to kiss your auntie, Mook." She laughed.

"Brina, leave that boy alone." Nick laughed, motioning for his nephew to return to his seat.

"Ewww, you got stuff on your lips." Marquise wiped the shiny lip prints off his cheeks, causing the family to laugh even harder.

"So, where is Mason?" her mother asked, looking toward the door.

Sabrina looked over at Nick, whose eyes were on the now-empty ring finger of her left hand.

"Ohhh, snap! Another one bites the dust." Her brother grinned, then turned to Tenille with his hand held out and said, "Pay up, sucker. Hahaha!"

"Pay what?" Sabrina snapped. "I know y'all ain't place bets."

"Fa sho, shorty." Nick winked.

"That better not be what your brother is talking about." Her mother shook her head and glanced over at Tenille and Nick.

Tenille was too busy reaching into her purse and taking out her wallet to notice her mother's stare. "I can't believe this. I swear, Nick, I thought this time—"

"You placed bets on my engagement? Now that's just—"

"Wrong," Sabrina's mother finished her sentence for her. "You both owe your sister an apology."

"I'm sorry, Brina. But at least I didn't bet *against* you, like some *other* people." Tenille looked over at her father.

"Daddy!" Sabrina gasped.

"Johnny, I don't believe you." Her mother swatted her father on the arm.

"It was all done in fun and in love, sweetie." Her father smiled.

"Hey, at least I put my money on you." Tenille passed her brother and father each a $10 bill. "A lot of good that did me."

"Y'all are just wrong." Sabrina shook her head. "Placing bets on my love life like it's some kind of game."

"Hey, don't get mad at me 'cause the odds of love are against you, sis," Nicholas said, folding the money and putting it into his pocket. "They're against me too."

"That's not true, Nicholas. I'm not even gonna let you sit here and say that." Their mother frowned. "Give me that money."

"The odds of love aren't against me." Sabrina suddenly felt the need for a drink. It was only eleven fifteen in the morning, and she rarely drank in front of her parents, but none of that mattered at that moment. *There's no way I'm gonna be able to deal with Ten and Nick if I don't have a drink.*

She motioned for their waitress. "Can I get a Cîroc and lemonade?"

"Dag, hard liquor in the morning?" Nick grinned. "I guess I struck a nerve."

"Nicholas, help Marquise make his plate," their mother commanded.

Nicholas didn't hesitate as he stood up. "Come on, Mook. Let's go get our grub on."

"Johnny, baby, make sure you get me some of that ham." Frances turned and lovingly stroked her husband's hand, slipping the tens out and passing both bills to Sabrina.

"I guess that's my cue to leave too." Their dad nodded. The three males headed off to the crowded buffet line.

"Make sure he gets some vegetables on his plate," Tenille called after them.

"Ten, it's breakfast. Why would he get vegetables?" Sabrina shook her head.

"Actually, it's brunch. He needs to put something healthy on his plate," Tenille answered, "other than chicken."

Sabrina laughed. There was nothing in this world Marquise loved more than chicken. He really didn't have a choice since that seemed like the only thing Tenille ate while she was pregnant. Fried, baked, broiled, barbequed, grilled, boiled, roasted, stewed, braised, fricasseed—as long as it was chicken, Tenille was gobbling it. She ate so much chicken that they just knew Marquise was going to come out clucking, and he should have been named Colonel.

"Leave that baby alone." Frances smiled. "Chicken is good for him."

The waitress returned with Sabrina's drink, and before she could place it on the table, Sabrina took it from her and took a long swallow. The smoothness set off an instant relief within her, and she felt her body relax. *Okay, that's better.*

"Well?" Tenille asked.

"Well what?" Sabrina asked as if she had no idea what her sister was referring to.

"You know what." Tenille gave her a knowing look. "What did poor Mason do, or should I be asking what did he *not* do?"

"Shut up, Ten." Sabrina rolled her eyes. "It's not even like that. And while we're getting all in my business, where is your husband?"

"Working, and at least I actually have one." Tenille sat back in her chair. "I'm trying to help you figure out how to get one. Now talk."

"I hate you." Sabrina squinted.

"Sabrina, you don't hate your sister, so don't say that." Frances sighed. "Tenille, just let her explain what happened. Go ahead, baby."

Whether Sabrina even wanted to explain what happened obviously hadn't crossed either one of their minds. It also hadn't crossed Sabrina's mind either. She knew if she didn't explain, they would harass the hell out of her until she did. At least her mother had been gracious enough to excuse the men from the table. Not that that mattered, because one thing about the Chambers family was if one person knew, the entire family knew.

"I just realized that it wasn't gonna work." Sabrina shrugged. "I wanted it to. I really did."

"I don't understand. Mason is such a sweet guy," Tenille said. "Great job, smart, nice looking. But then again, so were all the rest of your ex-fiancés."

"So, what are you saying, Ten?" Sabrina glared at her older sister, who always seemed to have a permanent chip on her shoulder these days. The vibrant, vivacious woman who smiled all the time seemed to be buried somewhere within, and Sabrina had been sensing something was off for a while. On the outside, Tenille was still as beautiful as ever, but there was a slight dullness about her.

"I'm saying that maybe you need to reevaluate what's really going on. You're developing a pattern," Tenille replied.

"First of all, I know what's going on. Let's get that straight right now." Sabrina felt herself becoming angrier by the minute. *What the hell is that supposed to mean? Reevaluate?*

"Tenille, that's enough. And why are you taking your sister's breakups so personally?" Frances frowned.

"Thanks, Ma. I'm sitting here wondering the same thing," Sabrina said.

"I'm not taking anything personal, especially not her breakup*ssssss*." Tenille stressed the plural.

"Sabrina, I think Tenille is right about one thing: there is a pattern here." Frances gave Sabrina a knowing look. "So, what was the problem with Mason? You two seemed happy."

"In a sense, we were happy, Ma. But then again, how happy am I if I have to explain my every move to the man I love? How happy can I be if I have to defend every relationship I have and jump through hoops to prove that I really want to be with him and only him?" Sabrina stated. "He wasn't the one. He just wasn't."

She saw the understanding in her mother's eyes and knew that breaking up with Mason was the right thing to do.

"If that's the case, then I'm glad you realized it before it was too late." Her mother smiled at her.

"I still don't understand what brought about this great epiphany." Tenille frowned. "Mason's had you on a short leash forever. That's nothing new. What happened? Details, please."

Just as she was about to speak, a loud voice seemed to come out of nowhere. "Looks like we came to the right place at the right time, baby. Look who's here."

Sabrina cringed as she looked up to see Khalil and his fiancée coming toward the table. "Oh, no, not now."

"Khalil!" Her mother smiled and stood up to greet him with a big hug. "It's so good to see you."

"You too, Mama C." Khalil kissed her on the cheek.

"K-Boogie, man, what's the deal?" Nick said with a wide grin as he returned to the table along with her father and

Marquise, who were equally excited to see Khalil. Before Sabrina knew it, her father had invited Khalil and his date to join them and they were making room at the table.

"I'm going to make my plate." Sabrina stood up and motioned the waitress for another drink. She turned to her sister and nodded toward Khalil, who was teasing Marquise. "By the way, *that's* what happened."

Chapter 2

Tenille

"Oh, my God, Tenille, they're gorgeous!" Bianca, the bride, gushed.

"Wow," was the only word Darrell, the groom, could utter.

Tenille knew the instant she saw the pictures that the newlyweds would be pleased. She had captured moments of the wedding that normally wouldn't even seem relevant. Brief, intimate snapshots of their perfect day included a close-up shot of the crystal-studded sandals Bianca wore, a photo of Bianca's wedding ring precisely placed in the middle of her bouquet, and a picture of Darrell's grandmother dabbing tears from her eyes as the minister prayed over the couple.

"I'm glad you like them." Tenille smiled.

"I can't believe you got all these great shots. I didn't even realize you were taking pictures half the time," Darrell told her.

"That's because the only person you noticed was her." Tenille pointed to Bianca. "And that's the only person you were supposed to notice."

"That's right." Bianca nodded. "I'm the one and only woman you're supposed to be noticing."

"Don't worry, Darrell, she couldn't take her eyes off you either," Tenille said. "Look at that picture right there."

Darrell reached over and stared at the picture of him talking to one of the guests. Bianca was standing right beside him, securely tucked in his arms, staring at him as if she were hanging on to his every word. They looked as if they were made for each other.

"I don't see how we're gonna decide which ones to buy." Bianca shrugged and stared at her new husband. The cute couple was still glowing from their Caribbean honeymoon cruise. "Awww, Darrell, look at this one with your brothers."

"I'll give you guys a moment to decide." Tenille stood up.

"Naw, we know what we want," Darrell said.

"No, we don't. Darrell, what are you talking about?" Bianca looked over at him.

"We'll take all of them," he said, smiling.

"Darrell, we can't afford all of these pictures." Bianca shook her head.

"Baby, what did you tell me the entire time you were planning our wedding and I said we couldn't afford something?" Darrell reached over and put his arm around her.

Bianca smiled. "I said that there were some things we couldn't afford *not* to do."

"We can't afford *not* to get all these pictures." Darrell pressed his forehead against hers.

Tenille watched the exchange between the two of them and smiled. *They got it. I see it. It's there.* She had been taking wedding photos for a decade and as a full-time professional for the past three years. Not only did she have a gift for capturing precise moments on film, but she had also developed a sixth sense for those couples who had a level of love that was so deep it radiated. Unable to resist, she worked out a deal for the happy couple to purchase all the photos.

"Another satisfied couple?" Noelle, her new office manager and assistant, asked as Tenille walked Darrell and Bianca out of the studio.

"Of course," Tenille replied. "They purchased every last shot."

"Wow, I knew they had to be balling to hire you." Noelle gave her a knowing look. "But I didn't know they were balling like that."

Tenille shrugged and admitted, "I gave them a deal."

"I figured that. So, you let them get everything for what? Four?"

"Thirty-seven."

"Thirty-seven? That's not a deal. That's a steal." Noelle shook her head. "Those pictures were worth way more."

Tenille was pleased. Perfect Ten Photography had come a long way since she opened. When she started, she only booked two to three weddings a month and charged a couple hundred dollars. Since then, Tenille had become one of the most sought-after wedding photojournalists on the East Coast, not only doing weddings, but also magazine and advertising layouts. The starting price for her wedding packages was now over $3,000, and she was booked nearly a year in advance.

"They definitely got their money's worth," Tenille agreed.

"So, are they going to be one of your LLCs?" Noelle asked with an inquisitive grin.

After years of shooting weddings, Tenille had developed a knack for spotting what she called "Long Lasting Couples." These were pairs who shared a connection so profound it seemed almost divinely ordained. It was a special kind of bond she had learned to recognize early on in her career.

"Yes, they are." Tenille nodded, and her eyes glanced at a photo of another couple displayed on the studio wall. The couple demonstrated the epitome of long-lasting love.

Thirty-five years, that's a long time, Tenille thought as she looked at the pictures of her parents that she took at their anniversary brunch. They had been married as many years as she had been alive. She would be celebrating her thirty-fifth birthday on Valentine's Day. She stared at the happy couple who raised her and smiled. *True love.* They were so happy, always had been.

She continued flipping through the pictures of her family. Sabrina stared back at her in the next photo, looking as gorgeous as ever, perfectly poised with their parents. At times, she wondered if her sister was crazy and would ever make it down the aisle. It was as if she would meet these great guys and accept their proposals, get the ring, and then miraculously realize that they weren't "Mr. Right" and break it off. Mason had been fiancé number four. *I hate to be the one to tell you, Brina, but perfect ain't possible.*

The next picture was of Nick, Marquise, and her father, all three men sharing the same mischievous grin. Her brother was a self-proclaimed, bona fide player. He barely dated the same girl twice and had come to the conclusion that he was destined to be single and satisfied the rest of his life. As far as Tenille was concerned, both her brother and sister had issues, serious ones, unlike herself.

A lie! her inner voice said. *Your issues are just as serious as theirs. Look at that picture.*

Tenille glanced up at her own wedding photo. There she was, dressed in a gorgeous gown, makeup and hair perfectly done, smiling as she stood next to Brandon, her husband. They looked like the typical married couple, but Tenille saw something that she wondered if everyone else saw when they looked at the picture. Her sadness. It was the weirdest thing. A woman's wedding day was supposed to be the happiest day of her life. The day that she had planned and been waiting for her whole life. The day she said, "I do," and was joined in holy matrimony with her soulmate. For Tenille, that wasn't the case. She was happy, in a sense, but instead of feeling overwhelmed with emotions of happiness, she felt empty and couldn't understand why. Brandon was a great guy and had everything a woman wanted in a husband. He was good-looking, a hard worker, a great provider, laid-back, nice, dependable, and he loved her. What more could she want? There was no reason for her not to marry him, so she did. Now, five years later, she was still empty.

"Tenille?" Noelle knocked on the door. "I have your itinerary for next weekend. I made sure you got a window seat."

"I'm more concerned with if you got me a first-class seat," Tenille teased. She didn't know how Noelle did it, but somehow she was always able to get her bumped up to first class without paying more or cashing in her frequent flyer miles. She was also able to get upgrades at hotels and resorts at no extra charge. Hiring her had been even more beneficial than she thought.

"Of course, you know I did." Noelle smiled. "Are you sure you don't need me to accompany you and assist?"

Noelle assisted Tenille with the last three weddings she shot, all of which had been larger weddings with over 200 guests in addition to large bridal parties. She knew this was one of the weddings she would love to assist with, especially since it was a destination wedding in Montego Bay, Jamaica. She didn't blame her for trying.

"I'm positive. You know the wedding is small, only about fifty people. No assistance needed. Thanks for offering though." Tenille smiled and took the file from her.

"I can't wait to go with you on the good trips," Noelle hinted.

"You just went with me to San Francisco," Tenille reminded her. "Not only was that wedding fabulous, but we got treated like royalty."

"I want to go on the exotic trips!"

"Believe me, you'll get to go. But remember, the more exotic the trip, the smaller the wedding."

"Tell the couples you can't travel without your new assistant. Then I can go," Noelle suggested. "The more the merrier."

"Okay, I'll suggest that," Tenille said.

"Your flight gets in late Sunday evening. You need me to pick you up, or will your hubby be there waiting with flowers?"

The thought of Brandon waiting for her at the airport with flowers almost caused Tenille to crack up laughing. She didn't think he had ever bought her flowers. Flowers and romance were not her husband's strong points.

"Sparkle is gonna pick me up. It's no big deal." Tenille shrugged. Sparkle was her best friend of over twenty years.

"Does he ever travel with you? It seems like the destination weddings would be a great chance for you and him to sorta hang out and spend some uber-romantic one-on-one time." Noelle winked.

Tenille almost laughed out loud again. Instead, she said, "You know he works a crazy schedule at the shipyard."

That was a true statement. Brandon was a longshoreman and worked a crazy schedule that included days, nights, weekends, and holidays. The pay was great, but he put in long hours.

"Well, it was just a thought," Noelle said as she walked out of the office.

Tenille looked back at her wedding photo and sighed. "Empty."

Chapter 3

Nick

Oh, Maria, Maria
She remind me of a West Side story
Growin' up in Spanish Harlem
She livin' a life just like a movie star

Nick sang along as he pulled his car into the parking lot of Horizon Telecom. Although there were plenty of empty spaces near the front of the building, Nick parked all the way in the back of the parking lot where he was sure no one would park near his car. He reached in the back seat and grabbed his new Armani blazer before stepping out and slipping it on. Clicking the alarm and checking his reflection, he was just about to walk off when a car came dangerously close to hitting him as it pulled into the space next to him, music blaring loudly.

"Man, you don't know how close you came to meeting your Maker," Nick yelled when the driver stepped out.

"Whatever, I know how to drive. Wasn't nobody about to hit your ass," Eric Thurmond, his coworker and best friend, laughed. "Nice jacket."

"Thanks." Nick adjusted his jacket. "A little something I picked up this past weekend."

"And you waited all week to wear it?" Eric shook his head. "Today is Thursday."

"Don't be mad because you wear your new gear on Mondays. I have self-control, bro."

"What the hell ever. So, you rolling out this weekend or lying low?" Eric asked.

"Haven't decided yet," Nick replied. Eric had been wanting to go on a road trip for a while. Normally, Nick would be packed and ready to go at the drop of a hat, but lately, he hadn't really had the desire.

"Man, what's wrong with you? You've been flaking out on hanging since Christmas." Eric shook his head. "Let me guess, you found a winter boo already. Who is she?"

"Naw, man," Nick replied.

"Then what's the problem? You getting old?"

"Never that," Nick told him, and he pointed to two women walking toward the building. "Look, Sheridan and Dannica."

"My, my, my, what a lovely sight to see early in the morning," Eric said loud enough for the ladies to hear.

The women paused, turned around, and smiled. Both dressed in high-end pantsuits and heels and carrying designer briefcases, they exuded professionalism yet still gave a hint of sex appeal.

"Oh, no, here comes trouble." Sheridan, the darker of the two women, shook her head at them.

"Where? I need to be running from it," Eric responded. They hurried and caught up with the ladies. Eric reached over and took the large box Sheridan was carrying out of her arm. "Let me help you out there."

"How noble of you," Sheridan said.

"What are you two doing here?" Nick asked.

"Interviewing for a new hire class," Dannica told them.

"Word?" Eric grinned. "Fresh meat."

"Calm down, man-whore," Sheridan snapped.

"Why am I a man-whore?" Eric smiled innocently.

"Boy, please." Dannica rolled her eyes. At five six, she was slightly shorter than Sheridan and a little thicker. Nick knew Eric had a thing for her.

"So, how long are y'all in town for?" Nick asked.

"Depends, maybe a month or so," Sheridan answered. "So, you guys have plenty of time to wine and dine us."

The four of them typically hung out when the ladies were in town from Dallas, where they were based in the home office. Their per diem cards covered meals at the city's trendiest restaurants and clubs, thanks to the company. The only expense they had to cover themselves was drinks, as company cards couldn't be used for alcohol. Nick always looked forward to these outings. Dannica and Sheridan were both great people. Plus, the fact that Nick and Sheridan had been discreetly seeing each other for the past year added a personal perk. They kept their relationship under wraps not only because company policy frowned upon fraternization but also because Nick wanted to avoid any misconceptions about them being a couple.

"Word." Nick nodded. "Where are y'all staying?"

"The Montclair downtown," Sheridan answered as they walked into the large glass building and headed toward the elevator. "It amazes me that as large as this company is, they're still not willing to spring for security. Anyone can walk in this piece and go postal."

"Don't be scared, sweetheart." Eric winked. "Big Daddy E will keep you safe."

"What the hell can you do to protect us, Eric? Flirt someone to death?" Dannica teased. Nick couldn't help laughing along with them.

"Oh, y'all just chock-full of jokes today, huh?" Eric snapped. "And you're supposed to be my boy and have my back."

"I do, E. But that was funny," Nick admitted.

"Whatever. Here, you carry this, Sir Laugh a Lot. This is my floor." Eric shoved the box into Nick's arms as the elevator stopped on the third floor and the doors opened.

"You're not gonna come upstairs with us?" Dannica pouted.

"No, I'm not. I have a team to manage, and I need to be there for them in case an intruder gets in the building and I have to flirt them to death." Eric stepped off the elevator and started to walk away.

"Don't be like that, Eric," Sheridan called after him.

"What time do you wanna go to lunch?" Dannica added.

"Twelve fifteen," Eric answered without even turning around. "I'll meet y'all downstairs."

"He is so damn sensitive." Sheridan laughed. "I don't know why you give him such a hard time, Danni. You know he has a crush on you."

"Because he's so damn cocky. He thinks all the women want him."

Nick glanced over at her and said, "Well, uh, most of them do."

Not only was his friend the epitome of tall, dark, and handsome, but he had a style and personality that attracted women. Much like Nick, he wore tailored suits that effortlessly accentuated his tall, athletic frame. His wardrobe was a blend of classic elegance and modern flair—crisp dress shirts, slim-fit trousers, and fitted blazers, often paired with the perfect pair of shoes that completed his ensemble. Accessories were carefully chosen: a stylish watch, a silk pocket square, or a subtle, high-quality tie. It was Eric's personality that made him a chick magnet. He had an innate ability to make others feel comfortable, enhancing his allure. It was this combination of impeccable style, self-assuredness, and genuine charm that made him irresistibly attractive.

"And that's what his problem is. He's used to women falling at his feet. I don't know why. I mean, look at Nick."

"Me?"

Dannica continued talking as if Nick weren't on the elevator with them. "He's cute, fine as hell, funny, and can dress his ass off. He has no kids, a good job, and his condo is the bomb."

"That's true. Nick does have it going on." Sheridan nodded. "He's definitely a catch."

"Exactly, but he doesn't try so hard. He knows he's a hot commodity and doesn't have anything to prove to anybody. Nick has . . ."

"Swagger," Sheridan said.

"Yeah, swagger," Dannica repeated.

"Ahem, I don't know if y'all realize it or not, but I'm still on the elevator with you," Nick told them.

"Uh, you work on the sixth floor, the same floor as us." Dannica stared at him like he was crazy. "Why wouldn't you be on the elevator with us?"

"You thought we didn't see you, Nick?" Sheridan glanced at him knowingly.

Nick felt an urge in his manhood and smiled, knowing he would be in for a treat sooner rather than later. Their "friends with benefits" relationship was casual, the way he liked it: no expectations, no strings, no emotions. And strangely enough, the same way it worked for him, it worked for her. Just two friends enjoying each other's company and, when the mood struck them, having great sex. What more could he want?

The doors of the elevator opened, and he followed the two women to the training room and put the box down on a nearby desk.

"So, twelve fifteen?" Sheridan asked.

"Twelve fifteen." He nodded.

Her comment on his being “a good catch” echoed in his head. As he headed to his office, he hoped she wasn’t trying to change the way things were. Right now, things were exactly the way he liked them.

Chapter 4

Sabrina

"Sabrina Chambers," Sabrina answered her desk phone.

"Brina!"

"Emily," Sabrina said.

"What are you doing?"

"Working."

"Yeah, right." Suddenly, Sabrina's office door opened, and Emily, her best friend, walked in and plopped down in one of the two chairs in front of Sabrina's desk. "Guess what?"

"Have you ever heard of knocking? I could be in here with a client or having a meeting." Sabrina put the phone back on the receiver.

"Then you wouldn't have answered your phone."

Sabrina shook her head and waited for Emily to talk. She was glad to see her and needed the comic relief she was sure she was about to receive. Emily worked as a nurse in the critical care unit of the hospital. She was bright, bubbly, and everyone loved her.

"So, are you gonna guess or what?" Emily said.

"Just tell me," Sabrina sighed.

"Ms. Edna wants to hook me up with her nephew."

"And what's wrong with that?"

"Don't you mean what's wrong with him?"

As soon as people found out Emily was single, they instantly went into matchmaker mode. Emily had gone on more blind dates than Sabrina could count, and sadly, none had ever resulted in a love connection. Most hadn't even been a "like" connection. But Emily, never one to say no, continued to go on the suggested dates on the premise that she enjoyed meeting new people.

"Why does something have to be wrong with him?" Sabrina asked.

"Well, according to Ms. Edna, he's thirty-one, no kids, a great job, owns his own home, and attends church," Emily replied.

"Wow, that does sound too good to be true. He's probably married."

"He can't be married. She wouldn't introduce me to him if he were married. That would be just plain wrong," Emily told her.

"Um, if I recall, didn't the other lady introduce you to her son who was married? The loan officer. What was his name?"

"Victor, and he was engaged, not married. Get it right." Emily laughed. "And she just wanted him to explore his options before he took the big plunge. That's all that was."

"She didn't like his fiancée, that's all that was."

"True."

"Is he shy?"

"From the way she describes him, he sounds really outgoing."

"Is he cute?"

"She says he's very handsome, and one of the other nurses confirmed he is."

"Hmmmm, good job, owns a house, which means good credit. Is he black?"

"Of course he's black. Why wouldn't he be black?" Emily's eyes widened.

"You've gotta be kidding," Sabrina said, amazed that Emily had asked that question.

"Everyone who knows me knows I don't play that." Emily's voice was full of attitude.

Sabrina stared at Emily, not saying a word, trying with everything within herself not to laugh. "I don't know, maybe because—"

"He's gotta be black," Emily said emphatically.

"Okay, so what if he's not? What difference does it make?"

"He's black."

"I mean, hell, men are men. Black, red, purple. Skin color doesn't matter. And it's not like any of us have had any luck with the black ones. Maybe it's time for you to broaden your horizons," Sabrina told her.

"Forget you. I don't see you going all Whoopie Goldberg these days and broadening your horizons."

"First of all, you know I don't have a problem with guys who aren't black. I just can't get past the whole 'pink' thing." Sabrina shuddered.

"You're crazy. They're not pink, Brina." Emily laughed.

"I've seen porn. They're pink."

"You really think he may not be black?"

"It doesn't matter, Emily."

"What doesn't matter?" a deep voice interrupted.

Sabrina looked up to see Khalil standing in the doorway of her office.

"K-Boogie! Happy New Year." Emily leaped up and hugged him.

"Emily, the finest nurse in the city. Happy New Year to you, sweetheart." Khalil smiled.

"Get out!" Sabrina snapped.

"Come on now, Sabrina, don't be like that," Khalil told her.

"Get out, Khalil. I mean it."

"Why are you being mean to Khalil? What did you do, K-Boogie?" Emily asked as she sat back down. She pointed to the empty chair beside her. "Come, sit, talk to me."

"Thank you, Emily," Khalil said as he plopped into the chair and crossed his legs.

Sabrina hated the fact that not only was he sitting in her office, but he was looking fine as hell. She noticed he was sporting a fresh cut, and his goatee was just as precise.

He even had the nerve to seem sincere when he said, "I didn't do anything. She's been pissed at me for a week, and I don't know why. She ignores my calls, my emails. She even ignored me the other day when I ran into her with the fam at breakfast."

"Sabrina!" Emily sounded shocked.

"What?" Sabrina asked.

"It's all good. I know she's going through a recent breakup." Khalil nodded. "Again."

"How dare you, Khalil? There wouldn't even be a breakup if it weren't for your ass," Sabrina hissed.

"So, you're blaming me for that? That's crazy."

"That is crazy, Brina." Emily nodded.

"Shut up, Emily," Sabrina said. Then she continued, "You! With all your drunk dialing and flower sending, you caused my breakup."

"I don't think that's fair." Khalil folded his arms.

"I don't give a damn what you think." Sabrina stuck her tongue out at him like a 6-year-old.

"Now, you do have to be fair, friend. You broke up with Mason because he was truly insecure. You said that yourself," Emily reminded her.

Sabrina gave Emily a dirty look.

"Everyone knew that brother was insecure, and it had nothing to do with me. Although a brother as fine as myself could be seen as some fierce competition."

"You damn sure didn't help the situation. Okay, if you knew he was so damn insecure and you were this big threat, then why the hell would you send me flowers?" Sabrina asked.

"I sent them to you at *work*. How was I supposed to know he was gonna show up here and see 'em? It was an apologetic gesture. And you still haven't thanked me, by the way." Khalil smirked.

"It was a nice gesture. You should really thank him." Emily nodded.

"Who made you Khalil's backup choir?"

"I'm just saying. You and Mason had issues. That was the reason you broke up with him." Emily shrugged.

"And Khalil made the issues worse."

"What? No, I didn't." Khalil frowned.

"Well, you definitely didn't help the situation, Khalil." Emily's head tilted to the side and she asked, "Why *do* you always call Sabrina when you're drunk?"

Khalil sat up. "I don't know. Probably because she's the only telephone number I remember when I'm drunk."

"Remind me to change my number," Sabrina said to Emily.

"Hmmmm, interesting. I don't know, I've always said that you two—"

"Don't go there," Sabrina and Khalil both said at the same time.

"Jinx!" Emily laughed. She looked down at her watch and jumped up. "Damn, I gotta get back upstairs. I love you both."

Khalil stood up and hugged Emily. "I love you too, girl."

Emily headed out the door but stopped and turned. "But, Sabrina?"

"Go on the date, Emily. It doesn't matter," Sabrina told her.

"It does matter," Emily said. "But I'll call you later and we'll discuss it."

When she was gone, Khalil said, "That's one crazy white girl. So, tell me, what doesn't matter?"

Sabrina stared at him with an evil grin. "Size. I mean, isn't that why you started hitting the gym and lost forty pounds?"

Khalil looked at her as he stood. Their eyes locked, and she braced herself for his response. To her disappointment, he turned and walked out without saying a word.

Sabrina knew she was being unreasonable, but she didn't care. Khalil was right. She was bitter over the breakup with Mason. It wasn't that she even missed Mason all that much. In a way, she was enjoying her freedom. But the reality was that she was alone, once again. She hated being alone. Being in a relationship made Sabrina feel special, significant, and most of all wanted. She enjoyed being the center of a man's world, being the one he desired, especially if he was a man she desired. She looked at the framed picture of her parents, which was sitting on her desk, and wondered if she would ever find a love as special as the one they shared. Before she knew it, she was crying and dialing Tenille's number.

"Perfect Ten Photography," Tenille answered.

"T . . . Ten." Sabrina sniffed.

"Brina? What's wrong?" Tenille's voice was full of worry.

"I don't know. I was talking to Emily, and then Khalil came in and . . . and . . . what's wrong with me? Why does this keep happening to me? I give up. Maybe everyone is right. Love isn't meant for me." Sabrina's lip trembled as she reached in her drawer and pulled out some Kleenex. Dabbing at her eyes, she waited for her big sister to comfort her. Tenille always made her feel better after her breakups, which often included a day at the spa and a great dinner at a fancy restaurant.

Tenille sighed into the phone, “Okay, Brina, get it together. I will not allow you to have another pity party over some nonsense.”

Sabrina was shocked by Tenille’s response. It was definitely not what she was expecting. “What do you mean, nonsense?”

“It’s nonsense. You know how special you are, and you know damn well you don’t need a man to validate that fact. The right man will come along at the right time, and you will have the right relationship. You’re beautiful, talented, smart, educated, and a good person. And that’s all the ego stroking you’re gonna get from me today. I’m packing, and I don’t have time to deal with you and one of your pseudo-psycho emotional breakdowns,” Tenille told her.

“Well, damn, I don’t know whether to thank you or hang up in your face, Ten.” Sabrina frowned.

“How about you thank me and then hang up so I don’t miss my flight.” Tenille laughed.

“Where are you going?”

“The beautiful beaches of Jamaica,” Tenille answered.

“You are so lucky. Who would have known that your nerdy knack for taking pictures would lead to all this? And how come you never ask me if I wanna come along?”

“Do you ever ask me to come along with you when you go to work? It’s not a vacation, Brina. I’m working.”

“I wish I could work in Jamaica. I would definitely find someone to occupy my time.” Sabrina laughed. “All those fine Jamaican men. You want them all to yourself. That’s why you don’t want me to tag along.”

“No, I don’t want any of them. I’m married, remember?”

“Whatever, you’re just as lonely as I am. That’s exactly what you need in your life, some excitement. You’re boring as hell these days. You used to be so much fun.”

“Whatever, Sabrina.”

"It's true. And your husband is even more boring than you are. All he does is work. He never hangs out with our family like—"

"I refuse to have this conversation with you, Sabrina."

"I'm just suggesting you have some much-needed fun while you're there. You know what they say—what happens in Jamaica stays in Jamaica."

"There's no such saying. I'm hanging up now."

"Bring me something back. Preferably a fine Jamaican man."

"I will. I love you."

"I love you too," Sabrina said before hanging up the phone. Although she didn't get the pampering and free meal she had hoped she would get, her sister did make her feel better. If nothing else, she realized that her life could be worse. She could be in a boring, routine marriage like Tenille was. There was no way in hell any man in his right mind would allow his wife, who was as gorgeous and outgoing as Tenille, to travel all over the world and work at weddings of all places. Weddings—the most romantic, sexy hookup events anyone could attend. And everyone knew the only reason men went to weddings was to meet women. Her brother-in-law was as dumb as they came. Yes, Sabrina definitely felt better.

Chapter 5

Tenille

The beautiful landscape of the Coyaba Beach in Montego Bay provided the perfect backdrop for Larry and Tiffany Crenshaw to exchange their wedding vows. They had met four years ago at Powell and Associates, the law firm where they were both competing for a junior partnership position. Neither one got the promotion, but they each found love, and it was apparent as Tenille captured each moment with her camera. Their wedding party was lively and full of laughter and rum, which made them a great group to shoot. It was one of the most fun weddings Tenille had ever done, and she enjoyed every minute of it.

"Tenille, you haven't stopped taking pictures since you got here. I need for you to put that camera down and enjoy yourself, girl," the bride's mother told her, yelling over the reggae band that was playing.

"I am enjoying myself. I'm doing what I love to do and having fun doing it." Tenille laughed as she turned the camera toward the woman and clicked another shot.

"Girl, stop it. Now, stop and have some food before I snatch that camera and smash it like you some paparazzi. You know how much this is costing me?"

"Okay, okay," Tenille sighed. "I got you."

"Come on, the bride and groom aren't even in here right now. They've gone to change clothes. Take a break." The woman grabbed her by the arm and pulled her along to the front of the buffet line, which Tenille was certain the folks behind her were not pleased that they had skipped.

As she piled her plate with curried shrimp, stewed chicken, and peas and rice, Tenille heard a voice behind her.

"Excuse me, do you have a card?"

Balancing her plate, she reached into her camera bag and pulled out one of her glossy business cards. She turned, their eyes met, and she felt the blood rush out of her head and from her face. Instantly, she felt faint, and he reached to grab her as she stumbled.

"Oh, my God," she mumbled. "What are you doing here?"

"You two know each other?" the bride's mother gushed. "What a small world."

"Yes, we've known each other for years," he replied, his eyes not leaving hers.

"What are you doing here?" Tenille repeated.

"I was invited, if that's what you're asking. Larry's brother and I are coworkers. Wow, you look amazing. Where's your partner in crime? You and Sparkle are always joined at the hip." He grinned at her. "I can't believe she's not here with you getting some poor, unsuspecting dude drunk and taking advantage of him."

"I'm here alone," she told him.

It had been years since she had seen him—six years, three months, and fourteen days to be exact. He looked the same, maybe a few more laugh lines in his dimpled smile. His hair might have been a little thinner, but his face was still strikingly handsome with his strong jawline and rich deep brown skin that seemed to glow. Her heart was pounding so hard that she wondered if everyone else heard it. Yes, he still had a way of making her lose her breath when she looked into his eyes.

"Let me carry that for you, Ten," he said, taking the plate from her. "I know you want some of these oxtails. Oh, and you gotta try this salt fish. You'll love it."

"Make sure she sits down and eats," the bride's mother told him. "She's working so hard that she's not having fun. Snap, snap, snap with the camera."

"I'm the photographer," Tenille explained.

"You're also a guest."

"I'll take care of her, Marie. I promise." He nodded.

"Thank you," Marie said, acknowledging that Tenille was in good hands before wandering off to make sure everyone else was taken care of.

"I can carry it." Tenille reached for her plate, but he shook his head.

"No, I got it," he said and gestured toward a nearby table. "Come on."

Her plate being held hostage, Tenille told herself that she had no other choice but to follow him. She tried not to admire the cream linen pants and shirt he wore with brown leather sandals. Instead, she adjusted the cream linen dress she wore and smoothed her hair.

Calm down, Tenille. It's no big deal. You run into people all the time while you're working. Today is no different. Just sit down, eat, be polite, and get back to work. Nothing more, nothing less.

They arrived at the table, and he pulled the chair out for her after placing her plate down. She thanked him and again nearly lost her breath when he leaned in close and whispered, "I'll go get you something to drink."

Tenille looked around the room, still somewhat in a state of shock, wondering if someone was playing some type of practical joke on her. At any moment, she expected Ashton Kutcher to jump out and say, "You've been punk'd," or, "Surprise, you're on *Candid Camera.*" Her unexpected reunion didn't faze her stomach, and it growled to remind her that it was empty and ready for the food sitting in front of her. She picked up a fork and started eating. It was amazing. The band softened, and the mood became relaxed.

"Here you go," he said, setting the ice-filled glass in front of her. "Your usual Arnold Palmer. I know you're working, so I didn't get any of the hard stuff. I figured we'll get something stronger a little later."

"Later?" she asked, putting down her fork and taking a sip. It was exactly the way she liked it: more tea with the exact right amount of lemonade. She wondered if that was a coincidence or if he'd ordered it that way.

"Later, when you're off the clock," he said.

"I'm leaving when I get off the clock," she told him.

"You're leaving tonight?"

"Yep," she lied. She wanted to discourage any ideas he had assumed about "later." There would be no "later."

He looked at her strangely. "Won't you be tired after working all day?"

"Yes, but I have to get home to my husband." She flashed her ring. Ironically, she often forgot to wear it, but she had slipped it on her finger after defending her marriage to Sabrina right before she left.

"That's right," he sat back in his chair and said. "You did get married. How's that going?"

"It's wonderful." She smiled. "I couldn't ask for a better marriage. You know, it's great. I mean, really good."

"That's good, Ten. I'm happy for you."

Tenille was relieved that she sounded so convincing. "I'm happy for me too."

"How're your parents?"

"They're good, and yours?"

"Mom and Pop are still hanging in there. They ask about you all the time. I still think Mom is a li'l mad at me." He laughed. "And how is Nick? Still a player?"

"Of course."

"And Brina? Did she and Khalil finally get married?"

"No, they're still friends, but she's single and he's engaged to someone else," Tenille told him.

"Whaaaaaat? I thought those two would be married with kids by now."

"I think she did too." Sabrina laughed. Then she asked about his daughter. "How is Fabian?"

"Fabian is still a good student, of course, but she's no longer shy. She's quite the social butterfly." He grinned.

"Like her father." Tenille laughed.

"If you say so. All right, now you know I gotta know." He leaned over and asked, "How is my boy?"

"Marquise is awesome. He's excited about going to middle school next year, you know."

"Middle school already? Wow, time really does fly." He looked into her eyes again. "Is he still playing ball? How tall is he?"

Tenille told him all about her son, and they ate and talked until the newlyweds reentered the room and the party reignited. She was having such a nice time that she forgot she was working.

"Well, my break is over," she told him, standing up. "It was nice seeing you and catching up."

"Indeed it was." He stood beside her. "I hate that you're leaving tonight. It woulda been nice to get a drink and talk some more."

"Time to cut de cake," the lead singer of the band announced, saving her from having to respond.

Tenille jumped into photographer mode and went back to capturing moments on film. As she snapped away, she forced herself not to think about his being there, in the same room, just feet away from her. Instead, she focused on Larry and Tiffany cutting the cake, Tiffany dancing with her father while Larry danced with his mother, the tossing of the garter, and the throwing of the bouquet. She concentrated on the best man making his speech and Tiffany's face as she fought tears while Larry raised a toast in her honor, instead of whether she was being watched while she worked.

A few hours later, the happy couple was off to enjoy their first night as husband and wife, and the crowd was thinning out.

"I can't wait to see the pictures," Tiffany's mother said as Tenille packed her camera up. "Thank you so much once again."

"It's been my pleasure," Tenille told her. "I had such a wonderful time."

"And you ran into your friend." She nodded. "He's such a sweetheart."

"We have a special request," the lead singer announced. "Dis one is for de fabulous photographer."

Tenille nearly dropped her camera as she realized what he said. The band began playing the familiar tune of Babyface's "Every Time I Close My Eyes," and she looked up to see him walking toward her, hand held out.

"Will you do me the honors? I had them play it just for you," he said.

"I told you he was a sweetheart," Tiffany's mother squealed, taking the camera bag and purse and pushing her toward him.

She must not realize I'm married. Or maybe she's too drunk to care.

Not wanting to be rude, Tenille took his hand and walked onto the dance floor.

"I can't believe you," she told him, clasping her arms around his neck and swaying to the music. The reggae beat the band gave the song made it even more sensual than she recalled.

"I couldn't resist, Ten," he whispered. "You always loved this song."

He was right, and the fact that he remembered made her love it even more. She closed her eyes and allowed him to pull her body closer to his. The familiar scent of Kenneth Cole Black and Dove soap filled her nostrils, and a chill went down her spine. They moved back and forth, not saying anything, just enjoying the music, the closeness, the moment, until, before she knew it, it was over. The crowd clapped, and Tenille quickly stepped back.

"Ten," he sighed and touched her cheek softly.

Tenille felt a lump rise in her throat. Although she loved seeing him, talking to him, even dancing with him, it was all too much. She walked over and took her belongings from Tiffany's mother and excused herself. The nearby bathroom offered a brief sanctuary and the privacy she desperately needed. She gazed at her reflection in the mirror, struggling to regain her composure and get herself together.

Tenille Chanel Chambers, get a hold of yourself. Chambers? That's not even your last name, fool. What's wrong with you? Are you that weak that you can't even handle seeing him after all these years? You are a married woman. You are here to do a job.

I've done my job, and I know that I'm married. You don't have to point that out. Granted, seeing him was shocking, but I'm good. The wedding is over, he's leaving, and so am I. I'm good.

Tenille checked her reflection in the mirror and reapplied her lip gloss. Satisfied with her appearance, she walked out.

To her disappointment, he was gone. She slowly walked into the parking lot and found her rental car. The long day had been exhausting, and she was drained.

The warmth of her luxurious hotel bed called to her. She hit the unlock button.

"So, you're really leaving?"

Tenille turned and saw him standing behind the car. "What?"

"You're leaving?"

"Yeah, I'm on my way to the airport now."

"That's funny, because Maria just called your hotel and left you a message about taking pictures at the bridal party brunch tomorrow."

Tenille shrugged. "I'm sure they told her I checked out already."

"Ten, you were always a bad liar." He stepped closer to her.

"I'm not a bad liar," Tenille told him. "I just could never lie to you."

"Come have a drink with me, Ten. I just wanna talk, that's all. There's this bar right on the beach."

"A bar on the beach? I don't think so."

"Okay, we can go to the bar at your hotel if that makes you feel safer."

Alone with him in the hotel, that's probably even worse, Tenille. This is wrong. Say goodbye, go to the hotel, and go to bed.

"What do you want from me?" She shook her head.

"I told you, Ten. I wanna talk. I get it. I know you're happy, and I'm happy for you. But hell, we're here, in Jamaica of all places, on this beautiful beach, and to be honest, I just wanna look at you," he sighed, then reached over and touched the necklace she wore: a white gold diamond-crusted X. "My perfect Ten. You still have it."

He had given her the necklace and charm for her birthday one year. She had never taken it off. Even after they were over, she could never bring herself to take it off. She had always been his "Perfect Ten," and she loved the nickname so much it was the name she gave her photography business when she opened it.

"I don't know."

One drink isn't too much to ask, Tenille. It's just a drink. A glass of wine will help me sleep better.

"One drink, Ten," he pleaded.

"One drink," she said and unlocked the door. He quickly jumped into the passenger side.

If anyone had told her that she'd be riding in a car with him, heading to a bar in Jamaica, Tenille would have thought they were insane. It seemed inconceivable. Their breakup years ago had been her decision, not his. The final conversation had been swift and amicable, making it easier to accept. They had even parted with a warm embrace. Yet for years, the heart-wrenching regret that gnawed at her whenever she thought of him lingered. The void left by their ended fairy-tale romance never healed, even during her marriage to another man. The only comfort she found was in pushing aside thoughts of him, burying the fond memories that once brought her joy. And now, here he was, sitting beside her and making her smile once more.

It's just one drink, she reminded herself.

Chapter 6

Nick

"Uncle Nick, can I get a margarita?"

Nick looked over at his nephew like he had lost his mind. "No, you can't get a margarita. You're not twenty-one, and furthermore, a margarita is a chick drink."

"It looks like a Slurpee," Mookie told him. "Does it taste like one?"

"No," Nick said, reaching across the table and taking the drink menu from him.

"How do you know what it tastes like? I thought it was a chick drink."

"Because I kiss chicks who drink 'em." Nick winked and held his fist out.

Marquise laughed and tapped his own fist against his uncle's. "That's why I wanna be just like you when I grow up, Uncle Nick. You are so cool."

"Stick with me, nephew, and I'll teach you everything you need to know."

"Know about what?" Nick's dad asked, taking a seat at the table.

They were at Scorekeepers, the local sports bar, preparing to watch the playoffs. The Chambers men were die-hard fans, and watching the games together on Sundays was routine for them. Nick appreciated the fact that it was a tradition that now included his nephew.

"Uncle Nick kisses girls who drink margaritas," Mookie informed his grandfather. "Isn't that cool?"

"I don't know about that. Women who drink liquor can be trouble."

"How?" Mookie asked.

"Well, Mook, alcohol can make women do some crazy things," Nick's dad told him.

"Like what, Granddad?"

"For starters, liquor brings out the wild side of women. There was this one time—"

"Dad," Nick interrupted his father before he started telling Mookie something he didn't need to hear. Nick had experienced firsthand his father's lack of discretion when it came to sharing what he thought was "manly advice." From the time he was 10 years old, an age when his father thought he was old enough to learn about being a man, Nick had heard more than his fair share of stories he was certain his father intended as life lessons that he would rather not have heard. He didn't want his nephew to endure them, especially since his father didn't really have a censor button when it came to certain subjects such as women, sex, gambling, and racism, to name a few. He would hate to think how he would have turned out if he didn't have his nurturing mother to counteract the tales his father told him of his life experiences.

"What?" his father asked.

Nick shook his head. "I thought you said Favre was injured this week."

"He was. Well, that's what they said on the sports channel." His father's attention now turned to the large screen showing Brett Favre warming up with the rest of the team. "I ain't worried. He's still probably aching from the whooping he took last week. He ain't a hundred percent, trust me."

"I don't know, Granddad. The Vikings always play harder during the playoffs."

The waitress came to the table, and Nick ordered their usual meal of hot wings, potato skins, a pitcher of beer, and instead of his desired margarita, a soda for Mookie.

"Is Eric coming?" his dad asked.

"No, he's still recuperating from last night, probably. I called him, but he didn't answer."

"That boy plays harder than I did back in the day, and I was a player."

"What did you play, Granddad?" Mookie turned and asked.

"Boy, you don't know? I played—"

"Dad!" Nick interrupted again.

"What? Everybody knows I played baseball. I was good, too! Better than Jackie Robinson. You know I used to play with Hank Aaron and his brother, Tommie. I was headed straight to the major league right along with them."

"Really?" Mookie's eyes widened. "What happened?"

Nick watched as his dad's eyes saddened. "Life happened, grandson."

Mookie's cell phone rang, and he pulled it out of his pocket. "Hey, Mom." His nephew excused himself from the table to go talk to his mother.

"You all right, Dad?" Nick asked. His father always seemed a little sad every time he talked about his near-successful baseball career. Nick, like his nephew, often wondered what happened, but his dad never spoke on it.

"I'm fine, son. So, how are things going for you at the job? Everything working out all right?"

"Everything is great, Dad," Nick told him.

"Nick, your mama was talking the other night, and she's worried because it's been quite a while since you've introduced us to any of your female friends."

Nick shook his head. "Why were y'all even talking about that, Dad?"

"I tried to tell her that you're just like your daddy, but she wasn't trying to hear that. I'm just giving you a heads-up that she's probably gonna say something to you about it."

"Thanks, Dad."

"Granddad." Mookie passed his cell phone to his grandfather.

"Your mom okay?" Nick asked.

"Yep, I told her about your margarita women," Mookie giggled.

"Mook, how many times have I told you that what is said between men stays between men, man? Come on, where's your loyalty?" Nick frowned.

"Mom says there are to be no secrets between us," Mookie answered.

"She's right," Nick told him, not wanting him to think that was what he was suggesting. "But it's not about keeping secrets. You don't have to tell everything that we talk about. You understand?"

"Yes." Mookie nodded.

The waitress brought the food and placed it in the middle of the table just before the game started. She smiled at Nick as she asked, "Did you want anything else?"

"Not right now." Nick smiled back. She was cute, in a Jada Pinkett Smith type of way, but a little too young for his taste.

"I'll make sure to check on you in a little while," she told him.

Nick said a quick prayer over the food, and they dug in, then became engrossed in the game, cheering and yelling.

"Come on, ref. Stop being soft and let the guys play!" Nick's father yelled.

"That was a foul and you know it. You were just complaining about them not calling one when one of your players got knocked down a few minutes ago, remember?" another fan of the opposing team yelled back.

"That was different. That was a real foul."

His dad's game commentary provided lots of entertainment for the other patrons who laughed and talked smack. Soon, it was halftime, and Nick was headed back from the restroom when he was stopped.

"Well, well, well, why am I not surprised to run into you here?"

He looked up to see Sheridan standing in front of him, wearing a tight-fitting Vikings jersey and jeans that showed off the perfect curves of her hips.

"Wow," was all he could mutter as she walked over and hugged him.

"The hotel bar was kinda wack, and the concierge told me this would be a cool place to watch the game," she told him.

"Yeah, this is my regular spot." He nodded.

"You here with Eric?"

"Naw, my dad and nephew," he answered, motioning with his head.

"This is the BS I keep telling you about, grandson," his dad yelled and pointed toward the televisions hanging over the bar. "The referees are biased against the NFL quarterbacks who didn't come from ACC schools."

"Yo, that's your dad? I was sitting back here laughing at him. He's off the chain." She laughed.

"Yeah, he's something," he told her. He thought about asking her to join them but felt that introducing her to his father may have been a bit much.

"Your nephew is cute, too."

"It runs in the family." He laughed. "Where is Dannica?"

"She won't be back until sometime later tonight. I came back early this morning to get a head start on work." She shrugged.

"So, does that mean you're gonna be busy later?" He reached over and put his hand on her hip.

"I guess you're gonna have to call me and find out." She winked and hugged him once more before walking away.

When he got back to the table, Mookie didn't waste any time asking, "Who is that lady you were hugging, Uncle Nick?"

Nick prayed his father was too engrossed in the second half of the game to hear what Mookie said, but when his father began looking around the bar frantically, he knew his nephew's question had been heard.

"What lady?" Nick's dad asked.

Nick rolled his eyes at Mookie and asked, "Didn't we just have this conversation like thirty minutes ago about loyalty?"

"I didn't tell Mama you were hugging a lady." Mookie blinked, looking innocent.

"What lady?" His father was now standing on his feet, still looking.

"Dad, sit down. She's just a girl I work with."

"You can't be hugging ladies you work with, Nick. You know they can get you fired, and you got a good job."

"It's all right, Dad. She's not gonna get me fired," Nick assured his father.

"Where is she?"

"Sitting at the table near the bar over there." Mookie pointed to where Sheridan was sitting. Nick reached over and playfully smacked him on the head.

"In the ugly jersey? Whoo, she is a cutie right there."

"Dad, sit down, please," Nick pleaded.

"I mean, she clearly has poor taste in football teams, but she is good-looking. Why didn't you invite her to sit with us? She's over there by herself. I'm surprised some hustler ain't made his move already and sent her a drink. You see, Mook, that's how you get a woman's attention when she's at a bar. You send her a drink."

"A margarita?" Mookie asked.

"Well, you ask the waitress to take her whatever she's having—"

"Come on, Mookie." Nick quickly jumped up and grabbed his nephew by the hand. They walked over to Sheridan's table. "Excuse me, miss. I was wondering if you'd care to join us over at the winning table even though you're wearing that loser jersey."

Sheridan gave him a look that let him know that if Mookie weren't there, she would have probably punched him. "Only if I get to sit next to the cutest guy at the table."

"Sure, I have no problem sitting beside you." Nick pretended that he didn't know who she was referring to.

"Not you, this handsome young man." She pointed at Mookie, who immediately began blushing, which, to Nick, was slightly odd considering the darkness of his complexion like his sister.

"Introduce yourself, Mook." He nudged him.

"Hello, I'm Marquise," Mookie said shyly.

"Nice to meet you, Marquise." She stood up, and Nick couldn't help notice Mookie's eyes glance at her cleavage.

My man. There may be hope for him after all, he thought as he led both of them to their table.

"Hello there, pretty lady." His dad immediately stood up and pulled out a chair for Sheridan.

"Sheridan, this is my dad," Nick said.

"Nice to meet you, Mr. Chambers." Sheridan shook his hand as she sat down beside Mookie.

The waitress came back to clear the table, and Nick noticed that the overt friendliness she had earlier was gone as she peeked over at Sheridan. "Will there be anything else?"

"I'd like to get the lady a drink," Marquise told her.

"And what would you like to order her?" Nick laughed.

"Whatever she's drinking, right, Granddad?" Marquise asked.

"That's right, Mookie. You're learning."

Sheridan laughed, then said to the waitress, "Strawberry margarita."

"Strawberry," Mookie repeated. Then he leaned over and whispered, "You should kiss her and see how that one tastes, Uncle Nick."

Chapter 7

Sabrina

Sabrina couldn't believe the weekend was over already. She had spent most of it indulging in retail therapy and pampering with Emily. After an early morning breakfast on Saturday, they went to their favorite beauty spa, After Effex, where they treated themselves to massages, manicures, pedicures, and facials, and then it was off to the outlet malls and dinner. Sunday, they were right back at it again after church, hitting all of the local malls, and her best friend even treated her to dinner at her favorite restaurant, Jaspers. Although Emily was just as much of a shopaholic as she was, Sabrina knew she was being extra nice to her. At first, she thought it was because Emily knew Tenille was out of town and didn't want her to spend the weekend alone, but as they pulled into Sabrina's driveway late Sunday night, Sabrina found out the real reason for Emily's undivided attention.

"Come on, Brina, it'll be fun. I promise," Emily said, referring to the charity singles auction she had submitted Sabrina's name and information to. "Best of the Bunch" was a list of the city's most eligible bachelors and bachelorettes who, after being featured in the newspaper, were auctioned off at the annual charity ball to raise money for the children's hospital.

"Uh, no, Emily. I can't believe you even agreed to that. You know it's not happening."

"It's for charity. I didn't think you'd mind since you're single and it's no longer a conflict of interest," Emily explained.

"No, I'm not doing it. End of discussion. Is this your Vicky's bag or mine?" Sabrina looked through the hot pink Victoria's Secret bags to make sure she got the one that belonged to her.

"Yours has the black lace set," Emily told her. "I would also like to point out that being asked to participate is an honor."

"I wasn't asked to participate. You volunteered me."

"I didn't volunteer you. One of the board members asked if I had any suggestions, and I mentioned you, that's all."

"You mentioned me to a board member for a singles auction, but you've never thought to mention me for a raise? A promotion? How about a grant?" Sabrina shook her head as she walked past Emily to unlock the door of her condo. The burglar alarm chirped, and she dropped the armload of bags along with her purse in the middle of the floor and rushed to enter the code into the keypad.

"Brina, your cell phone is ringing," Emily called out to her.

"Grab it out of my purse for me, please."

"It's the former groom-to-be!"

"Don't answer it. Send it to voicemail," Sabrina sighed.

"You didn't even ask which former groom-to-be it is." Emily laughed.

"I know which one it is. The same one who's been calling me all day."

Sabrina walked into the kitchen and poured two glasses of wine, then joined Emily, who was in her favorite spot in the den: the oversized lounge chair directly in front of the TV.

"Thanks," Emily said, taking one of the glasses from Sabrina. "Poor Mason. Why won't you talk to him?"

"There's nothing to talk about."

"Did you give him the ring back?"

"I told you I tried to, but he didn't want it. I told him I didn't want to keep it." Sabrina sat down on the nearby sofa, ignoring the house phone, which was now ringing.

"Maybe something's wrong." Emily kicked off her pink Coach sneakers. The shoes were a combination of Emily's two favorite loves: pink and Coach. Emily was a Coach fanatic. Shoes, purses, watches, jewelry, scarves—if it was Coach, she had to buy it, and if it was pink, she had to have it.

"Nothing's wrong," Sabrina told her, then, noticing Emily's socks, she added, "except for those socks you have on. Are those mismatched?"

Emily looked down at the footies she had on her feet, one light pink and the other pale pink, and replied, "They're both pink, they're both Fruit of the Loom, and they match my outfit."

A little while later, they were kicked back, watching TV and working on their second bottle of wine when Sabrina's doorbell rang. Sabrina glanced over at Emily and said, "That better not be Mason. He knows I don't play that popping up on my doorstep."

"Maybe if you'd answer your phone, you wouldn't have to worry about him popping up on your doorstep. Desperate times call for desperate measures."

"Well, he's about to get a desperate cussing out." Sabrina rushed to the foyer and snatched open the front door, ready to release some choice words. She was surprised to see it wasn't Mason standing on her doorstep, but Sparkle, Tenille's best friend, and her sister, Ivy.

"Where the hell is your sister?" Sparkle asked without even saying hello.

"Hello to you too, Sparkle. You know she wouldn't be all the way over here at my house," Sabrina said. "She had a wedding to shoot in Jamaica."

"I know she went to Jamaica, but she was scheduled to come back today. I got to the airport at four o'clock to pick her ass up, but she didn't show," Sparkle told her.

Sabrina frowned. "Was her flight delayed?"

"No, the flight she was supposed to be on from Atlanta arrived right on time. I tried to get some information from the airline to see if she got on the originating flight from Jamaica, but they wouldn't tell me anything. They were acting like I was a stalker or a terrorist. Speaking of stalker, did you know your boyfriend is parked over there?" Sparkle pointed.

Sabrina brushed past Sparkle to see what she was talking about, and sure enough, there was Mason in his green Infiniti SUV, parked a little ways from her house. Sabrina just shook her head as she went back inside, Sparkle and Ivy following her.

"Hey, Emily," Sparkle said, walking into the den.

"Hey, Sparkle, how are you? I haven't seen you in ages. How was your holiday?" Emily asked.

"It was great. You remember my sister, Ivy?"

"Yes, how are you?"

Ivy barely looked at Emily as she answered, "Cool."

Emily glanced over at Sabrina, who gave her a look that said, *she's got issues*.

Sabrina grabbed the cordless phone off the coffee table and dialed her mother's number.

"Helloooooo." Her mother sounded like she was singing into the phone.

"Ma, have you talked to Ten?"

"She called and talked to Marquise a little while ago," her mother said. "Why? What's wrong?"

Sabrina didn't want her mother to panic, so she quickly replied, "Nothing's wrong, Ma. Let me speak to Mookie right quick."

"Mookie, come to the phone."

A few seconds later, her nephew's voice came through the phone. "Hello."

"Hey, Mook, did your mom say anything when you talked to her earlier?"

"No," Marquise said, sounding distracted.

"Mook, put the game down and talk to me," Sabrina told him.

"How did you know I was playing the game?" Mookie laughed. "She didn't say anything, Aunt Brina. She just asked if I was okay and being good and she would see me tomorrow."

"Tomorrow?"

"Yeah. Then she talked to Granddad."

"Okay, let me talk to Daddy."

"Okay."

The line got quiet, and Sabrina waited a few moments, then yelled, "Marquise, let me talk to Daddy!"

"Oh, okay," Mookie said. "Granddad, phone!"

"Hey, Brina, I thought you were gonna come by this weekend so I could change your oil," Sabrina's dad greeted her.

"I was, Daddy, but I didn't get a chance to get over there. Hey, did you talk to Ten earlier?"

"You need to get that oil changed, Brina. It's way past time. If you don't take care of your car—"

"Daddy, I'll get it changed this week. I promise." Sabrina glanced over to see Emily giggling.

"You bring that car over here. Don't take that car to one of those overpriced commercial places. All they wanna do is—"

"Daddy, please, when you talked to Ten, what did she say?" Her father was just as unfocused as her nephew.

"She said she was delayed and asked if I could take Mookie to school. I told her that was fine. Then she told me to call Sparkle . . . I knew I forgot to do something."

"I'll call her, Daddy."

"Thanks, baby. You know, I was out with your brother and nephew watching the game, and this girl walked over and—"

"I gotta go, Dad. I love you."

"Love you too, baby girl."

Sabrina ended the call, then turned to Sparkle and said, "She called earlier because she had some kind of delay. She told Dad to call you, and of course, he forgot."

"Well, at least she's okay. She betta have the bomb souvenir for me when she gets back, and even if she does, I'm still cursing her out," Sparkle told her.

"I don't blame you," Sabrina said as she walked them out.

"I think loverboy's gone," Sparkle said, pointing to where Mason had been parked.

"Good."

"I can't believe you let a good man like that go. You're crazy as hell," Ivy sneered. "I would be doing any- and everything to make sure Mason was well taken care of, trust. I just don't know."

Sabrina was aware that Ivy was trying her best to provoke her, and unfortunately, she was succeeding. The history between them was far from friendly, dating back to their high school days. Ivy had always been trouble, believing she was better than everyone else. Though not particularly attractive, she matured early, and her curvaceous figure quickly drew attention from men, which gave her a false sense of entitlement and validation. Her desperate attitude and manipulative ways made her insufferable. Sabrina couldn't trust her as far as she could throw her, which wasn't far. She and her sister were like day and night. Sparkle was cute, well-liked, and had an outgoing personality. Sabrina wondered how they even had the same DNA.

"Ivy, you need to just shut up," Sparkle reprimanded her sister.

"Trust, you don't know, Ivy," Sabrina snapped. "Sparkle, thanks for coming by and checking on Ten. I'll be sure to let her know."

"No problem, girl." Sparkle gave her a hug before getting into her car. "Sorry about Ivy. You know you can pick your friends, but you can't pick your family."

Sabrina didn't respond. She just waved and walked back into the house.

"I know you already know this, but I can't stand that chick," Emily didn't hesitate to announce as soon as Sabrina returned to the living room.

"Join the club. I don't even know why Sparkle brought that bitch to my house. She knows I don't like her. No one does." Sabrina sighed. "The only reason we tolerate her is because Sparkle has been dragging her along since we were kids. It's annoying."

"Very," Emily agreed.

"I'm trying to figure out why Ten called my dad to say she was gonnna fly in later instead of calling me or Sparkle directly," she said. "Something's up."

"You think so?"

"I know so," Sabrina told her. "For her to change her flight and not say anything, there has to be an unusual reason. Elusiveness is not my sister's strong suit."

"You make a good point. It has to be something important if she's not even making it back in time to take Mookie to school. She does not play about that," Emily pointed out.

Sabrina's curiosity about what her sister had going on in Jamaica deepened. She couldn't wait for her to come home so she could hear the details of this trip.

"Hello?" Sabrina's voice was so deep she sounded like a man answering her phone. It was one thirty in the morning, and she had ignored the first two times it rang, thinking it was Mason. She was about to turn the phone off completely when she checked the caller ID and saw her sister's name and photo on the screen.

"Brina, wake up. I need for you to pick me up," Tenille told her.

"What? Where are you?"

"I'm in Charlotte, but my flight is about to board, and I'll be home in an hour. Brina, come on, are you up?"

"What?"

"Sabrina, I need for you to wake up and come to the airport."

Sabrina rolled on to her back and tried to understand what her sister was saying. "What time is it?"

"Time for you to get up and come get me! The plane is boarding now. I gotta go before I miss this flight. I'll see you in an hour. I'll be waiting for you in front of the airport."

Sabrina let out a groan of frustration. Few things irked her as much as being abruptly roused from a deep slumber—a fact that was well-known by everyone she was close to. Sleep was a cherished commodity, and she adamently upheld her need for a full nine hours each night to function optimally. She was so committed to rest that she rarely participated in weekday or late-night partying. Now, in the midst of a peaceful Sunday night, her sister was insisting on utilizing her as an Uber, interrupting her slumber.

I'll get up in five minutes, she thought as she closed her eyes. *Just five more minutes.*

"Brina, where the hell are you?" Tenille's voice screamed at her almost two hours later, causing Sabrina to regret that she had even answered the phone.

"I'm on my way," Sabrina said, jumping up. Five minutes of sleep had actually ended up being an hour and fifteen minutes. Grabbing her keys, she rushed out the door and into her car, quickly pulling out of the driveway. She fought sleep as she drove through the dark, empty streets and got on the interstate. Farther down the highway, another car merged into her lane, causing her to slow down. Just as Sabrina was about to switch lanes and pass the slow-moving car, it swerved into the right lane. Sabrina laid on her horn.

"What the hell are you doing?" she yelled as if the driver could hear what she was saying. The brake lights of the car flashed before her, and Sabrina realized that the car was now slowing down, almost causing her to miss the airport exit. She jumped into the left lane and sped by, giving the driver an evil look and the finger. The old white woman's eyes widened, and she nearly came back into Sabrina's lane. Sabrina blew the horn again, then pulled ahead.

Knowing her sister was probably seething because she still hadn't arrived, she leaned over to get her cell phone and realized that she had left not only the phone at home, but her purse as well. She was thinking things couldn't get any worse when she looked up and saw blue lights flashing in the rearview mirror. Sabrina couldn't do anything else except scream, "Damn! Damn! Damn!"

Chapter 8

Tenille

"About time! Where have you been? I've been calling you for the past forty minutes," Tenille said when Sabrina finally pulled in front of the airport where she was waiting.

"I don't have my phone," Sabrina said. "The trunk is open."

Tenille put her bags into the trunk of her sister's shiny Maxima and climbed inside. She looked over and saw that all Sabrina had on was a T-shirt and a pair of pajama pants. "Where the hell are your clothes? It's twenty degrees out here. You don't even have on a coat! What happened? You went back to sleep, didn't you?"

"No, I got stopped by the damn police!"

"The police?"

"Well, the state trooper."

"For what? Did you get a ticket?"

"No."

"That's good."

Sabrina passed her a handful of crumpled yellow papers. "Check this bullshit out."

"Wow, Sabrina, this is like three tickets," Tenille said, flipping through them.

"Actually, it's four."

"Four?"

"No seat belt, driving without a license—"

"Where's your license?"

"In my purse, which is at home along with my cell phone."

"Ohhhhhh."

"Improper lane change, and reckless driving."

"Reckless driving? Oh my God, how fast were you going?" Tenille laughed.

"I wasn't even going that fast," Sabrina lied. "That bastard cited me for reckless driving because I didn't have on any shoes."

Tenille leaned over and looked under the steering wheel and saw Sabrina's tiny, pedicured foot on the pedal. "I didn't know you could get a ticket for driving barefoot."

"I didn't either. His ass tried to get me for disorderly conduct, too."

"Ha! Sabrina, what on earth? Why?"

"Because I wouldn't get out of the car."

"Why didn't you?"

"Ten, look at me. I'm barely dressed. When you called, I literally got out of bed and into my car to come and get you. My hair is wrapped, and in case you didn't notice, I don't even have on a bra. There's no way that was gonna happen."

"Brina, you better be glad all you got were these tickets. He coulda taken you to jail, for real. You know you can't be playing with these state troopers. Now that I think about it, maybe you shoulda gotten out of the car and given him an eyeful. He mighta let you go with a warning," Tenille teased her. "You never know, he may be a fan of dark chocolate."

"Whatever, his wack ass was black as I am."

"And he still gave you four tickets? You must've had an attitude."

Sabrina's head tilted to the side and she sarcastically asked, "You think? I mean, I was awakened in the middle of the night by my sister to come and get her from the airport. So, being the good sister I am, I did, even though I'm currently being stalked by my ex-fiancé, who is probably behind us as we speak. All things considered, I believe I was entitled to have an attitude."

Tenille turned around. "I don't see anyone. And you are a good sister for getting up out of your warm bed and coming all the way out here to get me. Where is the music in this joint?"

"Okay, who are you, and what have you done with my sister?"

Tenille found the volume button and turned the music up to sing along with Mariah Carey. Had it been some other time, she would probably have been pissed about having to wait outside for almost an hour, but she was still floating from the weekend.

"Tenille!"

"What?"

"Why are you acting so weird?"

"What are you talking about?" Tenille asked.

Sabrina turned the music back down and said, "You're in a good mood. You hooked up with a Dexter on the beach while you were in Jamaica, didn't you? You got your groove back!"

"Girl, shut up. My groove was never gone, so how could I get it back?"

"You did something. Did you get high? You should have. I bet Jamaican weed is the best. Maybe that's what I need to do. I haven't gotten high in years. I need to mellow out."

"I didn't get high, Sabrina."

"You did something. Something's different. You seem . . . happy. And you haven't been happy in years."

"Years, Brina?"

"Yeah, years. You haven't been like this since you and Xavier were together."

Tenille's head snapped, and she glanced over at Sabrina. She couldn't believe what she had just said and wondered if her sister had some sort of psychic abilities. "What made you say his name?"

"I don't know. I guess because everyone knows that was the one man you were truly in love with, and when you were with him, you were happy. You didn't happen to hook up with Xavier all the way in Jamaica, did you?"

Tenille remained silent, unsure of how to articulate her feelings. There were never any secrets between her and Sabrina, but she wasn't ready to divulge the details of her surprise reunion just yet. Not because there was much to conceal, but because the experience felt too personal to share at the moment.

Her thoughts wandered to the remainder of Saturday night, which had unfolded with unexpected familiarity. Conversations flowed freely at the hotel bar, followed by a shared bottle of wine in her room.

"This feels like old times, doesn't it? I haven't laughed and talked like this since . . ." Xavier didn't finish his sentence.

He didn't need to. Tenille knew exactly what he was referring to because she felt the same way as they sat beside each other in the sitting room of her suite. The lighthearted banter they'd always shared returned as if it hadn't been years since they'd seen or talked to one another. She'd always had a level of comfort with Xavier that she'd never experienced with anyone else. He made her feel safe, desirable, and important. That hadn't changed.

"You always had plenty of jokes," she told him.

"Because I loved to make you smile, Ten," he said in a way that instantly made her nervous.

"Xavier, I—"

"I know, Ten," Xavier interrupted her. "You're married, and I respect that. Shit, it's one of the reasons why I stayed away all these years even though it's been the hardest thing I've ever had to do. As much as I wanted to be selfish, I didn't want to disturb your peace or disrupt your livelihood."

"Oh," Tenille muttered.

"You deserve a good husband, Ten, and I'm glad you found one. You're an amazing woman, and he's a lucky guy. My one regret in life will always be that I was stubborn and didn't realize it until it was too late," Xavier told her. "You were the love of my life. I miss you."

His words confirmed what she'd wondered during the times that she allowed herself to think about him and his whereabouts. She put her hand on his. The longing look in his eyes as he spoke made her nervous.

"I miss you too, Xavier," she confessed, allowing herself to lean closer into his arm that was now around her.

He held her for a lingering moment, then sat up. "It's getting late, and I should get out of here. I ain't even gonna sit here and act like there aren't some boundaries I wanna cross, Ten."

Tenille smiled. "See, plenty of jokes."

"I wasn't trying to be funny that time, believe it or not. I was being honest." He laughed, and they stood. "I'm glad it put a smile on your face, though."

"Don't go," Tenille said before she could stop herself.

"What?" Xavier asked.

"Stay for a little while longer," she told him. His eyes lit up, and she quickly added, "We won't be crossing any boundaries, sir."

"Damn," he said with a dramatic sigh. "Fine, we won't unless you decide that you want to."

"I won't," Tenille said more for herself than for him.

They drifted off to sleep during an episode of Saturday Night Live, *and she was awakened to a lazy Sunday morning and a tempting breakfast spread, complete with her favorite indulgence: chocolate-chip pancakes with whipped cream, compliments of room service ordered by Xavier.*

Although Tenille had a scheduled flight at eleven on Sunday morning, Xavier's persuasive charm convinced her to extend her stay and seize the opportunity to spend the day together. Knowing she may never get the chance to spend a day exploring paradise with him again, she threw caution to the wind and agreed, excited to embrace the moment. They explored the streets and shops while laughing and enjoying each other's company. Despite the lingering undercurrent of sexual attraction between them, they refrained from crossing any physical boundaries. The simple gestures of hand holding and hugs served as gentle reminders of their unspoken agreement to tread carefully. It was as if they both knew the potential consequences of anything more.

"Brina, don't take me home," Tenille said, returning to reality.

"What? We're almost there," Sabrina stated.

"Just take me to your house. I'll stay there. Is that okay?"

"That's fine. I just wish you would've mentioned it two exits ago. You may not have hit the blunt in Jamaica, but you are truly acting like you got a contact or something."

As they pulled up to Sabrina's house, Tenille noticed Mason sitting outside in his truck.

"Why is—"

"Don't ask," Sabrina said, jumping out of the car. Tenille laughed as her sister paused and stuck her middle finger up at him.

"You are so wrong, Brina," she said and waved at Mason, who waved back at her.

When they got inside, Tenille went straight into the guest room and plopped on the bed. Her body was tired as hell, but she was too wired to sleep. She thought about calling Brandon and telling him that she was staying with Sabrina for the night, but instead, she sent him a text message saying she was fine and would call him later. A few minutes later, he responded with a simple, Okay. She leaned back in the chair and stared at her phone.

Damn, I should have gotten his number.

"I enjoyed this, Ten," Xavier said as they prepared to leave the hotel.

"Me too," Tenille said.

"Can we keep in touch?" he asked.

As much as she wanted to say yes, Tenille knew that doing so would not be a wise decision for either one of them. Their brief platonic reunion in paradise had been more temptation than she could handle. Now, it was time for them to return to their reality.

At the time, it sounded like the noble thing to do. In hindsight, she regretted not exchanging contact information with him, even if it was just an email address.

"So, which one is it?" Sabrina asked, wrapping herself in an oversized blanket and climbing beside Tenille.

"What are you talking about, crazy?" Tenille asked.

"Smoking or stroking, which one did you do?" Sabrina innocently inquired as if she were asking about the Jamaican weather.

"Neither one." Tenille balked as she answered her sister's question.

Sabrina continued to press for answers. "Why didn't you wanna go home?"

"I just didn't feel like it." Tenille sighed, hoping her response would be satisfying enough to be left alone. She was wrong.

"Why not?"

"Because for one, you didn't need to be out in the cold without any clothes on," Tenille deflected.

"Bullshit." Sabrina smirked.

"Don't you have to be at work in the morning?"

"You weren't concerned about my work schedule when you called me in the middle of the night and asked me to pick you up," Sabrina snapped. "Come on, Ten, what's the deal?"

"There is no deal. Marquise is at Mama's, Brandon is working the night shift, and I just didn't want to go home to that empty house." Tenille shrugged.

Sabrina stared at her for a minute and finally said, "Fine, don't tell me. But I know you, and I know there's something you're not telling me. I will find out."

"There's nothing to find out." Tenille laughed.

"Oh, just so you know, Daddy forgot to call Sparkle, so she went to the airport to pick you up. She's kinda pissed."

"Great," Tenille sighed, wondering how her best friend would react if she discovered that she had spent the past twenty-four hours in the company of none other than Xavier Reynolds. Back when she and Xavier were dating, Sparkle had long held the belief that he failed to appreciate Tenille and had been quite vocal about her feelings about their relationship. It was Sparkle who convinced her that she was wasting her time.

"Ten, you and Xavier have been dating for three years. You mean to tell me that after all that time, he still hasn't decided to marry you? Girl, please, you need to think about your son," Sparkle had insisted on more than one occasion.

"What are you talking about, Sparkle? Xavier loves Marquise more than his own father does."

"If that's the case, then why doesn't he marry you and give Marquise his last name? Why isn't he trying to

make you all a real family? Tenille, you deserve better than what you're getting."

Whenever Tenille mentioned marriage to Xavier, his response fell into one of two categories: "in due time" or "when the time is right." Slowly, Tenille began to question why he was the only one who determined when the time would be right. She was happier than she had ever been and content with her life. Marquise had a love for Xavier that was more than she could have ever wanted, and they blended harmoniously with Fabian, his daughter. They all seemed like the perfect fit. But for some reason, Xavier seemed to be reluctant to take their relationship to the next level.

As time passed, Sparkle's words of wisdom gradually resonated with Tenille. A few months later, she met Brandon, who, unlike Xavier, was eager to commit and quickly put a ring on her finger. She transitioned from the uncertain realm of a committed relationship with Xavier into the stability of married life with Brandon. It was a decision made seven years ago, leaving the single life behind for what she thought would be a future filled with love and contentment. The harsh reality was that she didn't have either one, and seeing Xavier again reminded her of the intensity of her feelings, an energy she had never really felt with Brandon.

"Hey, how was your trip?"

"It was good," Tenille said to Brandon, who was sitting in the den watching television. "I thought you'd be at work. That's why I stayed at Brina's."

"I'm working a split today. I go back at two this afternoon," he told her.

Tenille went upstairs to their bedroom. The bed was still perfectly made, a telltale sign that Brandon had probably slept downstairs the entire time she'd been gone, which wasn't unusual. It had become a routine for him to doze off in the recliner and remain there through the night. In the early years of their marriage, Tenille would make an effort to wake him up and have him come to bed. As time passed, she gave up. His work hours were so crazy and erratic that she couldn't even tell when he came home.

She undressed and climbed into the hot shower. As she stood under the water, her mind wandered back to her weekend with Xavier. A pang of regret flowed over her like the water falling onto her body, and she contemplated Sabrina's advice. What if she had thrown caution to the wind and allowed herself to enjoy Xavier to the fullest? Now it was too late. In Jamaica, she'd had the chance to enjoy his touch, his taste, the feel of his lips on hers, his body, but she didn't.

"I love this cut on you." Xavier's fingers brushed through her hair as she lay beside him on the chaise longue. They had ventured away from the hotel to a secluded cabana on the beach, the perfect hideaway to enjoy the warm breeze, the ocean view, and each other's company.

"Thanks. I was nervous about cutting it at first, but I'm glad I went through with it," she replied.

"I feel you," he said. "Sometimes giving in to what we want, rather than holding back, turns out for the best."

Their eyes locked, and she sensed he wasn't just talking about her haircut. There was something more, something she had been yearning for throughout their time together. Xavier's face inched closer, his breath warm against her skin. Their lips were nearly touching when Tenille shifted, creating a small gap between them. Despite her intense desire to kiss him, she knew she couldn't allow it to happen. Giving into temptation would lead to more, something dangerous and forbidden, and something they could never undo once it was done.

You could have had it. You chose not to. Now, it's too late. She attempted to reassure herself that she had made the honorable choice by prioritizing her commitment to her marriage over fleeting desires and selfish indulgence. Yet, within her internal debate, Tenille couldn't shake the nagging question: did Xavier have similar regrets? Was he disappointed that he hadn't been more assertive and given into his own desires, meeting both of their obvious needs to be satisfied?

As she closed her eyes, an image of Xavier appeared in her mind. His striking good looks flooded her thoughts, stirring a familiar sense of passion that she only felt with him. She recalled the intensity of his gaze that confirmed that he felt that she was the most beautiful woman on earth. It was a turn-on each and every time he looked at her.

The shower door opened suddenly, causing her to gasp.

"Relax, T, it's just me." Brandon laughed, stepping behind her. He began kissing the back of her neck. "I missed you."

Tenille sighed and politely said, "I missed you too."

His hands began fondling her breasts, and she turned to face him, praying that he couldn't see the look of disappointment on her face.

Get it together, Tenille, she warned herself.

Sex with Brandon usually wasn't disappointing, but for some strange reason, she felt like he was interrupting her. Although her husband was a fairly decent lover, it wasn't him she wanted. Brandon's thick fingertips felt like claws on her skin, and his kiss was wet and sloppy. Instead of being aroused, she was irritated. His moans in her ear caused her to tense, and she trembled, wondering why her body was reacting the way that it was. The more he touched her, the more she wanted him to stop.

Sabrina was right. Something had definitely changed while she was away, and as she tried not to cringe as they made love in the shower, Tenille wondered if that something was her.

Chapter 9

Nick

"I heard about your new friend."

"What new friend?" Nick asked his mother, who'd called while he was on his way to work. He thought the morning conversation would be lighthearted entertainment during his morning commute. He was wrong.

"The one who watched the game with y'all on Sunday," his mother answered.

Nick didn't know which one had spilled the beans, but considering who was supposed to be keeping their mouths closed, he wasn't surprised. He specifically told his dad and nephew not to mention Sheridan to his mother, and they both promised not to say anything. Now here his mother was calling and making a big deal out of it.

"What about her?" Nick asked, hoping that if he acted as if it were nothing, his mother would do the same.

"I hear she's really pretty and a nice girl."

"She's a'ight."

"Well, I'd like to see how a'ight she is for myself. When can I meet her?"

This was exactly what Nick didn't want to happen. "Mom, it's no big deal. She's just a girl who works with me. We're not exclusive or anything like that. "

"Okay, well, let me ask you this. Is she someone you date?"

"Yeah."

"Do you date anyone else?"

Nick pondered the question and thought about the other women he'd been involved with over the past year. He would hardly call the chance meetings that occasionally resulted in an overnight rendezvous "dates." At least he did take Sheridan out for dinner and a movie, or drinks at a bar. "Well, not really."

"Then that's exclusive enough for me."

"But, Ma—"

"You're acting as if exclusive is a bad thing, Nicholas. It's not. I did not raise you to be a 'hit it and quit it' man."

"Ma—"

"And surely, I would hate to think of my son out here being some kind of man-whore!"

"I'm not," Nick insisted. He realized that there was no way he was winning this argument, so he simply said, "If you want to meet her, I'll introduce you, Ma."

"Well, Nick, if you think that's a good idea, I would love to meet your friend," his mother said.

I don't know which one I'm gonna kill first, but I'm either gonna be fatherless or nephew-less before this is all over.

"I'm telling you, that's definitely not a good idea," Eric said later that evening as they lifted weights at the gym.

"It's all good, man. Sheridan knows what's up. I'll just explain the situation and tell her that my dad made a big deal out of nothing and now my mom is in a tizzy."

"Tizzy?" Eric laughed.

"You know what I mean."

"I'm warning you, if you introduce her to your moms, it's over. She's probably already psyched about meeting Pops and shorty."

"No, she's not. Come on, her meeting them was simply a coincidence, and she knows it meant nothing. Nothing's changed between us," Nick said, putting the barbell back on the stand.

"Let me ask you this. Have you hooked up with her since that night?"

"Yeah." Nick nodded as he wiped the sweat from his face.

"And nothing was different? Nothing at all?"

Nick tried to recall if there was anything distinctively different about him and Sheridan. It was still great sex, nothing more, nothing less. "I'm telling you, she was still cool."

Eric shrugged. "Hey, I could be wrong. Maybe she's as cool with it as you say she is. But mark my words, introducing her to your mother is a no-no. You're about to complicate things. That good thing you've been bragging about is about to go bad."

"I got this, man." Nick laughed. As he got dressed in the locker room, again he tried to recall if he had missed any sign that Sheridan may have felt things between them had changed, but there weren't any. He'd made it clear where he stood early on when they began sleeping together, and Sheridan agreed.

"I know we've kept things casual, but I want to make sure we're on the same page. Right now, I'm not looking for anything serious, and I don't think I'll be ready for that with anyone, including you," he said one night when he accepted her invitation to have dinner in her hotel room. "I just want to be honest and up-front."

Sheridan's eyes widened slightly, but she nodded. "I appreciate that because I do too. I feel the same way. I'm focused on my career and shopping, and those are the things I'm committed to right now."

Nick's shoulders relaxed in relief. "I'm glad to hear that. It's important for me to know that we both agree on this."

Sheridan leaned back on her couch, looking thoughtful. "Yeah, I don't want anything to complicate things. I'm happy with how things are."

Nick smiled, feeling a weight lift off his shoulders. "Me too. I'm glad we could talk this through."

Sheridan grinned and gave a small laugh. "Me too. Now let's not let this ruin our evening. How about we order food and then I give you something else to eat for dessert?"

Nick nodded in agreement. "Sounds perfect."

Since that conversation, Nick proceeded with a sense of ease, knowing they were on the same page and could enjoy their time together without any further complications.

To be on the safe side, Nick called Thaddeus, his boy from back in the day. They had been friends since second grade and gotten into more devilment together than he could remember. Thad lived his life to the fullest, and there was never a dull moment with him. He always worked hard. Therefore, he played harder, and when it came to women, Thad was a pro. The flyest women would fall for what Nick thought were the corniest of lines when they came from Thad.

"Damn, there must be something wrong with my eyes. I can't take them off you."

"Do you believe in love at first sight, or should I walk by again?"

"So, apart from being sexy, what do you do for a living?"

Although he didn't have the striking good looks of his best friend Nick, Thaddeus LaTrell Montgomery had an undeniable charm that made him irresistible to women. While Nick's appearance, inherited from his mother, drew attention with its traditional attractiveness, Thaddeus's allure was his confidence and charisma. And in matters concerning women, Thaddeus reigned supreme. This predicament with Sheridan definitely called for reinforcement, and calling Thaddeus for his invaluable advice and guidance was a must.

"Whoa, I thought you said you and this chick weren't serious, man," Thad said.

"We're not. I mean, we hang out every now and then, but I'm not feeling her like that."

"I know that's what you're saying, but I'm kinda like Mama C. Why haven't you been dating other chicks? You been 'hanging' with Sheridan for a little while now, right?"

As Nick contemplated the situation, he came to the realization that he had been involved with Sheridan for over a year, a fact that somehow he hadn't noticed until now. Strangely enough, he couldn't find a compelling reason to pursue anyone else. Sheridan seemed to effortlessly fit into his life, almost like a seamless addition. She was, in essence, convenient. He didn't have to put in much effort, and that simplicity made dealing with her easy.

"It's been a minute," Nick admitted.

"Well, it could be that you really are feeling her. You haven't found a reason to hang out with anyone else, so she must be doing something to satisfy you." Thad laughed.

"She definitely does that."

"Oh, shit, let me find out she got you open. Don't tell me you're sprung, Nick. I taught you better than that."

"Hell no, never that."

"Then what is it? Look, man, I'm just joking. There's nothing wrong with taking a casual thing a step further. I'm all for commitment. If that's the direction you think this thing is going toward, then go for it. Let her meet the fam."

"But I don't know if I'm really ready for that. The whole meeting the family thing is to get my mom off my back. You know that. That's why I'm thinking if I tell her up front what the deal is, she'll be cool," Nick explained.

"What has she said about you and her?"

"Nothing. We never discuss it. She's fine with things the way they are now."

"Well, then there's nothing to worry about. Chill out. If you're not ready to take it to the next level, then don't. Don't let anyone pressure you into getting into anything you're not ready for. I love Mama C to death, you know that. But believe it or not, when all is said and done, she's a woman. And women have a way of trying to get men to do what they want them to do. Sabrina getting married anytime soon ain't happening, so she's moving on to get you down the aisle. Mookie's growing up. He's not a baby anymore. She wants more grandbabies."

Unlike Eric, everything Thaddeus said seemed to make sense. There was no need to get into something he knew he wasn't ready for, especially a relationship.

"I like Sheridan. She's a nice girl. But there's no hope for her, huh?"

"Don't get me wrong. She's cool, but I don't know. There's something missing. I can't explain it," Nick told him. "I definitely don't want anything more than what we have now. I'm sure of that. Sheridan's not it, and until I find a woman who makes me feel somthing real, I'll stick with her for now."

"Still holding out, huh?" Thaddeus sighed.

"I'm not holding out, Thad."

"Still waiting on the fireworks and violins. You remember that year we went to Beach Week?"

Nick knew where this was going, and he quickly changed the subject. "When are you coming home?" Thad worked as a project manager for FEMA and travelled all the time.

"A couple of weeks. I wanna sit down with you and see if you can help me with this app we're trying to develop. I don't know why you don't just let me hire you. You can go places, man, with your talent."

"I'm good, Thad."

"So, how is Emily? Is she still fine as hell and on the prowl? Let her know a brother will be home to make her smile."

Nick shook his head and laughed. For the longest time, Emily had had a crush on Thaddeus, and he flirted with her constantly. "I will definitely let her know."

"A'ight, I will see you in a couple of days. Until then, keep doing your thing. You wanna keep hanging out with Sheridan, there's nothing wrong with that. If you're ready to go to the next level, there's nothing wrong with that either. Whichever way, just let it happen naturally. If you're pressured into it, you'll regret it in the end."

"For someone who has never had a successful relationship with a woman in his life, you sure have some great advice. Thanks, bro."

"I'd like to think my romantic failures serve a purpose in some way." Thad laughed.

Talking to both Eric and Thad made Nick feel a little better. He liked Sheridan. She had a lot going for herself, and he also wondered if maybe he was holding out for something that didn't exist. But he was certain he'd felt it once before. It was years earlier when he was in college, a happenstance meeting with a gorgeous young lady that was brief and didn't end well. A woman he'd never forgotten.

His cell phone began vibrating, and there was a text message from Sheridan.

Come through later.

Nick smiled. *Maybe I'm worried about nothing. My good thing is about as good as it can get.*

***

Later that night, Nick showed up at Sheridan's hotel room. She opened the door and led him inside. He was shocked that she was fully dressed. Most of the time when he showed up, they went straight for the action. He would arrive, and the mood would already be set with the dim lights, candles lit, music playing, and Sheridan wearing nothing at all. There was even a time or two that he had arrived and she had gotten started without him.

"What's up?" he asked, trying not to sound confused by the non-sexual atmosphere.

"Nothing. Just finishing up some paperwork," she said. "How are you?"

"I'm good," he said, sitting in one of the two chairs in the room.

"Man, I had the longest day ever. This new training class is working my nerves. I'm trying not to be stressed. I swear, I feel like saying the hell with them and taking my ass back home."

"I feel you," he said.

"I didn't think you'd be here this early," she told him. "But since you are, let's hit the bar."

Nick was relieved as he realized it was only nine o'clock and still kind of early. *Man, stop tripping. Everything is all good.*

"Sounds like a plan," he said.

"Why are you smiling like that?" Sheridan asked him.

"Like what?"

She walked over to him and put her arms around his neck. He leaned over and kissed her, reaching his hand under her shirt. Her firm breasts were warm in his hands, and he brushed his fingers over her nipples until he felt them hardening.

"Mmmmm," she moaned, slipping him out of his leather jacket.

"I thought you wanted to hit the bar," he whispered, tugging at the zipper of her skirt.

"You look like you needed a drink," she teased.

"Naw, I got just what I need right here." The skirt finally gave and fell to the floor. In one swift movement, he picked her up off the floor and carried her to the bed.

Sex with Sheridan was something he always enjoyed and looked forward to. She was as exciting and ambitious in bed as she was at work. Her kinks were a turn-on: handcuffs, blindfolds, feathers, and hot wax. There was never a dull moment in bed or any other room they happened to be in. By the time they finished, he was beyond spent.

"That was better than a drink," she gasped as she collapsed on his chest.

"Damn right." He laughed.

"I think you may have even given me the inspiration I needed to stay and finish training my class."

"Hey, that's what friends are for," he laughed. "I'm always here to help."

"Well, if ever I can help you in any way, let me know." Sheridan smirked. "Now feel free to let yourself out so I can get back to work."

For some reason, Nick felt as if this was the ideal time to bring up his predicament. "Well, now that you bring it up, there is something you can help me with."

Sheridan lifted her head and asked, "With what? I thought I had already helped you with that."

"Not that. Something else. Well, remember Sunday you met my dad?"

"Oh, hell naw, I am not having a threesome with you and your dad. That's sick."

"Stop playing." He laughed. "Check it out. My dad went home and said all of these great things about you to my mom, and now she's all gung ho about meeting you."

"Really?" She sounded shocked. "What kind of good things?"

"I don't know. Some nonsense like you're pretty and nice."

"Awwww, he thinks I'm pretty and nice?"

"Well, it was either him or Mookie. Someone told her, and now she's pressed," he replied.

"Okay," Sheridan said.

"Okay what?"

"I'll meet her. No big deal," Sheridan told him. "But you owe me."

"Wait. I thought you just owed me a few minutes ago. I inspired you to not quit your job. How do I owe you?"

"Meeting your mom, Nick. That is so much bigger of a deal than me not quitting. As a matter of fact," Sheridan rolled over and said, "I think that maybe you should plan on coming over every night for the rest of the week in an effort to work out a repayment plan."

Chapter 10

Sabrina

"Sabrina, this is Mrs. Tolliver. Can you please give me a call when you get this message?"

Sabrina couldn't shake off her amazement as she deleted the voicemail. Mason's mother reaching out to her was unexpected, to say the least. While their interactions had always been polite, she and Mrs. Tolliver had never shared a particularly close relationship during Sabrina's time with Mason. Sabrina couldn't help but speculate whether Mason had influenced his mother's decision to call.

"Why are you doing this, Sabrina?" Mason asked.

"Because it's the right thing to do." Sabrina took a long sip of her coffee. After much contemplation, she'd agreed to meet him at the Starbucks near her house so that they could "talk things through" and resolve things amicably as Emily had suggested. She'd hoped that he would finally realize that her decision to end things was for the best and he'd accept it once and for all.

"For who?" He frowned.

"For everyone," she told him. "I know this isn't something you agree with right now, Mason, but I promise, eventually you'll see that I'm right."

Sabrina was calm and reasonable, unlike Mason, who was tense and combative. One of the reasons she was so confident in her decision to end their engage-

ment was that, unlike all the other times they'd broken up, she wasn't unsettled. This time, there were no tears, drunken phone calls to clear the air, or second thoughts. It was as if she'd arrived at some point of clarity.

"You're not right. You're wrong," Mason rebutted. "I love you, Brina, and I want to marry you. You love me."

"I do love you, but I don't want to marry you," Sabrina insisted.

"Why not? Because a few weeks ago, we were looking at venues and planning our honeymoon. What the hell changed? Where is this coming from?"

"Don't you see that this is a good thing?" she asked. "You should be glad that I came to this realization before it was too late."

"What realization? That you wanna be with Khalil? Is that what this is about?"

"Yes, that's exactly what this is about." Sabrina shrugged.

"I knew it. I knew there was something up with the two of you." Mason sat back and gave her a look of disgust.

"There's nothing going on between me and Khalil, and you know it." Sabrina shook her head.

"It's probably some other dude you're fuck—"

"I'm done." Sabrina stood and shook her head. "This conversation is over. I'd hoped we could end on good terms, but obviously that's not happening."

"Brina, wait." Mason jumped up. "I'm sorry. I just don't understand why you're doing this. Please tell me what I need to do to fix us."

"There's no us to fix," she said. "You're a good guy, Mason. You wanna know what you do need to fix? Your trust issues. If you don't, you're going to ruin any chances of being with the next woman you fall in love with."

Having said her piece, Sabrina turned and walked away before Mason could say anything else.

She felt that they'd parted on good terms, and the last thing she wanted to deal with was his mother.

The next message played. "Brina, call me."

Sabrina dialed her brother's number as she walked into her kitchen. As soon as he answered, she asked, "Nick, do you know a good lawyer?"

"What?" Nick asked.

"A lawyer. I need one." She began rambling through her cabinets in search of something to snack on. She wasn't hungry, but she was bored, and although she knew that eating out of boredom was one of the reasons she had gained five pounds in the past three weeks, she didn't care.

"Why do you need a lawyer?"

"It's a long story," she said, spotting a bag of Pepperidge Farm Milano mint chocolate cookies. *Jackpot!*

"Not offhand. I can ask around. Does this have anything to do with Mason? Is he still stalking you? You ain't kill the brother, did you?"

Sabrina opened the bag of cookies and began nibbling on one. "No, fool. Mason has accepted the fact that we're over, and we are cool. At least, I think we are. His mama is calling me all of a sudden, so I don't know."

"Maybe she saw your picture online and she called to tell you."

"What picture?" Sabrina asked, her mouth now full of cookie. Reaching into the cabinet, she took out a glass and went to the fridge for the milk.

"Stop chewing in my ear. The hospital's IG post about the gala and the singles participating in the Love Connection date nights."

Sabrina nearly choked. Nick had to be joking. There was no way she was in a post about the hospital gala, especially after specifically telling Emily she wouldn't do it.

"Then again, his mom may be a little pissed. After all, you did just break off an engagement with her son less than a month ago, and now you're on the auction block, literally." Nick began laughing as if his cornball comment were actually funny.

"I gotta call you back," Sabrina told him and hung the phone up. She quickly opened Instagram and went to the hospital's page. There, in full color, was her picture, among fourteen other of the city's supposedly most eligible bachelors and bachelorettes, including her best friend, Emily. "I'm going to kill her!"

"Sabrina, I swear, it's not my fault. I told the director that you declined," Emily explained.

Sabrina had arrived at the physical therapy department, where Emily worked, in record time. The receptionist told Sabrina that Emily had been expecting her and complimented her on her picture. It was a staff photo of her that Tenille had taken, and she was grateful that it was a great shot. Whenever Sabrina looked at it, she thought she resembled Laila Ali. The fact that this was the photo used in the announcement still didn't erase the fact that it was done without her permission, even if it was for a great cause.

"Then what the hell is this?" Sabrina held up her phone and pointed to the screen. "Did the page get hacked?"

"I swear, the day after you told me you didn't want to do it, I called her and left a message."

"A message? You didn't go to her office and tell her in person? You do realize how bad this makes me look, right? I literally just ended my engagement less than a month ago, and now I'm participating in a singles event."

"I'm sorry, Sabrina. I'll fix it. I promise."

"You better do something," Sabrina hissed. Her cell began ringing, and she answered it. "Hello."

"Brina, you didn't tell me you were gonna be on the internet," her mother said. Sabrina prepared herself for the lecture she was probably about to get.

"I didn't know I was gonna be on the internet, Mama. I just found out myself when Nick called me."

"Tell her she looks pretty," Sabrina's dad called out in the background. "Like her daddy!"

"I thought Eloise was lying when she called and told me. I guess you decided to start dating again, huh? That certainly didn't last long."

Sabrina rolled her eyes. "Ma, I'm not dating."

"Aren't they auctioning you off for a date? And don't get me wrong, I know it's for charity, but for some reason, this whole auction thing is kinda weird to me," her mother said. "First of all, having men pay for a date is one thing, but to pay to go out on a date is a tad bit disturbing."

"Reminds me of slavery. They used to put our people on the auction block and sell 'em to the highest bidder. That ain't right! And ain't next month for Black History?" her dad yelled louder.

"Johnny, be quiet," her mother told him. "So, are you gonna be on a stage or something? How does this work?"

"I don't know, Mama. I told you I didn't even know I was in it. Let me call you when I get home," Sabrina said, ending the call before her mother could say anything else.

She glared at Emily and folded her arms. "See what you've started? You know how my parents are. Lord, have mercy!"

"I know, I know," Emily replied. "I accept full responsibility for it."

"How the hell do you plan on fixing it?"

"I don't know. I'll call the director in the morning and tell them to withdraw you."

"That'll just make me look even worse."

"It's not a big deal, Sabrina. Look at it as great exposure for the clinic. You said yourself you wanted to work on getting more funding for the speech and hearing program. Here's your chance. You know for a fact that all of the hospital bigwigs will be there."

Emily was right. The most influential hospital staff would be at the ball, in addition to the biggest donors. It was the networking opportunity of a lifetime.

"I just don't like the fact that I'm being auctioned off. Like I'm so pathetic that I can't get a date without pimping myself out for one," Sabrina explained.

"Brina, you've got it twisted. Your being auctioned makes you the prize! Look at it as if you're so fabulous guys have to compete for your time—with their checkbooks." Emily nodded in excitement.

Sabrina tried to remain stone-faced and bit her lip to keep from smiling. Her best friend knew her like a book.

Emily walked over and put her arms around her. "And you're not in this by yourself. I'll be right there with you."

"And what if no one bids on me?" Sabrina peered at her.

"What? Are you kidding? That face with all that ass, you're a moneymaker for sure." Emily laughed. "Now I'll probably bring more money in, but you're definitely a close second."

Chapter 11

Tenille

"Ma, I don't want to go to Sheldon Prep next year."

Tenille looked over at Marquise. "Why not? What's wrong with Sheldon? You've been going there ever since second grade. It's a good school."

"I wanna go to Frazier Middle and play basketball."

"You play basketball now, Mookie."

"That's rec ball, Ma. I wanna play real basketball. And I'm tired of wearing uniforms. I've had the same classmates over and over again. Like you said, I've been going there since second grade."

"Marquise, I don't think you realize how blessed you are to be able to go to a private school. There's a reason we sacrifice for you to go. Your class size is smaller, and you get to do a lot more than kids in public schools. Remember the class trip last year where you spent a week in DC? Believe me, kids at Frazier don't get field trips like that," Tenille told him. "Your grades are excellent, and you're on the right path to go to college."

"Mom, Uncle Nick took me to DC last year and I had way more fun. I make good grades because I'm a good student, and if I go to Frazier, I can still get a basketball scholarship and go to college."

"Marquise, Frazier is a junior high school. They don't have college scouts at the games." Tenille laughed.

"That's not true, Ma. College scouts came to see Lebron James and Carmello Anthony play in junior high. They'll come and see me if I'm playing at Frazier."

"And they won't come and see you at Sheldon?" Tenille raised an eyebrow as she glanced over at him, then focused back on the road.

Marquise shook his head. "Not with that whopping zero-eight record the team has."

"Come on, Mookie. With you on the team, the record will be eight-zero, so you won't have that problem," Tenille teased. By the look on his face, she could tell her son was not amused.

"I'm gonna make headlines on the court, Ma. You know I'm good."

"Just like your father," she told him.

"No, I ain't nothing like him," Marquise quickly said.

Marquise's relationship with his father was virtually nonexistent, largely due to the influence of his father's wife, who failed to grasp that Tenille had no desire for any involvement with her husband beyond his parental duties. Over time, Marquise had been reduced to little more than a monthly financial obligation of $200 and sporadic phone calls. Tenille found solace in the fact that her brother and father stepped in to provide the attention and care that her son deserved.

"Don't be like that, Mook. Give credit where credit is due. You inherited the best of both your parents. You have his gorgeous eyes and athletic ability and my good looks and overwhelming intelligence. Take it for what it's worth." She winked.

"I know, Ma. I just don't think he deserves any credit from me. Let his other sons give him credit. That's whose names he has tattooed on his arm."

Tenille found herself speechless. She always made a conscious effort never to speak ill of Marquise's father, mindful that her son was beginning to form his own perceptions. As they arrived at Sheldon Preparatory, she felt relieved by the timing. The principal's friendly wave as Marquise stepped out of her SUV provided a reassuring moment amid her inner turmoil.

"Bye, Mook. Have a blessed day. I love you." She leaned over and barely kissed his cheek.

"Love you too, Ma," he said, grabbing his backpack, and then he paused before closing the door. "Will you at least think about it?"

Tenille looked at her son's handsome face. He looked so much like her younger brother, wearing the distinguished uniform that he hated so much. She said, "Yes, Mookie."

"Morning, boss," Noelle greeted Tenille as she walked into the studio.

"Good morning."

"Can you ask Sabrina if she can get me a ticket to the gala? I was checking out some of those bachelors in this year's Love Connection, and I'm trying to bid."

Tenille flipped through the stack of mail on Noelle's desk. "You can have mine."

"What? Are you serious?" Noelle asked excitedly.

"Yeah, I don't wanna go."

"Thanks, Ten. I appreciate it, and um, I'm gonna need an advance on my paycheck."

"You're planning on bidding on a bachelor, but you don't have any money?" Tenille glanced up from the mail.

"Don't be ridiculous. Of course I'll have money. As soon as you give me my advance, boss." Noelle laughed.

"Not happening." Tenille shook her head.

"You just don't want me to be great," Noelle sighed. "You know without my paycheck I can't bid on a bachelor. Do you want me to be single forever?"

The look on her face was so stoic that, for a second, Tenille had to wonder if Noelle was serious. She was relieved when she noticed a slight grin.

"Get some work done, crazy," Tenille said, "before I fire you and you'll have more to worry about than a pay advance. You'll be worrying about a paycheck."

"Fine. Just so you know, I will find love at the gala even without your help," Noelle declared, placing her hands over her heart dramatically.

"For the record, I do want you to be great, and should you happen to come across a guy you feel would benefit from your awesomeness at the ball, then good for you. Now get to work," Tenille reassured her.

There was something about Noelle that struck a chord with Tenille and was reminiscent of her own younger days. Noelle possessed a vibrant personality. She was bright, funny, creative, and diligently hardworking. Like Tenille, she proudly owned her curves, a natural "thick chick," but with more style. It was her undeniable beauty and impeccable sense of fashion that caught Tenille's eye a few months back at a local coffee shop.

Standing in line, Noelle exuded confidence in her attire: a yellow long-sleeved men's shirt paired with black patterned tights and the most eye-catching combat boots Tenille had ever seen. Her cropped hair was styled into an edgy spike, complemented by dangling gold earrings and flawlessly applied makeup. Tenille couldn't shake the impression that Noelle was destined for the runway, so she simply had to ask.

"Excuse me, do you model?"

"No way." Noelle laughed.

"Well, you should! You're gorgeous!" Tenille told her. "I mean it."

"Thanks. I appreciate the compliment. But I don't think I'm model material."

"Nonsense. I'm telling you." Tenille nodded.

The barista called her name, and she went to get her order. When she walked back to the table where Noelle was now sitting, she reached into her bag and handed her one of her business cards. "Hey, give me call so we can talk some more."

Noelle looked at her and shook her head. "Listen, I appreciate the offer, but I don't get down like that. I'm not gay."

Tenille's eyes widened, and she realized the young lady thought she was coming on to her. "What? Oh, no, it's not like that. You think I'm gay? I'm not gay. I'm a photographer, that's all. I'm always looking for great faces. I'm definitely not gay."

"Oh, I'm sorry. It's just that you'd be surprised how many women . . . well, they come at me, and I just thought . . . I mean—"

"It's okay. I can see how I could have come off like that."

The two ladies laughed and got to know one another. Within a week, Noelle officially joined the team as her office manager and personal assistant. As time went on, their bond grew deeper, evolving into a sisterly relationship rather than a typical employer-employee dynamic. This closeness prompted Tenille to go above and beyond to ensure Noelle's safety and happiness.

Having Noelle working at the studio not only made Tenille's life easier but also a little less lonely. She enjoyed having someone to chat with throughout the day and share creative ideas with. Plus, her protégé brought a fun, young energy that Tenille loved.

"I stopped by the post office and grabbed the mail on the way in." Noelle handed her a bundle of envelopes wrapped in a rubber band. "And the FedEx guy dropped off a few packages already this morning. I haven't opened them yet, but I will. I know you're waiting on the canvas prints of the Duvall engagement session."

"Thanks, Noelle," Tenille said with a grateful nod.

"And you didn't think I had done any work." Noelle winked.

"I was wrong," Tenille told her. "Let me know if those prints are in, and if they're not—"

"I'll call the printer and see what the holdup is, and if need be, I'll go pick them up myself."

"Keep this up and I may have to give you that advance you'll need for the gala." Tenille winked.

"Oh, let me hurry and get back to work." Noelle rushed back to her desk.

After sorting through the mail, Tenille retreated to her office in the back of the studio. The recent conversation with her son lingered in her thoughts, leaving her pondering whether to allow him to enroll at Frazier, a public middle school, in the fall. As she powered up her computer and began researching the school, she couldn't help but feel the absence of her husband's input on the matter. Brandon's indifference toward Marquise was a recurring theme in their relationship. Rarely did he express opinions on anything, content as long as he was working and the bills were paid. Despite being married, Tenille often felt like a single parent, longing for Brandon to play a more active role in their son's life.

During their courtship, Brandon had assured her that her having a son was not an issue, and he promised to be a reliable provider. True to his word, he maintained a cordial relationship with Marquise, but the emotional connection between them was lacking.

As Tenille delved into her research, consumed by thoughts of Marquise's future, she was caught off guard by Noelle's sudden presence in the room.

"Hey, do you have the proofs for the Bridal Boutique?"

"Huh?" Tenille looked up from the computer screen.

"Bridal Boutique. The proofs for their editorial spread. Are they ready yet?" Noelle clarified.

"Oh, yeah, I'll send the file over to you," Tenille told her.

"Are you okay?" Noelle asked.

"Yeah, I'm fine."

Noelle didn't press further. She left the office, and Tenille returned her focus to the school's website and discovered they were hosting an information session for prospective students. Without a moment's hesitation, she promptly registered to attend.

"Tenille." Noelle's voice came through the phone's intercom system a short while later. "Your mom is on line one."

"Thanks," Tenille said, picking up the phone. "Hey, Ma."

"Hey, Ten, how are you?"

"I'm good, Ma."

"You're not busy, are you? I asked Noelle if you were shooting because you didn't answer your cellular phone."

Tenille smiled at her mother saying "cellular phone." "No, I'm not busy. My cellular phone is in my purse."

"Well, I called to tell you I'm making reservations for your brunch, so I need to know how many people to plan for. Noelle says she's coming, and she even offered to help decorate. I'm going to call Sparkle and send Brandon a text. What about his mother and sister?"

"No," Tenille quickly answered. She was well aware that the likelihood of Brandon attending was slim to none. She'd learned early on in their relationship that, although he was a great provider, he wasn't big on holidays or special occasions. She had no desire to entertain his family alone, especially if he wouldn't be there. It was clear they didn't hold much affection for her, and the feeling was mutual.

"Tenille, they are your in-laws. Why—"

"Ma." Tenille interrupted her mother before she continued. "To be honest, I really don't feel up to celebrating this year. You're making a big deal for nothing."

"Nothing? What do you mean, nothing? It's your birthday. That's something. What's wrong with you? You came back from your trip the other week and you were in such good spirits. Now it's as if you're frustrated with the world."

Her mother was right. She was quite frustrated, mainly due to the looming approach of her birthday. Over the past few years, the once-exciting occasion had lost its sparkle. She couldn't shake the feeling that it was linked to the memories she held of celebrating with Xavier. When they were together, he turned her birthday, which fell on Valentine's Day, into something truly magical. From the moment she woke up until she drifted off to sleep, he orchestrated a day filled with surprises and delights. Ever since their parting, her birthdays had been lacking that special touch. Her family still upheld their tradition of a celebratory brunch, but beyond that, the day held little significance. Brandon's idea of marking the occasion was limited to lunch at a nearby restaurant, a heart-shaped box of candy, a hastily signed card with a generic "happy birthday," and a Visa gift card.

"I'm fine, Ma. I'm just a little distracted. Mookie is really trying to get me to let him change schools next year."

"I know. He and I talked about it the other night," her mother sighed. "What does Brandon say about it?"

"Brandon?" Tenille was confused by her mother's question.

"Your husband. Mookie's stepfather," her mother reminded her.

"Oh, I haven't even mentioned it to him," Tenille responded.

"Don't you think maybe you should?"

"I guess. I mean, I really didn't think about it."

"Well, talking to Brandon about your frustrations may help you and make you feel better," she suggested.

"You're right, Ma. I'll talk to him," Tenille lied.

"Good."

"Are you and Daddy going to the gala this year?" Tenille changed the subject.

"No. We already had plans to go to dinner with Frieda and Tommy," her mother said, referring to another couple her parents had been friends with for years.

"That's nice."

"Are you going? I know your brother said he would be there. You and Brandon should go and make a night of it."

Tenille understood her mother's intentions were good. It was evident that the lackluster state of her marriage hadn't escaped her family's notice, resulting in her mother's frequent, well-meaning suggestions. However, she had no inclination to even mention the event to her husband. She had no desire to attend with him. Just the thought of them going together gave her anxiety.

"I'm probably not going to go. Listen, I have a meeting I gotta get ready for, Ma. I'll call you later."

"Okay, Ten. You go ahead and enjoy your day. Love you," her mother told her.

"Love you too, Ma."

"Tell Marquise to call me later on my cellular phone."

Tenille couldn't help laughing as she hung up. She was grateful for her mother's humor, even if she didn't realize how funny she was.

Chapter 12

Nick

"You're coming back by next Sunday, right?"

"Yes, Nick." Sheridan laughed. "I'll be back in time for your sister's brunch. Dag, you're acting kinda pressed. Let me find out you're getting caught up."

Nick shook his head. "Never that. I'm just trying to get Mom off my back, that's all. If I bring you, she'll stop worrying me."

"You don't have to use your mother as an excuse. I know I got you open."

"Yeah, right. Don't you mean the other way around? You're the one who called me over here."

"Well, I had a good reason to, don't you think?" Sheridan smiled seductively at him.

"Damn right you did." His eyes admired her nude body lying beside him.

Nick was taken aback when Sheridan's late-night text summoned him to her hotel room. Given her usual preference for rest before an early morning flight, the request was unexpected. He'd just stepped out of the shower and was about to get ready for bed, but he decided to seize the opportunity. Knowing that Sheridan was going to be gone for over a week, which meant over a week with no sex, he decided he'd better take her up on her offer and immediately drove over.

As usual, Sheridan wasted no time getting down to business. She was ready and waiting by the time he arrived and helped him undress as soon as he walked in the door. Their sex was fast, passionate, hot, and satisfying.

"You wanna join me in the shower before you leave?" she asked, stroking his chest.

"Are you putting me out?" Nick laughed.

"Nope, you don't have to go if you don't want to. By all means, feel free to sleep over."

"Sleep over? How old are we? Six and seven?"

"I was thinking more like six and nine." She grinned, maneuvering herself on top of him.

"You are a freak," he told her, enjoying the feel of her mouth now on his manhood, which was slowly becoming erect. A moan escaped him, and he cupped her perfectly shaped buttocks in his palms, easing his fingers into her wetness. As she continued sucking him, his tongue replaced his fingertips, and he teased her clit as her legs opened wider, allowing him greater access. Her thighs tensed up, and Nick knew he had her just where he wanted her.

"Nick," Sheridan moaned as his tongue dipped deeper inside, continuing until she nearly drowned him as she climaxed on his face. Moments later, she was fast asleep.

"Night night," he whispered with a satisfied grin as he hopped out of bed.

"Where are you going?" Sheridan sat up in bed.

"To take a shower, and don't worry, you don't have to get up," Nick told her.

"Nick." Sheridan reached for him. "I want you to stay."

"The night?" Nick frowned.

"I was thinking maybe the weekend." She smiled.

"Aren't you leaving in the morning? I mean, don't you have a flight already booked? And you're not scheduled to come back until next weekend."

She'd never asked him to spend the night before, and staying wasn't something he'd want to do anyway. To him, overnight stays were for couples who were dating or at least pursuing some type of committed relationship, even if they weren't officially in one. That wasn't the level of involvement he had with Sheridan or anyone else. Sex was one thing. Intimacy was another, and spending the night was something he considered intimate.

"Yeah, but I can reschedule it. It's a business flight on the company card, and honestly, it's no big deal. I can just leave on Sunday instead. What's wrong? Is it a problem?"

Nick was caught off guard by her suggestion. Although they'd been sleeping together over a year, it had never been overnight and certainly not a full weekend. He had to wonder if this sudden request to spend the weekend together had something to do with his inviting her to join him for a family event.

"I mean, not really. It's just that I have plans already for this weekend, that's all," Nick explained.

"Oh, plans. That's cool. It was just a thought." Sheridan's tone had lost a bit of its warmth.

"I'm going to a charity event my sister's job is hosting. It's a gala."

"Oh, I heard a few people at the office talking about that. It sounds like it's a pretty big deal," Sheridan commented. "You didn't mention it."

"Nah, it's a big event, but it's not a big deal." Nick slipped his feet into his loafers, now damn near ready to sprint out of the hotel room. "My sister is a speech therapist at the hospital that hosts the gala every year as a fundraiser. We just go to support her, that's all."

"We? You're taking a date?"

"No, definitely not taking anyone. Me, E, and my boy Thad are going. It's kinda like the one guys' night when we get formal." Nick posed as if he were a fashion model. "We get to get our *GQ* swag on."

Sheridan's slight smile put him a little at ease, but then she said, "And bid on a Love Connection, too, right?"

Nick tensed again. This was a side of Sheridan he'd never seen before. She'd never questioned his whereabouts or activities before, and now she was a total inquisitor.

"I don't bid on anyone or anything. I prefer keeping my dollars in my bank account." Nick leaned over and gave her a quick kiss. "I gotta get outta here. We'll talk before your flight."

"We will. Drive safe." Sheridan nodded, then as if things were back to normal, she added, "And thanks for coming over tonight, Nick. I appreciate you."

"The pleasure was mine." Nick winked and hurried out of the room.

As he drove home, Nick's mind was all over the place. The impromptu pleasurable encounter with Sheridan went quite unexpectedly. He left quickly, and it confused him. It wasn't just her inquiry about his weekend plans, but also the suggestion that they spend it together. He was bothered. He liked Sheridan, but spending extended time together wasn't something he wanted to do. Casually kicking it was one thing, but she wasn't a woman he desired to have a true relationship with. Sexual compatibility was one thing, but the emotional connection was nonexistent. He'd dealt with her long enough to know. Their situationship would never be anything more than what it was, and Nick made sure to treat her with respect and made sure he didn't do anything to make her believe it was something else.

Now he wondered if having her attend brunch with his family next weekend would be a mistake. Then again, it was just brunch, and if nothing else, he figured it would satisfy his mother and get her off his back for a while. Right now, he was focused on enjoying hanging out at the gala with his boys and helping his sister.

***

"Man, you're late!" Eric's voice boomed across the grand ballroom of the Ritz-Carlton as soon as Nick stepped inside. The space was adorned with twinkling lights and heart-shaped decorations, setting a luxurious ambiance for the evening. Tuxedo-clad waitstaff welcomed guests with glasses of champagne and delectable hors d'oeuvres, inviting them to mingle and socialize amid the elegant surroundings.

"I know, I know. It's not my fault." Nick's eyes shifted over to Thaddeus, who was standing beside him. "Someone had to make a pit stop at the mall after they left the airport this afternoon."

"Hey, I forgot my tuxedo shoes. What did you expect me to do, wear my Js?" Thaddeus shook his head. He raised his arm and dapped Eric as the two men greeted one another. "What's up, E? You looking smoother than Tyrese singing a damn love song."

Eric struck a pose as if he were on the cover of *GQ* magazine and said, "What's up, Thad? You know how a brother does. I knew this place was gonna be full of women, so I had to come correct."

"Yeah, Nick told me there would be plenty of women here, and he definitely didn't lie." Thad looked around.

"But there is one particular woman here who is pissed at you, Nick. So, get ready." Eric laughed.

"Who?"

"It's about time you got here. What took you so long?" Sabrina demanded.

Nick shouldn't have been surprised by how beautiful his sister looked, but for some reason, he was. She wore a rose gold sequined dress that was striking, and her hair was pulled up into a tight bun on top of her head. Her face seemed to be glowing.

"Damn, Sabrina!" Thaddeus said. "You are gorgeous."

"Thanks," Sabrina responded, then turned back to Nick. "You were supposed to be here thirty minutes ago."

"Did I miss the auction? It's only ten o'clock. I thought it didn't start until ten thirty." Nick frowned. He had promised Sabrina that he would bid on her so she wouldn't have to risk going on a date with some lame.

"I know what time it is. Did you register for the auction?" Sabrina asked.

"Calm down, Brina. I registered." Nick showed her the heart-shaped paddle with the number 145 in the center. "I got you. I don't even know why you were worried. Eric is registered too."

"Hell, I am too." Thaddeus held up his paddle as well and winked. "I'm definitely bidding."

Sabrina ignored him and continued talking to her brother. "I didn't give Eric my two hundred dollars to spend, did I? Nope, I gave it to you," Sabrina told him.

"Wait, you're paying for your own self? Is that legal?" Thad laughed.

"Shut the hell up, Thad," Sabrina said.

The music died down, and a small woman onstage asked all the auction participants to report to the back.

"Guess that's your cue to go," Nick told her. "Look, I got you. And Thad is right, you look amazing."

"She looks beyond amazing."

They all turned to see Mason smiling at Sabrina. No one said anything for a few seconds, until Nick broke the silence. "What's up, Mason? Glad to see you. How've you been?"

"I'm good, Nick. How's life been treating you?" Mason asked, his eyes never leaving Sabrina.

"Hello, Mason. Nice to see you." Sabrina sighed and gave Mason a quick, half-hearted smile before excusing herself. "I have to go."

"Good luck," Thad said, waving his paddle at her.

"You're really trying to get cussed out tonight, huh?" Nick laughed. "Why do you insist on getting on her nerves?"

"Because she treated us like crap when we were kids. This is payback and you know it. She's always been fine as hell, though, that's for sure," Thad told him.

"Man, you never stood a chance, and I ain't even know you as a kid," Eric said. "Sabrina don't play when it comes to dating, and she will drop you like you never existed if you push her to her limit. We all know that."

Nick realized that Mason was still standing beside them, and he felt bad for his sister's ex. "Mason, man, I'm sorry about the way things went down with you and Sabrina. You're a cool dude."

"It's okay," Mason told him. "I got a plan to win her back. Don't worry."

Nick didn't have the heart to tell him that he knew his sister well enough to know that she would never give Mason another chance. Once she was done, she was done. He had seen it happen time and time again over his lifetime.

"Well, good luck, man." Nick nodded.

"I'll check you guys later." Mason turned and disappeared into the crowd.

"I can't believe Sabrina was even engaged to that cornball," Thad commented. "He doesn't even seem like her type. For as long as I've known her, she's always been with a hardcore, bodybuilder-type dude who would look like he stepped out of a scene from a rap video. That cat looks like he teaches psychology at the local community college."

"Man, you're crazy." Nick laughed.

"He's right, though, Nick. Everybody knows that Mason was definitely *not* Sabrina's type," Eric agreed.

The three men walked over to the bar and were standing in line when Nick noticed a familiar face across the room. She was a little on the thick side, but she definitely owned the room as she walked. Several people stopped and stared, including Thad and Eric. Her form-fitting black dress clung to her curvaceous body just right, revealing enough cleavage to make a man want to see more. Nick was a breast man, and he couldn't help but notice. She wore her hair short now, but she still had the brightest eyes he had ever seen, with thick, long lashes.

"Hey," Eric asked, "don't we know her?"

"I think so," Nick said, unable to take his eyes off her.

"Have you guys seen Sabrina?"

Emily's voice interrupted his thoughts. He turned around and was pleasantly surprised to see his sister's friend decked out in a sapphire blue ball gown, looking very much like a young Heidi Klum.

"She went to wherever the auction participants are. Isn't that where you should be?" he asked.

"That's where I was, but I didn't see her over there," Emily told him, looking around the room.

"There she is over there," Eric said.

Nick looked in the direction Eric was pointing and spotted his sister near the dance floor, in what looked like a heated conversation with Mason. Nick was about to go and make sure Sabrina was okay when he saw Khalil walk over and say something. Within seconds, Sabrina walked away, and so did Mason.

"Oh, shit," Emily said. "See you guys later."

"Definitely," Eric said. As she departed, Eric commented, "That's one sexy-ass white girl. I swear, I just might put a bid in for her myself."

"Man, you're crazy." Nick laughed.

"Hey, I got a couple of stacks I would be willing to spend, and besides, this is a charity event, right? I suddenly feel inspired to give back." Eric shrugged with a smile.

The small woman who had made the previous announcement came back onto the stage and introduced the auctioneer, Chet Peterson, a local TV news anchorman who seemed a little too excited about his job for the night.

"Ladies and gentlemen, welcome to the Love Connection Gala's dating auction." Chet's voice boomed with an almost theatrical flair, visibly excited. "Tonight, we're not just raising funds for a great cause. We're giving you the chance to bid on some of the most eligible singles right here in our very own hospital."

The crowd erupted in applause and laughter. Onstage, the first participant, Dr. Claire Turner, took her place. She was dressed in a stunning lavender gown that highlighted her radiant smile.

"Let's start the bidding with Dr. Turner," Chet announced. "A well-known figure here, admired for her dedication and a heart of gold. Who's ready to bid on an evening with this incredible doctor?"

Hands shot up as the crowd responded enthusiastically. Chet guided the bidding with exaggerated gestures, enjoying the lively interaction. "We're starting at one hundred! Do I hear one fifty? Yes, there's one fifty! How about two hundred? Two hundred, anyone?"

As the bidding war for Dr. Turner ended, Chet moved on to the next participant. Nick was pleasantly surprised when Emily took a step forward and stood onstage.

"Next up, we have pediatric nurse Emily Harris." Chet's voice took on a playful tone. "Not only is she a star on the floor, but she's also a fantastic cook and an avid fan of classic movies. Who's ready to bid for a delightful evening with Emily?"

"One hundred dollars!" Eric immediately held his paddle up.

"We have one hundred here. Do I hear two hundred?" Chet asked.

"Two fifty!" someone yelled.

"Two seventy-five!" Eric countered.

"Five hundred dollars!"

Quickly realizing that his attempt at winning the date with Emily was diminished by the tall, tuxedo-wearing guy in glasses standing directly in front of the stage, Eric politely bowed out and took his loss like a true gentleman.

"Five hundred going once, going twice, and the date is sold," Chet announced.

"Sorry, E. Let me buy you a drink." Nick patted his back.

"Where's Thad?" he asked when they reached the bar.

"I don't know." Eric shrugged.

"Oh my God, I need a drink *now!*" Emily appeared out of nowhere and leaned between them.

Nick put his arm around her. "Eric, buy her a drink. You got a couple of stacks."

Eric gave him a dirty look, then turned and said, "What you drinking, Em?"

"Something strong . . . please." Emily sighed.

Eric ordered them both a vodka and cranberry juice.

"Eric did try really hard to win a date with you," Thad said, appearing out of nowhere. "That other guy was a little more determined. He's been checking you out all night. I watched him."

"Where? What guy? I don't even know who won the auction," Emily said.

"The guy over there next to the lady in the silver dress." Thad motioned.

"Ewwwwwww, I don't wanna go out with him."

"Why not?" Nick asked.

"Because she wants to go out with me." Eric grinned, passing Emily her drink.

"That guy is *not* my type."

"How do you know? Do you know him?"

"Because . . ." Emily sighed.

"Because what?" They all waited for her to respond.

"Because he'ad s white."

They laughed uncontrollably.

"It's not funny, Nick." Emily pouted.

"Yes, it is," Nick told her. He reached over and put his arm around Emily and gave her a hug. She really seemed devastated.

"Excuse me. I believe that's my prized possession you're embracing."

Nick and Emily both looked over to see the guy who won the auction smiling at them.

"Hello, I'm Brady," the guy said.

"Nice to meet you, man." Nick extended his hand. "I'm Nick, and you're right, she is a prize. Emily, this is Brady."

Nick caught the evil look Emily gave him, then watched as she plastered the fakest smile on her face and said, "Nice to meet you."

"All right, ladies and gentlemen, are you ready for our next auction item? Coming to the stage is someone who's not just a standout clinician in the speech and audiology clinic, but also an absolute gem of a person. Let's give a warm round of applause for Ms. Sabrina Chambers," Chet announced.

The crowd erupted into applause as Sabrina stepped onto the stage, her slightly visible discomfort overshadowed by her undeniable beauty and elegance.

"Now, Sabrina isn't just known for her expertise in helping others find their voices," Chet continued with a grin. "She's also known for her incredible sense of humor and kindness that brightens up everyone's day. So who's ready to spend an evening with this delightful and talented clinician?"

The crowd responded with laughter and enthusiastic applause, including a high-pitched whistle from Eric.

"All right, folks, let's start the bidding at one hundred dollars. Who's in for one hundred?" Chet called out.

"One hundred dollars!" Nick raised his paddle, hoping to secure the winning bid uncontested. However, the goal was short-lived.

"I see one hundred. Now who's going to make it one fifty?"

A hand shot up from the back, and Chet pointed to the bidder. "One fifty! Thank you. Now who's going to go two hundred?"

"I got two hundred," Eric offered, trying to help out his friend.

As the bids rolled in, the excitement in the room grew. But Sabrina's facade of composure began to fade, replaced by a look of distress. Nick quickly realized her panic was for good reason as a familiar face in the crowd raised his hand.

"I'll go two fifty!" Khalil called out, his voice filled with determination.

The crowd murmured with curiosity as another hand went up. This time, it was Mason, Sabrina's ex-boyfriend.

"Three hundred," Mason announced, his tone defiant.

Khalil wasn't backing down. "Three fifty," he shot back quickly.

Mason narrowed his eyes and raised his hand again. "Four hundred."

"Oh, my God," Emily muttered.

"This is crazy," Eric commented.

"Nick, do something. Raise your paddle!" Emily pleaded.

Nick was too shocked to move as the bidding war heated up, with Khalil and Mason exchanging higher bids, their rivalry on display for everyone to see. Chet stood and smiled at the drama, his excitement growing.

"Four fifty!" Khalil called out.

"Five hundred!" Mason countered.

The room buzzed with anticipation as the two men continued to raise the stakes. But just as it seemed the bidding might go on forever, a new hand shot up in the crowd.

"One thousand dollars!" Brady called out, his voice confident.

The crowd gasped and then erupted into applause. Chet's eyes widened in surprise. "One thousand dollars! Wow, that's a substantial bid. And it looks like we have a winner."

Khalil and Mason both looked disappointed as Brady's bid ended the war. Chet turned to Sabrina with a broad smile.

"Well, congratulations to you again, sir, for winning this exciting bid, and a huge thank-you to everyone who participated. Sabrina, you're going to have a fantastic evening, and all the proceeds are going to a wonderful cause."

Sabrina, visibly flustered, turned to exit the stage.

Chet shook her hand warmly. "Thanks again, Sabrina, and thanks to our generous bidder. Now let's keep the gala going with more exciting auctions."

"What are you, some kind of perv? You want two women at one time?" Emily turned and asked Brady, her face red with anger.

"You wanted someone to do something, so I did. I was trying to help. Besides, I think she'd be a great date for my best friend."

Emily glanced over at Nick, who was still trying to figure out what had just happened. "Your sister is going to kill you. I hope you know that."

Nick shook his head, desperately hoping Emily's prediction was wrong, although deep down he knew there was a good chance it wasn't. Scanning the crowded ballroom, his gaze finally locked on to the person he sought. Their eyes met, and a smile graced her lips, the dimple in her left cheek adding to her charm. Just as he prepared to make his way toward her, Sabrina stepped in front of him.

"What the hell, Nick? How could you let that happen to me? I've never felt so humiliated in my life. You just stood there while Khalil and Mason battled it out in front of everyone?" Sabrina's voice was full of anger and hurt.

"Brina, it wasn't my fault. There was nothing I could do," Nick responded, his tone slightly agitated. He knew his sister was upset, rightfully so, but he was now on a mission.

"That's it? That's all you're going to say?" Sabrina scowled.

"Hang tight. I'll be right back," Nick assured her, gently pushing past her. As he navigated through the bustling ballroom, darting through the sea of elegantly dressed attendees, he could hear Chet as the auction continued, but his focus was on one thing: finding the woman he'd locked eyes with moments earlier. She had been standing by the grand piano, her presence both magnetic and elusive.

He moved through the crowd, each step quickening with anticipation. His eyes scanned the room, searching for a glimpse of her dress—a stunning shade of emerald green that had caught his attention. He weaved past groups of people engaged in what was happening on the stage, occasionally pausing to glance around, hoping she might reappear.

A pang of frustration crept in his chest as he reached the edge of the ballroom. She was nowhere in sight. His heart sank slightly as he moved toward the bar, thinking maybe she had stopped for a drink. The bartender offered a polite smile, but Nick shook his head and sighed as he adjusted his suit jacket. He had no other choice but to accept the fact that she was gone.

Chapter 13

Sabrina

"I'm free!" Sabrina squealed into the phone as she pulled out of the parking lot of the courthouse on Wednesday.

"I'm glad you're free. I guess your court case went well?" Tenille asked.

"The judge threw everything out. The asshole cop didn't even really have the chance to say anything. I explained exactly what happened, showed him my insurance papers, and he dismissed all the charges. The asshole cop just stood there looking stupid."

"Stop calling him an asshole cop."

"He is an asshole cop, no correction. As of today, he is a stupid asshole cop."

"Aren't you glad you didn't waste your money on a lawyer? See? Nick was right," Tenille told her.

"Don't bring that name up. I'm still pissed at him," Sabrina snapped.

"Brina, what did you expect him to do? You know Nick ain't have money like that. Where the hell was he supposed to get eleven hundred dollars from? And from what Noelle told me, the bidding may have gone even higher than that."

"He could have combined the money he had with money from Eric. He had money. His ass was bidding on Emily."

"And between the two of them, they probably had about two hundred dollars." Tenille laughed.

"I gave him two hundred myself, so they had to have more than that," Sabrina informed her. "Anyway, what are you doing tomorrow for your birthday?"

"Well, I have an engagement shoot tomorrow afternoon, and then Marquise has a basketball game, so I will be cheering for my son."

"That's it?"

"Yep, that's it. What excitement do you have planned?" Tenille asked.

"Nothing at all. I'm single this year, remember?" Sabrina sighed. She tried to remember the last time she had been single on Valentine's Day, and for the life of her, she couldn't. Whether it was a boyfriend, a fiancé, a significant other, a boo, or even a potential boo, she always had a valentine. It was odd for her not to have any plans at all.

"There's nothing wrong with being single on Valentine's Day. Hell, some people wish they were single on Valentine's Day."

Sabrina wondered what Tenille meant by that and was about to ask her to explain, but the beeping sound of her call waiting through the car's Bluetooth interrupted her. She glanced at the screen of her dash and saw that it was Emily. She asked Tenille to hold on and clicked over.

"What's up, Em?"

"Just checking on you. How did it go in court? I see you answered your phone, which means they didn't throw you in jail."

"Nope, the judge threw the case out, thank God."

"Good for you! I told you you had nothing to worry about."

"Let's meet for drinks to celebrate. My treat, of course."

"Ummmmm, I can't," Emily told her. "I have plans already."

"Plans? With who?"

"I'm meeting Victor for brunch at Cascades," Emily replied.

"Oh my God, Emily, he's married!" Sabrina yelled. "What the hell is wrong with you?"

"I keep telling you, he's not married," Emily whined.

"He's engaged and about to be married. The point is he has a woman, one who is preparing to have his last name soon. This is stupid."

Sabrina couldn't fathom why Emily continued to see this guy. One principle they had always upheld was that married men were strictly off-limits. They prided themselves on their intelligence, beauty, and success, knowing they deserved partners who were fully available. They had never felt the need to resort to someone else's man when they were more than capable of finding their own.

"Calm down, Sabrina. It's just lunch, that's all. Look, I have to go. Don't forget we have reservations at Magnolia Tavern on Friday night. Seven thirty. Please be on time."

"On time for what? Magnolia Tavern?" Sabrina frowned, wondering why they would be going to the overpriced restaurant.

"Don't pretend like you don't know our Love Connection date is this week, Brina."

"I thought it was next week, I swear."

"Sabrina, I sent you a text Sunday night asking if Friday night was cool, and your response was, 'Whatever, I'll probably be locked up,'" Emily snapped.

Sabrina couldn't even argue as she suddenly remembered the text she had gotten in the middle of the night. She had been so sleepy she thought it was a dream.

"Emily, that's not fair. You sent that text to me at like two in the morning while I was asleep."

"You weren't too sleepy to respond with a smart-ass comment, were you?"

"Emily, I'm not going."

"Yes, you are. You have to go. I'm not going out with this guy by myself. The only reason I agreed to dinner instead of lunch was because it was a double date and you would be there. We can't cancel. Let's just go and get it over with. We'll be done by nine at the latest. I promise."

"Emily."

"Victor's calling. I gotta go." Emily hung up before Sabrina could say another word.

"Uuuuuuggggggghhhh!" Sabrina groaned.

"What the heck is wrong with you?"

She had forgotten that her sister was even on the phone.

"I forgot about this stupid Love Connection date with the stupid white boys. Emily set it up for Friday night." Sabrina leaned her head back.

"Don't be like that. You were just complaining about not having any Valentine's plans, and now look at you. You got a date," Tenille teased.

"First of all, it's not a date, it's an obligation. It's a charitable contribution as a matter of fact." Sabrina sighed. "Second, Valentine's Day is tomorrow, not Friday. I can't do this. You know I don't do white boys, Ten. I just can't."

"Girl, stop it. Go. It will probably be fun. Like you said, it's not a date. It's only gonna be for a couple of hours, and it's for charity. Besides, isn't Emily gonna be there with you?"

"Yeah, but that's probably gonna make it even worse. Me at dinner with three white people."

"Now you know Emily ain't really white." Tenille laughed. "Hell, she probably is hating the fact that she gotta go on this date with a white boy more than you are."

"It's *not* a date!" Sabrina corrected her.

"Fine, this charity event. Look, I gotta go get some work done. Call me later."

As Sabrina reached down to adjust the volume of her car radio, she couldn't help but notice the state of her nails, desperately in need of a manicure. Suddenly, it dawned on her that Mason had booked a couple's pampering package at her favorite beauty spa: massages, manicures, pedicures, the whole nine yards.

No sense in letting that appointment go to waste, she thought as she quickly redialed Tenille's number.

"Ten," she said, "I have a birthday gift for you. Meet me at After Effex tomorrow at two."

"What?"

"After Effex, meet me there tomorrow at two."

"I can't. I have an engagement photo shoot tomorrow, Brina."

"Shit, that's right. Hold tight. Lemme see if I can get an earlier time. I'll call you right back."

Sabrina instructed Siri to call After Effex.

"Thanks for calling After Effex, where before and after are never the same. This is Kai. How can I help you?"

"Hey, Kai, it's Sabrina Chambers."

"Hey, Sabrina, how are you?"

"I'm good. Listen, I have an appointment for tomorrow afternoon. I need to see if I can change it to tomorrow morning instead," Sabrina replied.

"Now, Sabrina, you know we're booked solid tomorrow. You do realize what tomorrow is, don't you? Wait, and it's for a couple's package."

"Ummmmm, but it's my sister's birthday," Sabrina said innocently.

"Hold on, lemme go check and see what I can do. You'd better be glad I like you." Kai sighed. She placed Sabrina on hold, and a few minutes later, she was back on the line. "I have good news and I have bad news."

"Oh God. What's the bad news?" Sabrina groaned.

"Well, I'll just tell you the good news first. I can change your appointment to ten in the morning."

"Great. What's the bad news then?"

"You won't be able to get the facials with Taryn," Kai explained apologetically. "She's completely booked solid. However, I can arrange for you to have full-body massages with the masseuse, and I'll schedule you in with Monya, our nail tech, and her assistant for the manicures and pedicures. Consider yourself lucky to be one of her regulars. That's the only reason I can work this scheduling magic for you."

"I know, I know. And I appreciate it, Kai. We can cancel the facials. You're the best." Sabrina became excited at the thought of not only spending time with Tenille for her birthday but also having something to do for the dreaded holiday. "I will see you tomorrow."

"Be on time, Sabrina. You can't be late."

"I promise, I won't."

"Happy Valentine's Day! Welcome to After Effex, where before and after are never the same." Kai greeted Sabrina and Tenille when they walked into the spa the next morning.

"Kai, you really have to say that to everyone who walks in here?" Sabrina laughed.

"Each and every one, girl." Kai laughed. "You're actually a few minutes early, Sabrina. That's a first. Good job!"

"That's what I told her." Tenille nodded.

"Neither one of you are funny." Sabrina smirked.

"Hey, Sabrina." Monya, her favorite nail specialist, walked into the reception area of the salon. "You're early."

Sabrina couldn't help laughing along with her sister and Kai. "I know, I know. Monya, this is my sister, Tenille. Today's her birthday."

"Well, happy birthday," Monya said, giving Tenille a quick hug.

"And here I was thinking Sabrina was just saying that so I would change her appointment time." Kai smiled. "Let's get you two to the back so you can change and get started."

After what was the most amazing massage, Sabrina and Tenille made their way to the open area of the spa, where Monya and her assistant were waiting for them at the pedicure stations.

"You good?" Sabrina asked.

"I feel awesome." Tenille nodded, taking a seat in the chair beside her.

Sabrina eased her feet into the water and continued to relax. Between the warm water, the feel of Monya's hands working their magic, and the massage, it felt like heaven. Sabrina began telling Monya about her pending Love Connection date.

"Hey, you never know. From what some of my clients are telling me, once you go white, everything's right." She laughed.

"No, thanks. I like my men the same way I like my coffee: strong, black, and smooth," Sabrina said. She didn't realize how loud she was until she heard a couple of the other clients in the salon giggle, all of whom were black.

"I had a guy who was convinced collard greens were just fancy lettuce. He tried to make a 'healthier' version of my mom's recipe and ended up with what looked like a green swamp on a plate. He served it with a side of quinoa and was like, 'It's gourmet!'"

"I went out with this guy who didn't understand why I needed to spend so much time on my hair. He was like, 'Can't you just, you know, brush it and go?' I had to explain that my hair is more like a full-time job, not a five-minute task."

Monya shook her head, still amused. "And let's not forget the guy who tried to impress me by saying he was 'down with the culture.' He showed up wearing a dashiki he bought online, which was about three sizes too small and looked like it was made of bedsheets. He thought it was his 'ethnic statement piece.'"

Another woman burst out laughing. "Oh, my goodness. The effort is sweet, but sometimes it's just way off. I had a guy who tried to impress me by learning some dance moves from a video he saw. He showed up doing what he called the Electric Slide, but it looked more like he was having a seizure."

The ladies all laughed together, nodding in agreement. Kai grinned and said, "It's clear that no matter the race, men are going to be men. They might mess up our favorite recipes, misunderstand our hair routines, or completely misinterpret our cultural references, but they all have their quirks."

Tenille raised her glass of wine, toasting to the shared experience. "Here's to the good, the bad, and the hilariously awkward. At the end of the day, we all just need to laugh it off and remember that we're all a little bit of a mess, and who knows? Maybe it will be fun. You never know. This could be your Mr. Right."

"It won't be. Besides, you were the one who told me not to date for a year, remember? I need to get myself together. Isn't that what you said?"

"Yes, and I meant it. But you never know what could happen."

"A whole year with no di . . . I mean, dates?" Monya looked at Tenille for confirmation.

"I just suggested she take a breather. Over the past few years, my sister has had more than her fair share of—" Tenille explained.

"Whoa, whoa, whoa! You're making it seem like I'm a ho!" Sabrina interrupted.

"I was gonna say fiancés! And you have. Five, if I'm not mistaken."

"Five fiancés?" Monya's assistant gasped.

"Four," Sabrina corrected her.

"Fine, four," Tenille relented.

"What are you, a runaway bride?" Monya asked.

"No, I just realize that they're not the one before I say 'I do' and it's too late. I refuse to be one of these women who are stuck in a horrible situation." Sabrina shrugged.

"Well, damn," Tenille said under her breath.

"What?" Sabrina asked.

"Nothing. I understand. But, Sabrina, you broke up with a guy because of what he gave you for Christmas," Tenille commented.

"What did he give you?" Monya asked.

"He gave me an emergency car care kit," Sabrina replied. "And that was after he gave me a cheap-ass manicure set for my birthday along with a card that read, 'Happy Birthday, Princess.' What the hell? I turned twenty-five, not five!"

"I got one better than that," another woman spoke up from the chair she was sitting in. "I had a guy give me a box from the jewelry store. I'm all excited and open it to find a picture of a necklace in it. Then that joker had the nerve to say it was what he wanted to give me but he couldn't afford it."

"That's kind of sweet," Tenille told her.

"It might have been if he hadn't been wearing some brand new Jordans when he gave it to me. And when I pointed them out, he admitted that he had purchased the sneakers right before going to the jewelry store."

"Please, I had a guy give me a teeth whitening kit for Valentine's Day." Monya's assistant sighed.

"What?" Sabrina laughed.

"And for my birthday, he gave me a gift certificate for electrolysis."

"Now that's just wrong right there."

"And offensive."

"And none of y'all are with these guys, are you?" Sabrina asked the room.

"Nope."

"Hell naw."

"Not me."

The ladies reassured her.

"And so you should understand my decision. I refuse to stay with a guy who doesn't even know me well enough to buy me a gift that I would enjoy. It's not even about the price. He could've bought me a bottle of bubble bath and a bottle of wine, and I would've been good with that. A sister loves to relax," Sabrina explained.

"That's true," Monya said. "And I gotta respect your fearlessness. A lot of women would stay in these dead-end, lifeless relationships knowing they don't even like the dude just for the sake of saying she got a man."

"Nope, I refuse to." Sabrina shook her head emphatically.

"Get out while the getting's good," another woman said with a laugh.

"I need to go to the restroom."

Sabrina looked over at her sister. A few moments ago, Tenille had been enjoying the conversation. Now she looked a bit uncomfortable.

"You're actually all set," Monya's assistant told her. "You like it?"

"I love it," Tenille said, flexing her perfectly painted toes.

"Y'all can go ahead and get changed," Monya said to Sabrina. "You're all done too."

The two sisters went back into the changing area.

"Thank you so much for this," Tenille said after they had gotten dressed and were preparing to leave.

"No thanks needed. You know I had to hook you up for your birthday," Sabrina told her. "Besides, you deserve it. You've been working like a crazy woman for the past year."

"Hey, in my line of work, I gotta get it while I can. I'm just lucky that so many people are getting marr . . ." Tenille stopped mid-sentence. "I'm sorry, Brina. I didn't mean anything by that."

"I know you didn't, and you don't have to apologize. I was the one who broke up with Mason, remember? It was my decision. I'm fine." She gave her sister a quick hug. "But, Ten, with the way you and Brandon work, when do you have time for each other? Damn, I never see y'all together. Today's your birthday. He couldn't take at least the afternoon off?"

Tenille shrugged. "He comes home at night. We see each other then. We are fine."

Sabrina decided not to push the issue. She was the last person to give relationship advice, especially considering her track record. At least Tenille had made it to the altar.

They proceeded toward the reception area to leave, pausing as they walked through the main area of the spa to thank the staff.

"Thank you so much for your impeccable service, Monya. Ladies, thanks so much for the conversation," Sabrina told them. Monya walked them out to the receptionist desk.

"I feel amazing. This was incredible. Thanks again," Tenille told them.

"Enjoy the rest of your birthday, Tenille. Sabrina, I can't wait to hear how everything goes," Monya said.

"I'll fill you in when I come for my appointment in two weeks," Sabrina said. "Right, Kai?"

Kai laughed. "You know I already got you on the books."

"Awesome. How much do I owe you?"

"Nothing. It's already taken care of. Everything including the tip was paid when the appointment was booked. Since it's a holiday, we required it up front."

Sabrina blinked. "Uh, all righty then."

The door chimed as it opened.

"Welcome to After Effex, where before and after are never the same," Kai said, greeting whoever had come through the door.

"Hi, we're here for the couple's package."

A familiar voice caused the hairs on Sabrina's neck to stand up. She glanced over and saw the look on Tenille's face, and she froze.

"No problem. Do you have an appointment?" Kai asked.

"Yes, at two. Last name is Boyd."

Sabrina looked up and locked eyes with Kai. The young receptionist glanced down and began clicking the computer keyboard. "I'm so sorry. Your appointment *was* at two."

Sabrina slowly turned around and faced Mason, standing near the doorway with his arm around a woman's waist. His eyes met hers, and she slowly grinned. The look on his face was priceless.

"Hello, Mason," she spoke.

"Uh, oh, uh, hey," he stuttered, then looked at Tenille. "Um, hello, uh, Tenille."

"Hey, Mason." Tenille nodded.

"How are you?" he asked.

"I'm wonderful. Hello," Sabrina said, noticing and greeting his companion standing beside him, a short, petite woman with fair skin and a reddish weave. The colorful bodycon dress she wore clung to her curves. Mason looked a bit underdressed compared to her in his black sweats, long-sleeved T-shirt, and black shell-toe Adidas.

The woman stared at Sabrina for a second before finally saying, "Hi."

Sabrina noticed the woman's scrutinizing gaze from head to toe, and she couldn't help but feel relieved that she had opted not to wear the casual sweatsuit she had initially considered for the spa visit. Instead, she exuded confidence in her sleek black pantsuit. Despite the slight pain of her black peep-toe stiletto heels, they added a touch of elegance, complemented by her freshly done pedicure. And although she hated that she didn't have the opportunity for a makeup session with Taryn, the baddest makeup artist in the salon, Sabrina reassured herself that the minimal makeup she applied herself still added a polished touch to her appearance.

"Uh, um, Sabrina, this is Janae," Mason said, still looking a bit awkward. "Janae, this uh, is uh, Sabrina and Tenille."

Sabrina held her hand out and said, "Nice to meet you, Janae."

The woman shook Sabrina's hand lightly and then eased back into Mason's arms, tightening her grip on him.

"Can you squeeze us in?" Mason turned and asked Kai. "I mean, I already paid for it and everything."

"You ready, Ten?" Sabrina said quickly, reaching into her purse and pulling out her Chanel shades. She put them on her face and headed toward the door. "See you in two weeks, Kai!"

As they passed Mason and Janae, Tenille gave them a quick wave. "You two have a great day. Happy Valentine's Day."

Tears were streaming down Sabrina's face as they got to her car. "Oh, my God, Ten." She could hardly breathe.

"Are you okay?"

Her body shook as she leaned over and gasped for air.

"Sabrina, calm down. It's gonna be okay. I'm so sorry this had to happen to you. Please don't be upset." Tenille ran over and began rubbing her back. "That was a bitch move and just goes to show how trifling Mason really is. You were right to break up with him. You dodged a bullet for sure."

Sabrina took a few deep breaths, steadying herself until she could speak. It was only then that Tenille realized her sister was laughing, not crying, and she found herself joining in the laughter.

"Wait, can you believe he actually brought some random to the nail spa that happens to be the only one you go to? Who the hell does that?" Tenille giggled.

"But the kicker is he paid for our appointment." Sabrina began laughing all over again and unlocked the car.

"Oh my God, Sabrina. You're lying! You told me you did this for my birthday."

"I mean, I was gonna pay for it. I didn't realize it until Kai told me. He's gonna be pissed."

"Do you care?" Tenille asked as she climbed into the passenger side.

"Nope, but I think we'd better get the hell out of here before he finds out," Sabrina said with a sense of satisfaction.

"Sabrina, wait."

Sabrina turned to see Mason rushing toward her car.

"Uh-oh," Tenille moaned.

Just as Sabrina prepared herself to get cursed out for using the appointment for herself and her sister, Mason stated, "My mom has been trying to reach you."

"I know," Sabrina snapped.

"She says she needs to talk to you, and it's important. I mean, I know you and I are having issues right now, but you can still speak with her."

"Issues? Mason, we broke up and aren't together," Sabrina reminded him. "And whatever she needs to talk about, she needs to be having that conversation with Janae."

"That's not—"

"Bye, Mason." Sabrina got into her car and drove off.

Chapter 14

Tenille

Tenille navigated her way through the crowded bleachers of the school gymnasium where Marquise's team was playing. She found a spot midway up the stands, strategically positioning herself right behind her son's team. She wanted to offer support without overwhelming him with her presence. Tonight was significant for Marquise. He was facing off against the school he hoped to attend in the fall, and she knew he was eager to make a strong impression.

As the announcer called out the starting lineup, Tenille couldn't contain her excitement when Marquise's name rang out. Despite the sheepish glance her son gave her, she let out a proud scream before quickly settling back into her seat, applause echoing around her. As the game began, she found herself fully immersed in the action on the court. The energy was high, with the sounds of fans and the rhythmic bounce of the basketball filling the air. She watched intently as Marquise darted across the court, sweat gleaming on his forehead, his determination evident in every move.

"Let's go, Mook!" Tenille yelled, conveniently forgetting not to use her son's nickname despite his numerous requests.

Marquise was on fire, charging down the court, dribbling with a precision that spoke of countless hours of practice. His focus was unwavering, a stark contrast to his teammates, who seemed to be playing in slow motion. The opposing team quickly capitalized on the lackluster defense, sinking basket after basket.

As the scoreboard continued to favor the other side, Tenille's heart sank. She could see Marquise's frustration mounting. Each missed pass, each lack of defensive effort from his teammates seemed to chip away at his resolve. She could see his shoulders slump slightly each time the opposing team scored, his frustration transforming into a visible struggle to keep his head up.

The game clock ticked down, and Tenille noticed Marquise's energy beginning to wane. He tried to rally his teammates with a few encouraging words, but his calls were met with indifferent nods. She saw him attempt to make a steal, only to be met with a series of careless errors from his teammates. His head dropped, and he seemed to slow down, his once-fiery movements now marked by a growing resignation.

Tenille's hands clenched around her water bottle as she felt a pang of sympathy for her son. She knew how much he cared about the game, how hard he worked to improve his skills. It hurt to see his efforts overshadowed by the lack of commitment from his team. Her heart ached as she saw him attempt a shot from the three-point line, only for it to miss the mark, his frustration evident as he stared at the ball bouncing away.

"What's the score?"

Tenille turned to Sabrina, who was taking a seat beside her. "What in the world are you doing here?"

"Well, I ain't have anything better to do, so I may as well come and support Mookie. I decided to make him my valentine."

"I'm sorry, but he's already *my* valentine." Tenille laughed.

"You have a man. I don't. You don't get to keep all the men. You have to give me one."

"You can have Brandon," Tenille said.

"Uh, no, thanks." Sabrina shook her head. "I'm good."

"Come on, Marquise! Keep hustling! You got this, Mook!"

At the sound of someone calling Marquise's name, both ladies scanned the crowd to locate the source. Sabrina's mouth fell open in surprise as she spotted the guy standing and yelling across the court. Following his gaze, she noticed the smile spreading across Marquise's face as he nodded in acknowledgment.

"Oh, my God. Is that Xavier? Shit, that is Xavier!" Sabrina stood up.

Tenille tried to pull her sister back down. "Brina, sit down."

Marquise dashed toward the net and effortlessly executed a layup. As the opposing team gained possession of the ball, Marquise swiftly turned, snatching it away, and sprinted back to the basket, sinking a three-pointer. The crowd went wild, swept up in the excitement of the moment.

"Yeah, Mook!" Sabrina yelled, then told her, "We're at a basketball game. My nephew just made a shot. I'm not sitting down."

Tenille tried to focus on the game, but she couldn't help wonder how the hell Xavier had found out about the game.

"Hey, Ten." A bubbly teenage girl came up the bleachers and gave Tenille a big hug. "Happy birthday."

"Fabian! Oh my goodness! How are you?" Tenille grinned as she held the girl tightly. "You've gotten so big, and you're as beautiful as ever."

"Hey, Fabulous." Sabrina greeted the pretty girl.

"I can't believe you remember that," Fabian said, taking a spot between the two sisters as they made room for her.

"You're always gonna be Fabulous to me," Sabrina told her. "What are you doing here?"

"This is my school. I go to the upper school, though," Fabian replied. "I was so excited when Mookie messaged me and told me about the game. You know I wasn't gonna miss it."

Tenille glanced at Fabian, noting the striking resemblance she bore to her father. She remembered how she had been a cute, chubby 5-year-old when she and Xavier first started dating. Now, Fabian stood almost as tall as Tenille, her long hair pulled back into a ponytail, a subtle hint of makeup enhancing her features.

"You see my dad?" Fabian pointed at Xavier, who was now sitting but staring intently at the game.

"I . . . we did see him." Tenille nodded.

The buzzer sounded, announcing that it was now halftime. The other team was leading, but Marquise's team was now only down by six points.

"My dad told me about Jamaica. I thought that was so great. I'm gonna go see my friends, but I wanna come back and watch the rest of the game with you guys. Is that okay?" Fabian asked.

"Of course," Tenille told her. She hoped Sabrina hadn't heard Fabian's comment about Jamaica.

"Tenille," Sabrina said when Fabian had walked away.

"What?" Tenille looked at her innocently.

"What in the world?"

"I don't know what you're talking about. I didn't know they were gonna be here. Mookie hasn't mentioned anything to me about Fabian at all."

"I'm not talking about Fabian."

"Who are you talking about then?"

"Xavier. That's why you were in Jamaica? You sneaky, sly devil. No wonder you're trying to push Brandon off on me." Sabrina shook her head.

"That's not why I was in Jamaica. He was actually a guest at the wedding I shot," Tenille explained.

"That's why your ass came back all happy. I knew something happened," Sabrina squealed.

"Nothing happened. We just talked, that's it. I swear. He took me to the airport the next morning."

"You spent the night with him? At the hotel? In Jamaica?"

"We sat on the sofa in his room, talking and catching up."

"What a waste."

"What is that supposed to mean?" Tenille asked.

"I mean, if you're gonna spend the night in a hotel room, in Jamaica, with the man who is the love of your life, you may as well do more than just talk." Sabrina sighed. "I definitely woulda gotten more from him than conversation, that's for sure."

Tenille shook her head. "You sound crazy. I'm married. Or did that seem to slip your mind?"

"Nope, but just because you're married doesn't mean you're happy. And when I picked you up from the airport, you were ecstatic."

"Shut up, Sabrina." Tenille could not believe what her sister was saying.

"So, now what happens?"

"Nothing happens."

"You haven't talked to him? Not once since you got back?"

"No, not once."

"So, what are you going to say? I mean, he's here now. You know you're going to have to say something," Sabrina insisted.

"I'm not going to say anything other than hello. What do you think I'm gonna say?"

"'Hey, X, great to see you. You look amazing.' He does look amazing, Ten. That brother has always been fine as hell."

"I'm not having this conversation with you. I'm going to get something to drink. Come on," Tenille declared, rising from her seat. They made their way into the crowded concession area and joined the line.

"Hello, beautiful ladies," a voice greeted them.

Taking a deep breath, Tenille turned around. There stood Xavier, looking amazing in a white collared Polo shirt, jeans, and a pair of black designer loafers. His hair was freshly cut, and his beard was a little fuller than the last time she'd seen him. Once again, her sister's observation rang true—Xavier was fine as hell.

"Xavier!" Sabrina gave him a big hug. "Damn, you smell good."

"Brina, you are still crazy as hell." Xavier laughed. "Happy birthday, Ten. I see you get more and more perfect every year."

Tenille didn't say anything. She just looked at him and shook her head.

"Xavier, you still got a way of making my sister blush," Sabrina teased. "It's so good to see you."

"It's good to see you too. It's been a long time."

"Not as long for some of us," Sabrina hinted.

"Can I help the next customer?" the old lady behind the counter yelled.

Before Tenille could answer, Xavier was in front of her. "Can I get a Sprite, a bottle of water, one Coke, an orange soda, and four popcorns? Y'all want anything else?"

"Nope, sounds right to me." Sabrina shrugged.

He handed the cashier the money, and in return, she passed him the food and drinks. Xavier distributed a box of popcorn to each of them. Then, in a smooth motion, he handed Tenille the bottle of water and the orange soda to Sabrina as though it were the most natural thing in the world.

"Thank you," Tenille told him. She couldn't believe he remembered exactly what they liked.

"Now where is my daughter?" he asked, picking up the remaining two boxes of popcorn and sodas.

"She's probably looking for us. She wanted to sit where we are," Sabrina remarked. "You're welcome to join us if you'd like. It's not safe to be cheering for Marquise in enemy territory. We want you to stay safe, right, Ten?"

Tenille's eyes widened, and she stared at her sister. "Um, okay."

They reentered the gym, where both teams were shooting around and warming up for the second half. Just as Tenille was about to head to their seats on the bleachers, Xavier stopped her.

"Take this for me. I'll be there in a few minutes," he instructed, passing his bottle of water to Sabrina and handing Tenille the other items.

Tenille watched as Xavier made his way behind the team chairs and called out to Marquise. Her son dashed over, and they exchanged fist bumps and a brief hug. Then Xavier leaned in to whisper something into Marquise's ear, gesturing toward the net and the floor. Marquise listened attentively, nodding in understanding.

"Are you coming?" Sabrina nudged.

Tenille hesitated before joining Sabrina, hesitant to tear her gaze away from the touching scene between her ex and her son. Xavier had always been close to Marquise—almost like a father figure alongside her own father and brother. He had been the driving force behind Marquise's participation in various sports, attending all his games and practices while also supporting Fabian's equally busy schedule consisting of dance, Girl Scouts, and piano. During their five years together, their lives had been filled with nonstop activities, and there had never been a dull moment. No matter what Xavier had going on, he made spending time with her and the kids a priority. She missed it.

"Yeah," she finally said, turning to follow Sabrina.

By the time they made it to their seats, Fabian was already there waiting. Tenille passed her a box of popcorn and the Sprite.

"Thanks, Ten." Fabian smiled.

"Thank your dad. Slide down. He's coming to sit up here," Sabrina instructed, making room for Tenille to sit. Tenille positioned herself so that the only available space would be on the other side of Sabrina, ensuring there was no empty space near her. Her efforts in doing so were in vain. When Xavier joined them, he remained focused on the game unfolding on the court, seemingly unconcerned about the seating arrangements in the bleachers.

As they all cheered and screamed throughout the remainder of the game, the tension on the court escalated. Despite Marquise's exceptional performance—he scored twenty-six of his team's forty-three points and provided eleven assists—they ultimately fell short, losing the game by two points. The disappointment on her son's face was heartbreaking, but Tenille resisted the urge to rush down and gather him into her arms, knowing it would embarrass him.

While Xavier went down to talk with the coach, Tenille, Sabrina, and Fabian waited for Marquise.

"You did so good, baby." Tenille greeted him when he finally came out of the locker room.

"Thanks, Ma. But we lost."

"You were awesome." Fabian didn't seem worried about embarrassing Marquise as she ran over and hugged him tight. "My little brother was the star on that court. It doesn't even matter what the score was. All eyes were on you."

"She's right. I saw all the little fast-tail girls checking you out." Sabrina rubbed his head.

"Stop it, Aunt Brina." Marquise ducked away from her. "Thank you guys so much for coming. I didn't expect anyone but Mom."

"You know I told you the other day when we talked I would be here." Fabian smiled.

"When y'all talked, huh?" Tenille raised her eyebrow at Marquise. She had no idea her son and Fabian were even in contact with each other. He hadn't mentioned it to her at all.

"Good game, Mook." Xavier rushed over and grabbed Marquise. "My man!"

"Thanks, X. I'm so glad you came. And thanks for the advice. When I posted up to the left and took a step back, it made a difference. I never thought about that."

"Your left side has always been your strong side, Mook. You favor that side, so that should be the side that you shoot from," Xavier told him.

"A'ight, Commanders! Load up!" Marquise's coach yelled across the gym.

"You riding back to the school with your team?" Sabrina asked.

"Well, actually I was gonna take my mom to dinner for her birthday and Valentine's Day," Marquise said sheepishly as he glanced at Tenille, causing her heart to melt.

Her son meant more to her than life itself, and the thought of him wanting to take her to dinner made her day.

"Awwwwwwww," Sabrina and Fabian said at the same time.

“Sounds like a great idea. How about we treat all these beautiful ladies to dinner, Mook?” Xavier suggested.

“Yes!” Fabian clapped. “Just like the old days.”

Tenille glanced at Sabrina, silently questioning whether she shared the same reservations about the suggested dinner plan. Judging by her response, it seemed she didn’t.

“Hell, having two handsome men take me out to Valentine’s dinner is way better than none. Let’s go,” Sabrina affirmed with a nod.

They all piled into Xavier’s SUV. Knowing that most restaurants in town would be busy with Valentine’s Day crowds, they opted for The Golden Egg, a cozy Chinese eatery they had frequented during the early days of dating. The restaurant was relatively empty. They feasted on pu pu platters and house fried rice while catching up and reminiscing about birthdays past.

Marquise sat next to Tenille, his face brightening as he dug into a plate of orange chicken. Across from them, Sabrina was animatedly recounting a story about a particularly memorable birthday party.

“Remember that time,” Sabrina began, her eyes sparkling with nostalgia, “when we tried to throw Fabian a surprise party, but the whole thing turned into a disaster?”

Xavier chuckled, nodding in agreement. “Oh, I remember that day well. Fabian was so excited, thinking it was a party for her teacher. Little did she know we had something else planned.”

Fabian, now a teenager, grinned at the memory. “I was so thrilled when I saw all those decorations and balloons before I left for school. I didn’t even realize the surprise was for me.”

Marquise leaned in, curious. “What happened with the party? I don’t remember.”

Tenille laughed, her voice full of amusement. "Well, we had this elaborate plan to surprise Fabian at school, but the problem was we didn't realize how early we were supposed to be there. By the time we showed up with the cupcakes, balloons, gift bags, and the presents, all the kids were already gone, including Fabian. It turned out they had early dismissal that day."

The table erupted in laughter, with Xavier shaking his head. "Man, it was crazy. We had to bring all that stuff back to the house and pretend it was just a normal birthday celebration."

Tenille added, still smiling at the memory, "And Fabian's face when she finally figured out what was happening—priceless! She was so confused but happy."

Fabian grinned sheepishly. "I was wondering why everyone kept talking about Ms. Lovejoy's birthday instead of mine. But when I finally got the surprise, it made all the confusion worth it."

"Oh, yeah, now I remember. We had cupcakes for days and all of those candy bags, too. It was great," Marquise said, then looked over at Fabian. "I think my favorite birthday memory was the time you and I tried to make a homemade piñata for Sabrina's party. It was a total mess, but we had so much fun."

Fabian snorted with laughter. "Oh, I remember that! It was supposed to be a fun, colorful piñata, but instead, it looked like a sad paper bag."

"It was still one of the best birthday gifts I've ever received." Sabrina put her arm around Fabian and hugged her.

Xavier looked over at Tenille. "We had plenty of those unforgettable birthday celebrations and a lot of fun. It's the little things that make life special."

To their delight, the staff serenaded them with a rendition of "Happy Birthday" in Mandarin. Before they realized it, the clock had nearly struck midnight.

"Jeez, is it really this late?" Sabrina said, looking at her cell phone.

"These kids got school tomorrow. We gotta go," Tenille said, causing Fabian and Marquise to moan in protest.

"Funny how time flies when you're having fun." Xavier stared at her.

"It really does." She nodded. He was right. The entire night had been fun. She hadn't expected her birthday to be so eventful, but between the spa day, the basketball game, and the impromptu family dinner, she was happier than she'd been in a long time.

They arrived back at the school parking lot to find a police car behind Sabrina's car. Xavier had barely put his truck in park before she jumped out to see what was going on. The lot was dimly lit, and they could make out the shadow of a uniformed officer walking around her vehicle.

"Excuse me. Is there something wrong?" Sabrina asked. Tenille hurried behind her sister.

"Is this your car, ma'am? I was just checking to—" the police officer began.

"Oh, hell no! No way," Sabrina whined.

"You gotta be kidding me." The officer groaned.

"Sabrina, what's wrong?" Tenille asked.

"What seems to be the problem?" Xavier took a step in front of them.

"There's no problem, sir." The officer sighed.

"Yeah, there is!" Sabrina exclaimed. "This is the asshole cop."

"Whoa," Tenille commented.

"What's your deal? Why do you have such a problem with me?" Sabrina asked.

"I don't have a problem with anyone," the officer explained. "I was doing my job patrolling the area because there've been several vehicle break-ins, and I saw your car sitting here."

"Well, my car is fine, and we were just leaving if that's okay with you," Sabrina sneered.

"Officer, thank you for your service," Tenille offered, causing Sabrina's jaw to drop. She couldn't believe her sister's disloyalty, especially after she had explained exactly who this guy was.

"Enjoy the remainder of your evening." The officer nodded before returning to his patrol car and leaving.

"Wow, that's the cop, huh? He's kinda fine," Tenille told her.

"Traitor." Sabrina shook her head and flipped the bird at her sister, now laughing.

Chapter 15

Nick

"Wow, you look nice."

"You look nice too." Nick smiled at Sheridan as she got out of her rental car. "But you're late."

"Oh my goodness, by like five minutes."

He noticed the birthday card she carried in her hand along with the designer handbag. "You brought her a card?"

"It's her birthday, isn't it? You didn't bring a gift?" Sheridan asked.

"Uh, it's on back order."

"You're terrible."

They entered the crowded restaurant, and Nick led them to the back room his mother had reserved for the occasion. His parents were already seated along with Sabrina, Marquise, Tenille, her best friend Sparkle, and a few other of her friends and family members. He was surprised to see the room decorated from top to bottom in black and white. This was the same room they reserved every year, but he had never seen it look like this. Normally, they only had balloons tied to whichever chair Tenille sat in. He also noticed that instead of the traditional sheet cake from the neighborhood grocery store, there was a custom black-and-white cake with a camera sitting on top and Tenille's name in the corner, along with a red, black, and white candy bar.

"Happy birthday, Ten!" he said as he walked into the room. "Hey, everybody."

"Hey, Nick," everyone spoke at once.

"Wow! This is different," Nick said as he made his way over to hug his sister and parents.

"So is this," Sabrina said, her eyes turning to Sheridan. "Hello there."

"Hello." Sheridan smiled.

"Uncle Nick." Marquise jumped up and ran over.

"What up, Mook? You remember my friend Sheridan?"

Marquise nodded. "Yeah, nice to see you again."

"Same here," Sheridan told him.

"Everyone, this is Sheridan," said Nick.

"Nice to meet you, Sheridan." Nick's mom stood up and hugged both of them.

"Nice to meet you as well," Sheridan said. "I've heard so much about all of you."

"How you doing, pretty lady?" Nick's dad smiled. "I'm glad you could join us."

"Let's go sit over there," Nick said, pointing to two empty seats near the end of the table. He paused as they passed Tenille, and Sheridan gave her the birthday card.

"Oh, thank you so much." Tenille stood up. "I really appreciate it, and thanks so much for coming."

"That's from both of us, Ten," Nick told her.

Sheridan playfully hit him on the arm. "Stop it."

"Don't worry, Sheridan. This dude hasn't given me a card or a gift since he was like six, so I know he was lying."

"Hey, that ceramic fish I made you in art class and the handmade card were priceless. I shouldn't have to give you a gift after that," Nick teased. They took their seats, and he commented, "This place is really decked out."

"Isn't it gorgeous?" Sabrina nodded. "Ten's new assistant, Noelle, did it. She's awesome. Where's Eric and Thad?"

"They should be here at any moment," Nick said, looking down at his phone to make sure he hadn't missed any calls from his friends. Thad always ran late, but Eric was normally the punctual one of the group.

"Nick, who is that girl staring at me?" Sheridan leaned over and asked.

Nick glanced to see who she was talking about. Sure enough, Ivy, Sparkle's sister, was glaring at them from a nearby table. Nick had made the mistake of sleeping with Ivy a few years ago, despite Tenille's warnings, and it did not end well.

He had just moved back home after college graduation and was at a barbeque Tenille was hosting when he saw her. He asked his sister to put him on, but she refused, saying it was a bad idea. That night, they all went to a nightclub. Ivy was all in his ear, telling him how she had always considered him sexy and was curious about how he was in bed. She invited him back to her place, and he wasted no time accepting her offer. Sex with Ivy was incredible. It was as if she couldn't get enough of him. When Tenille heard that he was hanging out with her best friend's sister, she was livid and told him to stop, but he brushed his sister off. Then Ivy started getting weird. She would pop up at his parents' house unannounced and even at the job where he was working at the time. She would call constantly, asking his whereabouts. What Nick thought was a mutual understanding, that they were just "kicking it," turned out to be wrong. Nick was out playing pool with another woman when Ivy walked in. She began ranting and raving, calling him a cheater and embarrassing him. She then went to Tenille, Sparkle, his parents, and anyone else they both knew and told them how he had disrespected her and broken her heart. Everyone was pissed at him for months.

"Oh, that's just Ivy. She's an old friend of the family. Her sister and Tenille are best friends," Nick explained. He gave Ivy a slight smile, and she flipped him off. Clearly she was still feeling some type of way.

"She doesn't seem too happy to see you," Sheridan responded.

"Ivy is never happy about anything," Nick told her. "She's crazy."

"Hmmmm, interesting. Was she crazy before dating you, or did you make her that way?"

Nick gave Sheridan a surprised look. "What makes you think I dated her?"

"Why else would she be looking at me like I shouldn't be here? I know the 'who the fuck are you?' vibe when I feel it. Should I be concerned about anyone else here?" Sheridan leaned in and asked him. "Come on, tell me."

Nick pretended to look around the room and point out various women. "Her, her, oh, and her. Wait, I think I banged that waitress too."

"Now you're trying to be funny." Sheridan laughed.

"I can't believe you even asked me that." Nick shook his head.

"You know I was just kidding, Nick. Calm down," Sheridan told him.

"So, Sheridan, you work with my brother?" Sabrina asked.

"Yes, we both work for Horizon. I'm a corporate recruiter in the HR department," Sheridan answered.

"Oh, so you're a bigwig." Tenille nodded. "Impressive."

"It pays the bills." Sheridan shrugged.

"I keep telling my son that's all that matters at the end of the day," Nick's dad told them. "It's hard to get a good job these days."

"I know, Dad, I know," Nick groaned.

"Well, he has a great job, and he definitely makes more than enough to pay his bills. I should know because I set the company salaries." Sheridan laughed.

"Where's the birthday girl?"

Nick glanced up to see Thad walking in along with Eric. He was about to get up and go greet his friends when he stopped in his tracks. There she was again, standing right beside Thad. Nick couldn't believe it. She looked amazing dressed in a simple denim jumpsuit with a colorful kente cardigan worn over it. Her hair was big and curly, and she wore stylish thick black glasses on her face. Nick wondered how she had ended up with his friends.

"It's about time. I just asked Nick about you guys," Tenille yelled.

"You know I wasn't gonna miss the birthday celebration. Come on now, Ten, you know better than that." Thad walked over and gave his sister a big hug. Eric followed suit along with the girl.

"Noelle, where did you disappear to, and how the hell did you run into Frick and Frack?" Tenille asked, pointing to Eric and Thad.

"I realized I left my cell phone at home, so after I finished the room, I ran home to get it. I just happened to walk in at the same time these two handsome fellas did," Noelle said.

"Noelle, everything is gorgeous," Nick's mom said. "You really outdid yourself."

"It was nothing," Noelle said, taking an empty seat near the opposite end of the table.

"Noelle, this is my brother Nick." Sabrina introduced them. "And his, uh, coworker . . . uh, friend . . . well, this is Sheridan."

Nick watched as Noelle's attention turned to them. He could see the slight flicker in her eye as she recognized who he was.

"Nice to meet you, Noelle." He smiled at her.

"Well, now that everyone is here, can we go ahead and pray and eat?" Sabrina asked. "A sister is hungry."

"All right, everyone," their mother said, her voice carrying a comforting authority. "Let's take a moment to give thanks before we start this wonderful meal."

The room quieted down as everyone turned their gaze toward her.

"Heavenly Father, we come before you today with hearts full of joy and gratitude. We thank you for this beautiful day and for the many blessings you have bestowed upon us. We are especially grateful for this precious time together celebrating Tenille's special day. We thank you for the gift of family, for the love and support we share, and for the way you continually guide and protect us."

Nick's heart swelled with emotion as he listened. His mother's prayers had always been a source of comfort and strength for him.

His mother continued, "Lord, we ask that you bless this food to our bodies and grant us nourishment and joy. We pray for continued health and happiness for Tenille and all of us gathered here today. We thank you for the gift of this day, for the laughter, and for the memories we are about to make. In your name, we pray. Amen."

"Amen," the family echoed, their voices harmonizing with a sense of unity and shared warmth.

The main dining area of the restaurant buzzed with the pleasant hum of conversation and the clatter of utensils. The breakfast buffet, a feast for the senses, was spread out along a long, elegantly dressed counter. As Nick and his family approached, the waitress gestured toward the array of dishes with a welcoming smile.

The buffet was a vibrant display of breakfast delights. At one end, a towering stack of golden-brown pancakes was nestled beside a tray of fluffy waffles, along with a selection of fresh berries, whipped cream, and warm maple syrup. Nearby, a platter of buttery croissants and assorted pastries glistened under a soft light, their flaky layers promising a melt-in-your-mouth experience.

Fresh fruits were artfully arranged in a large bowl, offering a colorful mix of strawberries, blueberries, melon, and pineapple. Next to it, a selection of yogurt and granola stood ready for those who preferred a lighter option.

A large chafing dish held light and fluffy scrambled eggs, crispy bacon, and savory sausage links. Another dish featured golden hash browns with perfectly crispy edges. There was a carving station with a succulent roast, and a smaller pot of rich, creamy grits sat nearby, inviting guests to ladle some onto their plates.

A variety of juices—orange, apple, and cranberry—were neatly arranged alongside a large coffee urn, and a small selection of teas offered even more choices.

As Tenille and her family began filling their plates, the warm aromas of freshly cooked breakfast mingled with the lively chatter around them, setting the stage for a delightful meal and a joyful start to the day.

"This is really nice," Sheridan said once they sat back down to eat.

"Yeah, we come here all the time for special occasions," he told her. He looked down the table to see Thad and Noelle laughing and talking. His friend was a little too close to her, and for some reason, Nick was bothered by it.

"Nick, are you okay? Nick?"

"Huh? Oh, yeah," Nick said, realizing Sheridan was talking to him. He tried to enjoy his food, but he was too distracted to eat. He could hear the conversation about the Love Connection Gala, but he wasn't really listening.

"And then the next thing you know, some white boy starts bidding," Sabrina whined. "And he wins!"

"He actually won her and Emily." Thad laughed.

"It all happened so fast, I swear," Eric added.

"It was pretty hilarious." Noelle giggled, glancing over at Nick. Their eyes met, and he tried smiling at her, but she looked away.

"Sheridan, did you go to the ball with Nick?" Ivy asked out of nowhere.

"No, I actually wasn't in town," Sheridan answered. "I'm sure it was a lot of fun. I wish I could've attended."

"Ummmm-hmmm." Ivy gave her a fake smile.

"And then here comes Khalil, after everything done went down, asking me what was going on," Sabrina said.

"How is Khalil?" Nick's dad asked. "I miss him. That's my boy. I need his number so I can call him."

"Khalil's engaged, Daddy. He's someone else's problem now." Sabrina shook her head.

"Ma, can I get some more chicken?" Mookie asked.

"Yes, Mook. Come on." Tenille got up and followed Marquise back to the buffet.

"So, Noelle, arc you a photographer as well?" Sabrina asked.

"I know my way around a camera and a darkroom, but I'm more into set design. That's my forte. But I'm learning a lot working at Perfect Ten, and I know it's going to give me experience in a lot of other areas," Noelle replied.

"Well, from what Ten tells me, you are very talented, and from what you've done in this place, I can definitely see what she means. It looks amazing. You may wanna add party decor to your repertoire, young lady," his mom said.

"Yeah, you did a fabulous job," Sheridan added.

"Thank you." Noelle smiled. "It was nothing, really."

Nick glanced at Noelle, and their eyes locked. In that brief moment, he saw that she recognized who he was, but she quickly broke the stare and gave him a dismissive smile, turning her attention to Thad.

"It's almost as beautiful in here as you are," Thad said.

"I think I'll get another plate." Nick stood up, struggling to hide his irritation.

"You haven't even eaten everything on the one you have." Sheridan frowned.

Nick ignored her and walked off. He found his sister over at the salad bar.

"Ten, what's the deal with Noelle?"

Tenille looked at him as if he had just told her someone stole her car. "Hell no, Nick."

"What? I'm serious. How long has she been working for you?"

"Long enough. Stay away."

"I just asked—" Nick said.

"Nick, she's a nice girl, and she's my assistant. Please leave her alone. I'm asking . . . no, I'm telling you, I'm not dealing with this again." Tenille moved a step farther in the line.

"Dealing with what?" Nick's eyebrows furrowed, and he stared, waiting for her answer.

"You know what. Hell, remember Ivy? My best friend's sister? The one in there giving everyone attitude and giving you the evil eye? You being a man-whore almost cost me my friendship with Sparkle. I'm not dealing with that shit again. No! Stay away from her."

"Away from who?" Sabrina walked up.

"Noelle," Tenille answered.

"Ohhhhhhh." Sabrina laughed. "No, don't do that, Nick. She's a nice girl. Besides, I think Thad is making a move on her."

"I'm not gonna let that happen." Nick shook his head.

"Why not? I think Thad would be great for her," Tenille told him.

"What? You're kidding, right? You want me to leave her alone but have no problem with Thad? This is a joke, huh?" Nick couldn't believe his sister.

"No, I'm serious. Thad is a decent guy." Tenille began putting lettuce on her plate.

"And I'm not?"

Tenille and Sabrina both looked at him and said, "No."

"That's that bullshit," Nick told them.

"Let me ask you a question, Nick. Did you bring a date here today?" Tenille asked.

"Well, technically she brought herself. We drove separate cars."

"Nick, she's your guest. Don't do that," Sabrina coaxed.

"Fine, I brought a guest with me today."

"Exactly, your guest at a family gathering. So, don't you think it's kind of disrespectful for you to even be asking about Noelle right now? This is the exact foolishness I don't want her to get caught up in."

"She has a point, Nick." Sabrina sighed. "Noelle is a nice girl."

"Y'all are bugging. Just because I brought a coworker to brunch with me doesn't mean she's my girl." Nick was trying not to become angry at his sisters.

"Does she know she's not your girl?" Tenille asked.

"There you are. I was wondering what was taking you so long." Sheridan walked over to where they were standing.

Nick looked over and said, "Just chatting with the birthday girl, that's all."

"I'm gonna get some more of those fried green tomatoes from the other buffet. You want me to get you anything, sweetie?" Sheridan smiled at him.

"Nah, I'm good," Nick told her as he avoided Tenille's stare.

"I rest my case, sweetie," Tenille said. "You know how much I love you, Nick. You're my baby brother. But Noelle doesn't need that type of drama in her life, and neither do I. Stay the hell away."

"You good, homie?" Thad asked when he returned to the table.

"I'm great," Nick answered.

"I was telling Noelle that I feel like we've met before." Thad put his arm around Noelle's chair. "But that can't be true because I would never forget a woman this gorgeous."

"Thad, you're so funny." Noelle giggled. "I'm sure I would've remembered you as well."

"The way Nick gets around, he barely remembers anyone." Ivy cut her eyes at him from across the table.

"I beg to differ. Nick's memory is almost photographic. He never forgets anyone worth remembering," Sabrina stated, saving him from having to respond. Little did his sister know how profound her statement was in that moment. He glanced at Noelle once again. This time her gaze held his a little longer.

"I had a great time. Your family is awesome," Sheridan said as Nick walked her to her car.

"Thanks, I had a great time too."

"I couldn't tell. You were exceptionally quiet. Did this have anything to do with that other girl?"

Nick stopped and wondered if his distraction had been that obvious. "What girl?" He frowned.

"Ivy, your ex."

Nick didn't even attempt to hold his laughter inside. "Ivy? That chick is not my ex."

"She just seemed a little bothered by my being here, and then you were acting all weird. She may not be your ex, but there is some type of history there. I know that for a fact." Sheridan waited for him to explain.

"Let me find out you're jealous," Nick said smugly.

"Never that," Sheridan told him. "Do you really think that I would be jealous of her?"

There really was no comparison between the two ladies. Sheridan was high-class, poised, and bourgeois, for lack of a better word. Ivy, on the other hand, was a typical around-the-way girl with a big ass and an even bigger personality.

"I can't imagine you being jealous of anyone, Sheridan." He laughed.

"You're a smart guy, Nick. It's one of the many reasons I'm feeling you." Sheridan smiled.

A confused look came across his face. "Feeling me?"

"Yes." Sheridan nodded, then added seductively, "So, are you coming to my room so I can show you some of the other reasons?"

Nick glanced down at Sheridan's hand, which was making its way from his chest to his crotch. His mind was elsewhere, but the bulge that was now in his pants seemed to answer Sheridan's question for him without his having to say a word.

"Text me when you're on your way." Sheridan climbed into the rental car, and he waited as she pulled off.

After making sure there was no evidence of his momentary erection courtesy of Sheridan, Nick turned to go back inside to say goodbye to his parents when he spotted Noelle walking out of the restaurant carrying a large box. He didn't hesitate to rush over to help.

"Let me grab some of that for you."

"It's okay, I got it." Noelle glared at him. He ignored her and took the box out of her hand anyway.

"What kind of man would let a beautiful woman like you carry this thing?" He smiled at her. "Believe it or not, I'm a gentleman."

"I choose not to believe it," Noelle said. "My car is over here."

Nick walked beside her until they reached the black Nissan Altima. She popped the trunk open, and as he placed the box inside, he noticed a sketchpad and other art supplies. "You're really talented."

"What?"

"I said you're very talented. The way you transformed that room was amazing. We've rented that back room for the past five years, and it's never looked like that," Nick told her.

"Thanks," Noelle told him. "I really didn't do that much. Just a few balloons, tablecloths, crystal containers, and candy. That's about it."

"Well, the fact that you were able to create all that magic with the stuff you named speaks volumes about your creativity." Nick pretended to clap. Noelle just stared at him, her face expressionless, so he stopped and became serious. "Listen, I just wanna say I know today was kinda awkward."

"Awkward for who? Not me. I had a great time. You, my friend, were sweating bullets, and I must admit, it was quite entertaining. There was the one chick who I'm assuming is your ex-girlfriend based on the way she kept giving your new girlfriend the evil eye."

"One, she's not my ex-girlfriend. She's just crazy. And two, she's not my current girlfriend—she's just a co-worker."

Noelle raised her hands in the air. "You don't owe me an explanation. And I'm sure if she is crazy, you contributed to her mental state."

"That's a low blow," Nick told her.

"I'm surprised that you even recognized me. I mean, you did have a lot going on."

"I saw you the other night at the Love Connection Gala. You looked right at me, and then after all that drama with Sabrina popped off, I turned around and you were gone. I looked for you." Nick sighed.

"Ha. You looked for me. That's so funny." Noelle laughed.

"Don't be like this, Nori. Wasn't that what you said your name was?" Nick countered.

Noelle's mouth opened to speak, but nothing came out, and she quickly closed it. Nick knew that she didn't have a comeback.

"Look, I'm sorry."

"For what?" she asked.

"For today, and for . . . I had no idea that—"

"That you would ever see me again?" Noelle interrupted him.

"No, that's not what I was gonna say. I mean, I didn't know that you worked for my sister."

"Okay, so you're apologizing because I have a job?"

"That's not what I'm saying either." Nick tried to think before he spoke. As hard as he tried to get his words together, nothing seemed to come out right. "I just want to—"

"Nick, you don't have to apologize. It's cool," she said. "Now can you move so I can get into my car?"

Nick didn't move. "Nori . . . I mean, Noelle, can we go somewhere and talk?"

"There's nothing to talk about. We were both grown, we both got what we wanted. We were drunk, it happened, it's over."

"We still need to talk."

"About what? There's nothing to talk about."

"Noelle . . ."

"Besides, I already have plans. I'm meeting Thad for drinks. Now, excuse me. I have to be going."

Nick watched as Noelle got into her car, and as she drove out of the parking spot, a large pickup truck pulled in. The driver opened the door and stepped out, and Nick thought he was seeing things.

"Brandon?" Nick asked to make sure it wasn't a case of mistaken identity and that it was indeed his brother-in-law.

"Uh, hey, Nick." Brandon walked over and shook Nick's hand. "Good to see you."

"Same here," Nick said. "It's been a while." Nick tried to remember the last time he'd seen his sister's husband. It had to have been almost a year. The man was a true workaholic and rarely took a day off, even holidays.

"It has," Brandon agreed.

"Is that Brandon?"

Nick turned to see his mother rushing over and the remaining party guests who were exiting the restaurant.

"Yes, ma'am." Brandon hugged Nick's mother and gave his father a nod, then pointed at Sabrina and Marquise carrying Tenille's balloons and wrapped gifts. "I guess I missed the party."

"We just finished," Marquise told him. "There's leftover cake though."

"I tried to get here on time," Brandon explained. "I got tied up at work."

"It's fine." Tenille walked over and gave him a hug.

"It's the effort that counts," Ivy spoke up. "You really didn't miss much, and the food wasn't all that."

"Everything was perfect," Sabrina corrected her, "especially considering some guests didn't pay for themselves."

"That's my cue to get out of here." Nick giggled. "Ten, happy birthday. I love you."

As Nick hugged his sister, she whispered in his ear, "Remember what I told you. Stay away from Noelle."

"Relax, Ten. You have nothing to worry about," Nick reassured her, knowing that staying away from her was the last thing he planned on doing.

Chapter 16

Tenille

Tenille was in her office going through her weekly schedule when she heard the buzzer of the front door. She wasn't expecting anyone, so she tried to listen as Noelle opened it and talked to see exactly who it was.

"Hello, I'm Catherine Baldwin with Windstar Resorts. I'm looking for a Tenille Holmes," a woman's voice said.

"One second. I'll see if she's available," Noelle told her. A few moments later, she tapped on Tenille's door and peeked in. "There's a woman named Catherine from Windstar Resorts here?" It sounded more like a question than a statement.

"You can bring her back here." Tenille shrugged.

Windstar Resorts stood out as one of the premier destinations for weddings and bridal shoots. Tenille was well aware of the venue's high-class reputation and its extravagant pricing, which was probably why none of her clients had ever opted to utilize it. Although the financial standing of her clientele had improved significantly since she first opened her doors, she had yet to attract clients who could afford to host their weddings at Windstar.

"Good morning." Tenille stood up and greeted the woman Noelle led into her office. She was an attractive older woman dressed in a nice pantsuit and carrying a briefcase, which Tenille instantly recognized as Italian leather. "I'm Tenille. Welcome to Perfect Ten Photography."

"Nice to finally meet you, Tenille. I'm Catherine Baldwin."

They shook hands, and Tenille motioned for the woman to have a seat. "Nice to meet you, Ms. Baldwin. Can I get you anything to drink? Coffee, tea, water?"

"No, thank you. And please call me Catherine," she said as she sat down.

"Thanks, Noelle." She smiled. Noelle exited and closed the door behind her. Once they were alone, Tenille said, "So, how can I help you today?"

"Well, first of all, I am a fan of your work. I've been following you for a while now, and I've gotta tell you, you are a true talent," Catherine said.

"Thank you. I'm flattered." Tenille couldn't help grinning. To hear that someone had not only taken notice of her work but actually admired it made her heart swell with pride.

"Not only do I watch your work on social media, but Maggie from The Bridal Suite gave me a sneak peek at the work you did for their spring catalog, and it was breathtaking. I've also actually seen pictures from a couple of weddings that you've captured. However, when I saw this, I knew I had to come and meet you. A friend of mine got it in the mail, and she showed it to me." Catherine reached into the briefcase, took out a small envelope, and slid it across the desk. "I swear, I was so moved by it that it almost made me cry. I showed it to our marketing director, and he insisted I come and speak with you in person about a proposal."

Tenille looked down at it, then picked it up. It was addressed to a recent client, and Tenille's logo and return address were on the front, but she had never seen it before. She opened it and took out a card. The front of the card read, "How do you say thank you to those who make us smile?" Tenille opened the card, and on the inside was a picture of the bride and her mother, smiling as they admired her bouquet, along with the words, "With the Perfect smile, of course! Thank you for allowing us to share in your special day. Perfect Ten Photography." It was a beautiful card. The words, the sentiments, and the photo were everything she would have wanted as a thank-you card. It was perfect. But it wasn't hers.

"Wow, it's a beautiful card, but I'm sorry. It's not mine." Tenille shook her head.

"But aren't you Perfect Ten Photography? My friend assured me that you were the one who took the pictures at her daughter's wedding. Are there two businesses with the same name?" Catherine looked confused.

"No, I took the picture. But I didn't create the card, and I didn't mail it. Wait, hold on one second." Tenille picked up the phone and hit the intercom button. "Noelle, can you come back here?"

"You think she knows anything about this card?" Catherine asked.

"We're about to find out," Tenille told her.

A few moments later, she peeked through the door. "What can I do for you ladies?"

"Noelle, have you seen this card before?" Tenille held the card up.

Noelle nodded. "Yeah, it's the thank-you card I sent out to the Burke family after the wedding. Is something wrong?"

"You designed this card?" Tenille asked.

"Yeah, I design all the thank-you cards we send out to clients."

Tenille didn't know whether to be angry because her assistant had done this without her knowledge or elated because she had done a phenomenal job.

"Oh, mystery solved," Tenille said. "Can you come in and join us for this meeting?"

"Me?" Noelle looked confused.

"Yes, you. Now please have a seat."

"Okay." Noelle sat in the chair beside Catherine and looked at Tenille as if she were crazy.

Tenille ignored her and continued, "It seems as though your beautiful card has caught the attention of Catherine and the marketing director at Windstar Resorts."

"Really? That's awesome." Noelle smiled. "But it's not so much the design of the card. It's the picture that Tenille took."

"Well, let's just call it the result of a team effort," Catherine told them. "And at this time, Windstar Resorts would like to contract your company and bring you on as part of the marketing team for our new national campaign."

Tenille was stunned. It was something she had often dreamed about but never dared to talk about with anyone. The idea of her work being featured in a major marketing campaign seemed almost inconceivable.

"That's incredible," Tenille said, trying to maintain her composure.

"That's awesome." Noelle clapped, unable to contain her excitement.

"What exactly would we be doing?" Tenille asked.

Catherine opened a folder on the table and began outlining the role. "We're looking to bring you on board as part of our marketing team for our national campaign. Your primary responsibility would be handling the photography shoots for our various locations across the country."

Tenille's eyes brightened. "That sounds intriguing. What would that entail?"

"You'll be responsible for capturing high-quality images of our resorts," Catherine explained, "highlighting their unique features and amenities. This means working closely with our on-site teams to ensure that each shoot aligns perfectly with our brand's vision. You'll also coordinate with local vendors, manage the logistics for each shoot, and handle the editing and final delivery of the photos."

"That sounds like a comprehensive role," Tenille said thoughtfully. "What about compensation and expenses?"

Catherine nodded, ready with the details. "We offer a competitive salary that reflects your experience and the scope of the work. On top of that, we cover all travel expenses, including flights, accommodation, and a per diem for meals. You'll also receive a travel allowance for any incidental costs while you're on location."

Tenille's interest was piqued. "That's great to hear. Are there any other benefits or specifics I should be aware of?"

Catherine smiled, clearly pleased with the offer. "In addition to the salary and travel expenses, you'll have access to our comprehensive employee benefits package. This includes health insurance, retirement contributions, and performance bonuses based on the success of the campaign and your contributions."

"Sounds like a well-rounded offer," Tenille said, her mind already turning over the possibilities. "When would you need a decision from me?"

"We'd like to have a commitment by the end of the month if possible," Catherine said, her tone both friendly and urgent. "This way, we can start planning the upcoming shoots. But please take the time you need to review everything and let us know if you have any more questions."

"I appreciate the detailed information, Catherine," Tenille replied. "I'll review everything and get back to you shortly."

Catherine extended her hand with a smile. "Fantastic. I'm excited about the possibility of working together. Thank you for considering this opportunity, Tenille."

Tenille shook her hand, feeling a mixture of excitement and anticipation. "Thank you, Catherine. I'm excited as well."

"I can't believe this!" Noelle squealed when Catherine left the office. "We have to celebrate. This is incredible. A national campaign. Like, this is big, Tenille. Congratulations."

"I should be congratulating you. It was your creativity that caught their attention," Tenille said. "I had no idea you created thank-you cards and were sending them out."

"I mentioned them to you the same day you got back from Jamaica. You were like, 'Sounds great.'"

Tenille could barely recall her arrival at work following Jamaica. Her mind had been so consumed with thoughts of everything from Marquise's potential new school to her birthday brunch, and fighting thoughts of Xavier, that Noelle could have requested a million-dollar raise and she would have agreed without hesitation. Something as trivial as a thank-you card hardly registered on her radar. Now, after seeing the thoughtfulness behind Noelle's gesture and its flawless execution, she realized she had been overlooking the depth of talent possessed by her assistant. Although aware of Noelle's background in marketing and graphics, Tenille had primarily valued her exceptional administrative and organizational skills. Since joining Perfect Ten, Noelle had not only managed the company's demanding schedule and assumed control of the front office, but had also undertaken tasks such as organizing files, paperwork, and decluttering the storage room, significantly streamlining Tenille's daily operations and making her life easier.

"So, what else have you been working on that you haven't shown me?"

"Well, I have been playing around on the computer with a few other ideas you might like to see. Nothing is finalized, but the pictures you take are so inspiring that my mind sometimes goes wild. Check this out." She turned on the screen of the large iMac that was on her desk and began showing Tenille all the creative projects she had been working on featuring photos from the last few weddings she shot. Tenille was blown away as she looked at the designs.

"Noelle, why didn't you tell me you could do all of this?"

"I showed you my portfolio when you hired me, remember?"

The door chimed again, and for the second time that day, Tenille was speechless as she watched Xavier walk in looking as handsome as the first day they met.

"Hello there." He smiled.

"Hello, can I help you?" Noelle asked. Tenille could see that she found him just as attractive by the way her face lit up.

"I'm actually here to see Ms. Chambers," he said, staring at Tenille.

"Who?" Noelle frowned.

"That's my maiden name," Tenille told her. "Hello, Xavier."

"I'm sorry, I don't know your married name. Hello, Ten."

"How can I help you?" she asked, trying to remain as nonchalant as possible. She didn't dare let him see how happy she was to see him, and she especially didn't want Noelle to notice. She prayed that neither one could see the beat of her heart, which was increasing with each step he took toward her.

"Well, two things. First, I want to schedule a shoot for Fabian and me. You know, a family photo shoot."

She gave him a sarcastic look. As much as Xavier had supported her dreams when they were together and helped her get her business started, one thing he was not fond of was being photographed. She would fuss at him all the time because he never wanted to be in front of the camera.

"Xavier." She shook her head.

"I'm serious, Ten. She's getting older. I swear, one day she was walking around carrying Barbie dolls and asking for Pop-Tarts, and I blinked and she's in high school carrying an iPhone and asking for a car. My baby is about to leave for college in three years."

"Two years." Tenille laughed as she corrected him.

"She hasn't finished her sophomore year. Let me hold on to as many months as possible."

"Awwwww. That's so sweet," Noelle said. "I'd be more than happy to schedule a shoot for you if it's okay with the owner."

"I never turn down paying customers." Tenille shrugged.

Xavier smiled even harder as he walked over to the desk. Some of the images that Tenille and Noelle were looking at were displayed on the screen.

"Wow, these are beautiful," he said. "Tenille, you were good when you first started, but now, no words."

"She's amazing. But I'm sure that's why you want her to shoot you and your daughter."

"You're right." Xavier turned and stared at Tenille. "She's the absolute best, always has been."

"That's not just my work. I did the pictures, but Noelle did the graphic design. She has a degree in graphic design, and she's in grad school to get her MBA in marketing," Tenille added.

"Smart girl. You two make a great team." Xavier nodded. "Do you mind if I see more?"

Noelle looked over at Tenille for confirmation, and when she nodded, Noelle clicked through more files.

"That's what the lady from Windstar Resorts said. They want to hire her, well, us to become a part of their marketing team for their nationwide campaign they're launching," Noelle bragged.

"What? That's great. I'm not surprised at all," Xavier told her. "I hope you told them they could contract your company to do the work."

"What do you mean?" Tenille walked over to the desk and stood beside him.

"I mean, why not hire Perfect Ten to handle the campaign?" he asked as if he were suggesting that she try French dressing on her salad instead of ranch.

"We can't do that. I mean—"

"Why not?" Xavier interrupted her. "You can expand Perfect Ten Photography into Perfect Ten Design Company. You gotta think big, Ten. I've always told you that."

"He's right, Tenille. There's so much more we can offer than just photography services. Catherine Baldwin walking in here just to find and talk to you just proved that," Noelle agreed.

"But what about my bridal clients?" Tenille sighed. "I'm already trying not to overbook as it is."

"You won't. The weddings are mainly on weekends, Tenille. You can take on other clients during the week. Isn't that when you took the photos for The Bridal Suite photo shoot?"

"But during the week is when I edit photos, Noelle," Tenille told her.

"Didn't you say Noelle had a degree in graphic design? I'm sure she can help with editing. And before you even say it, we know how you are about your photos, Tenille. She can make sure you give final approval on everything," Xavier said.

Tenille looked at him. As much as she wanted to tell him he was wrong, he wasn't. She was very particular when it came to editing her shots.

"Exactly." Noelle nodded.

For a few moments, Tenille remained silent, trying to process the whirlwind of events that had unfolded in the past hour of her life: a job offer from a prestigious resort, an unexpected visit from Xavier, and the prospect of expanding her freelance photography business into a full-scale design firm. The myriad of surprises left her uncertain if she could handle any more. She turned to face Xavier. "You said you came here for two reasons. What was the second one?"

He stared into her eyes and simply said, "I wanted to take you to lunch."

Chapter 17

Nick

Nick sat in his car, grappling with his thoughts and wondering what the hell he was doing. Originally planning to grab some food on his lunch break, he found himself driving past restaurants and fast-food joints until he arrived in the parking lot. His mind had been in a fog since Tenille's brunch. Taking a deep breath, he glanced at his reflection in the mirror before heading inside. She spotted him before he could even open the door, her face registering surprise.

"Hey." He spoke first as he approached the desk she was sitting behind.

"Hello," she said politely.

He had hoped that she would be a little friendlier, but her demeanor was professional, a little too professional. He was going to have to try a little harder than he thought. "How are you?"

"I'm fine," she answered.

He was tempted to respond by telling her she was definitely that, but he knew the chances of her being receptive to him flirting were slim. "Well, that's—"

"If you're looking for Tenille, she's not here. She's gone to lunch." She interrupted him.

"I'm not here to see Tenille. I'm here to see you," Nick told her.

"Why?"

"You know why."

What he knew was he wanted to see her and talk to her. He wanted to tell her that he remembered how he knew her and how they met. He wanted to tell her that the memories came flooding back to him of that weekend, the time they spent, what they did. Most of all, he wanted to apologize.

Nick and his frat brothers had been planning to attend Black Beach Weekend in Tampa for a year. They saved their money, booked their hotel room well in advance, and when they arrived in Florida, they planned to drink, party, and have a good time. Nick was enjoying nonstop partying and having the time of his life when, on the second night, he ran into a girl on his way to the bar, literally. She spilled her drink on her blouse.

"I am so sorry," he said, attempting to wipe the liquid from her shirt. The last time he had spilled a drink on a girl, she cursed him out so bad that it ruined his night. He prepared himself to get cussed out.

"It's fine. No harm done." She laughed.

He noticed she was cute. Her voice was melodic, and there was a vibe about her that made him like her.

"Let me buy you another one to make up for it."

"How about you dance with me first and then you can buy me one?" she told him as she pulled him on the dance floor. He wasn't really a dancer, but that didn't seem to matter, and he enjoyed pressing against her thick curves. She was taller than most girls, and the girl could move. They danced, had a round of drinks, and danced some more. When the club closed, they were tired, drunk, and happy. Nick asked her to hang out the following day, and she agreed.

"Wait, what's your name?" he remembered to ask.

"Oh my gosh, I didn't tell you my name. Nori."

"Nori." He repeated the name she gave him at that moment, then said, "I'm Nick."

"Good ol' Saint Nick."

"Jolly ol' Saint Nick." He winked. "You gonna sit on my lap and tell me what you want?"

"I don't know. I may have been a naughty girl."

"That's exactly the kind of girl I like."

"I'll see you tomorrow. Wet Willies at four o'clock, right?" she said as one of her girls came over and pulled her by the arm.

"Wet Willies. Four o'clock," Nick yelled behind her. "Bring your girls."

"Bring your boys," her friend yelled back.

The next day, they both arrived right on time, and sure enough, she brought her girls, and he brought his boys. They barhopped and ended up partying poolside at the hotel where he and his boys were staying. Nori was easygoing, fun, and cool. She was also sexy as hell in the cropped top and cutoff shorts she wore. The entire night, he couldn't keep his eyes off her enticing cleavage, and his hands stayed on her thighs.

They were relaxing by the pool when he couldn't take it anymore, and he leaned over and kissed her. It was soft, wet, and sweet. He instantly wanted more, and from the way she responded, he could tell that she did too. They were both drunk and horny.

He took her by the hand, and they went to his room. He barely got the key into the door, and when it finally opened, they wasted no time tearing each other's clothes off. He fumbled in his suitcase, found the box of condoms, and took one out. The sex was hot, passionate, and gratifying, leaving them exhausted, and they both passed out.

The next morning, he was awakened by the sound of yelling. He forced his eyes open and instantly sobered as he recognized Lauren, his girlfriend of the past year, standing over him.

"I knew you were gonna do this, Nick! I knew it."

Nick sat up, and Lauren slapped him.

"What's going on?" Nori leaned up off the bed, looking just as hungover as Nick felt.

"I can't believe this. I came down here to surprise your trifling ass, and you down here fucking a fat girl? At least you could've screwed someone cute, Nick."

"Who are you calling a fat girl?" Nori sat all the way up in bed but held the sheet to cover herself.

"The bitch who's in bed with my man, that's who. Correction—my ex," Lauren snapped.

Nick panicked. He hadn't planned on any of this happening. Not hooking up with Nori and especially not having Lauren show up in his room. He didn't know what to do. Lauren began crying uncontrollably and ran out of the room. He reached on the floor and grabbed his shorts, slipping them on before he got out of bed and took off behind her. He caught her before she could get to the elevator.

"Baby, listen. Look at me." He reached for her, but she pulled away.

"Don't touch me, Nick," she yelled.

"Lauren, come on now." His voice softened. "I don't even know that girl. Come on. Do you really think I'd do that to you? I admit I was drunk, really drunk. I came in from the pool party, and when I got into my bed, I was by myself."

Lauren looked up at him. "You're lying."

"I'm not. You saw that girl. Do you believe I would do that?"

"I don't know what I believe." Lauren sniffed.

"That chick was at the pool party. She was drunk too, and she probably just climbed into bed with me. Nothing happened. I swear."

"You swear?" Lauren stared back at him. She was the total opposite of Nori: small, petite, with fair skin and hazel eyes. When he had convinced her to be his girlfriend, he felt like he had a winner. Now after a year of dating, he wasn't so sure, but he also didn't want to lose her. Not like this, anyway. He could see the hurt in her eyes. She was heartbroken.

"I swear," he lied. "You know I love you and would never cheat on you, especially with a fat girl."

Lauren smiled briefly, and then her eyes turned cold. "Then why the fuck was there an empty condom wrapper on the floor, Nick?"

Nick didn't have an answer, and Lauren didn't wait for one. She took off down the hallway. He turned to head back to his room and then stopped as he saw Nori standing in the doorway. She looked as hurt and disappointed as Lauren had, and he realized that she had heard the entire conversation.

"Hey, listen—"

"Don't bother." Nori held up her hand. She was now dressed in the same halter top and denim shorts, carrying her sandals in her hand.

"Nori, wait."

She brushed past him in the same direction that Lauren had gone. He felt like shit, not just because of the hangover, but also because of the heartbreak that he had caused two women. In that moment, he promised himself that he would never put himself in a position to hurt another woman again.

Never in a million years did he think he would ever see her again. Now here they were, standing face-to-face in his sister's office, where she now worked. It was awkward, but he was determined to say what he felt needed to be said.

"Nori—"

"That's not my name."

"Noelle, I'm sorry," he said. "I was wrong, and what I did was . . . I want to explain."

"You don't owe me an explanation."

"Yes, I do."

"I don't want an explanation."

"But—"

"Nick, let it go. Listen, like I told you the other day, we were young, drunk, and stupid. It was what it was, it happened, it's over. We don't have to talk about it. I don't want things to be awkward between us. I work for your sister. She's my boss, it's that simple. No one has to know anything. I haven't mentioned it, and you don't have to. It was a long time ago. I've definitely moved past it, and so have you."

Her words were curt and simple, and although she tried to seem indifferent, Nick could see the emotion in her eyes. She was angry and hurt, and he was the cause of it. Now he wanted to be the one to take it away.

"Nori . . . Noelle, I truly am sorry. Can we just sit down and talk for a little while?" he asked.

"There's nothing to talk about."

"Yeah, there is. How have you been? What made you live here? I want to catch up." He really did want to talk and catch up. Although she was giving him the cold shoulder, he could still feel that same energy coming from her. That vibe that made him want to just relax and enjoy hanging out with her.

"Nick, please. Just don't." She shook her head.

"But—"

"Fine, apology accepted." Noelle sighed. "Are you happy?"

"I would be happy if you let me take you out to dinner."

"That is not happening."

The door chimed and opened, and Nick turned to see Tenille walk in. He did a double take because right behind her was her ex-boyfriend, Xavier, who he hadn't seen in years.

For years, Tenille and Xavier had one of the best relationships he had ever seen. Nick thought they would eventually get married. Tenille had ended up marrying Brandon, who popped up out of nowhere, before Nick even realized she and Xavier had broken up. Everyone loved Xavier. Brandon, not so much, but Tenille stuck with him.

"What are you doing here?" Tenille's voice was two octaves higher than normal.

"X?" Nick asked, walking over and giving him a pound with his fist and a man hug.

"What up, Nick? It's great to see you, man. I see you're still dressing like a white dude who works in the shoe section at Saks," Xavier teased.

"Man, I see you still hating on my style." Nick adjusted the silk tie he wore along with his sports jacket.

"Um, why are you here?" Tenille asked again.

"I . . . I . . ." Nick tried to think.

"He came to take you to lunch," Noelle answered for him, "but I told him you were already gone, and he was just about to leave when you walked in. Right, Nick?"

Nick looked over at her and nodded. He then turned and said, "You two went to lunch together?"

"Yes, we did," Tenille said.

"Belated birthday lunch," Xavier added.

"Cool," Nick said. "Well, I guess I should head back to work. Nice seeing you again, X. We gotta hang out, watch some football. I know Pops would love to see you. He was just asking about you at Ten's birthday party."

"Really? She didn't tell me that. I gotta call Pops and check on him," Xavier said. "Nick, take my number and call me this week, man."

"Will do." Nick took out his phone, and they exchanged numbers. Nick made sure to say his number loudly, hoping that Noelle would hear it and write it down. He glanced over and saw that she was staring into the computer instead.

"See you later, Nick," Tenille said, rushing him out the door.

"Goodbye everyone," Nick said. Again, he looked over at Noelle, but she wasn't looking his way.

He got into his car and started the ignition. The clock on the dashboard let him know that if he didn't hurry, he would be late getting back to work. His meeting hadn't gone as planned, but he glanced up one final time before pulling out of the parking lot. This time, his eyes met Noelle's, and even though she shook her head at him, he knew that this wasn't the last conversation they would be having.

Chapter 18

Sabrina

"Hey, beautiful."

Sabrina looked up from her desk and stared at Khalil standing in her doorway. She was finishing up her client files and preparing to leave for the day. "What do you want, Khalil?" she asked, stacking the folders on her desk.

"Come on, Brina. You can't still be mad at me. Don't be like this," Khalil pleaded as he entered her office. It was the first time she had seen Khalil since the night of the gala, though they had spoken on the phone. The first couple of times he called, she had cussed him out and hung up, followed up by a round of angry texts. Sabrina knew he would eventually show up either at her office or her house. He probably felt that making an appearance at her office would be a safer choice, since he knew she couldn't yell at him there. Truth was, she was over the entire fiasco. She was more concerned with the blind date she was going on as a result of the auction.

"Khalil, I don't have time to deal with you and your nonsense right now. I'm about to leave," she told him.

"I know. That's why I came by. I wanna take you to happy hour." He grinned. "My treat at your favorite spot, Jaspers."

If it were any other day, Sabrina would have grabbed her purse and keys, locked the door, and headed off with her longtime friend. Jaspers was their ultimate spot, one they had frequented plenty of times over the years. It had been a while since their last visit. The last few times she had invited him, he'd declined, mainly because his fiancée had started keeping him on a tighter leash since the drunk dialing incident.

"Don't pop up in here trying to be all nice to me, Khalil," Sabrina warned him.

"Brinaaaaaa. I'm always nice to you." Khalil sat on the edge of her desk. "You know that. Come on. Let's go hang out. It's been a minute."

"I'm surprised Tyra is letting you hang out, especially with me." Sabrina looked at him.

"What the hell does that mean? I'm a grown-ass man. I hang out where I want, when I want, and with whoever I want." Khalil puffed his chest out.

"That's a lie and you know it." She shook her head. "You don't believe that your damn self, and neither do I."

"Naw, Brina. You know Tyra don't have no problems with us hanging out. As long as I get home at a decent hour, she's cool." He shrugged.

"Mmmmmm-hmmmmmm. If you say so." Sabrina grabbed the coat off the back of her chair and slipped it on.

"Come on, I miss my friend. Let's go get some drinks and some fried fish and get our dance on." Khalil walked behind her desk, grabbed her by the hand, and spun her around.

"I can't." Sabrina sighed.

"Why not?" Khalil looked disappointed.

"I have a date."

"A date? With who? Don't tell me you and cornball Mason—"

"No, not with Mason." Sabrina clicked her computer off.

"With who?" Khalil ignored her and waited for an answer.

"It's a double date with Emily and the guy from the gala."

"The white guy?" He began laughing.

"Yes, the white guy. It's not funny. And I'd just like to point out that I wouldn't even have to be going on a date with a white guy if you hadn't been so cheap. You wanted to be all bad and bid on me, but your ass got scared and quit," she snapped.

"That dude paid like a G to win that damn auction. Ain't nobody have money like that. Hell, and I just wanted to beat Mason and save you the headache."

They walked out of her office, and she locked the door behind them.

"Have a great weekend, Gracie," Sabrina called out to the receptionist as they walked out of the building.

"Good luck on your date," Gracie yelled.

"So cancel," Khalil told her. "You know you don't wanna go anyway."

"I can't do that. First of all, I wouldn't do that to Emily."

"Okay, leave early then. What time is the date?"

"Seven thirty."

"Where are y'all going?"

"Magnolia Tavern."

"Daaaaaamn." Khalil was clearly impressed. "Big ballers. Who is this dude?"

"I don't know," Sabrina told him.

"Well, listen, here's what you can do. Happy hour is until nine. All you gotta do is dip out at like eight and meet me over at Jaspers."

"I can't leave in thirty minutes. That would be kind of obvious." Sabrina shook her head.

"Fine, leave at eight fifteen, eight thirty at the latest."

Sabrina considered Khalil's suggestion. Truth be told, having drinks and hanging out with him at Jaspers sounded much more appealing than spending time with

Emily and two unfamiliar, seemingly dull guys. Plus, going along with Khalil's plan could serve as an escape route for Emily as well.

"I don't know." She hesitated.

"Listen, I can make it easy for you. I will call you around ten minutes after eight and tell you to come and get me. It's an emergency." Khalil grinned. "And don't act like you haven't done that shit before. Remember ol' boy at Ruby Tuesday?"

"God, don't remind me of that clown," Sabrina groaned as she thought about one of the worst blind dates she had gone on. Once again, another coworker had suggested that she go out with her cousin after one of Sabrina's breakups. She swore he was tall, handsome, and everything Sabrina was looking for and more. Well, turned out that the guy, Denard, was average height, grungy looking, and at about 300 pounds, he weighed more than what Sabrina was looking for. As she stared at him across the table, Sabrina wondered if he didn't have time to shave or get a haircut before their date, or he just chose not to get one. She convinced herself to get past his looks. She told herself to ignore the fact that he ordered a strawberry daiquiri and drank it through a straw, but when he began explaining that the reason his baby mama broke up with him was because she caught him getting orally served by her sister in the bathroom during their family reunion, she knew it was time to go. She quickly excused herself, saying she had to use the restroom, and sent Emily a text saying, help. By the time she got back to the table, Emily was calling and yelling loud enough through the phone that her car had a flat tire and she needed Sabrina to come and help. Sabrina jumped up and said she was on the way. Denard was nice enough to offer to tag along, but Sabrina told him no, she would just call AAA, and they would be fine. It had to have been one of the worst dates of her life.

"So it's settled. I'll call you, and then you can come hang out." Khalil didn't even give her a chance to agree. He just gave her a quick hug and walked off.

Magnolia Tavern was an upscale restaurant known for its elegant ambiance, exquisite food, and elaborate prices. The building was actually a former country club located near a golf course, and it sat on a beautiful lake. Sabrina had only eaten there twice: the first time was after prom, and the second was when she was a debutante and they went for their "fine dining experience" along with their escorts. It was where most guys took their girlfriends to propose, where people celebrated wedding anniversaries, and where men who were trying to be overly impressive took their dates. Sabrina figured this was exactly why they were invited here. She gave her keys to the valet and checked her reflection in the door as she approached the entrance. Her simple black-and-white print dress belted at the waist fit just right, and the leather biker jacket she wore gave her the perfect balance of class and chic. She felt the weight of every gaze as she walked into the lobby of the restaurant, and she prayed it was because she looked so damn amazing and not because she was black. Of course, they were all white. There definitely weren't many people of color in the establishment, at least as far as she could see. She checked her coat and then walked to the maître d' standing behind a wooden podium.

"Good evening, madame," he greeted her. "Will you be dining alone?"

"No, I'm actually meeting someone. Well, actually a couple of people," Sabrina said politely, then bit her lip as she realized she didn't know the last name of her nor Emily's dates. She reached into her purse to take out her phone and text Emily.

"Your name wouldn't happen to be Sabrina, would it?" he asked before she could dial.

"That would happen to be my name." She laughed.

"Then your party is actually waiting for you at the bar," he said and pointed to the bar area.

"Thank you," Sabrina said as she walked in the direction he was pointing. She saw Emily sitting along with Brady, the guy from the auction. She tried to peek and see if she could see her date, but there wasn't another white guy sitting with them. *Oh God, I hope I'm not being stood up. Then again, I hope I am. Then I can leave.*

"Here she is." Brady turned around just as she walked up. He was a nice-looking man who put her in mind of a Calvin Klein model. He was tall, muscular, and very handsome with a strong jawline and dimpled chin. His dark hair was a little longer than it had been at the Love Connection Gala, but neatly trimmed. The navy blue suit he wore was recognizably Italian and custom fit, and his black shoes were the ultimate choice. He looked perfect, but she could tell that he was nervous.

"Hello." Sabrina smiled at him.

"Hello yourself, gorgeous!" Emily swiveled around in her seat, looking like she just stepped off the runway. For someone who swore she didn't want to come on this date any more than Sabrina did, she had put a lot of effort into her hair, makeup, and the outfit she wore.

"Wow." Sabrina giggled. "Look at you!"

"Stop it," Emily whispered into her ear as she leaned over to hug her. "It's Magnolia Tavern. I didn't want to risk running into my Prince Charming while we're here and looking a mess. You know all the classy NFL and NBA players come in here."

"It's nice to see you again," Brady told her. "I'm so glad you're here."

"You too," Sabrina said. "Um, where's your best friend? He isn't here?"

"He's running a little late himself, but now that you're here, we can go ahead and be seated. I mean, if you want to. We don't have to." Brady shrugged. "He shouldn't be much longer. Emily and I just decided to hang out over here and wait. Our table is actually ready."

"We can go to the table." Sabrina didn't know if he was asking or making conversation.

The maître d' led them through the crowded dining area to a table overlooking the lake. Brady made sure she and Emily were seated by the window so they would have a view of the water. Sabrina checked her watch to see how much time she would still be there.

"I'm not going to be a third wheel," she said after they were seated and Brady ordered a bottle of wine.

"I promise, you won't be." Brady gave her a nervous smile. "As a matter of fact, I see him coming now."

Because she sat across from him and Emily, she couldn't see the direction in which he was looking, and she didn't want to be rude by turning around in her seat. She tried to read Emily's face to prepare herself.

"Where?" Emily frowned. "I don't see anyone."

"In the brown jacket."

Sabrina continued watching her best friend and then noticed a slight look of surprise right before they locked eyes. Sabrina didn't know if her friend's reaction was a good or a bad thing, and she didn't have time to figure it out.

"Sorry I'm late. Traffic was horrible."

Slowly, she turned and stared into the eyes of the last man she expected to see.

"Sabrina, Emily, this is my best friend, Jarrett." Brady stood up.

"You're kidding," Jarrett said.

"Oh, hell no." Sabrina looked over at Emily and shook her head.

"Brina, what's wrong?" Emily's voice was full of concern.

"What? Do you guys know each other?" Brady asked.

"This is the asshole cop."

"This is the loudmouth chick."

Sabrina and Jarrett spoke at the same time.

Brady and Emily looked from Sabrina and Jarrett back at one another.

Sabrina grabbed her purse and stormed from the table into the restroom. She entered a stall and tried to calm down. This had to be some kind of prank or cruel joke. There was no way in the world that God or the universe could allow this to happen. Of all the people in the world for her to be with on a date, it couldn't be him.

"Brina, are you okay?" Emily called out to her.

"Yes. I'm fine. I'm leaving."

"Brina, don't leave."

Sabrina flushed the toilet and walked out. "You can't be serious."

"It would be rude." Emily shrugged.

"Rude was that bastard giving me all those damn traffic tickets for no reason."

"The judge threw them out, remember?"

"You said yourself that you didn't even want to come on this charity white boy date, you remember? Now you're trying to get me to stay? For what?"

A flush came from one of the other stalls, and an older blond woman walked over to the sinks. Sabrina could see her trying not to stare at them as they talked. She gave them a polite smile, but Sabrina cut her eyes and went back to washing her hands.

"Just stay. At least for a little while. Please don't leave yet," Emily pleaded. "Brady is kinda nice, and I don't want to cause like a scene."

"Wait, don't tell me you like him."

"I didn't say that, and no, I don't like him. Hell, I don't even know him well enough to like him. Don't be ridiculous. We've had two phone conversations including the one we had today confirming I was on the way. But he's kinda interesting, and I just don't want you to go yet. Hang out for a little while please, just for me?"

The other woman at the sink seemed to be waiting on her answer just as much as Emily was.

Sabrina looked down at her watch and saw that it was seven fifty. Khalil was scheduled to call at eight ten anyway, so she figured she could tolerate another twenty minutes as a favor for Emily.

"I'm not staying for dinner. I'll finish my glass of wine, and then I'm outta here." Sabrina checked her hair and reapplied her lipstick. She noticed the other lady smiling at them, and this time she gave her a fake smile in return.

"You beautiful ladies enjoy the rest of your evening," she said as she exited.

"You do the same." Sabrina gave her a dry wave.

"Thanks, Brina. And Jarrett may be an asshole cop, but he is fine as hell. You ain't tell me that." Emily put her arm through hers as they walked out of the bathroom.

Sabrina gave her a look that showed she was not amused by her statement. "Too soon, Emily."

"Everything okay?" Brady asked when they returned to the table. He and Jarrett stood as the ladies took their seats.

"Everything is fine, right, Brina?" Emily looked over at Sabrina for confirmation.

"Yeah, everything is just peachy." Sabrina's voice dripped with sarcasm. She glanced over at Jarrett, who seemed just as irritated to be there as she did.

"Awesome," Brady said, reaching for the bottle of wine in the middle of the table and pouring some into each of their glasses.

"I'm gonna need something a little stronger than wine," Sabrina announced. "I think I'm gonna go to the bar and get a real drink."

Brady and Jarrett started to stand again, but she held her hand up and stopped them.

"I'll come with you," Emily offered.

"I'm fine, Em. I'll be right back. I promise."

Sabrina walked to the bar and ordered a shot of SKYY on the rocks.

"I'll take one of those too."

Sabrina didn't even bother turning around this time. Her eyes stayed focused on the bartender as he poured her drink. He put the shot glass in front of her, and just as she was about to pay, Jarrett handed him his credit card.

"Just the two drinks?" the bartender asked.

"Go ahead and start a tab. We're probably gonna need a lot of drinks."

Finally, she looked at him. "You don't have to do that. I probably won't be staying long anyway."

"It's no big deal. And buying you a drink is the least I can do."

"You think?" She downed the shot and turned to face him.

"Hey, this is just as awkward for me as it is for you. I'm just trying to extend the olive branch and be cordial."

"You gave me *four* tickets for no reason."

"First of all, you were going seventy-one in a fifty-five mile per hour zone at four in the morning. Then, you had the nerve to be disrespectful and call me an Uncle Tom MF who had nothing better to do but pull you over so I could make my quota for the month. You also screamed that if you had been a white girl—oh, I'm sorry, a Becky—I would've let you go."

Hearing Jarrett repeat everything she said to him that morning made Sabrina cringe a little. She was determined to stand her ground and reminded him, "Then you were about to have my car towed from the school parking lot after my nephew's game."

"No, I was making sure your car was safe in the parking lot of a school that had recently been targeted for vandalism. But you were so busy going off I couldn't explain." He shook his head.

The bartender set Jarrett's drink in front of him, and after downing it, he motioned for another round for both of them. Sabrina caught a whiff of his intoxicating cologne, mentally confirming Emily's description of him as sexy. She hadn't noticed it before, but now his allure was undeniable. His tall, muscular frame stood out in black slacks and a crisp white shirt, accentuating the smoothness of his caramel-toned skin. Without his police cap, she could see his wavy hair and neatly trimmed beard, with a hint of gray adding to his charm. Sabrina couldn't help but wonder about his age.

"Aren't you concerned about drinking and driving?" she asked him in an effort to change the subject.

"I know my limits. I also know how to Uber or Lyft, or if I need to, I'll just get Brady to take me home." Jarrett shrugged.

"He's drinking too." Sabrina nodded toward their table. "He ordered a bottle of wine and poured himself a glass."

"And he probably won't even finish that single glass. Brady doesn't drink." Jarrett laughed. "You can't leave. Listen, Brady is my boy, and he's been through a lot this past year, especially with women. This date is a huge step for him, and I promised I would be there to support him."

The bartender returned with their drinks, and Jarrett held his up toward her. "Truce?"

Sabrina glanced over at the table and observed Emily and Brady laughing together. She noticed that Brady's glass of wine remained untouched, yet Emily appeared to be genuinely enjoying herself. It was surprising, considering her earlier reluctance to socialize with someone who was "clearly" interested in her.

Sabrina's phone buzzed, signaling the call from Khalil. Despite the temptation to answer and proceed with their plan, she hesitated. Curiosity and a hint of intrigue urged her to stay. Though Sabrina was initially caught off guard and irritated by Jarrett's presence, she couldn't deny her desire to see how the evening would unfold. She retrieved her phone from her bag, stared at it for a moment, then made a decision and powered it off before returning it to her bag.

"Truce." She touched her shot glass to his, then gulped down the vodka.

After the truce between her and Jarrett at the bar, they rejoined the table and settled into an enjoyable evening. The food was superb, and the conversations were not only engaging, but entertaining. Emily's intuition was spot-on. Brady proved to be quite captivating, and surprisingly, so was Jarrett. Both men were charming and witty, and it didn't hurt that they were also easy on the eyes.

"Wait, wait, wait. So you mean to tell me you don't lose your mind over Mrs. Carter?" Brady seemed shocked. "I don't believe it. Every woman in the world is her biggest fan, seems like."

"Nope," Sabrina told them, taking a bite of her crème brûlée, relieved that she had decided to stick around.

"She's not lying. She was actually given tickets to a concert and didn't want to go. She gave the tickets away. I was so pissed because, unlike her, I am a card-carrying member of the fan club," Emily announced.

"So what do you have against who has been called one of the world's greatest female entertainers?" Jarrett asked.

"I don't have anything against her. I'm just not a rah-rah type chick. I'm more laid-back and mellow," she explained.

"You know I don't agree with that, right?" Jarrett shook his head. "Until tonight, you were the most rah-rah chick I've ever met. I've seen you in action twice."

"Okay, those were unusual circumstances. And I just prefer a different type of vibe when it comes to music."

"Yeah, she likes boring people," Emily added.

"They're not boring."

"Trust me, they are. You've dragged me to plenty of concerts, and they're boring."

"Give me some examples of who you like," Jarrett said.

Sabrina paused and then said, "I'm more of a Jill Scott, Erykah Badu, neo soul kind of chick."

"See? Boring," Emily said matter-of-factly.

"I can dig all of them." Brady sat up in his seat. "*The SunRoom* is one of my favorite albums, and 'Nothing to Something' is one of my favorite songs. But Leela James does it for me each and every time."

Sabrina stared at him, stunned by what he was saying. She glanced up and saw that Emily was surprised by his response as well.

"Brady's not your typical white boy," Jarrett leaned over and said in her ear.

"I see," she said. "I must tell you, I'm impressed. So I guess you're the Beyoncé fan?"

"Whoa, whoa, whoa. All men are Beyoncé fans," Brady said.

"You got that right." Jarrett reached over and gave him a high five. "She's got the best—"

"Don't," Sabrina told him.

Emily shook her head. "Men are so typical."

"What? I think she has a great . . . work ethic," Jarrett responded.

"Awwwwwwww, come on!" She couldn't help laughing.

"What?" Jarrett stared at her innocently. "She does. She works hard and rehearses sixteen hours a day."

"You ladies do realize how impressive a sixteen-hour workday is, right?" Brady asked.

"I work as a pediatric nurse," Emily told him. "I'm very familiar with sixteen-hour shifts."

"And her . . . work ethic is just as impressive." Sabrina laughed.

Brady pretended to glance down at Emily's rear in the chair. "Can you stand up for a second?"

Laughter erupted at the table, and Sabrina couldn't remember the last time they'd had such a great time on a double date.

"Are you sure you're okay to drive?" Jarrett asked two hours later as they waited for the valet to bring their vehicles. Emily and Brady were still inside, talking at the bar.

"I'm fine. My two shots have worn off, and I didn't even finish my wine."

"Yeah, I noticed that. I just wanted to make sure."

"I'm good."

The valet pulled up with her car and brought her keys.

"Well, I'm glad you didn't leave." He smiled.

"I'm glad you called a truce. I can't believe Emily is still in there."

"It's definitely a blind date to remember. Definitely wasn't what I expected."

"Oh, my goodness. Were you expecting me to be white? I have to confess, I was expecting a white guy."

"No, I was really surprised that you were black."

"What? Why?" Sabrina was even more confused.

"Because Brady doesn't date anyone except black girls. You were actually supposed to be his date, and Emily was supposed to be mine."

Chapter 19

Tenille

To say that Tenille was exhausted would be an understatement. Over the past two weeks, she had been running on fumes, starting her days before dawn to drop Marquise off at school for his morning workout sessions, then heading straight to the office, where she remained until it was time to pick him up. Noelle had been putting in just as much effort, arriving early and leaving late. With prom and graduation season on the horizon, their already-packed schedule was becoming even more hectic. The meeting with Catherine had ignited a newfound determination in Tenille to reach her full potential and expand her business.

Then, there was Xavier. Since his sudden appearance and impromptu lunch date, she had crossed paths with him a few more times. Nothing extravagant—just a casual cup of coffee at Starbucks one afternoon, or a glass of wine at a bar another time. Their meetings allowed her to unwind and bounce ideas off someone she trusted. While there was never any physical contact beyond a friendly hug hello and goodbye, she sensed the lingering attraction between them. They exchanged texts throughout the day, and although she acknowledged that hanging out with her ex might raise a few eyebrows, she cherished the renewed friendship and resolved to keep things platonic.

When her best friend texted, expressing feelings of neglect, Tenille knew they both needed some "girl time." Instead of retreating home, taking a hot bath, and climbing into bed on Friday night for a cozy solo night in, her plans changed to ordering Chinese food, uncorking bottles of wine, and tuning in to the Mary J. Blige Pandora station. Just as she changed into comfortable yoga pants and a T-shirt, the doorbell rang.

"Well, it's about time," Sparkle said when she walked in and gave her a hug. "I feel like I haven't seen or talked to you in forever."

"Girl, I know. I've been swamped at work."

"Where's Mookie?" Sparkle handed her a bottle of wine.

"At his friend's house for the night. Thanks, but you know I already got one chilled and ready."

Tenille poured them each a glass of wine, and they walked into the den, taking their fave spots on the sofa.

"I thought things would lighten up a little after you hired an assistant. What's her name? She's not working out for you?"

"Noelle, and yes, she's amazing. The girl is talented. That's part of the reason we've been busy. We've started doing a couple of new things using her graphic design skills."

"Oh, that's good. I was about to say if you wanted to let her go and hire someone else, Ivy is looking for a job."

"She's not working at the community center anymore? What happened?"

"She said they kept changing her hours all the time and not telling her. So, she ended up going in on days she was off and not being there when she was supposed to come in. You know how unorganized black folks can be."

The fact that Ivy had kept her job as long as she had was more surprising to Tenille than her getting fired. Ivy had always been spoiled. It had to be her way or no way.

That was one of the main reasons she had warned Nick not to mess with her. He insisted it was just a casual thing, but Tenille knew that, like most women, Ivy would talk a good game but eventually want more, which her brother was not going to give. Sure enough, it ended, and it didn't end well at all. The chaos and commotion that erupted from Ivy when Nick stopped responding to her constant calls and text messages had almost ended Tenille and Sparkle's friendship.

"I hope she finds something soon. She's a smart girl."

"Well, since your business has picked up, maybe you can find something for her to do in the office part-time."

There was no way Tenille was going to hire Ivy. It would not be a good idea, and she wasn't even about to put herself or her friendship with Sparkle in another jeopardizing position.

"I'm not at that point where I can afford anyone else right now, not even part-time. But if I hear anything, I will let you know. You know I'm always out and about. I'll keep my ears open."

"I'd appreciate it because if she loses her apartment, she cannot come and live with me. No, ma'am," Sparkle laughed. "So, what else has been going on?"

"Nothing much, really."

"You're lying. And don't tell me you're not because I know you. I don't care how hard your ass has been working, I can tell you got something else going on."

Tenille picked up her glass of wine and took a long sip. Sparkle was her oldest and dearest friend. Sharing secrets was something they had always done. But for some reason, Tenille was hesitant to tell her about Xavier.

"There's nothing to tell," she lied.

"Is everything okay with you and Brandon?" Sparkle became serious.

"Why would you ask that?" Tenille frowned.

"I was glad to see him at the end of your birthday brunch, but the two of you seemed so . . . cordial."

"Was that a bad thing? How were we supposed to be?"

"I don't know. You both just looked uncomfortable."

Brandon showing up at her brunch after it ended had been unexpected to everyone, including Tenille. She mentioned it to him more so out of obligation, thinking that he would be working like he always was. When she walked out of the restaurant and saw him standing with her brother, she didn't know how to react. Brandon didn't have a relationship with her family at all. That alone probably added to the weird tension Sparkle was talking about.

"Brandon and I are good. I need a refill and so do you." Tenille stood and picked up both of their glasses. As soon as she entered the kitchen, the doorbell rang. "That's probably our food."

"You want me to get it?" Sparkle called out.

"No, I got it." Tenille paid for the food and then set it out on the large marble island in the middle of her kitchen. "You want me to fix your plate?"

She waited for Sparkle to answer, and just as she was about to ask again, she turned and saw her standing in the doorway of the kitchen, holding Tenille's iPhone.

"Was someone calling me?" Tenille asked.

"Nope, you actually got a text. Two, as a matter of fact."

Tenille's eyes widened as she remembered Marquise had changed her phone to display her texts on the screen without her having to open it. She stared at the screen and stared at the two text messages that were displayed, both from Xavier.

Hey, beautiful.

Great seeing you today. Never doubt yourself. Remember what I told you. You are exactly what your brand represents. "A Perfect Ten." TTYL.

"I knew something was going on with you. I knew it." Sparkle shook her head.

"It's not what you think, Sparkle. I swear." Tenille put down the phone.

"Ten, don't do this."

"Do what?" Tenille asked.

"Don't go backward."

"Oh my God, Sparkle. I'm not going anywhere. It's nothing."

"You saw him today, you talked to him today, that's something. How long have you been dealing with him?"

"Marquise and Fabian reconnected a couple of months back, and they showed up at his basketball game the night of my birthday. We all went out for pizza afterward. Since that night, we've had lunch once and coffee a couple of times. That's all. It's Xavier, Sparkle. We talk and laugh."

"Have you slept with him?"

"No. I haven't."

"But you want to."

Tenille stared at her and didn't say a word. She did want to sleep with him, and the more time they spent together, the more she craved him. It wasn't just about sex. She missed the intimacy they shared, the touching and caressing before, during, and after they made love. She missed laughing in bed because she was so clumsy, and she missed the way he would whisper how good she felt to him each and every time. And despite her desires for him, it was her own fault that she couldn't have him. She was the one who walked away from it, not him.

"The food is getting cold," Tenille said, picking up a plate and putting food on it.

"Tenille, look at me," Sparkle said, taking the plate from her hand. "I love you. You are my best friend. You are smart, you are beautiful, you are talented. You have an amazing son, and your business is thriving. Your husband works hard to make sure you all are taken care of. That's what you wanted, remember? There was no security with Xavier. He did not want to marry you. All he wanted to do was play house instead of buying one. You wanted more for you and your son, and you have that. Do not risk everything you have by going backward. It's not worth it."

"Sparkle, I'm not."

They made their plates and filled their wineglasses and returned to the den.

"All I'm saying, Ten, is I know how you are with Xavier. He's always had this kind of spell over you."

"Spell? Really?" Tenille picked her plate up.

"It's like he can tell you whatever and you're fine with it."

"Like what?"

"Like the child support situation with George," Sparkle said, taking a bite of lo mein.

Tenille groaned, "Not this again."

"I'm just saying, Tenille. There's no reason why you shouldn't be getting child support. You're owed it. I gets my coins every single month, and so should you. And you would be getting it if it weren't for Xavier."

"That's not true."

For years, Sparkle blamed Xavier for Marquise's dad not paying child support. When he was small, Tenille went back and forth to court month after month in an effort to get a decent support order in place. The last time she appeared before the judge, George lied and said he had no income and was looking for a job. The truth was that he was working for his friend who owned a corporate moving company and getting paid decent money under the table. The judge ordered him to pay a whopping $62 a month, not even enough to cover a third of what she was paying in childcare weekly. She was so upset when she got home that she was in tears. After she told Xavier what happened, he told her to drop the case, not accept a dime from George, and leave the entire situation alone. He told her they didn't need him or his money and that Marquise would be better off without both, he would make sure. From that moment on, until she left him, Xavier had made sure Marquise had everything he needed.

Sparkle did not agree with the situation at all, saying that Xavier was involving himself in a situation that he had nothing to do with. No matter what he did or said, it meant nothing to Sparkle, who insisted that if he truly loved Tenille, he'd marry her and adopt Marquise. Over time, Tenille realized there was some truth to what her best friend said, and she decided that if she was indeed going to be a single mother, she may as well be single. The breakup was heart-wrenching. Xavier was devastated but understanding and insisted his decision not to get married had nothing to do with her and was a personal choice. He was the one to explain the ending of the relationship to Marquise, once again making things easier for her. Xavier always seemed to make their lives better, and although Brandon was a decent husband, she missed having a partner who always made her feel at ease about everything.

"Ten, please listen to me. You have a great marriage to a good man, a thriving business, and a stable home for your son. Don't risk ruining all of that for a fling with a guy who didn't respect you enough to marry you. Xavier isn't worth losing everything you have," Sparkle pleaded.

"Sparkle, you're being ridiculous. I'm not risking anything. The few times I've seen or talked to Xavier, he's been nothing but respectful of me and my marriage. See, this is why I haven't said anything to you about him."

"Don't project that shit on me. I've known you our entire lives. The reason you didn't mention it is because you know you're dead-ass wrong, Ten." Sparkle put her fork down and stared at Tenille. "I love you too much to not call you out on your bullshit."

"It's not bullshit." Tenille's voice was a little louder than she intended, causing both herself and Sparkle to jump a little. She quickly calmed down. "Sparkle, I promise you, it's nothing. I know you don't care for Xavier, but I do, and we are still friends, that's it. Trust me, I won't be crossing any lines with him."

"I pray that you don't, Ten." Sparkle went back to eating her food. "You are my best friend, and I love you too much to watch you mess up a good thing."

"I love you too, and I know you do." Tenille grinned.

"And even though I trust you, I'm not the person you truly need to be worried about."

"What do you mean?" Tenille frowned.

"What if Brandon had been the one to see those text messages from Xavier, and not me? How do you think he'd feel about you and Xavier being so 'friendly'?"

Tenille thought about Sparkle's questions but didn't answer. She honestly didn't know how Brandon would react. She'd never seen him angry or upset and couldn't remember them ever having an argument or him being jealous of anyone. Then again, she'd never given him a reason to be.

There's no reason for Brandon to be jealous of anyone. I'm not doing anything wrong, Tenille told herself. One thing was for certain, though. She was going to change the settings on her phone ASAP so her texts couldn't be seen on the screen.

Chapter 20

Sabrina

"Awesome session today, Jada." Sabrina beamed with pride. She had been working with the adorable 6-year-old for almost three months. When she first started speech therapy with Sabrina, she could barely say simple words. Now she often spoke in complete sentences. It was the sessions like today's that made Sabrina love her job.

"May have treat?" she asked with wide eyes.

"You were so great today that I'm going to give you two treats." Sabrina reached for a box where she kept all types of toys and goodies. She opened it and held it toward Jada, who reached inside and took out a sticker and a small pack of Twizzlers.

"What do you say to Ms. Sabrina?" Jada's mom said.

"Please?" Jada asked.

Sabrina laughed and said, "Well, I'll take that even if it's after the treat is given."

"Say thank you."

Jada hesitated and then signed, "Thank you."

Sabrina signed back to her, "You're welcome," and they left. She had just sat down at her desk when her cell phone rang.

"Hello."

"Yo, you're not gonna believe who I saw today," Nick said.

"Some random chick you slept with." Sabrina sighed. It wasn't unusual for her brother to call with some story about running into one of his past conquests. Her brother had been knocking chicks off left and right since college and showed no signs of slowing down.

"Funny. But no," Nick said.

"Who?"

"Xavier."

"Oh."

"With Ten," Nick added.

"Okay."

"That's all you have to say? You're not wilding?"

"No, I saw him with Ten the other night." Sabrina laughed.

"What? When? Where?"

"He came to Mookie's game. We all went to dinner afterward, too. It was fun."

"What? Why am I just finding out about this? So, what the hell is going on? Is she gonna leave Brandon?" Nick asked.

"Nope, I don't think so." Sabrina grabbed her purse from her desk and headed out to meet Emily for lunch. They hadn't really talked since their double date.

"So, she's just gonna cheat on him? That's not right. I told her ass not to marry Brandon anyway. He's a lame. I knew this was gonna happen."

"Wait? Where did you see them?" Sabrina asked.

"At Ten's office," Nick replied.

"Why were you at Ten's office? You didn't have to work?"

"I was gonna take her to lunch for her birthday," Nick told her.

"You're a damn liar. You've never taken either one of us to lunch. The only people you take to lunch are your hoes." Sabrina laughed. "Wait, you went to see Noelle.

Oh my God, Nick. Tenille told you to stay away. I'm with her on this one. She's really cool. We're supposed to hang out."

"When?" Nick asked.

"I don't know. We haven't made plans yet, Nicholas. And even if we had, I wouldn't tell you."

"You're tripping."

"I'm not. The girl you brought to the brunch seems nice, and you need to chill. You're getting a little too old to be a man-whore."

"Whatever, Brina."

"But listen, I am about to go meet Em for lunch."

"Oh, yeah. How did your date with the white boys go?"

"It was surprisingly decent, and you're not going to believe who the other guy was."

"Mason."

"Hell no. You're trying to be funny."

"I wasn't. Who was it?"

"The cop who gave me all those tickets."

"You're kidding."

"I'm not. It was awkward at first, but it turned out to be okay."

They said their goodbyes, and Sabrina hurried into her car and down the street to the sushi restaurant, where Emily was already waiting.

"Oh my goodness, are you ever on time?" she asked as soon as Sabrina sat at the table across from her.

"Sorry. You could've ordered for me. You already know what I want."

"I know, and I did." Emily laughed. She reached onto the seat beside her and handed Sabrina a gift bag.

"What is this?" Sabrina asked, taking it from her.

"It's a thank-you gift."

"For what?"

"For being such a great friend. You did the auction and gala even though you didn't want to. And then you didn't leave me stranded and hung out with the asshole cop. I appreciate it," Emily told her.

Sabrina looked across the table. "Em, you didn't have to get me a gift. You would've done the same thing for me."

"True, but you've been through a lot the past couple of weeks. I know you act like you're okay about breaking up with Mason, but even if you're not upset, I know you're still a little disappointed."

Emily knew her well. Even though she knew breaking up with Mason had been the right decision, she was disappointed. She was right back at square one and had to wonder if maybe she was looking at relationships all wrong. She was adamant about dating men she felt were compatible mentally, emotionally, spiritually, and financially, and who she was physically attracted to. She weeded them out quickly and definitely made sure she set the standard early on in dating and let them know what her expectations were. Mason exceeded in all areas, with the exception that he was possessive and he had a jealous streak, especially when it came to Khalil. No matter how many times she told him that they were just friends and that's all they would be, he didn't believe her.

But it wasn't just Khalil. When she would hang out with Nick and his friends, whom she'd known for years, Mason would question her continually about where they'd gone, and God forbid they posted pics on social media. He would complain even more. She couldn't live like that, not until death, which was exactly what marrying him would mean.

"Have you talked to him?" Emily asked.

"Just texted. It's always one extreme or the other with him. One minute he's saying he loves me and wants to talk, and the next he's saying I overreacted and clearly never loved him because I tossed our future away like a torn piece of notebook paper. You know how poetic his ass can be." Sabrina sighed.

"Don't you miss him, though?"

"Not as much as I thought I would. I'm actually enjoying not having to check in, report my day, and make sure I've done everything I'm supposed to. I didn't realize how needy Mason was until we broke up." She thought about what Tenille and her mother had suggested. "I'm thinking about taking a sabbatical."

"From work? Oh my God, why?"

"Not from work, Emily. From relationships. Just take some me time and figure out exactly what I want."

"You already know what you want. Hell, Sabrina, you're the pickiest, most selective woman I know. You're picky about everything: food, clothes, shoes, and men. I don't think you're picking the wrong guys. All of your exes have been smart, fashionable, had great jobs, a solid future, and most of all, each and every one of them have been fine as hell. You have never dated a buster as long as I've known you."

"Yeah, they are all of those things, but they don't last. And I've gotta figure out why."

"How are you gonna do that? Especially if you stop dating?"

Sabrina shrugged. "I don't know. But I'm done dating for a while. The one I went on with you last week was my last one. Speaking of which, have you heard from Brady? You two seemed to have hit it off."

"No, not yet. He texted me that night to make sure I made it home safely, and he told me he had a nice time and would stay in touch. I was unexpectedly pleased with him. He was really cool for a white guy." Emily smiled.

"Does that mean you're gonna see him again?"

"I'm open to going on another date if he asks."

"Good for you. I'm glad. Now maybe you can leave that married fool alone."

"He's not married. He's engaged," Emily corrected her. "But I do think he's dateable. I thought he would have called and asked me out by now."

"He'll call."

"I hope so. We'll see. You gotta admit he was fine, funny, and financially stable, three things that are so sexy in a man."

"I can't believe you actually seem excited about a white guy."

"Stop it. He's not *white* white."

The waitress brought their food. Sabrina looked at the plate in front of her and laughed. Emily had gotten her order exactly correct: shrimp tempura roll, no tails, extra eel sauce on the side, no wasabi on her plate at all, and steamed rice in a separate bowl.

"See, Sabrina, even as picky as you are, sometimes people do get it right." Emily picked up her chopsticks.

"I see." Sabrina laughed.

After they'd finished their meal and paid the check, Emily insisted that Sabrina open her gift. Sabrina took the tissue paper out of the bag and looked inside.

"Awwww, Emily," she said, taking out a silver picture frame that Sabrina had admired when they were looking at things for her wedding. At the time, Sabrina had mentioned that it would be the perfect frame for her wedding photo. Inside, Emily had placed a picture of Sabrina from the gala standing center stage during the auction, looking amazing.

"I bought it as a wedding gift, but I figured what the hell. I hope you're not mad."

"Of course I'm not mad. I love it," Sabrina told her. "And I love you."

"I love you too."

They both stood and hugged before heading out the door and leaving.

Sabrina walked into her office and picked up the ringing phone on her desk. "Sabrina Chambers."

"Hey, Sabrina."

"Um, hey." She tried to recognize the male voice on the other end.

"How is your day going?"

"Okay." She still couldn't catch the voice.

"You don't know who this is, do you?"

"Ummmmm, I can't say that I do."

"It's Brady. Brady Richardson."

"Oh, Brady," Sabrina said.

"I'm sorry I'm calling you at work. I didn't get a chance to get your number Friday night before you left."

"It's okay. What's up?" Sabrina asked.

"I was calling to see if you had plans this weekend."

She didn't know how to answer his question and wondered if he was about to suggest another double date. On one hand, she knew how much Emily was looking forward to seeing him again, but on the other, it would mean seeing Jarrett again. And although they had gotten through the initial awkardness at the beginning of the date, she wasn't sure if she would want to go out with him again.

"I'm not really sure," she told him.

"Well, I know you mentioned that you were a fan of neo soul, and there is a great band performing at this place called Jaspers. I was wondering if you wanted to check it out and maybe have dinner Sunday night."

Sabrina waited for him to add, "with Emily and me," or maybe, "with me and Jarrett," but he didn't. She sat at her desk and paused a few seconds, hoping he would realize that he had somehow forgotten to include her best friend's name. She realized that what Jarrett told her at the end of their evening possibly had been true.

"Wow, Brady, um . . ."

"I'll tell you what. Why don't you take my number, think about it, and call me when you've made your decision? I know you're working," he said. "Will that work?"

"Sure, that will work," Sabrina said, relieved that she didn't have to give him an immediate answer. Hell, she knew whether it was now or later, the answer would still be the same. She was not going to go out with him. She took his number and said she would give him a call.

"I look forward to hearing from you and hopefully seeing you this weekend," Brady told her.

"Talk with you soon," she said before hanging up the phone. She remained seated for a few more moments, trying to understand what had just happened. The guy her best friend had the hots for had just called and asked her out.

"So, you gonna go on the date with the white boy or what?" Khalil asked.

It had been two days since Brady called and asked her out, and Sabrina still hadn't called him back. She had been trying to think of the best way to handle the situation. Had it been any other time, any other scenario with any other guy, her first call would have been to her best friend. Her mind was all over the place. She thought about calling Tenille, but her sister had her own situation she was dealing with, so she called the only other person she could think of, Khalil.

"Hell no, I'm not going out with him. Are you crazy?" she snapped into her Bluetooth. She was headed home from work and was considering whether she would stop and pick up something for dinner.

"I'm still mad that you flaked on me. Had me waiting at Jaspers like a dummy blowing your phone up."

"Oh my goodness, Khalil. I told you I was sorry. Let it go."

"It's cool. So, do you really wanna go out but you won't because Em is feeling him?"

"No. I mean, yes. I mean, no, I don't want to go out with him, but if I did, I wouldn't. I would never do that."

"You gonna tell her?"

"Do you think I should? I mean, I don't know. Think about it—I don't say anything, he doesn't call her, and she moves on. No big deal, right?" Sabrina suggested.

"That's true, but what if he calls her and mentions that he asked you out?"

"He wouldn't do that, would he?"

"I don't know. Hell, he may call her and ask her to put a good word in for him." Khalil was teasing, but Sabrina thought that could have been a possibility.

"You're not helping me, Khalil."

"I gotta take this call."

"Uggggghhhhhh," Sabrina groaned.

"I'll call you right back," Khalil said before ending the call.

Sabrina spotted a Jamaican place that she liked and decided to stop and grab some takeout. She had just ordered her food and was waiting at the bar. She looked up from the drink menu and caught the eye of a guy walking in. She shook her head at him, and they both laughed as he approached her.

"I'm really starting to believe you're stalking me," she told him.

"We definitely have to stop meeting like this," Jarrett said, sitting beside her. "How've you been?"

"I've been okay. What about you? Busy meeting your quota for the month?" she teased. He was casually dressed in black sweats and a pair of Adidas running shoes. As he sat down, she again noticed how good he smelled.

"You do realize that's just a myth, right? We don't have a quota."

"Sure you don't."

"I'm serious."

"If you say so."

"I say so. You order?" he asked, nodding toward the menu in front of her.

"I ordered food. I was thinking about getting a glass of wine. I need it."

"Bad day at work?"

"Not really."

"Good day at work?"

"Fine, I don't need a glass of wine. I want one."

He ordered a beer for himself and a glass of pinot grigio for her, then turned and said, "I heard you got a dinner date invitation."

Sabrina sighed. "He told you?"

"Yeah, he contemplated it for a couple of days. I didn't think he was gonna do it, but he did."

"I was surprised myself."

"I also heard you haven't called back with an answer. So, I guess that's your answer, huh?"

"I'm really not interested. I mean, he seems like he's a nice guy, but he's not my type, and then there's the fact that my best friend is really interested in him."

"Really? I thought she didn't date white guys."

"Well, she says Brady isn't really *white* white."

The dreadlocked bartender brought their drinks at the same time the waitress brought her food.

"Too bad you already ordered. We could've hung out a while longer and eaten together." He shrugged.

Sabrina paused and looked down at the white plastic bag in front of her. She didn't have anything else to do. Since her breakup, her nights mostly consisted of take-out, reality TV, and watching her friends on social media. Strangely enough, she was enjoying sitting and talking with Jarrett and wanted to hang out a while longer. "I can eat it here while it's still hot."

Jarrett looked surprised. "Cool. You wanna stay here or get a table?"

"We can hang out here at the bar," she said, taking out the Styrofoam box that contained her oxtails, peas and rice, and cabbage. When she opened the top, she turned her nose up.

"What's wrong?" he asked, peeking at her plate.

"I told them no plantains." She sighed, irritated but glad she found out while she was still there and not after she had gotten home. There was nothing she hated worse than having her food order messed up and having to come back to have it fixed or replaced. It was one of her pet peeves and a big one.

"Just pick them off."

"No, they're touching my food," she told him.

Jarrett reached over and picked the two yellow pieces off the plate and popped them into his mouth. "See? They're not touching anything now."

"Did you just put your hands on my plate?" she asked, horrified.

"No, I picked my plantains off and ate them."

"I can't believe you did that. I don't know where your hands have been."

"They're clean. I promise."

"I believe that about as much as I believe you don't have a quota," she told him. She continued staring at the plate without touching her food.

"You're kidding, right? Are you really worried because I touched your food?"

Sabrina looked at him. "That, plus the fact that the plantains touched it. I hate plantains."

"They're gone."

"But what if my food has that taste still on it?" she asked.

"You are crazy. You know that, right?" He beckoned for the waitress, and she came over. Before Sabrina had the chance to explain or complain, he looked over at her plate and began ordering. "Can I get some oxtails, peas and rice, and cabbage, please? Is that what you got?"

"Yes." Sabrina nodded.

"Exactly what you got?"

"Well, no. I got jerk sauce on the peas and rice and told them to be careful not to have any get on the cabbage. Oh, and no plantains."

"What?" He looked at her again as if she were crazy.

"Dat's exactly what she ahdhered." The waitress nodded.

"Then that's exactly what I want." He then slid her plate in front of himself. "Can I get some silverware?"

"What are you doing?" Sabrina asked, taking the plasticware out of the bag and passing it to him. He bowed his head and closed his eyes, and she waited.

"I'm eating my food. Yours is coming. Calm down," he said after he finished blessing his food. "And I asked God to please let them get your order right, just in case."

It was almost nine o'clock when they walked out of the restaurant. Jarrett had kept her laughing, and she felt at ease while they talked. It actually felt good to hang out with a guy without an agenda.

"So, are you gonna mention to Brady that we ran into each other?"

"Probably, but don't worry, it won't be a big deal."

"I feel bad about not calling him back, but I didn't really know what to say, especially because Emily likes him."

"I'll handle it. I promise," he said as he walked her to her car. "What's this?"

He removed a flyer tucked under her windshield wiper and handed it to her. She looked at it and read aloud, "'Trap Karaoke.'"

"Interesting. Kinda sounds like fun."

"Maybe." Sabrina tucked it into her purse.

They said their goodbyes, and he waited until she pulled off before he walked away. She was thinking about how much she had enjoyed hanging out when she heard a beeping coming from her seat. It was then that she realized her phone had been in her car the entire time. She hit the screen and saw that she had six missed phone calls, all from Khalil.

Chapter 21

Nick

Nick had every reason to be in a good mood. It was Friday, it was payday, and he had plans to hang out with Eric, Sheridan, and Dannica. But for some reason, he just wasn't feeling it. His friends had been hyped all week about a new event people had been talking about called Trap Karaoke. According to one of his team members, it was the ideal mixture of thug, thot, and theatrics as amateurs got on stage and performed their favorite trap songs karaoke style. The first time they tried to get tickets, it was sold out, but this time they were lucky. Sheridan not only got them tickets to get in but also a VIP table located upstairs with a private bar and overlooking the stage and dance floor.

The venue was packed by the time they arrived and made their way to the table they had reserved. Nick looked around, scanning the crowd for any familiar faces as they ordered a round of drinks and appetizers, and he nodded his head to the music.

"Are you gonna perform?" Sheridan leaned over and asked.

"Nah, I'm more of a spectator," he told her. "I like to watch."

"Yeah, I know." She gave him a naughty look, and he forced a smile. They hadn't been hanging out as much as and hadn't slept together in a while. She hadn't done anything wrong. He just didn't seem as interested for some strange reason. Eric had to convince him not to cancel an hour before they were supposed to meet the girls. The only reason he agreed to come was so he wouldn't leave his boy hanging.

"Hey, isn't that your sister?"

"Where?" Nick turned in the direction Eric was pointing, and sure enough, he spotted Sabrina near the stage. His eyes shifted, and he froze. Standing beside her, looking sexy as hell, was Noelle. They were laughing and talking to a couple of guys.

"Yeah, that's her," Nick said as he stood up. "I'll be right back."

The club was packed, and he had to maneuver his way through the crowd. It was taking so long that he was relieved to find them still there.

"What the hell are you doing here?" Sabrina looked just as surprised to see him as he was to see them.

"I should be asking you the same thing. You don't even like rap music," he answered. He nodded at the two guys standing with them and then looked at Noelle. "How are you?"

"I'm good," she said, and then her attention went back to the guy standing closest to her.

"Jarrett, this is my brother, Nick," Sabrina said.

The guy reached over and shook Nick's hand. "What's up. This is my partner, Chad."

He was caught off guard by the word "partner" because they certainly didn't look like they were a couple. The other guy briefly looked up from Noelle and spoke, "Sup."

Nick nodded.

"Who are you here with?" Sabrina asked, looking around.

"Oh, Eric and the crew," Nick said, conveniently not mentioning Sheridan. "We got a table."

"Damn, y'all are fancy," Sabrina laughed.

"Looks like it's more fun down here," he said, again trying to make eye contact with Noelle, who refused to look in his direction.

"You can always come down and hang out with us regular folks." Sabrina shrugged.

"Nah, I'm good," Nick told her. "Where's Emily?"

"She had other plans. Are you getting on stage?"

"Definitely not. Are you?"

"I dared her to get up there, but she's too chicken." Jarrett laughed.

"That's because she doesn't know any trap songs for real. She only likes soft rappers like Drake," Nick told him.

"That's not true." Sabrina punched Nick playfully in the arm.

"What about you?" Nick addressed the question to Noelle, who had finally turned and was listening to their conversation.

"I might," she replied, then turned to Chad and added, "if I have someone who's not afraid to be up there with me."

"Why would someone be afraid to be with you?" Jarrett asked.

"You know how some guys are intimidated by girls like me." Noelle smiled innocently. Her comment stung Nick's pride, and he could tell that she knew it by the way she looked at him.

"You must be hanging with the wrong guys," Chad told her. "Because you are gorgeous."

Any thoughts of the two men being gay immediately left his mind, especially since Chad's hand was now placed on Noelle's waist.

"Well, I guess I'll holler at you later," he said. "Nice to meet you fellas. Good to see you again, Noelle."

"Bye, Nick." Sabrina waved.

By the time he made it back to his table, the show had started. The music was up full blast, and the crowd was going wild as a group of guys performed a song by Wu Tang Clan.

Being at a reserved table provided a place for them to sit, but as the crowd got thicker, they couldn't see everything that was going on. Eric and Dannica hopped up and decided to go downstairs. Sheridan stood up and danced but didn't leave the table. Nick eventually stood up to get a closer look.

"Are you okay?" she yelled over the music.

"Yeah, I'm fine," he told her. "You can go up there if you want. It's cool."

"No, I'm good right here."

He tried to enjoy himself, but he was distracted with thoughts of Noelle. He thought about suggesting that they go downstairs just so he could see her again, but he didn't want to run the risk of, one, having her see him with Sheridan again, and two, seeing her hugged up with Chad's corny ass. He looked over the balcony and saw Eric and Dannica waving their hands and jumping up and down with the rest of the crowd as a fat guy finished his energetic performance of Busta Rhymes's "Put Your Hands Where My Eyes Could See." The host announced that the next performers would be the last of the night. Nick was about to take his seat when he saw the group come onstage. Sure enough, Sabrina, Jarrett, Noelle, and cornball Chad ran onstage as music began blasting through the speakers.

"That's your sister!" Sheridan screamed as if Nick didn't already see her.

He couldn't believe that they were actually up there. Ms. Goody Two-shoes, Prim and Proper, My Way or No Way, I Don't Support Thug Music was on stage rapping along with Lil' Kim. She knew the words, which was even more shocking to him. He became just as excited as the crowd, quickly taking his phone from his pocket and recording their performance.

"Go, Brina! Go, Brina!" he yelled, trying to steady the phone as she danced with Jarrett. Then he stopped as it was Noelle's turn to take center stage with the microphone. She rapped the lyrics with ease and moved with just as much skill as she had when they first danced together at Black Beach Week.

Suddenly, he realized she was looking at him as she stood under the spotlight and said, "'I'm not the one you sleep wit', to eat quick/Want a cheap trick, better go down to FreakNik,'" and then she pressed her body against Chad's seductively. Chad looked as happy as a kid in a candy store who had just been given a gift card with no limit. Nick stared until the song ended and watched the four of them in a group hug.

"Nick? *Nick?*"

He turned to see Sheridan standing with her coat and purse in her hand.

"Huh?" he said.

"I asked if you were ready. What is going on with you?" She frowned.

"My bad. I didn't hear you over the music. Yeah, we can go. Don't we have to wait for E and Dannica?"

"I texted her and told her we would meet them at the car."

"Oh, okay," Nick said. He glanced back at the stage one more time, but it was now empty with the exception of the deejay.

When they finally made it to the parking lot, he heard Sabrina calling his name.

"Nick!" He turned around, and she ran up to him. "I know you saw me."

"Man, I can't wait to send this to Ten." He laughed.

"You did not record it, did you?"

"Hell yeah. You think I didn't? I'm about to post it to my Facebook, Instagram, and Twitter accounts."

"You'd better not. But that was so much fun."

"You killed it, Sabrina," Sheridan said. Nick had forgotten that she was beside him. "Who was your date?"

"Girl, not a date. I didn't even know he would be here. That's Jarrett. He and Chad are state troopers."

"Wait, is that the guy who gave you the ticket?" Nick was confused. "How the hell?"

"It's a long story, but hey, I gotta catch up with them. We're about to go grab some food. Don't tag me in that video, Nick. I mean it."

Nick stared at his sister. There was an excitement behind her smile that he hadn't seen in years. She gave Nick a quick hug and then took off.

They got to his car, where Eric and Dannica were already waiting. The girls suggested they go somewhere else and hang out, but Nick declined. He took them straight back to their hotel and parked directly out front, a sign that he wouldn't be staying for long. He could see that Sheridan was disappointed when he got out to open her car door. When she got out, he gave her a hug.

"Are you sure you're okay, Nick? You've been acting weird all night. Hell, actually all week."

"I'm good. I've just got a lot on my mind, and I think I'm coming down with something," he told her. He could tell that she wasn't satisfied with his answer, but she didn't say anything more as she kissed his cheek and went inside.

Fifteen minutes later, Eric got into the car. "A'ight, man, what's really going on?"

"What are you talking about?" Nick told him as he pulled off.

"You been quiet all night, and now Dannica is asking me all types of questions because Sheridan is asking her all types of questions. You're messing up my game plans, dude."

"Man, it's nothing. I'm just not really feeling her, I guess."

"Why not? What happened? She started tripping once she met your moms, didn't she?" Eric asked.

"Naw, she hasn't even really been tripping. I don't know what it is."

"If she ain't tripping, then we know what it is."

"I'm serious. I don't."

"Come on, Nick, I've known you for a long time now. You know what it is. Who is she and how long you been screwing her?"

Nick took his eyes off the road and looked over at Eric, who was now looking at him. "I don't know what you're talking about. I haven't been seeing anybody else. I swear."

"You don't have to lie to me. You know I ain't gonna say nothing."

"I know you wouldn't, and if I was seeing somebody else, you know I would tell you. I just gotta figure some stuff out."

Technically, Nick wasn't lying. He wasn't seeing anyone else. There was a big difference between thinking about someone and sleeping with them. The problem was that the person he couldn't stop thinking about wouldn't give him the time of day.

"Well, I hope you figure it out and figure it out quick." Eric took out his phone and then began laughing. "Yo, your sister tonight, bro. That was classic. I gotta post these pics I took of her onstage."

"Yeah, that was crazy."

"But that chick who was wit' her, Tenille's assistant, that girl is hot. Man, look at her."

Eric held his phone up, and Nick glanced over. There was a picture of Noelle holding the microphone in one hand and the other on her hip in a perfect pose. He stared and smiled until the car swerved, causing Eric to yell, "What the hell?"

"My bad. You're the one showing me pictures while I'm driving. Calm down."

"Damn, I thought you could multitask. But now that I see you can't, I won't show you nothing else. You can look at them on my page when you get home."

He dropped Eric off and then headed to his own condo. After getting undressed and climbing into bed, he grabbed his iPad and went straight to Eric's Facebook page, clicking on the pictures from the night. There were a few of Sheridan and Dannica that must've been taken when he had gone down to the main floor to speak to his sister. Nick smiled again when he got to the picture of Noelle. He took his own phone out of his pocket and replayed the video. There was something about her that drew him in. He went to Sabrina's page and was happy to see that his sister had also posted pics from the night. Unfortunately, Noelle wasn't tagged in any of them, so he couldn't get to her social media page. He went to search for her by name, but then he remembered he didn't even know her last name. He thought harder, and an idea came to him. He went to Instagram and searched for the name of the venue.

Don't be stupid. You are in a perfect situation with a girl who is smart, sexy, and great in bed, while you're sitting here cyberstalking a chick who doesn't even want to be bothered. Why? Why are you turning down guaranteed ass for someone who barely speaks?

His phone began to vibrate, alerting him that he had a text message. It was from Sheridan, checking on him. Nick didn't respond. Instead, he closed his eyes, and with Noelle still on his mind, he drifted off to sleep.

Chapter 22

Sabrina

"I know you're lying to me."

"I wish I were. But it's the truth, I swear."

"Four? Really?"

"Four." Sabrina nodded.

"You actually had four different guys put a ring on it, and you changed your mind and gave the ring back all four times."

"Actually, it was only three if you want to get technical. I was actually engaged to the same guy twice, and he gave me the same ring twice. At least it looked like the same ring, and I think it was, but I've been engaged four times."

Jarrett looked at her and shook his head. It was almost three thirty in the morning, and they had been sitting in Waffle House for almost two hours.

Sabrina hadn't even planned on going out, but she got a text from Noelle. The two had been planning to hang out for a couple of weeks, and going out with her sounded more fun than sitting home alone eating pizza, drinking wine, and watching reality TV on Bravo. Clubs weren't really Sabrina's thing. She was more of a bar kind of girl, so she was nervous and apprehensive as they got out of the car.

They had just gotten in line when she heard someone call her name. Sabrina turned around and saw Jarrett and another guy approaching. He introduced his friend

Chad, who was also a state trooper, and told them they could skip the line and all go in together. The club was crowded, but they found a nice spot near the stage, and as they talked and had a couple of drinks, she loosened up a bit and relaxed. Seeing Nick was also an added surprise, but for some reason, she felt like there was a weird vibe between him and Noelle. She was out of her element with a group of people she didn't really know that well, but Sabrina was having the time of her life, and when Jarrett and Chad dared them to go on stage, Noelle immediately accepted the challenge, and Sabrina couldn't resist. It was one of the most fun moments of her life, and she was glad that she had done it.

After leaving Trap Karaoke, they decided to continue their night at Waffle House. The diner was packed, and the four of them couldn't get a table together, so while Noelle and Chad sat and ate at one table, she and Jarrett were seated at the counter. For the past hour, they had talked about everything from childhood cartoons to their dream cars. Somehow the conversation turned to Emily and Khalil, and then Mason, which led to Sabrina telling him that she had been engaged four times.

"So what are you, some runaway fiancée?" he asked. "You wanna get engaged but don't wanna get married?"

"No, I want to be married. I just want to be married to the right person," she explained.

"Don't you know that it's the right person when you agree to marry them?"

"I think I do, but then the more I get to know them, the more I realize that they may not be. So I get out before it's too late."

"But why accept the ring if you're not sure?"

Sabrina thought about the question for a moment before answering, "Because I love them, and they love me enough to ask."

"How long are you dating these guys before they ask?"

"Well, the guy I was engaged to twice, we dated throughout high school. He asked me to marry him the summer before we left for college. We definitely weren't ready. Then he asked again two years later, and we realized we still weren't ready. The third guy I dated for a year, and the last one for nearly two."

"Interesting," Jarrett told her.

"What?"

"You."

"What about me?"

"You're just interesting."

"I don't know if that's a good or a bad thing. I just don't go around accepting proposals from random guys. I make sure we're compatible before we even . . . I mean, I know them very well. It takes a year to really know a person anyway," she said matter-of-factly. "But now I'm on sabbatical."

"Uh, what does that mean?"

"I'm not dating for a year. I'm taking some time to figure it all out."

"What exactly are you figuring out? And is that going to help?"

"I don't know."

Jarrett laughed heartily. "So let me ask you this."

"Ask away." Sabrina turned to face him. He was handsome, and she had been forcing herself not to stare at him all night. This time, she gave in to the urge to look right into his dark eyes, and she immediately regretted it. His gaze, combined with the baritone of his voice along with his scent, was too much, and she was captivated.

"Have you ever had a one-night stand?"

"What kind of question is that?" She quickly looked away, picking up her fork and swirling the remaining bites of her waffle on her plate.

"It's a simple question that can be answered with yes or no."

Sabrina had never indulged in a one-night stand. Every guy she had ever slept with had been one she was in a relationship with. She had never even considered having one.

"No, I haven't," she finally answered. "I guess you have had plenty, huh?"

"Of course."

"That's a shame," she teased him. "You sound exactly like my brother. You don't believe in love and commitment."

"That's not true. I believe in love, and I believe in marriage, too. But like you, I believe it will only work with the right person."

"And how will you know if it's the right person if all you're doing is having sex with them?" She frowned, anxiously awaiting his answer.

"Are you saying sex isn't important in a relationship?" He laughed.

"That's not what I'm saying at all. I'm just saying that you have to build on a foundation, and it has to be deeper than sex in order to know if the person is right for you."

"Could it be that you're setting yourself up for failure every time you date someone in anticipation of their being 'the one' rather than just a person you enjoy hanging out with? Why put all these expectations and what-ifs into a situation? In my opinion, it takes all the fun out of getting to know someone."

"I think you just enjoy being a man-whore." Sabrina laughed. When they were in the club, several women had spoken to him, and he acknowledged them, but he didn't act like it was a big deal, and he never left Sabrina's side.

"And I think you need to have a one-night stand," Jarrett told her.

"Are you offering?" she asked jokingly, but she was curious as to what his answer would be.

"Me?" Jarrett pointed to his chest. "Oh, no, definitely not with me. I don't want you falling in love and becoming a stalker."

"That definitely wouldn't happen." She laughed. "It would end up being the other way around, trust me."

"You guys ready?" Chad walked up and asked. Noelle was right beside him.

"Yes." Sabrina nodded.

Jarrett picked up the check, which was lying on the counter in front of them, and motioned for their waiter. Sabrina stood and picked up her jacket from the back of her stool. As he helped her put it on, their eyes met.

"Too bad you're on sabbatical and we can't find out which one of us is right." He winked.

"Yeah, too bad."

He walked Sabrina to her car, and she allowed him to hug her. As they embraced, she enjoyed the feel of his muscled torso and his strong arms around her. Most of her exes were on the slender side. Jarrett definitely worked out.

"Once again, I had a great time," he told her as he opened her car door.

"So did I," Sabrina agreed.

"Get home safely." Jarrett winked, then looked down. "And keep them damn shoes on while you're driving."

Sabrina laughed. "I'll try."

As she drove home, she thought about how much she'd enjoyed hanging out with him.

Too bad I'm on a sabbatical. Jarrett might have been just what I would go for.

"Oh my God, you were at Trap Karaoke?" Emily squealed so loud into the phone that Sabrina held it from her ear. "You know how bad I've been wanting to go."

"It was no big deal, and I didn't even know where we were going until we got there," Sabrina explained.

"No big deal? You got on stage and performed. That's a big deal. And you rocked it. I didn't even know you knew who Lil' Kim was."

"You're trying to be funny." Sabrina pulled her duvet tightly around her body. She had been sleeping peacefully until Emily's phone call. She should have known her plans to sleep in all day would be cut short. Once Sabrina was awake, she could never go back to sleep. The only reason she never cut her ringer off to prevent being disturbed was that she was afraid something would happen and she would be unreachable. *Maybe if my ringer had been turned off the morning Khalil drunk dialed me, I would still be engaged,* she wondered to herself as she rolled over in bed and looked at the time. It was only eight thirty, and she had only gotten four hours of sleep. "Why the hell are you up so early?"

"Actually, I have a gym date this morning," Emily told her. "But this phone call isn't about me. It's about you."

"A gym date with who? Didn't you just go on a date last night?"

"It's a date with the same person, if you must know."

"You spent the night with the married guy?" Sabrina sat up.

"Oh my God, Brina, stop saying that. He's not married. He's engaged, and that's not even who I went on a date with. Now back to you and Trap Karaoke. Was that Jarrett on stage with you? And the girl who works for Tenille?"

Sabrina was wide awake now. When Emily mentioned that she had a date, she naturally assumed it was with Victor, so she didn't even act interested. Now she was curious and wanted to know everything.

"Yeah, that was them. Who the hell did you go out with?"

"Brady finally called and asked me out," Emily told her.

"You spent the night with Brady?"

"No, I didn't spend the night with him. We just went to dinner and then drinks, that's it. We had a really nice time, and he asked if I wanted to meet him for a run this morning, and I said yeah."

"Emily, you hate running. Hell, you hate jogging." Sabrina laughed. "You hate exercise, period."

"I know that, but he doesn't. He commented on how fit I was and asked where I worked out. I told him at the hospital gym."

"We don't even have a hospital gym. I swear, those white girl genes are something else. You can eat pizza, ice cream, and those horrible burrito bowls from Chipotle every day of the week and still have a guy comment on how fit you are."

"First of all, don't talk nonsense about Chipotle. That's blasphemous, and I won't stand for it."

"Wait. When did he call and ask you out?" Sabrina was curious, especially since he had just asked her out on Wednesday.

"He called me Thursday, and I know, I know. That is totally against the rules, but it was kind of early Thursday and slightly longer than the twenty-four-hour window, so I let it slide just this once. Besides, you know I'd been kinda waiting on his call."

Sabrina thought about Jarrett's promise to mention Emily to Brady, and she wondered if he had really made good on it, especially since he didn't mention it.

"Well, I'm glad he called, and I'm glad you had a good time."

"Me too. Now back to you and Jarrett. Why didn't you tell me you were going out with him?"

"I didn't go out with him. Well, we did all go to breakfast after the club, but that was a group thing. It wasn't a date. He and his friend just happened to be at Trap Karaoke when we got there, so we all kinda hung out. Us getting on stage was totally unplanned, and the only reason I did it was because he dared me. But it was fun." Sabrina laughed.

"Which part? Hanging out with him or getting on stage?"

"Both," Sabrina admitted. "The entire night was just fun. I had a ball. Noelle is so much fun, and Jarrett and his friend were cool too."

"Are you feeling Jarrett now, Sabrina?"

"No, Emily, we're just cool. I'm not feeling him." Sabrina sighed. She didn't mention to her best friend how she felt slighted when at the end of the night he hadn't asked for her number. She was going to ask for his but decided not to, thinking that if he had been interested in her, he would've asked. Jarrett didn't seem like the type of guy who didn't make a move when he saw something he wanted. Based on the attention he got at the club, and his own admission at breakfast, he wasn't lacking female companionship.

"Good, because he's pretty much a man-whore," Emily told her.

Sabrina paused for a second before saying, "What?"

"Brady commented that he gets around. I don't think he thought I caught it, but I did. And I'm glad he said it so in case he tries to holler, you'll already know what the deal is."

"Well, it wouldn't matter anyway, Emily, because you already know I'm chilling with the whole dating thing for a while. So I'm good. Jarrett is cool, and so am I," Sabrina told her. Emily saying that Jarrett got around was somewhat disappointing. Not that she was at a point that she'd consider dating him, but it would've been nicer to hear that he was more on the faithful side.

"Well, you don't have to be so snippy about it, Brina. Goodness."

"I'm not being snippy. I was just saying. How did you even find out I went to Trap Karaoke or, better yet, that I got on stage?" Sabrina asked.

"Nick posted the video on his page."

I'm going to kill him, she thought as she put Emily on speakerphone and pulled up her Facebook page. Sure enough, there was a notification stating that Nicholas Chambers had tagged her in a video and, so far, there were over 200 likes.

"I told him not to post this."

"Why? It's a great video," Emily giggled. "I'm about to watch it again right now."

"Goodbye, Emily. Call me after your gym date."

"Okay, will do."

When the call ended, Sabrina clicked on the video. She couldn't help but smile as she watched their impromptu performance. Emily was right. She did a fairly decent job, and you could see that they were all having a ball, especially from Noelle and her seductive dance moves. If Sabrina didn't know any better, she would've thought that she was staring directly into the camera. It was one of the most memorable nights Sabrina had had in a long time, and despite her brother posting the video without her permission, she was glad she was able to watch it and enjoy it all over again. His doing so had also made her quite popular, because she had several friend requests. She went to view them, and though she tried to resist, she smiled as she stared at the list.

To her delight and surprise, Jarrett Moore had requested to be her friend. Sabrina went to his page and admired his profile picture. Her cyber research included going through his past posts, which mainly consisted of comments about sports and television. The only photos of females seemed to be group pictures or family members. He liked to travel and had vacationed in Jamaica, the Dominican Republic, Vegas, and even Italy. He volunteered for a boys mentoring group, and he also rode a motorcycle, which was an immediate turn-on.

He's a man-whore. You already know what the deal is, Sabrina. Don't do it, her mind told her.

"It's just a friend request, and he's just a friend. It's not that serious," she said aloud to the voice in her head as she quickly changed her relationship status from It's Complicated to Single and then went back to his request and accepted it.

Chapter 23

Nick

"Man, what's going on with you?" Eric asked as he entered Nick's office without knocking.

"What are you talking about?" Nick glanced up from his computer.

"For starters, you went MIA after Trap Karaoke. You didn't show up to play ball yesterday and ain't responding to nobody's calls or texts." Eric sat on the corner of the desk. "Then I get to work and your car is already here. When the hell did you become an early bird?"

Nick smiled. "I just got a jump start on the week. That's all, man. It's no big deal."

"It is a big deal when your girl is blowing up my phone asking about you."

"What did you tell her?" Nick sighed.

In an attempt to avoid the guilt of ignoring Sheridan's calls and texts, he had chosen to isolate himself and turned his phone completely off, avoiding everyone. He skipped his weekly pickup basketball game at the gym with the guys, knowing that conversation would inevitably turn to Sheridan, a topic he desperately did not want to discuss. It seemed that encountering Noelle at the karaoke event had ignited something within him. Thoughts of her had consumed his weekend. He spent the rest of his time alone, yearning to see her, talk to her—anything to bridge the gap. He even arrived at work an hour early just to steer clear of Sheridan. Deep down, he knew he couldn't avoid her forever, but right now, he wasn't ready to face her. Luckily, Sheridan hadn't ventured down to his office to see him.

"I told her you had something going on with your family." Eric shrugged.

"And what did she say? Was she cool with it?" Nick asked, wondering if Eric's lie was believable enough.

"She didn't have any follow-up questions, so I guess so."

"Cool, man. Thanks," Nick told him.

"You sure you a'ight?" Eric asked.

"I'm good, E. You know these team reports are due, so I've been focusing on getting them done." Nick pointed to the computer.

"Damn, you're right. I forgot they gotta be turned in. Lemme go and get mine done." Eric jumped up.

"Yeah, the sooner you turn them in, the sooner corporate can see that my team is blowing yours out of the water, my guy," Nick teased.

"I doubt that. Now I see why you've been avoiding us—to save the embarrassment of knowing your stats." Eric laughed as he walked toward the door. "I can't wait for the leadership meeting at the end of the month. Gonna be a good one."

"We'll see," Nick told him.

"Wanna wager?" Eric asked.

"Sure thing. Loser buys lunch for an entire week, winner's choice," Nick stated.

Eric paused for a minute before answering, as if pondering that Nick's dining choices for lunch were a little pricier than his. Then, as he walked out the office door, he finally said, "Bet."

Once Eric was gone, Nick took out his phone and turned it back on. As he'd suspected, there were several texts from Sheridan and Eric, and there was a voicemail from his dad, giving commentary about the football games. As he was listening to the comical message, Thad called.

"What's up, Thad?" Nick answered.

"Nothing, man, just checking in. Haven't talked to you since last week. You good?"

Nick leaned back in his chair. "Honestly, I'm not."

"What's going on?"

"You remember Noelle, Ten's assistant who was at the brunch?" Nick purposely omitted the fact that Thad had invited her for drinks.

"What about her?" Thad asked.

"I saw her Friday night, and it's kinda messing with me," Nick told him. "It's like I can't get her out of my head or something."

"Damn, Nick. You sleep with her or something?" Thad laughed. "She got you open like that?"

"No, I ain't sleep with her. I just saw her, that's all. We barely had a conversation," Nick explained. "That's what makes it even worse. This chick barely gives me the time of day."

"Wow, I mean, she is a beautiful woman, so I can't blame you for thinking about her." Thad laughed again.

"I'm glad this has you so amused, Thad," Nick said.

"It is amusing, Nick. If you're interested in Nori, then why don't you just tell her?"

Nick sat up. "Thad, what the hell? You know who she is? How?"

"Because I was there the night y'all met back in the day, and the energy between the two of you was interesting. While everyone else was focusing on the tension between Ivy and Sheridan, I was checking out the way you and Nori were avoiding looking at each other. That brunch was entertaining as hell. I knew having a concubine was going to catch up with you one day." Thad laughed again. "So, what's your game plan?"

"There is no game plan, and I don't have a concubine. I'm damn sure not interested in Ivy, Sheridan and I are just cool, and Nori—I mean, Noelle—isn't even an option," Nick said, standing up to close the door to his office so the private conversation wouldn't be overheard. The last thing he needed was for someone to tell Sheridan they heard him discussing other women.

"Why isn't she an option? Clearly there is some unfinished business between you, and then you're telling me you can't stop thinking about her." Thad pointed out the obvious.

"I've tried talking to her multiple times, and let's just say she hasn't been very welcoming. I even pulled up to Ten's studio and tried to holler at her, but she wasn't tryin'a hear anything I had to say. I let it go, and then I ran into her Friday night." Nick gave the recap of his and Noelle's interactions. "Ever since then, she's all I think about."

"Then tell her," Thad said as if it were as easy as peeling a banana. "You need to get her attention first, though, so she'll know you're serious, Nick. You're gonna have to make a gesture."

"You think that'll help? I can send her some flowers, maybe."

"Dude, I said a gesture. You send flowers to randoms all the time. You've been talking about this woman for ten years. Think of something to show her that you remember why."

It was moments like this that made Nick realize why Thad was his best friend. The man had always been wise. "You're right. Thanks, Thad. You're a damn genius."

"I know I am," Thad agreed. "I'm sure E's advice was quite different from mine. What did he have to say about this?"

"Honestly, I didn't tell him," Nick said. "You know Eric is tight with Sheridan. I didn't want to put him in a position to have to lie."

"Lie? About what? You and Sheridan aren't together, are you?"

"No, we aren't," Nick emphatically confirmed.

"Then you're free to pursue whoever you want, the same way she is, with no explanation," Thad told him. "And I would hope that as your friend, Eric wouldn't speak on it to her or anyone else. That's code, man."

"Nah, that's not what I'm saying. He wouldn't tell her anything I got going on with anyone else. E is my boy the same way you are," Nick explained. "It's just that I don't wanna talk about Noelle with anyone right now. You feel me?"

"I do, and I got your back," Thad told him. "I think it's cool that you randomly ran into her, Nick, for real. That weekend in Tampa was a long time ago, and you've always stood on there being a real connection. I know we've always teased you about it, but you may have been right."

"I guess we'll find out soon enough." Nick nodded in agreement. "Thanks again, Thad."

"Keep me posted, and don't forget, make sure the gesture is meaningful enough to show how serious you are," Thad reminded him.

"Will do," Nick said and ended the call. As he stared at the computer screen, the reports he'd been working on were no longer a priority. He pulled up a blank document, and instead of fighting thoughts about Noelle, he embraced them and began brainstorming about what he could do to show that his intentions were sincere.

It took three days for Nick to decide on what he felt would be the ideal gesture to show Noelle that he was sincerely putting forth the effort to get reacquainted. As he stared at the photo of the package that he'd scheduled to be delivered, he smiled, knowing that he'd done a good job. Buying gifts for women he dated wasn't something he typically did, but Noelle was far from typical. She was worth the effort even if things didn't go the way he'd hoped.

He waited an hour after receiving delivery confirmation with her signature before he made the call.

"Perfect Ten, this is Noelle."

"Hey, it's Nick. How are you?"

There was a brief silence, and for a moment, he wondered if she'd hung up.

"Nick, thank you," she told him. "I can't believe you did this."

"You like it?"

"I more than like it. The chocolate, the wine coolers, the bracelet, the book—it's all just . . ." Noelle sighed. "I don't know what to say."

"Say you'll let me take you to dinner this weekend." Nick was excited that she loved the gift basket that included a collection of her favorites: Tony's chocolate bars, Jamaican Me Happy wine coolers, a book about John-Michel Basquiat, her favorite artist, and a starfish bracelet. Everything was symbolic of the brief but eventful two days they had spent together years ago.

"What? Nick, I don't think that's a good idea," Noelle told him.

"So, are you saying having dinner with me is a bad idea?"

"It's not the best idea. How about that?"

"Nah, I don't agree with that at all. I knew I should've delivered the basket myself. There's no way you would've turned me down if I had asked in person," Nick said with a fake sound of disappointment. "Your answer would be totally different."

Noelle laughed. "No, it would be the same."

Nick opened the door to his sister's studio and strolled in, a bouquet of flowers in hand. "Prove it."

Noelle's eyes widened and were almost as big as the grin on her face. "What are you doing here?"

"I just wanted to give you these," he said, placing the flowers on her desk, "and prove you wrong. Now, Noelle Ridley, will you have dinner with me this weekend?"

Noelle folded her arms and rolled her eyes. "I'll think about it."

Nick shrugged. "Fine. Well, that's better than no, I guess. Can I at least get your number?"

Noelle became serious. "Nick, look. I appreciate the gifts, I do, but the last time I gave you my number, I didn't hear from you at all. And when I tried calling you, I was blocked."

"I know, and I apologize for that. I was young and dumb. But the fact of the matter is that I have never stopped thinking about you. I swear. That's why I sent this." Nick pointed to the basket sitting in the middle of her desk. "I remember our conversations on the beach while watching the sun set, and while everyone else was taking shots, you sipped those wine coolers. You told me how your mom would buy you Tony's chocolate every time you made honor roll and Basquiat inspired you to follow your passion. I also remember going into the store and you insisted that we couldn't just buy condoms, so I picked up the plastic starfish bracelet near the register and bought it for you."

"I was still embarrassed about the box of condoms." Noelle laughed, then became serious. "I accept your apology, and I'm grateful that you remember that weekend because it was special for me too."

"Then why won't you go to dinner with me?"

"Let me ask you a question."

"Ask away," Nick told her.

"What's the deal with the girl you brought to Tenille's brunch? Aren't you seeing her?"

"No, she's just a friend who works with me, and I invited her so my mom would stop harassing me about . . . never mind. To answer your question, no, she and I are not dating. I told you that in the parking lot," Nick insisted. "I'm not dating anyone, Noelle, I swear."

"I'm not trying to get caught up in no drama, Nick. I have a lot going on for me right now, and the last thing I need is a distraction."

"I'm not going to distract you from anything, and before you even go there, I'm not trying to play any games either. I just want to get to know you again, for real this time," Nick said sincerely.

"Fine, I'll give you my number. We can start there," Noelle said. "Give me your phone."

Nick didn't hesitate to take out his phone and unlock it before placing it into her hand. "Here you go."

Noelle typed her name and number in, and as soon as she gave it back, he called her.

"What are you doing?" she asked, picking up her vibrating cell phone.

"First, I wanted to make sure you gave me the right number." Nick laughed. "Second, I wanted you to see that you don't have to worry about me not calling."

"Whatever." Noelle chuckled. "Now, can you please get out of here so I can get some work done? The last thing I need is Ten firing me."

"You don't have to worry about that happening. As a matter of fact, I'm going to suggest that you get a raise," Nick teased. "Definitely Employee of the Month, for sure."

"Nick, no. You can't say anything to your sister about me," Noelle stated. "She can't know that we're even talking."

"What? Why?" Nick frowned.

"Because Tenille is my mentor and one of the best things to happen to me in life. I look up to her with love and respect. But one of her pieces of advice to me was to not become involved with you," Noelle continued. "I'd like to keep things between us between *us*. And if that's going to be a problem, then we can't talk."

Nick suppressed the anger he felt rising in his chest. The fact that Tenille had taken it upon herself to issue a warning to Noelle was preposterous and unnecessary. Instead of responding with anything negative about what was said and his sister's words of caution, Nick simply smiled and said, "What happens between us stays between us. I'll call you later. We can discuss dinner plans for the weekend."

"Get out, Nick."

Nick exited the office with a smile on his face. The air had been cleared, his intentions made known, and even with being blindsided with what his sister said, the gesture paid off.

As soon as he got into his car, Eric called. "Yo, Nick, what time you coming back to the office?"

"I'm not. What's going on?" Nick asked.

"We were gonna try this new sushi spot after work. Dannica said they heard it was amazing," Eric said.

"Nah, man. I'm chilling and working from home for the rest of the day," Nick said. "Y'all go have fun and let me know how it is, though."

"A'ight, bet. I'll holla at you later."

"Cool," Nick said, then hung up. In a sense, he knew that not returning to the office was another way of avoiding Sheridan, whom he'd barely spoken to all week.

When they did chat, it was brief and he told her he was swamped with a couple of new work projects. She offered to help, but he declined. There was a twinge of guilt, but he remembered what Thad had told him.

"You're free to pursue whoever you want, the same way she is, with no explanation."

Chapter 24

Tenille

Tenille stared at the thick brochure on her desk and rubbed her temples. When she had left the house, Brandon asked if she had looked it over, and she promised him she would do it. Now here it was sitting in front of her, and she didn't even want to open it. The words "Broughton Home Builders" seemed to jump off the glossy page at her. A new house. Their new house. Their dream house.

"I have something to show you," Brandon had told her as they were about to walk out of the restaurant after her birthday brunch. She had thanked her guests for coming and was planning on meeting Sparkle at the mall. Marquise had gone home with her parents.

"What is it?" She paused and looked at him.

"I actually have to drive you there," Brandon told her.

"Um, okay. Am I following you?"

"We can ride together. I'm sure your car will be safe here. It's only gonna be for an hour or so."

Tenille wondered where they were going, especially since he hadn't mentioned anything about going anywhere. She prayed it didn't have anything to do with his family. Had she known Brandon was going to attend brunch, she would have invited his family like her mother suggested. Seeing them now would be rather awkward.

"I'm supposed to meet Sparkle at the mall in a little while," she said.

"Tell her you have something else to do . . . with your husband." Brandon sighed while gesturing with his shoulders. Tenille could tell that he was getting agitated, which was unusual for him. Brandon never got upset. Hell, he never got angry, not that she ever gave him a reason to. He was pretty emotionless, and as long as the house was clean, his favorite beer was in the fridge, and he had snacks, he was fine. He was easy to please, and their marriage was just that simple. He paid all the bills, they went to breakfast after church on the one Sunday a month he was off, and they had sex every Wednesday night. Their lives were routine, and neither one complained.

Tenille sent Sparkle a text telling her that something came up and she would call her later and then climbed into Brandon's pickup truck. He seemed to relax a bit after they were headed to their destination, which to her was still unknown.

"Where are we going? Is your mother going to be there?" Tenille asked.

"No, she's not," Brandon said. "Why would you ask that?"

Tenille wanted to tell him that because, other than their den, his mother's house was the only place he went when he wasn't working. Instead, she said, "I don't know. I'm just trying to figure out where you're taking me."

"Chill, Tenille. I'm not taking you to the hood. I know better than that."

"Don't do that, Brandon." Tenille cut her eyes at him.

"I'm just teasing, but everyone knows how you feel about my neighborhood. You hate going to my mama's house."

"That's not true."

Brandon's mother still lived in the house he was raised in, located in the projects. Visiting her meant visiting an area that was constantly on the news and not for good reason. People were constantly robbed, assaulted, and killed in their neighborhood. Brandon had suggested that his mother move, even offered to help pay for her to live somewhere else, but she insisted she was safe because after living in her place for almost forty years, everyone in the neighborhood knew her. Tenille didn't feel safe at all the times that they would visit. Gunshots constantly rang out, strange men would always stare at her, and she couldn't relax because she feared their vehicle was being vandalized while they were inside. Her apartment was small, and because she had so much furniture, it was cramped and constantly smelled like smoke. Marquise hated visiting even more than she did, more so because he couldn't get a cell phone signal, and even if he wanted to go outside, Tenille refused to let him.

"Is that why you never wear jewelry or carry a purse when we go?"

Tenille hadn't realized he had noticed her safety precautions. "I have no problem with your mother's place."

"Liar," Brandon said, causing them both to laugh. She began to relax a bit as they passed the exit leading to his mother's. Brandon turned the radio up, and they enjoyed the sound of John Legend. As they continued traveling, Sabrina realized they were leaving the city.

"We aren't going far, are we?"

Brandon turned the music down, his head turned slightly toward her, but his eyes didn't leave the road. "Tenille, can I ask you a question?"

"Yes."

"Do you trust me?"

"Why would you ask me that?"

"Because sometimes you act like you don't. I wonder."

Tenille looked over at her husband. He wasn't overwhelmingly handsome, but he was nice looking. When Sparkle first introduced them, her first thought was that he wasn't really her type. He was tall, which she liked, but he was slender and had a fair complexion: a red bone, for lack of a better term. He was also quiet, and Tenille felt as if she had to force conversation. But her best friend insisted that he was a good man and exactly what Tenille needed in her life: stability. After dating for a few months, she introduced him to Marquise and her parents, who all agreed he was nice. When he proposed a month later, she was totally surprised. For years, she had dated a man who didn't even want to discuss marriage, and now, here was one she had only been dating months asking her to marry him. A hardworking man who would make sure she and her son were taken care of. There was nothing she would need and not have. Now, here they were seven years later, and she had to ask herself if Brandon's question was valid.

"Tenille?"

She realized her mind had drifted and she missed what Brandon had said. "Huh?"

"Never mind." Brandon turned the music back up. He drove another twenty minutes, and Tenille resisted the urge to ask where they were headed again. He finally exited the highway and drove into an area she had never seen before. She glanced at the surroundings as they entered a neighborhood that was newly constructed.

"Do you know someone who lives over here?" Tenille finally spoke.

"Yep." Brandon smiled.

"Who?"

"You'll see in a few minutes," he said. Moments later, they pulled in front of what appeared to be a model home, and a white guy walked out to greet them as soon as they parked and got out of Brandon's truck.

"Mr. Holmes, so glad to see you again." The guy shook Brandon's hand, then turned to greet Tenille. "And you must be Mrs. Holmes. Nice to finally meet you."

Tenille gave him a confused smile and glanced at the huge house with its perfectly manicured lawn. It had to have been at least 4,000 square feet, and it was so gorgeous that her first thought was that she wished she had her camera to take pictures.

"How are you, Frank? Good to be here," Brandon told the guy as he led them up the driveway and opened the front door for them to enter. The inside of the home was just as beautiful as the outside with its open foyer, cathedral ceilings, and ceramic tile floor.

"Wow, this is gorgeous," Tenille commented as she took it all in.

"Isn't it? And this is just the model. The ones that are custom constructed are even better. I told your husband you two are going to enjoy designing your home. It's fun and so much easier than going around and searching for a house. This way, you can ensure that your home has everything exactly the way you want it."

Tenille paused for a second. Her eyes met Brandon's, and she realized exactly why they were there.

"Tenille takes pictures, and she's really particular, so I'm sure she will enjoy this. Right?" Brandon winked.

"Well, let me grab something out of my office right quick. I'll be right back so we can tour the model, and we can get started. Feel free to take a look around," Frank said and walked off.

"So, what do you think? Are you surprised?" Brandon grinned.

"Brandon, what is this?" Tenille asked, hoping he hadn't done what she was thinking he did.

"It's our new house. Well, not this one, but it's what our house will look like when they finish. Unless you pick another design. But I like this one, and it's up to you. They have six different floor plans we can choose from. This one has five bedrooms and five bathrooms. Oh, and it has a utility room with a storage room, so you can use it for your camera stuff. And get this. It has a finished basement with surround sound so I can really have a man cave."

Tenille was still speechless as she listened to him go on and on about the details of the home. She couldn't believe he had done this.

"Tenille, say something."

"Brandon, don't you think we should've talked about this? I mean, this is a bit much, don't you think?" she asked. "You never even mentioned wanting to buy a house. What's wrong with the house we live in now?"

"There's nothing wrong with it. And you've always talked about your dream home. Isn't this it?" He lifted his hands as if he were presenting it to her.

"Hell, everyone talks about their dream home, Brandon. It's what people do."

"Well, now you don't have to talk about it. You can design it and live in it. I thought you would be a little more excited about this, Tenille." He seemed disappointed, and she couldn't blame him. It wasn't every day that a man presented his wife with not only the house of her dreams, but the opportunity to have it built to her specifications.

"Can we even afford this?"

"What kind of question is that? Do you think I would put us in a house we can't afford?"

"I'm not saying that. I just don't want to be put in a position where we are financially stressed, you know, house broke."

"I handle all the finances now by myself, and I ain't stressed, and I would never put myself in a position to be any kind of broke," he snapped. "I bust my ass seven days a week, twelve, sometimes fourteen hours a day. I work hard to pay our bills and make sure they get paid."

"You choose to work those crazy hours. I don't ask you to. And exactly what are you saying?" Tenille snapped back. "I don't work hard? I contribute to our household account every month, and my contribution ain't small either."

"I'm not saying that it is. And I've told you time and time again that you don't have to. But the fact that you do just proves my point, that we can afford this house."

"Ahem." The sound of Frank clearing his throat caused their attention to turn from one another to him. Tenille was immediately embarrassed.

"Sorry. We were having a discussion, and this is definitely not the time or place for it," she apologized. "I think I'm just in shock about this."

"Yeah, I tried to surprise my wife with a house for her birthday. Big mistake on my part." Brandon's voice dripped with sarcasm, causing Tenille even more embarrassment.

"I understand," Frank told her. "Maybe we should do this another time."

"I think that would be best." Tenille nodded. Frank gave her a thick folder containing the details of the construction and other paperwork, including the contract that Brandon had already signed.

The first half hour of their ride home was spent in silence. Brandon didn't even turn on the radio. Tenille stared out the window, her mind all over the place. This was the first time she and Brandon had argued about anything, but she didn't care. To make a big decision like this without her was just unbelievable, and she could not understand the rationale behind his thinking.

"Brandon, did you even consider Marquise when you made this decision?"

He didn't answer immediately, which let her know that he hadn't. Finally, after a few seconds, he said, "What about him?"

"How far he would be living from his friends, his school, my family."

"Nope, I figured you would just drop him off like you do now."

"Brandon, this area is almost an hour from where I work. Hell, from where we both work. And what about the house we're in now?"

"I'm gonna give it to my mom."

Tenille's eyes widened and her mouth opened. "What?"

"I told her we were buying a new house and she could have the one we're in now." He said it so simply, as if he had decided they would have chicken for dinner instead of steak.

"I'm so confused by all of this. I am. And why do we need five bedrooms? We have two bedrooms now that we aren't using. And what made you even want to do this?"

"Honestly?"

"Yes, honestly. Help me to understand why all of a sudden you felt the need to go and buy a big-ass house without even consulting me."

"I guess in my mind the house was going to be a segue."

"A what? What the hell is that?"

"Like, a transition."

"A transition to what?"

"Tenille, do you love me?"

"Why the hell do you keep asking me these crazy questions?" She was becoming more and more frustrated by the minute.

"Because deep down, I don't really know. Sometimes I feel as if you would rather be anywhere else in the world than with me when we're together."

"Brandon, how can you even say that?"

"And I really bought the house because I needed to show you that I love you and I would do anything in the world for you, even buy you your dream house. And I hoped that you, love, would be happy and feel the same way."

"I do feel that way, Brandon."

"I bought the house because I want us to have a baby."

A baby. When they had first started dating and it became serious, they talked about children. She told him she didn't want to have any more, and he didn't seem concerned about not having any of his own, which made her decision to marry him even easier.

"A baby?" This time she said the words aloud instead of in her head.

"Yes, Tenille, a baby. Our baby."

"But you said—"

"Tenille, I know what I said. But things are different now. My mom is getting older, and she wants grandchildren."

"So who wants a baby? You or your mother?" Tenille asked him.

"I do. The question is, do you love me enough to have one?"

Chapter 25

Sabrina

The driveway of Khalil's house was packed with cars by the time Sabrina arrived, so she parked her freshly detailed BMW SUV on the street behind several others. She glanced at her reflection in the rearview mirror to check her lipstick and hair, then grabbed the bottle of wine from the passenger seat. She walked confidently toward the front entrance. Despite being a frequent visitor and knowing the security code, Sabrina opted to ring the doorbell.

"Sabrina, you're here!" Tyra, Khalil's fiancée, squealed when she opened the door.

A successful bank manager, Tyra was captivating. Her high cheekbones, slender nose, and full, expressive lips that often curved into a warm smile reminded Sabrina of Meagan Good. Her almond-shaped eyes, deep and soulful, held a mix of intelligence and kindness. But it wasn't beauty but her genuine warmth and charisma that drew people to her. Sabrina understood why her best friend was so smitten.

"I am." Sabrina accepted Tyra's hug as she stepped inside, then held out the bottle of wine. "This is for you."

"Girl, you did not have to bring anything. We have plenty of libations. But you can never have enough wine," Tyra took the bottle. "Come on back. The party is in full swing."

Sabrina had promptly RSVP'd for Tyra's girls' night after receiving the invitation, which had arrived weeks before Khalil's drunken phone call and her subsequent broken engagement. Truthfully, she had been so engrossed in work and everything else, particularly Jarrett, that she had completely forgotten about the event until she received a reminder on her phone. Normally, she might have skipped it and apologized for her absence, but she genuinely liked Tyra and wanted to attend.

"Everyone, you all know Sabrina, Khalil's best friend," Tyra announced when they joined the other guests.

The party was taking place in the great room, decked out with vibrant decorations that set the stage for a lively night ahead. Strings of twinkling fairy lights crisscrossed the ceiling, casting a warm glow over the space. Colorful paper lanterns and streamers hung from the walls, adding pops of bright tones to the room. In one corner, a sleek margarita machine churned out refreshing cocktails, and across the room in another corner, a festive taco bar offered choices of beef, chicken, and spicy shrimp.

Around the room, ten women, each dressed in chic, comfortable attire, mingled and laughed. Sabrina stood out in a stylish denim jumpsuit paired with a colorful kente cardigan, her curly hair cascading freely while other attendees rocked a mix of trendy outfits: flowy maxi dresses, fitted jeans with fashionable blouses, and designer shoes. The atmosphere was a perfect blend of casual elegance and ratchet fun, with guests twerking while drinking high-end champagne. Sabrina immediately knew she had made the right decision by coming.

"Hey, Sabrina," they all greeted her.

Tyra wasted no time handing Sabrina a drink, and before she knew it, she found herself line dancing in the middle of the floor with everyone else. The evening continued with several hilarious games that had them all laughing to the point of tears. Despite meeting most of the ladies for the first time, Sabrina felt like she was hanging out with her homegirls from college.

"Hey, Brina, can you come with me for a second? I have something to give you," Tyra whispered.

"Sure." Sabrina stood and followed her into the kitchen.

"So, I probably should've given this to you a couple of weeks ago, but life got hectic and I decided to just wait until you came to girls' night." Tyra handed her a shiny metallic gift bag with her name personalized on the front.

"What's this?" Sabrina asked.

"Open it and see." Tyra gave an innocent shrug.

Sabrina removed the crinkled tissue paper from the top of the box, reached inside, and pulled out a candle with the words "Smells Like You're a Bridesmaid," along with Khalil and Tyra's names and their wedding date. Overwhelmed, she stared at it in silence.

"In a perfect world, you would be Khalil's best woman, but my traditional, pastoral parents wouldn't understand, and I don't have the time or energy to explain it to them. You're such a major part of our journey, so I'd love for you to be a part of our bridal party." Tyra smiled.

"Did Khalil know about this?" Sabrina finally spoke. "Because that joker hasn't said nothing."

"I threatened him not to. This was my moment." Tyra laughed.

"I can't believe this, T." Sabrina fought tears as she stared at the candle. "I'm tripping right now. I'm shocked."

"Why? You know how much I adore you. I never told you this, but as much as Mason hated Khalil and the friendship you shared, I appreciated it. You never said or did anything to make me feel uncomfortable." Tyra faced her. "In a lot of ways, you make Khalil a better partner because, unlike his homeboys, you call him on his bullshit."

"I definitely do that . . . a lot." Sabrina nodded.

"And I know it comes from a place of love."

"I do love Khalil, Tyra, and I love you. I want him to be the best version of himself because you deserve that from him. You deserve that from each other. That's why I've always rooted for the two of you."

"So, does that mean you'll do it?"

Sabrina smiled and nodded. "Of course I will. I'd be honored."

Tyra threw her arms around Sabrina's neck. "Thank you, Brina. This means a lot to me. Well, to us."

"It means a lot to me too. I've known Khalil since college, and I know he could be a lot to deal with at times over the past three years that you've been together. But there's no doubt in my mind that he loves you more than anything. I'm happy for you." Sabrina hugged her again.

"I know the timing of all of this is odd, especially considering you were planning your own wedding a few months ago. I felt kind of bad asking, but there's no way we could do this without you being a part of it."

"There's no reason to feel bad. Breakups happen for good reason. Better for it to be before the vows than after." Sabrina shrugged.

"True, and, girl, you were too good for Mason's pompous ass anyway. You deserve someone who allows you to be yourself and embraces all of you, your family and friends, including Khalil."

"We are a package deal." Sabrina laughed.

"And now I'm part of the package too." Tyra gave her a high five. "Now let's get back to this party before they have all the fun without us." Tyra put her arm around Sabrina's neck as they walked out of the kitchen.

***

After an unforgettable night with Tyra and her friends, and getting home well after three in the morning, having brunch was the last thing she felt like doing. But it had been a few weeks since she and Emily had hung out face-to-face, and cancelling at the last minute was not an option. A long, hot shower, a strong cup of coffee, and two Excedrin gave Sabrina that boost she needed to get dressed, toss on a baseball cap, and make the fifteen-minute drive to the restaurant where her best friend was already seated at a table with mimosas ready to drink.

"How was girls' night?"

"Lit as hell. Plenty of food, plenty of liquor, plenty of fun," Sabrina answered, hugging Emily before taking her seat.

"That's good. I like Tyra a lot. She's amazing. I still can't believe Khalil convinced her to marry him."

Sabrina laughed, especially since she'd often thought the same thing. "Girl, she deserves that ring after the work she's put in with that man. I'm happy for them though. She asked me to be a bridesmaid."

"What? Are you serious? That's so dope, Brina."

"I know. I damn near cried." Sabrina smiled.

"And you have a plus one now you can take to the wedding."

"Em, you're already invited. You don't have to be my plus one," Sabrina reminded her.

"I'm not talking about me, silly. I'm talking about your latest little secret," Emily pretended to whisper.

"What are you talking about? No, who are you talking about?" Sabrina shifted in her chair.

"Fine, I wasn't going to say anything and just wait until you told me, but I know about you and Jarrett."

"What about us?" Sabrina questioned.

"That you've been enjoying one another's company,"

Caught off guard, Sabrina tilted her head to the side. "I need coffee. Where's the waitress?"

Emily motioned for the waitress and said, "Can we get coffee please?"

"Sure." The waitress nodded. "Coming right up."

"It's coming right up," Emily repeated to Sabrina.

"Thanks, and what makes you think Jarrett and I are enjoying each other's company?"

"Because I . . . you see, um . . ." Emily, who was never at a loss for words, suddenly started mumbling.

"Spit it out, Emily. Explain yourself." Sabrina raised an eyebrow and tried not to become agitated. Luckily, the waitress brought their coffee to the table. Needing another caffeine boost to settle her nerves, Sabrina took a sip before adding her usual cream and sugar, then said, "I'm listening."

"Brady told me," Emily said. "I've been seeing him."

"Oh my God." Sabrina gasped. "Well, I'll be damned."

Emily telling her that she knew about Jarrett was surprising, but learning that she was dating Brady was even more shocking to hear. Not just because of the fact that Brady asked her out, but it also made her understand why Emily had been just as "busy" as she was these days. She was keeping secrets of her own, not that Jarrett was a secret. The reason she hadn't mentioned anything to Emily was because she wanted to keep the fact that she was enjoying him to herself. She didn't want to risk contaminating the unexpected friendship with the opinions of others, at least not yet.

"I know, I know, I should've told you before now. It's just—" Emily gave her an apologetic look.

"No, I get it, Em," Sabrina interrupted. "I'm not mad. I just wasn't expecting to hear that."

"Hell, I wasn't expecting to like him as much as I do. But I do, a lot. And I get it, he's not typically what I go for, but in a way he is. We like a lot of the same things: movies, TV shows, music, and Brady is just as liberal minded as I am," Emily explained.

"His best friend is black, Em, so I believe it. He seemed cool the night we went out." Sabrina sweetened her coffee and smiled. "I guess Ms. Edna was right—you and her nephew are perfect for each other."

"And to think, had I listened to her months ago, I might be engaged and asking you to be in my wedding too." Emily giggled, then stopped. "I'm sorry, Brina, I didn't mean it like that."

"Em, relax. You're being weird. You of all people should know that I'm glad that I'm not engaged anymore." Sabrina smiled. "And I'm glad to hear about you and Brady."

"And I'm glad you're not engaged to Mason anymore because now you met Jarrett and it's going well for you."

"What makes you think it's going well?"

"Because when I mentioned knowing about the two of you, you didn't deny it or cuss me out. And you wanted to smile but didn't. You like him and he likes you," Emily told her. "Am I lying?"

"Maybe, maybe not. Yes, we have been getting to know one another, but it's still too early to determine whether we'll be more than friends, and I'm fine with that." Sabrina thought about the late-night conversations that she shared with Jarrett while he was on duty and the random texts during the day that would make her smile. One thing she'd learned to like about him was that he was attentive without being clingy, and caring. He even made sure she got home safe after leaving Tyra's get-together, offering to send an Uber if she wasn't safe to drive. Had that been Mason, he would've insisted that he drop her off and pick her up by a certain time under the guise of "protecting her."

"It's fine for you to like him, Brina. He's a good guy."

"I know he is. But I just got out of a two-year relationship, Emily. I'm on sabbatical, remember?" Sabrina reminded her.

"Fine, call it what you want. I really do like Brady though, and I'm going to focus on seeing where things go with us." Emily sipped her mimosa, then took a deep breath. "I cut things off with Victor."

"Oh, shit, you do like Brady." Sabrina gasped.

"It was time, and I recognize that even in these beginning stages, Brady has shown me that I'm worthy of so much more than Victor's almost-married ass can give me."

"I'm proud of you, bestie. You definitely deserve better than Victor."

"And you deserve everything Jarrett has to offer, Brina. Just be open and give him a chance," Emily pleaded.

"I hear ya," Sabrina answered.

"Well, would you at least be open to a double date next weekend? You can do that while on sabbatical, right?"

"Yes, I guess I'd be open to that."

Emily's face lit up like a Christmas tree. "Thank you. I promise it'll be fun."

Chapter 26

Nick

Nick and Noelle glided across the skating rink, the soft glow of neon lights casting a playful ambiance around them. It was their third date, and Nick couldn't remember enjoying himself more. Noelle had chosen skating, a refreshing change from the usual dinner-and-movie routine.

Nick stumbled a lot on the rink, his attempts to glide gracefully often ending in awkward flails. Noelle, with her steady balance and patient demeanor, helped him each time, allowing him to constantly touch her hands and, occasionally, grab her waist.

As a slow song began to play, the deejay announced while the lights became dim, "Couples' skate!"

Noelle hesitated as other couples whirled past them. "We can sit this one out."

"No," Nick refused. He turned backward, holding Noelle's hands firmly as they glided across the smooth surface. It was then that Noelle realized he had been faking his clumsiness all along—he could skate perfectly well. Caught in the moment, they stared into each other's eyes, sharing a silent understanding that went beyond words.

"Nick, you didn't have to fake it," Noelle whispered with a smile.

Nick laughed, shaking his head. "I wanted you to feel comfortable, Noelle. Plus, it gave me an excuse to hold your hands longer."

Noelle chuckled as he spun her gently on the rink. "Well, I appreciate it."

Their laughter mingled with the music as they continued skating under the dim lights. As the song came to an end, they turned to leave the floor, but Noelle stumbled. Nick reached out instinctively to steady her, but they both ended up on the floor, laughing uncontrollably.

"You okay?" Nick asked, his eyes full of amusement.

"Yeah, I'm fine," Noelle replied. "Guess I'm not as graceful as I thought."

Nick grinned, pulling her closer. "You're perfect just the way you are."

They lingered on the floor for a moment longer, enjoying each other's company before Nick helped her to her feet. Their fingers intertwined instinctively as they stood together, the connection between them undeniable.

In that moment, Nick knew he was completely smitten with Noelle. It had taken some time and effort, but being consistent, attentive, and persistent had paid off. Every date they'd gone out on had been enjoyable, each one better than the last, filled with easy conversation and smiles. Tonight was no exception as they discovered a deeper connection on a simple skating rink.

"That was fun," Nick said as they exited the rink and walked in the parking lot.

"I told you it would be." Noelle held on to his arm.

The night air was exceptionally warm and signaled that spring was right around the corner. Nick had already been looking at events and places they could enjoy once the weather permitted it. He was looking forward to sharing new experiences with her.

"And I admit, you were right," he told her, kissing the top of her head.

When they arrived at her place, he escorted her to the front door and faced her. "I don't wanna go home yet."

Noelle looked down at her watch, then back at him. "It's after eleven. What do you want to do?"

"Stay with you longer," Nick told her. "What do you want to do?"

"I could go for something sweet," Noelle suggested.

"I could definitely go for that." Nick grinned, then leaned down and pressed his lips against hers. The kiss was just as perfect as the one they shared a decade ago. Although he'd contemplated it every time he saw her, Nick had held off on kissing Noelle, waiting until the time was right. Based on the way Noelle returned the kiss, she was just as anxious for the inevitable moment as he was.

"That was tasty," she told him. "I was thinking about us going to get ice cream."

"Fine." Nick laughed and reached for her hand. "Come on, sweetie."

Noelle took her hand back and shook her head. Nick's head tilted in confusion as she turned toward the door and unlocked it. When it was open, Noelle turned back around and gave him a seductive smile as she pulled him inside.

"Welcome to my humble abode." Noelle shrugged, leading him through the condo.

"Nice," Nick commented as he glanced around, taking in the stylish and modern aesthetic that reflected Noelle's vibrant personality and creative flair. The living area was adorned with abstract art pieces on the walls. A cozy sectional sofa strewn with colorful throw pillows that matched the artwork sat in the center of the room in front of a large television. He could picture the two of them cuddling while watching a movie or game.

"Thank you." Noelle smiled and continued pulling him past the compact but perfectly organized kitchen down the hallway.

Nick caught glimpses of photographs on the walls displaying moments of Noelle's adventures while traveling. The brief tour ended in Noelle's bedroom, where she stopped and put her arms around his neck and pulled him in for a long, passionate kiss that left them both breathless. A moan escaped Noelle's lips, turning Nick on even more. His hands slipped from her waist and cupped her perfectly round ass. Noelle tugged his shirt from his jeans and slipped it over his head. She caressed his shoulders, then his torso, her fingers tracing the cross tatted on his chest before moving lower. Nick gently moved her shoulder-length curls so he could freely kiss her neck while he unbuttoned her blouse, revealing the black lace bra she wore. Her nipples, already hard and erect, protruded through the fabric, signaling that they wanted to be free. Nick obliged by unhooking the bra with precision and fondled the double-D breasts that he'd fantasized about.

"Mmmm." Noelle gasped as she reached into his pants and wrapped her fingers around his hardness that was waiting to escape.

Nick unbuttoned her pants as he eased her toward the bed, and as she lay back on the all-white comforter, the moonlight streamed in the window. He stared at how beautiful she looked, half naked and smiling as he removed her calf-length heeled boots, jeans, and finally her lace panties. Noelle let her legs fall open, touching herself while looking into his eyes, giving him a full view of her wetness.

"Damn." He sighed, taking in her voluptuous body. "You're so fucking beautiful, Noelle."

"And you're so damn sexy, Nick," she replied.

Nick pulled her to the edge of the bed, opening her legs as he kneeled in front of her. He slowly licked her inner thigh, his fingers replacing hers, teasing before his tongue dove in for a taste. He savored her dripping center, taking his time as he gently sucked her clitoris before plunging his tongue deeper inside.

"Oh, shit, Nick." Noelle grabbed at the top of his head, but he pushed her away, continuing his oral exploration until she erupted on his face. Even then, he didn't stop until she whimpered softly in satisfaction.

He stood and smiled as he undressed. Noelle's eyes widened as she stared at his dick, now standing at attention. Amused, he said, "You act like you've never seen it before."

"I think it's gotten bigger over the years," Noelle told him. "Let me see it before you wrap it up."

"Okay, and then you can wrap it for me," Nick whispered.

"Deal. Where's the condom?" she asked.

Nick remained quiet, thinking about the box of rubbers at home in his nightstand. "I didn't bring one. You don't have any?"

Noelle sat up and shook her head. "No, I don't. This isn't something I usually do, Nick."

For some reason, her saying that made Nick even more excited to be with her. But it still meant that they wouldn't be going any further. "I mean, I didn't plan on this happening, Noelle, so I didn't prepare."

Noelle began laughing uncontrollably. "This is crazy."

"What? What's so funny?" Nick asked.

"I was just thinking about you lying to your girlfriend and her seeing that condom wrapper on the floor."

"Uuuuughhhhh," Nick groaned and fell on the bed beside her. "That was not funny."

"It wasn't funny then, but it is now." She giggled. "I don't know what was worse, the look on your face when she pointed it out, or when you saw me standing in that hallway listening."

"I'm so glad you're finding humor in one of my most humiliating moments." Nick smiled and pulled her close so that they were face-to-face.

"Sorry." Noelle sighed. "I swear, I've thought about that moment a million times since it happened, but this is the first time I've laughed about it."

Nick brushed a curl from her face. "No lie, I've regretted that moment a million times. Mainly because I was dead-ass wrong and neither one of you deserved it, but also because I never thought I'd see you again."

"Guess it was fate that our paths crossed again."

"That was more than fate. That was prayer," Nick told her.

Noelle looked surprised, then gave him a doubtful look. "Okay, prayer."

"That's the truth. I really hoped and prayed that I'd find you one day," he said. "And I said if I ever did, I would make up for lost time."

"I guess I don't have to worry about you ghosting me again."

"Never." Nick kissed her hand. "You're stuck with me."

"Good." Noelle smiled and reached for the colorful throw blanket, pulling it over them.

Nick rolled onto his back, and she put her head on his chest. As they drifted off to sleep, despite the fact that the lovemaking he'd been looking forward to didn't happen, Nick felt complete.

The next morning, Nick woke up to the aroma of butter, syrup, and bacon. After using the bathroom and putting on his boxers, he sauntered out to the kitchen. Noelle, dressed in a satin robe and bonnet, hummed softly as she flipped pancakes.

"Good morning." Nick hugged her from behind, kissing her neck as he reached past her and grabbed a piece of bacon.

"Good morning yourself." Noelle smiled. "Keurig and coffee cups are over there, and juice is already on the table."

"Thanks." Nick chewed the bacon and opted to pour himself a glass of orange juice. "How'd you sleep?"

"Once I got used to your snoring, I was fine." She shrugged.

"My snoring?" Nick gasped. "I'm surprised you could hear it over your talking in your sleep."

"I did not." Noelle balked as she carried their plates to the table.

"Oh, but you did. I know all about Taco Tuesday." Nick raised an eyebrow and repeated the incoherent phrase she'd mumbled throughout the night. "'No guac, no cilantro.'"

"Oh my God." Noelle shook her head in embarrassment. "Why didn't you wake me up?"

"Why didn't you wake me when I was snoring?" Nick asked as they sat at the table. "Wow, this looks amazing by the way."

"Thank you." Noelle nodded. "And I tried waking you, but every time I moved, you just held me tighter. So I just remained still."

"And kept talking." Nick chuckled softly while drizzling syrup over the stack of golden-brown pancakes, his mouth watering in anticipation. As he took the first bite, he closed his eyes, savoring the delicious flavors that didn't disappoint. "Mmmmmm."

"Best pancakes you've ever had, right?"

"They are." Nick nodded, taking another bite.

"So, how's work going?" Noelle asked, her voice carrying a hint of curiosity.

Nick's expression brightened. "It's going better than I expected, actually. I've started training the other team leads, and they're picking up everything quickly. Plus, I introduced this workshop with techniques for improving team stats, and everyone loved it."

As he spoke, Nick couldn't help but feel a swell of pride in his chest. He had developed the workshops and training sessions independently, resisting the urge to run his ideas by Sabrina, and it had paid off. Though it was still in the beginning stages, the fruits of his labor were already evident. Even Eric commented about seeing a difference in his team's performance, making Nick feel even more confident in his leadership skills.

"That's amazing, Nick. I'm really proud of you."

He grinned, taking another bite of the fluffy pancake. "Thanks, Noelle. When I get promoted, as promised, you're going to wine and dine me, right?"

Noelle chuckled, leaning in to kiss him gently. "Absolutely. We'll celebrate properly, and I'll even make sure we have the condoms."

Chapter 27

Tenille

"Can I have a one-night stand while I'm on sabbatical?" Sabrina asked.

Noelle, who was in the back seat, giggled, and Tenille rolled her eyes at her sister. "Sabrina, you're so dumb. How are you gonna ask a question like that and we're about to go to the mall?"

"What? Can I? I mean, does it count? Because I know you said no dating or relationships, so I was just wondering."

She had just parked her truck in the mall parking lot. Tenille turned to face her sister. Sabrina wasn't smiling at all, and she realized she was serious.

"Did you get it in with Jarrett?" Noelle asked.

"Who's Jarrett?" Tenille was confused.

"One of they guys we were hanging with Friday night. I knew he was into you. Good for you. He is fine and he's funny," Noelle commented.

"Jarrett, the ass . . . I mean, the cop I ended up on the blind date with from the Love Connection auction," Sabrina told her.

"I thought you went on the date with some white guy."

"That was Emily's date. Well, I thought it was Emily's date. Never mind all that. Just answer the question. One-night stand, yes or no?"

"You had a one-night stand with the asshole cop? The one who was in the school parking lot? Are we talking about the same guy?" Tenille was trying to keep up with Sabrina, but it was too much.

"Yes, it's the same guy, and no, I didn't have a one-night stand with him." Sabrina sighed.

"You should have. He has an amazing body. He's probably great in bed." Noelle laughed.

"Noelle." Tenille looked at her assistant in the rearview mirror.

"Sorry, but it's the truth. I'm just saying." Noelle shrugged.

"We should not be having this conversation right now," Tenille told them.

"Well, I thought it was going to be a simple yes or no answer. You're the one who turned it into a whole conversation," Sabrina said.

"Do you want to have a one-night stand with him?" Tenille asked.

"I would. He is fine," Noelle commented again.

"We get it, Noelle, he's fine." Tenille shook her head.

"And funny," Noelle added. "Funny guys are great in bed, too."

"Have you had a lot of one-night stands?" Sabrina turned around in her seat and asked Noelle.

Noelle shook her head. "Nope, just one. Years ago. And it did not end well."

"What happened? Did you catch feelings for him?" Sabrina asked.

"No, nothing like that. I mean, he seemed really cool, and we really vibed. It was a weekend situation. He was fine, too, and funny. I think I have a weakness for fine, funny guys, especially the good-looking ones. I have to be on the lookout for them."

"Noelle, stay focused. What happened?" Tenille hit the back of the seat.

"For someone who thought this was an inappropriate conversation, you sure seem interested now," Sabrina said sarcastically.

"Be quiet and let the girl talk. Go ahead." Tenille nodded.

"Well, we had a great night. Like I said, we vibed, and we vibed even more in the bedroom. Sex was amazing. And we were asleep in bed when his boy showed up and told him they had to go. Never heard from him after that."

"What? He never called, texted, nothing?"

"Nope."

"Wow. That's so trifling." Sabrina and Tenille spoke at the same time.

"And when I swallowed my pride and reached out to him, I was blocked."

"That bastard."

"No the hell he didn't." Again, Tenille and her sister spoke simultaneously and continued listening to Noelle.

"Yeah." Noelle's voice drifted off, and she looked like she wanted to cry.

"Wow, Noelle, I'm so sorry you had to deal with that." Tenille reached through the seats and squeezed her leg.

"Me too," Sabrina said.

"It was one of the most humiliating moments of my life. But I got over it. It's his loss, not mine, and it was a long time ago." Noelle perked up and smiled at them.

"He's an asshole who didn't deserve you. I can't believe he just left like that without saying anything." Sabrina sighed. "Especially after clearly having a connection."

"Definitely a connection. The way we clicked when we met, it was so unique and unexpected. Our ending up in bed was just a part of the process."

"That's deep," Sabrina said.

"There's nothing like having a connection with someone." Tenille thought of Xavier and their bond. She had never connected to someone the way she had with him. Nothing was ever forced between them. Their love was natural and all-encompassing. He had the ability to know exactly how she felt without her having to say a word and always knew exactly what she needed before she even knew herself. Her instincts for him were comparable.

"So to answer your question, yes, I have had a one-night stand. And believe it or not, I would probably have another one." Noelle laughed. "Definitely under the right circumstances."

"We know he'd have to be tall, funny, and fine," Tenille said.

"Definitely." Sabrina nodded.

"And it would have to be the same type of situation as the last one. We'd have to have that same type of vibe."

"Wait, you haven't vibed with anyone since that guy? Didn't you say that was years ago?"

"Don't get it twisted. I've been with other dudes, but I can't say none of them have been as organic as that one," Noelle explained.

"You haven't had a climax with anyone else?" Sabrina's eyes widened.

"Organic, Brina, not orgasmic." Tenille tapped her sister.

"Oh, my bad."

"Get this. The gag is I recently ran into him," Noelle told them.

"Here?"

"Stop playing."

"Yeah. And he had the nerve to ask for my number."

"Stop." Tenille balked, then asked, "Did you give it to him?"

"Of course she didn't." Sabrina took it upon herself to answer for Noelle. "Who on earth would give an asshole who ghosted them another chance?"

Tenille glanced in the rearview mirror and saw Noelle's head going back and forth as if watching the two sisters in a tennis match.

"This is true, but, Brina, don't act like you haven't let anyone spin the block. You've been engaged to the same man twice."

"Which is exactly why I don't want Noelle to make the same mistake twice like I did." Sabrina tossed her hands in the air.

"What if he's matured over time and realized he made a mistake?" Noelle spoke up. "I know I've grown up a lot over the past ten years. People grow, right?"

"They do," Tenille agreed. "And people do realize the value of the person they lost."

"So that means there are circumstances that warrant people being given second chances, especially if it's meant to be." Noelle's words caused a chill to go down Tenille's spine.

Meant to be. Since reconnecting with Xavier, she had wondered if that's what they were. And when the reality of being married snatched the fantasy away, she was willing to accept that they could never truly be together the way they'd hoped in the past, but there was no denying the emotions were still there. Maybe they were meant to be just friends. She needed him, Marquise needed him, and they needed each other.

"Maybe the one-night stand with the cop is meant to be," Tenille suggested, hoping to lighten the mood that was suddenly heavy.

"I agree." Noelle laughed. "The way the two of you crossed paths all those times, that's gotta mean something. May as well indulge in some intimacy if that's what you wanna do."

"Fortune favors the bold." Tenille repeated the words Xavier had told her.

"She's right. Being bold is why Perfect Ten is expanding and becoming a full-service media company." Noelle nodded as she conveniently changed the subject.

"What? Are you serious?" Sabrina squealed and grinned at Tenille.

"Let's just say we have a very lucrative contract on the table that I'm considering." Tenille shared the news she'd been holding on to since speaking with the rep from Windstar.

"Considering? What's there to consider?" Sabrina asked.

"It would require a lot more of my time and Noelle's, and I'd need a bigger space and more equipment, maybe even hire another staff member." Tenille pointed out all the reasons she'd been thinking about before signing the contract she'd received.

"I told her I have no problem taking on more responsibilities. I believe in her and Perfect Ten," Noelle leaned forward and announced.

"I believe in you too, Ten, and so do Mom and Dad and Nick. We all do. We've got your back."

"I know you do." Tenille nodded.

"What did Brandon say? He's gotta be happy about this. It's what you've worked for all this time," Sabrina said.

"I didn't tell him," Tenille admitted.

"What? Why not?"

"Because Brandon wants to buy a new house and have a baby," Tenille told her.

"Well, that ain't happening." Sabrina said the first thing Tenille had thought about when Brandon mentioned it.

"It's definitely not what I have planned." Tenille sighed.

She and her husband had yet to discuss the house or baby again. Tension between them was thick, even though, as usual, they barely saw each other at home. Brandon was working more shifts, and when she wasn't taking Marquise to practice or some other event, she was at the office, creating and recreating a business plan for a possible expansion. Until today, the only person other than Noelle she'd spoken to about growing her business was Xavier.

"You know I'll give you whatever you need to make this happen, Ten, right?" he said after offering her a congratulatory hug.

"I know you would, but I can't accept it," Tenille told him.

"Why not? How about you think of it as an investment, not a gift? I can be your silent partner." He playfully pulled one of her braids.

"I can't let you do that either," she told him.

"You know I got you. You don't have to stress about this. I mean it."

"And I appreciate that, Xavier, but this is something I'm going to have to figure out on my own," she told him.

As much as she had wanted to accept his help, she knew she couldn't. This was a major move that she was going to make on her own if she decided to make it. Still, it was a lot to deal with: her husband, her son, her business, and her friend.

Overwhelmed with her thoughts, Tenille looked at her sister. "You know what I really need?"

"What?" Sabrina asked.

"Some retail therapy, which is why we're here, remember? Why the hell are we still sitting in this truck?"

"Technically because Sabrina wants to have a one-night stand," Noelle answered, causing all of them to laugh as they opened their doors and got out of the truck.

Chapter 28

Sabrina

Sabrina gripped the axe tightly, focusing on the target in front of her. With Jarrett's guidance, she adjusted her stance and let the axe fly, watching with satisfaction as it landed dead center. Filled with excitement, she instinctively threw her arms around Jarrett, hugging him before she could stop herself. His arms enveloped her, and she enjoyed the strong embrace a little longer than she expected. When they finally released one another, she felt the magnetic energy between them that was so strong it caught her off guard. They smiled at one another and exchanged a triumphant high five before strolling back to join Emily and Brady at the table.

As they settled back at the table, everyone was buzzing with adrenaline and playful competitiveness. Sabrina couldn't resist teasing Brady a bit.

"You know, Emily," she started with a mischievous grin, "Brady might need a few more lessons from Jarrett before he can match our axe-throwing skills."

Brady raised his hands in mock defense. "I doubt that. I hope you know that was just a warm-up. Next round, you better watch out."

Emily joined in, nudging Brady playfully. "You're right. Sabrina and Jarrett make a pretty good team, but we got this."

"Yeah, y'all got it all right, this L that we're giving you." Jarrett leaned back, a proud smile spreading across his face as he put his arm around Sabrina's shoulder. "We're the dream team of axe throwing."

Sabrina laughed, enjoying the friendly banter. "Well, I have to admit, Jarrett's coaching definitely paid off," she said, nudging him affectionately.

The conversation flowed effortlessly between the two couples, highlighted with lots of laughter and friendly jabs. After a while, Emily and Sabrina excused themselves to visit the restroom, leaving the guys to chat.

They'd barely stepped into the ladies' room when Emily turned to Sabrina with a curious look and quietly asked. "So, what do you think about Brady?"

Sabrina thought for a moment before admitting, "I like him. He seems great for you. There's definitely something there between you two."

Emily smiled and raised her eyebrow. "And what about you and Jarrett? You two make a good team out there."

Sabrina sighed softly, her expression serious. "I won't deny the attraction. We do have chemistry. But you know I'm on a dating sabbatical. I'm just not sure if I should jump back into dating yet."

"Why not?" Emily pressed. "I know it's only been a couple of months since your breakup, but you said you aren't harboring any feelings for Mason and you were glad when it ended."

"This has nothing to do with Mason. I am over him and all of my other exes. But maybe one of the reasons none of those other relationships worked out is because I jumped into them too soon." Sabrina shrugged.

"Or maybe they didn't work out because they weren't the right guys for you," Emily insisted. "Brina, I've never seen you like this with a guy."

"Like what?" Sabrina frowned.

"You're relaxed and carefree, just enjoying the moment and being present. It's like you're vibing on another level, girl," Emily explained. "The only other person I've ever seen you chill this hard with is Khalil."

Sabrina paused, her mind racing. She understood what Emily was getting at—the comfort, the ease, the natural connection she had with Khalil. It was undeniable. But as she thought about it, she couldn't ignore the difference. There had never been any kind of attraction between her and her closest guy friend, especially the kind she shared with Jarrett. To be honest, she'd convinced herself that the reason she could be so comfortable with Jarrett was because she didn't think that there was any potential romantic interest and they would just be friends. Now, she wondered if there was something more.

"Yeah, I get what you mean," Sabrina replied softly. "Khalil is amazing, and we're like family. But with Jarrett it's different."

Emily nodded. "I can see that. It's like, with Jarrett, you're not just comfortable. There's more to it, and there's this spark, isn't there?"

Sabrina smiled wistfully, her thoughts drifting to Jarrett's smile, his warmth, and the way he made her feel every time they talked whether in person or on the phone.

"Exactly," she admitted to herself and her best friend. "I wasn't expecting any of this."

Emily squeezed Sabrina's hand reassuringly. "I get that. But sometimes the best things happen when we least expect them. Just keep an open mind. You don't have to rush into anything. Just enjoy the experience for whatever it is."

Sabrina nodded, grateful for Emily's understanding and encouragement. "Enjoy the experience."

Although she didn't say it, the one thing she wanted to experience was something that she'd been thinking about for a while: sex with Jarrett.

As Sabrina and Emily returned to the table, they were surprised to find Khalil and Tyra joining Jarrett and Brady. Khalil greeted them with a teasing grin.

"Well, well, look who's finally decided to join the party," Khalil exclaimed, his voice playful.

"Khalil, what the hell are you doing here?" Sabrina blinked, shocked to see him.

"I got tired of T telling me she wanted to come and try this place out. So, I brought her." Khalil gave Sabrina a side hug.

"Yes, he did finally." Tyra hugged her. "I kept hearing about how fun it is. We had no idea you guys would be here."

"We sure didn't." Khalil gave Sabrina a matter-of-fact glance.

She'd purposely failed to mention the double date or anything else about Jarrett, not wanting to hear any snide comments from him.

"Well, the more the merrier." Emily clapped and looked over at Brady. "Now we have another team to beat."

"I see you're drunk already, Em." Khalil scoffed. "My gorgeous lady and I have been together longer than anyone else at this table."

"What is that supposed to mean?" Sabrina asked.

"It means that our unity is strong and teamwork is solid. We're gonna handle you rookies like the MVPs we are," Khalil bragged.

Jarrett put his arm around Sabrina. "We're not worried, are we, Brina? We can't wait to beat all of y'all."

"I love a good challenge," Tyra squealed. "This is gonna be fun."

As Jarrett predicted, they were the winners, and after clinching the victory in axe throwing, their celebration was nothing short of spirited. Sabrina, usually reserved and composed, couldn't contain her excitement as she twerked against Jarrett, clapping her hands with a wide grin on her face. Jarrett joined in the moment, laughing and pumping his fists in the air.

"Did you see that? We nailed it!" Jarrett exclaimed, still beaming with pride.

Sabrina nodded enthusiastically, her eyes sparkling with joy. "I can't believe we actually won."

Emily and Brady exchanged surprised looks, their eyebrows raised in amusement. Emily chuckled softly. "Wow, Sabrina, I've never seen you so hype."

"Yeah, you're usually the tame one," Tyra added with a grin, nudging Jarrett playfully. "What did you do to her, sir?"

Jarrett shrugged, still catching his breath from their victory. "I guess we make a good team," he replied, giving Sabrina a playful wink.

Sabrina blushed slightly at the attention but couldn't wipe the grin off her face. "I guess so," she admitted, feeling a rush of adrenaline.

As they gathered their belongings and headed back to the table, Sabrina glanced at Jarrett, his arm around her shoulders, and realized how much she enjoyed being herself around him—carefree, competitive, and completely at ease. This night was turning out to be more than just fun. It was opening her heart to new possibilities.

"To the victor go the spoils," Sabrina announced as they took their seats. "Drinks on you, K-Boogie."

"A'ight, I'll be a graceful loser." Khalil nodded. "Jarrett, you must be something special. Sabrina here is usually so uptight, especially in public."

"I guess I must be doing something right then." Jarrett gave Sabrina a warm smile as he leaned back, surveying the group, then whispered in her ear, "So, is Khalil one of your infamous ex-fiancés?"

"Absolutely not," she clarified with a laugh. "Khalil is my best friend. We go way back."

"I was just curious." He shrugged.

The evening continued on a high note, with laughter and easy conversation flowing among the group. Khalil and Jarrett found common ground quickly, sharing stories and jokes that kept everyone entertained. Khalil, always the social butterfly, suggested they all hang out again soon.

"Yeah, we should make this a regular thing," Tyra chimed in, her voice warm and inviting. "We could invite Nick and his new girlfriend."

Sabrina paused, her brow furrowing slightly as she gently corrected Tyra. "Sheridan isn't Nick's girlfriend. She's just a coworker."

Khalil grinned knowingly, causing Sabrina to raise an eyebrow.

"Oh, I wasn't talking about Sheridan," Tyra remarked casually. "I saw Nick with the same girl who was in that karaoke video with you, Sabrina."

Sabrina's heart skipped a beat as she processed Tyra's words. She exchanged a stunned glance with Emily, suddenly feeling a mix of surprise and curiosity. The evening had taken an unexpected turn, leaving Sabrina wondering what other surprises might be in store.

"I haven't had that much fun in a long time." Sabrina leaned back into her seat, the night air swirling around them as Jarrett maneuvered the car through the city streets. They were on their way home, the thrill of the evening still evident.

Jarrett glanced at her with a grin. "I definitely enjoyed myself too. Your friends are great, especially Khalil. He's a cool guy."

"Yeah, he really liked you," Sabrina replied, her voice tinged with affection. "He's serious about us all hanging out again."

Jarrett reached over and gently clasped Sabrina's hand in his. "I'm also looking forward to another date with you, just the two of us. They're equally as fun."

Sabrina smiled warmly, her heart skipping a beat at his touch. As they drove, her phone buzzed with a message from Khalil. She couldn't help but grin as she read his words. "Speak of the devil. It's Khalil. He says he likes you," she said, showing Jarrett the text. "And he's happy for us. Thinks you're a great guy."

Jarrett chuckled, glancing at her with a playful look. "Tell him thanks. And that you deserve a guy like me."

Sabrina's smile widened. "He also said not to mess it up by thinking too hard."

"He knows you," Jarrett remarked, his eyes meeting hers briefly before focusing back on the road.

Sabrina got quiet, consumed by her thoughts. She didn't realize how long she'd been silent until she heard Jarrett's voice, which seemed to come out of nowhere.

"Everything good with you?"

"Everything's great," she assured him with a nod. "Actually, there's something I've been thinking about for a while."

Jarrett raised an eyebrow, curious. "Oh, yeah? What's that?"

Sabrina's smile turned mischievous. "Remember that conversation we had at the diner after karaoke?"

He glanced at her, a grin spreading across his face. "Yeah, what about it?"

She leaned closer, her voice dropping to a conspiratorial whisper. "Well, about your offer for a one-night stand . . ."

Jarrett laughed, his face full of surprise. "Oh, that? What about it?"

Sabrina gazed at him. "I accept."

"Hold up. You sure you can handle that?" Jarrett teased. "I told you I don't need you becoming a stalker."

"Believe me, that should be the least of your worries. You should be more concerned with how you're not gonna be able to stop thinking about me afterward," Sabrina told him.

"I mean, what's there to be concerned about? I already do that now."

"Oh, wow," Sabrina said.

Jarrett became just as quiet as she had been moments earlier, then told her, "Listen, Sabrina, we do need to make one final decision before we embark on this pleasurable adventure."

"What's that?" Sabrina asked, wondering if he was going to say he didn't think her acceptance of his offer was a good idea.

"Your place or mine?" Jarrett's voice deepened, and he reached over to touch Sabrina's thigh, sending a wave of excitement over her body.

Sabrina didn't hesitate to answer, "Mine."

Chapter 29

Nick

Nick stood in his cozy living room, making sure the warm glow of the flickering candles provided enough lighting. The air was filled with the rich aroma of sautéed garlic and herbs coming from the kitchen, where pots were simmering on the stove. Smooth R&B music played softly in the background, setting the relaxed and romantic mood he was aiming for.

As he sipped on a glass of red wine, Nick heard a knock at the door. Expecting to see Noelle, he hurried over and swung it open without checking the doorbell camera and was surprised to see Eric.

"Hey, man, what's going on?" Eric greeted him, stepping inside and taking in the scene. His eyes widened. "Whoa, candles, music, and you're actually cooking? Well, damn. You could've told me sooner, man. I thought we were gonna hang out tonight."

Nick shrugged apologetically. "Sorry, I should've mentioned it. But hey, next time for sure."

"It's cool. I can't believe you're finally doing something romantic for Sheridan."

Nick chuckled and shook his head. "Nah, man, it's not for Sheridan. Actually, I've got a date coming over—Noelle."

Eric's grin faded slightly, and he looked disappointed. "Noelle, huh? So, what's the occasion? You really pulling out all the stops."

Nick smiled, a hint of excitement in his eyes. "I just wanted to do something nice, you know? Noelle's special. I'm looking forward to spending time with her."

"So, you're seriously dating this Noelle girl now?" Eric finally asked, his tone rigid.

Nick nodded, sensing Eric's disapproval. "Yeah, man. Things just clicked between us."

Eric sighed heavily. "Nick, I don't agree with this. Especially knowing how Sheridan feels about you. She's been opening up to me about how she was looking forward to you all finally taking this a step further, and now you're dating someone else?"

Nick's defensive stance stiffened. "Look, Eric, I've been clear with Sheridan from the start. I always told her I'm not looking for anything serious. Hell, I told her that not too long ago."

"Words, Nick. Words," Eric responded sharply. "Your actions are saying something else. You took her to meet your family. You don't do that with someone you're not serious about."

Nick exhaled, frustration building. "I told you, I did that to get my mom off my back. Sheridan knows where I stand."

"Does she know you're dating someone else now?" Eric pressed, his voice rising. "Or are you keeping that from her, too?"

Nick hesitated, caught off guard by Eric's accusation. "I haven't told her yet. It's still early with Noelle."

Eric shook his head with a look of disbelief. "Nick, that's not cool, man. You're being dishonest with Sheridan. You can't just string her along like this."

"It's not like that," Nick protested in defense. "I'm not stringing her along. I've been up-front about my feelings."

"Up-front about not wanting a relationship, maybe," Eric shot back. "But you owe it to Sheridan to be honest about your actions. She's starting to care about you, man."

The tension between them was evident, thickening the air in Nick's living room. He felt conflicted, torn between his loyalty to Sheridan and his potential relationship with Noelle.

"I'll talk to Sheridan," Nick finally said. "But I'm not apologizing for seeing Noelle. We're just getting to know each other."

Eric sighed heavily, shaking his head. "Just be honest with her, Nick. That's all I'm saying."

"I hear you." Nick nodded solemnly, realizing the weight of Eric's words. The conversation had stirred up emotions and forced him to confront the complexities of his relationships that he'd been avoiding.

"Wait, does Noelle know about Sheridan?" Eric asked as if he'd just realized the other party involved in the complicated situation.

Nick hesitated, knowing where Eric was going with his line of questioning. "Yeah, she knows about Sheridan. She was at Tenille's birthday brunch too, remember?"

"And does she know that you've been dating Sheridan for over a year?"

Nick shook his head slightly. "No, she doesn't know that. And I wouldn't necessarily call what Sheridan and I are doing 'dating,' man. We just casually hang out, that's it."

Eric's expression darkened with disappointment. "Nick, this is not good, man. Someone is going to end up hurt here. You can't keep juggling these women and expect everything to turn out okay."

Nick's jaw clenched as he listened to Eric's words. "I know, Eric. It's complicated."

"Complicated because you're making it complicated," Eric replied sharply. "You're not being fair to Sheridan or Noelle. And you're setting yourself up to end up alone."

"I never wanted things to get this messy."

"Then you need to figure out what you want and be honest with these women," Eric urged, his voice softer but firm. "They both deserve that much."

Nick nodded slowly. "You're right, Eric. I need to sort this out."

"I hope you do, Nick. For everyone's sake."

With that, Eric turned to leave, leaving Nick to confront the tangled web he had woven between Sheridan and Noelle. As he watched his friend go, Nick knew he couldn't avoid the difficult conversations any longer. He had to find a way to be honest with both women before someone got hurt irreparably.

"Hey, you."

Nick's heart raced as he heard Noelle's voice behind him, her presence instantly soothing the tension that had gripped him during his argument with Eric. He turned to see her standing there, face full of concern as she glanced past him at Eric rushing off.

"Hey," Nick said softly, reaching out to take her hand and guide her inside. He closed the door behind her, enveloping them in the quiet comfort of his home.

Noelle furrowed her brow slightly. "Is everything okay? I heard you guys . . . yelling."

Nick sighed, running a hand through his hair nervously. "Yeah, everything's fine. We were just talking about work stuff."

Noelle studied him for a moment, her gaze searching his face. "Work as in Sheridan?"

Nick nodded slowly. "Yeah."

She took a step closer, her concern deepening. "Nick, is everything okay between you two?"

He hesitated, knowing he couldn't keep hiding the truth from her. "Noelle, there's something I need to tell you."

Her eyes widened slightly with anticipation and worry. "What is it?"

"Come over here, let's sit." Nick guided her to the dining room table, and they took their seats. This wasn't the conversation he had anticipated when he meticulously set the table with lit candles, a bouquet of flowers, and a chilled bottle of wine. He took a deep breath, gathering his thoughts. "Okay, so Sheridan . . . she's my coworker, but I had been seeing her for a while."

"A while. What does that mean? How long?"

Nick swallowed hard, feeling the weight of his confession. "Over a year."

Noelle took a step back, processing his words. "And you didn't think to mention that little detail to me?"

Nick reached out, wanting to comfort her. "I'm sorry, Noelle. I should have told you sooner. Honestly, I didn't think it was a big deal, but now I realize I need to."

She shook her head, pulling away slightly. "I don't understand, Nick. Why are you telling me now?"

He looked into her eyes, regret and sincerity written across his face. "Because you deserve to know the truth. I care about you, Noelle."

"This is a lot, Nick." She sighed in frustration, then looked at him curiously. "Does she know about us?"

"No, she doesn't. I haven't seen her outside of work in weeks. Ever since you accepted our first date, I've been nothing but professional. I admit, I've been avoiding her."

"You've been ghosting her?"

"No, we talk, but I keep it very professional, and I've been telling her I'm busy," Nick admitted. "But Eric seems to think that Sheridan started developing feelings for me."

"Yeah, I guess I can see why. You were casually dating for over a year," Noelle said. "Nick, you need to be honest with her. It's the right thing to do."

Nick nodded solemnly. "You're right. I'll talk to her and explain everything."

Noelle reached out and touched his hand. "And we also need to be honest with Tenille. She's your sister, my boss, and someone we both love and respect."

Nick nodded again. "I promise I'll talk to Tenille too."

"We will talk to her together," Noelle corrected him.

Nick gently took Noelle's hand, his eyes serious as he spoke. "Noelle, I mean it when I say I care about you a lot. There's something between us, something real."

"Nick, I feel the same way, but I can't allow myself to think about a future with you until you deal with your past and we tell Tenille. It's the only way we can move forward."

Nick nodded slowly, his grip tightening slightly on her hand. "You're right, Noelle. I need to sort things out with Sheridan and be honest with Tenille. I don't want anything hanging over us."

"Good, because I don't either."

Nick leaned in and kissed her, but as he pulled away, her frown caught him off guard.

"Is something burning?" she asked, wrinkling her nose slightly.

Realization struck him like a lightning bolt. "Oh, no."

Jumping up from his seat, he hurried to the stove, where he had left the pots simmering, forgotten during the conversations with Eric and Noelle. The dinner he had meticulously prepared—intended to impress Noelle—was ruined.

"Damn it," he groaned.

"We don't need to call the fire department, do we?" Noelle walked beside him and stared at the stove. "Oh, my."

"I'm so sorry, Noelle. I got caught up and forgot all about it."

Noelle hugged him. "It's okay, Nick. The thought was sweet."

"We can go out. I'll take you somewhere nice," he said. "It probably won't be as good as what I made, but . . ."

Noelle glanced over at the pot of burnt noodles and began laughing uncontrollably. "I'm pretty sure it would be."

"Wow, I'm glad you're so amused. I slaved all day over this home-cooked meal. This is all Eric's fault." Nick chuckled.

"Don't blame Eric for this." She pointed at him.

"I'll make it up to you, I promise," he said, feeling fortunate to have her patience and support. "Where do you wanna go?"

Noelle put her arms around his neck. "How about we order in instead?"

"We can do that. Besides, I already have my dessert right here." He kissed her again, happier than he'd ever been with anyone else.

A few days later, Nick stood by Sheridan's cubicle, his heart pounding with anticipation. He hadn't planned to approach her at work, but the conversation with her needed to happen sooner rather than later. He'd been putting it off long enough.

"Sheridan," he began tentatively, "can I talk to you for a moment?"

Sheridan looked up from her computer screen, surprise flickering in her eyes at seeing Nick standing there. "Sure, Nick. What's up?"

Nick shifted slightly, feeling the eyes of their colleagues on them. "I need to holler at you. Can I come by later?"

A hint of concern crossed Sheridan's face, but she nodded. "Of course. Is everything okay?"

Not wanting to alarm her, he remained cool and nonchalant. "Yeah, I just . . . I'll tell you when I get there."

Sheridan's brow furrowed with curiosity and a touch of apprehension. "Okay, Nick. Dannica and I are hitting the gym after work, but I'll be home by seven, seven thirty."

Nick nodded. "All right, I'll see you then."

He waited until almost eight o'clock, and as Nick drove to Sheridan's apartment, he felt a knot tighten in his stomach with every mile. He knew this conversation would change everything between them, and not necessarily for the better. When he arrived, Sheridan greeted him with a warm smile, dressed in a sexy lingerie set that usually would be a turn-on.

"Nick, I've missed you," she said, her voice full of as much longing as the look she gave him.

Nick managed a weak smile, trying to delay the inevitable. "I've missed you too, Sheridan."

He accepted the hug she offered, but before she could transition to kiss him, he stepped back and motioned toward the sitting area. They settled onto the sofa, the air thick with tension.

"What's going on? How are things going? I feel like we haven't talked in ages now that you've been so busy coaching. How does it feel to be a part of my side of the world?" Sheridan asked, running her finger along his arm.

"It's going good. I'm enjoying it," Nick told her. "Seales asked how I'd feel going to a couple of other offices and offering feedback."

"I heard," Sheridan told him. "I think that's a dope idea, and that would mean we can see each other while we're both traveling."

Nick took a deep breath, gathering his thoughts. "Sheridan, we need to talk."

The smile on Sheridan's face faded into a look of concern. "What's wrong, Nick?"

Nick hesitated, the words getting caught in his throat. "I've met someone, Sheridan."

Sheridan's eyes widened in surprise, then quickly filled with hurt. "What? Is it Ivy?"

Nick shook his head. "No, it's not Ivy."

"Then who is it, Nick?" Sheridan demanded, her voice quivering. "You can't just drop this bombshell and not tell me who it is."

Nick looked down, then back at her. "Sheridan, you know we've always agreed to keep things casual. I value our friendship, and that's why I want you to know that I've started seeing someone else."

Sheridan's expression hardened, hurt turning to anger. "So, that's it? You're just moving on?"

"I didn't mean to hurt you, Sheridan. You mean a lot to me, but I have to be honest about how I feel." Nick spoke softly, hoping it would ease the tension.

"How you feel? What about how I feel? Does that even matter?"

"It does, and I don't want you to think that I don't care about you, Sheridan, because I do," Nick explained.

"If that's true, then why are you here telling me about some other woman you're seeing?"

"Because I care about you, that's why," Nick replied. "If I didn't, I wouldn't tell you anything. Technically, I really don't owe you an explanation, but I value you and our friendship."

"Oh, really?" Sheridan's eyes widened as if she were stunned. "What the fuck am I supposed to say? Thank you?"

"No."

Sheridan turned away from him. "Just go, Nick. I can't believe this."

"I'm sorry, Sheridan," he apologized.

Sheridan told him, her voice cold and distant, "Just go."

Nick left quietly, the weight in his chest a result of a combination of his honesty and the sadness of ending something that had been comfortable but ultimately not enough. He had never wanted a future with Sheridan. As he drove away, he felt a mix of relief and sorrow, knowing he had to focus on moving forward with Noelle and resolving things with his sister, Tenille.

"Hello." Noelle sounded like she was asleep.

"Hey, babe, did I wake you?"

"Not really. What's going on?" she asked.

"I talked to Sheridan and told her what was up," Nick said.

"How did that go?"

"As expected, but at least I told her what was up."

"Are you okay?" Noelle asked.

"I'm great." Nick sighed. "And I'm grateful for you, Noelle."

"I'm grateful for you too, but there's still something left for us to do," she told him.

"I know—talk to Tenille. We can talk to her together." Nick smiled. "I need her and the world to know that I've found the woman of my dreams, and this time, I'm not losing her."

Chapter 30

Tenille

As Tenille stepped out of the corporate office of Windstar Resorts, clutching the signed contract that marked a pivotal moment in her career, she was greeted with a sight that caught her completely off guard. There, waiting for her in the parking lot, was Xavier, holding a vibrant bouquet of flowers in his hands.

"Xavier, what are you doing here?" she exclaimed, her voice a mixture of surprise and delight. They'd talked as she was driving to the meeting, and she appreciated the encouraging pep talk and voice of confidence he'd provided. Seeing him waiting beside her car was unexpected.

He smiled warmly, extending the bouquet toward her. "Congratulations, Ten. I knew you could do it."

She accepted the flowers with a grateful smile, inhaling the scent of lilies and roses and becoming overwhelmed with emotion. "Thank you. This means so much to me."

Xavier nodded, his expression serious yet supportive. "I know this is a big step for you. I'm proud of you and wanted to be here for your moment."

Tenille shifted slightly, her mind racing with thoughts of the future. "I'm excited, Xavier. Truly. But I'm also nervous. This changes everything for my business, and . . . well, I'm not sure where to start with expanding. I don't even have the space for it."

Xavier's eyes gleamed with a hint of mischief as he gestured toward his own car parked nearby and told her, "Follow me."

Tenille raised an eyebrow, her curiosity piqued. Without hesitating, she got into her car and trailed his Audi SUV. They drove for a few minutes until they arrived at a small office building in a newly developed commercial area.

Xavier parked, and Tenille pulled up beside him, her heart racing with anticipation and uncertainty. He got out of his car and walked over to her, holding out a set of keys.

"Here," he said, handing them to her. "It's your new office."

Tenille stared at him, stunned. "What? Xavier, how . . ."

He shrugged nonchalantly. "I knew you were thinking about expanding. So, I took the liberty of finding this place for you. It's not huge, but it's enough to get started. And it's close to Frazier Middle School."

"Xavier, I—"

"Listen, Ten, my boy Rick owns the property. He bought it a year ago, and I did all the general contract work for him at a huge discount. He still owes me for it, so we worked out a deal. He gave me a six-month lease to see if you like it. It's already been paid for, and you can move in whenever."

Tenille stood in the parking lot, stunned by Xavier's generosity and belief in her dreams. She hugged him tightly, whispering, "Thank you."

Xavier returned her embrace, his voice filled with pride. "You deserve this, Ten. I can't wait to see what you do with it."

As they stood there, gazing at the building, Tenille felt a surge of gratitude and determination. But reality soon set in. It was an incredible opportunity, but she knew she couldn't accept it as it stood. Talking to Xavier occasionally and meeting for coffee was one thing. This was another. It would complicate her life in ways she didn't want to imagine.

"Listen, Xavier, I appreciate you doing this, but I can't let you do this," she said, trying to convince herself as much as him.

"There's nothing to do. It's already done," Xavier insisted. "When you stepped out on faith and opened Perfect Ten years ago, I told you I would support you no matter what. Now here's my chance. What's the issue?"

Tenille hesitated. She didn't want to admit that the real issue was her internal struggle since reconnecting with Xavier in Jamaica. She had shared the details of the Windstar contract, expanding her business, and even her son, but she hadn't mentioned any of this to Brandon, her husband. She realized how little she shared with Brandon compared to the easy, effortless conversations she had with Xavier. She shared a home with Brandon, but she felt at home with Xavier. She was supposed to be picking out a floor plan for a new home and deciding whether to have a baby, not accepting keys to a new office space from her long-term ex-boyfriend. As much as she wanted to say yes, she couldn't.

"It's not right." Tenille's voice was barely above a whisper, tears threatening to fall as she held out the keys to him.

"Okay, I get it," Xavier said gently, lowering her hand. "What if I sublease the building to you?"

"What do you mean?" Tenille asked, uncertain but intrigued.

"You pay me rent," Xavier explained.

The idea of paying rent made Tenille feel more comfortable with the opportunity. "I want it in writing."

"Hell, if that's what you wanna do." Xavier shrugged.

"Wait, how much is the rent?" Tenille asked cautiously, wondering if she had spoken too soon.

"How much do you pay now?" Xavier inquired.

"Sixteen hundred a month," she answered.

"You'll pay me five dollars more for the first six months, and then we'll determine if there's another increase. Sound fair to you?" Xavier extended his hand for her to shake. "Deal?"

It was an offer Tenille couldn't refuse. She accepted his handshake and smiled. "Deal."

"I expect that you'll pay on time every month," Xavier warned.

"I will." Tenille grinned, relieved and excited about the new chapter ahead.

"Good. Now come on. Let's go inside and check out your new spot." He winked.

"It's a done deal!" Tenille burst into her office, waving the freshly signed contract.

Noelle, who had been waiting eagerly, leaped up and enveloped Tenille in a tight hug. "That's amazing!"

"Noelle, I couldn't have done this without you," she said sincerely. "You've been such a huge part of Perfect Ten. Thank you for pushing me to accept this contract and for believing in our vision to expand."

Noelle's face lit up with a wide smile. "Tenille, I'm so grateful to you too. Thank you for hiring me and giving me the chance to use my skills and creativity. It means everything to me."

"And there's more," Tenille said as she reached into her bag and pulled out the set of keys. "I've also got the keys to our new office space. We're moving to a bigger place."

"Oh my God!" Noelle jumped up and down, shedding tears of joy before Tenille even shared the news that her assistant would also be getting a raise and a promotion.

Their celebration was abruptly interrupted by the sound of the office door swinging open.

"Hi, can I help you?" Tenille immediately asked. There was something familiar about the woman whose face was contorted in a scowl. She'd seen her somewhere before but couldn't remember where.

"Hello, Tenille. I'm not here to see you." The woman looked past Tenille. "I'm here to see her."

Tenille tensed as she took a step forward, instinctively sensing trouble. "I'm the owner of this establishment. You can speak with me directly."

"Like I said, I prefer to address her," she retorted.

"What do want, Sheridan?" Noelle stepped beside Tenille.

As soon as Noelle said the name, Tenille realized who the visibly angry woman was: Nick's date from her birthday brunch.

"I know all about you and Nick," Sheridan spat. "Eric told me everything about you two."

Hearing her brother's name caused Tenille to become even more agitated than she already was, in addition to being confused by what Sheridan was referring to.

"What's your point?" Noelle snapped back at her.

"My point is you need to know the truth. Nick is a liar, and you shouldn't trust anything he says," Sheridan continued. "He's manipulative, opportunistic, and he's a bitch ass."

"You need to leave," Noelle commanded before Tenille could say it. "I get that you're in your feelings right now about Nick, but that has nothing to do with me."

"She's right. You need to leave," Tenille told her. Despite being rightfully angry at Nick for being the cause of the interaction between the two women, she wasn't going to allow Sheridan to disrespect him. "Whatever issue you have with Nick you need to address with him."

"Oh, it's already been addressed, trust me. I just came here as a personal favor to warn her," Sheridan yelled and pointed at Noelle.

"You don't need to do shit for me," Noelle yelled back.

Sensing that the verbal altercation would soon turn physical, Tenille moved so that she was standing between the two of them. "Sheridan, leave now before I call the police."

"And before I swing on your ass," Noelle added. "Either way, get the hell out of here."

"You've been warned, and tell Nick it's over for him, too." Sheridan issued the threat of her own before scurrying out the door.

"I'm sorry, Ten, we—" Noelle began.

"No, don't." Tenille held up her hand. "I don't even wanna hear it. I can't believe this shit. I swear to God, I'm going to kill Nick. This is why I told you . . . I knew . . . He always . . ."

She was so upset that she couldn't even form a coherent sentence. Time and again, she had warned Nick about his indifferent attitude toward the women he dated, his disregard for their feelings. She knew this recklessness would one day cause chaos and confusion, but to have it explode in her own place of business was unforgivable. What made it even worse was seeing Noelle in tears, a clear indication of the heartbreak Nick's actions had caused someone she deeply cared about.

"It's okay." Tenille hugged Noelle. "This isn't your fault."

"He said he talked to her, and then we were going to talk to you," Noelle explained through her sobs. The pain in her voice was heart-wrenching. "I can't believe he lied to me."

"Noelle, I don't know what the hell my brother has going on, but I swear I'm going to get to the bottom of it," Tenille reassured her. "How about we both take the rest of the day off? We need it."

"I'm sorry. This is your big day and now it's ruined, Ten." Noelle sniffled.

"The day isn't ruined, just a little disrupted, that's all. And we'll have plenty of other big days to celebrate. This is just the beginning." Tenille hugged her again. "This isn't on you. It's on that bigheaded brother of mine. I'm going to handle him."

"Don't worry. I'm going to handle him first."

Tenille sat in her car, the weight of the day pressing on her shoulders. She scrolled through her contacts, hesitating briefly before dialing Nick's number. No answer. Sighing, she considered calling Xavier but decided against it. Instead, she headed home.

As she pulled up to the house, Brandon's truck caught her eye in the driveway. She entered the house, finding Brandon in the living room dressed in jeans, a polo-style collared shirt, and sneakers instead of his work uniform.

"What are you doing home?" she asked.

Brandon looked up from his phone, a slight frown on his face. "My mom had a doctor's appointment, so I took the day off to take her. What are you doing home this early?"

Tenille set her bag down. "I have some news."

"I hope you're about to tell me you finally picked out a floor plan. The builder has been blowing my phone up. It's been damn near two weeks."

"I know, but, Brandon, listen. I don't think we need to buy another house. I think where we live now is fine. It's close to the school Marquise is attending next year," Tenille told him. "And I've decided to expand Perfect Ten. I signed a huge contract today with Windstar Resorts that's going to double my income."

Brandon's expression hardened. "Seriously, Tenille? I've been working night and day, trying to build a future for us, for our family. And you're talking about your business?"

"It's not just about me," Tenille responded, feeling a familiar sting of frustration. "It's about our future, too."

Brandon shook his head, his voice rising. "You're so selfish, Tenille. You always put your shit first."

She felt her temper flare. "And you're selfish for wanting a baby when you're hardly ever here," she shot back. "I'm practically a single parent already."

Brandon's eyes narrowed. "What do you mean by that?"

"You're never home," she said bluntly. "You don't spend time with me or Marquise. We never do anything as a family. You've never been to a PTA meeting, a sports event, hang out with him one on one. And don't blame work, Brandon. You could make time if you wanted to. You have no problem taking off work when you want to."

Brandon balked. "Wasn't I just with your family at your event?"

"My birthday brunch that you showed up for after it was over?" Tenille snapped.

"But I was there, wasn't I?" He glared at her. "You never spend time with my mother, but you make plenty of time for other folks too."

"Brandon, you're being unreasonable."

"And you're being unfair," he told her. "I have somewhere important that I need to get to."

Brandon shook his head at her as he walked past. Tenille couldn't believe her husband hadn't even congratulated her when she shared her good news. This contract was going to change their lives, and he dismissed it as if she'd told him she'd gotten her car detailed. What began as one of the best days of her life had quickly taken a turn, and she couldn't believe it. She grabbed her cell and called the one person she needed to talk to: her sister.

Chapter 31

Sabrina

The hot water cascaded over Sabrina's skin, washing away the remnants of sleep and refreshing her senses. Each droplet felt like a gentle caress, soothing away the fatigue that had settled into her muscles after a much-needed afternoon nap. As she stood under the showerhead, steam filling her bathroom, she closed her eyes and let out a contented sigh.

"You're stealing all the hot water."

Sabrina smiled as she leaned her head back and whispered, "Maybe you should move closer then."

Jarrett didn't waste any time taking her suggestion, and within seconds, she felt his muscled body against hers as he nuzzled her neck. Showering together was the perfect ending to the incredible day that they'd spent together. He took the bottle of vanilla-coconut bodywash from her hand, along with the loofah, and lathered her, taking his time on the parts of her that he'd quickly learned were her sensual spots. She turned around and returned the gesture, enjoying the smile on his face as she touched him. The sensual kiss he gave her was as hot and steamy as the water they stood under. Sabrina instinctively touched his manhood, erect and ready for whatever was about to happen next. To her disappointment, Jarrett reached past her and turned off the water.

"What are you doing?" she whined, her immediate thoughts of satisfying sex in the shower vanishing.

"Quitting while we're ahead." Jarrett gave her a quick kiss on the forehead as he grabbed a towel and wrapped it around the rock-hard penis she'd hoped to enjoy. "My shift starts in an hour, remember?"

He stepped out of the shower and reached for her hand. That was the kind of guy he was: attentive, chivalrous, and affectionate. Even something as simple as helping her out of the shower and wrapping her in a towel. It was the little things he did that she'd learned to not only expect but also enjoy and accept over the past few weeks that they'd hung out heavily.

"Jarrett, don't go," she said playfully, hugging him from behind as he began getting dressed for his overnight patrol shift.

"See, I knew that one-night stand would lead to this." He laughed.

Sabrina stepped back and put her hands on her hips. "Hey, you were the one who called me at six o'clock this morning telling me not to go to work, Officer Carmichael."

"Sergeant Carmichael," he turned around and corrected her. "Wait, is that my T-shirt?"

"Maybe." Sabrina posed in the "State Patrol Officer" T-shirt she'd slipped on after drying off that did belong to him. "I figured I'd borrow it."

"I guess that means you'll be keeping it, huh?" he asked.

"Feel free to take it back," she seductively suggested.

Jarrett pulled her close and kissed her. "If I didn't have to get out of here and get to the station, you know I would."

"Fine." Sabrina pouted.

"Yes, you are." Jarrett nodded. "That's why I gotta hurry and get the hell up outa here before I end up calling out. Thank you for a perfect day, though."

"You're welcome," Sabrina told him.

The day had been perfect, and she was grateful she'd taken the day off. When she had arrived at Jarrett's house, breakfast was ready. They ate together, then cuddled in his California king bed and binge-watched *Yellowstone,* a favorite show they both loved. They snacked on popcorn and chocolates throughout the episodes, pausing to discuss plot twists or share a laugh. At one point, their attention shifted from the television to each other, and they entered a marathon lovemaking session, leaving them both exhausted. Drifting off to sleep in each other's arms, they shared the most peaceful nap Sabrina had ever experienced.

"I'll call you later," he promised after they were dressed and walking out the front door. He escorted her to her car, parked in the driveway beside the same cruiser he'd been driving the first night they met. "We still on for dinner tomorrow night?"

"Of course. I love a free meal, especially when it comes with great company," Sabrina teased.

"Who said I was paying?" Jarrett's fake frown was as adorable as his smile.

"You did when you asked me out. You ask, you pay."

"I'll remember that next time you invite me out." Jarrett pulled her in for a hug. "I'll call you on my break."

"Please be safe, Jarrett." Sabrina put her arms around his neck. Now that he'd become close, the reality of the dangers of his job set in. His safety while working had become a concern.

"I will. And you don't be speeding, and keep them damn shoes on," he said, kissing her once more before opening the door for her to get in, then closing it. Sabrina watched him get into his car before finally backing out and driving away.

A loud vibration startled her. She looked down at her console and saw her cell phone, which she'd purposely left in the car, not wanting her time with Jarrett to be interrupted. Although they'd been routinely dating, because of both of their busy schedules, finding a way to spend an extended amount of time together had become tricky. It was also something that seemed to be more pressing to both of them since the "one-night stand" they shared that left them both wanting more.

Sabrina picked up the phone, looked at her missed call log, and saw that, had she taken her phone inside, the day definitely would have been interrupted. There were countless calls and texts. A couple were from Emily, as expected, asking why she wasn't at work even though she had Sabrina's location and knew where she was and who she was with. But there were also calls from her siblings, both of whom had been trying to reach her. Sabrina began to panic, thinking something had happened to one of their parents or both. She opted to call Tenille first.

"Hello."

The shakiness in her sister's voice instantly caused alarm. "Tenille, what's wrong?"

"Brina, where are you?"

"Uh, out and about." Sabrina hoped her vague answer would suffice and quickly deflected, "Why do you sound upset? What happened?"

"I don't even know where to begin. Jesus Christ, my day totally went from sugar to shit," Tenille groaned. "I can't believe it. It's like I'm not supposed to be happy at all."

"Ten, calm down," Sabrina told her sister as she pulled up her location. "I'm on my way."

Relieved that Tenille's distress wasn't the result of a family emergency but rather an emotional breakdown of some sort, Sabrina headed her way to find out what was troubling her. While en route, she called her brother.

"Nick, call me when you get this message," Sabrina said, leaving a message when he didn't answer. Disregarding Jarrett's instruction to not speed, she pressed the gas pedal to the floor and hauled ass to get to her sister.

"Damn, your day really did go from sugar to shit." Sabrina sat beside Tenille on the sofa, listening and sipping the oversized glass of wine that was waiting for her when she got to the house. "First, congratulations on landing the contract with the resort. That's huge, and I'm proud of you. You deserve it."

"Thanks." Tenille gave her a weak smile. "At least someone is proud of me."

"I'm sure Brandon is too. He knows how much blood, sweat, and tears you put into your business. Everyone does."

"I can't tell." Tenille shook her head. "All he cares about is a baby and a new house. That's all he talks about."

"Brandon doesn't have any children of his own. You can't be mad at him for wanting one now."

"The hell I can't. I told him from the jump that having more children wasn't something I wanted. I made that very clear before we got married." Tenille turned and glared at Sabrina. "Buying a bigger house damn sure won't make me change my mind. That's unfair to me. I don't want a baby with Brandon or a new house. At this stage in my life, I'm trying to build my brand and follow my dreams. If he really loved me, he would support me a helluva lot more than he does, the way other people do."

"But, Ten, you didn't have those dreams when you first got married either," Sabrina told her. "People change, including you. And as far as the way other people support you . . . no comment."

"Whose side are you on, Sabrina?" Tenille asked.

"I'm on your side, Tenille."

"I can't tell," Tenille yelled. "You sound like you're defending Brandon."

"I'm not defending anyone. I'm just stating the facts." Sabrina shrugged and gulped down the remainder of her wine.

"Wait, what's up with that shirt?" Tenille stared at the T-shirt Sabrina had forgotten she was wearing.

Sabrina put her glass down and tried to cover Jarrett's name and the law enforcement crest with her arms. "Nothing's up with it."

"You're lying. You usually dress up for work," Tenille's inquisition continued.

"I didn't go to work today. I took a mental health day."

"You were with the cop, weren't you? That's his shirt."

Sabrina's silence was all the answer her sister needed to confirm that her assumption was correct.

"Brina, you've gotta be kidding me. You're moving on too fast. It's too soon, and you shouldn't be dating anyone right now."

"What? It's not a big deal. We hung out today, that's all," Sabrina told her. "He's cool."

"And that's how it starts with you. You hang out because he's cool, and next thing you know, you're gonna be all caught up and have yet another ring on your finger that you'll end up taking off."

Sabrina's head snapped, shocked by Tenille's comment. "What the hell are you trying to say, Ten?"

"I'm saying that I thought you were taking a break from dating until you regrouped and figured out what it is you truly want in a partner. It hasn't even been three months since your breakup, and now here you are with a new guy." Tenille shook her head judgmentally. "You and Nick are just alike, and it's fucking ridiculous."

"What the fuck is that supposed to mean?" Sabrina slid to the edge of the sofa and turned toward Tenille.

"It means you're both selfish and have no regard for other people's feelings."

"That's not true and you know it. Nick may be a commitment-phobe, but I'm far from it," Sabrina said in defense.

"Please, you pride yourself on being engaged when the truth is you aren't in love. Being someone's fiancée just makes you feel less guilty about fucking the guy you're with. The only difference between you and Nick is that you get a ring out of your temporary flings, and he doesn't. If you both don't start doing some real self-reflection before jumping into these so-called relationships, you're gonna end up miserable."

Sabrina stood and stared at her sister. "I see why Brandon wants a new house, because that glass one you're in right now got you fucked up. If I recall, you got married six months after leaving the love of your life, and look at you now—miserable and stuck with the guy you were fucking. Guess you didn't reflect on yourself too much either."

Her words were hurtful but true, and Sabrina didn't regret them. The silence between them was deafening. Tenille didn't respond, and Sabrina didn't have anything else to say, so she left.

Chapter 32

Nick

"Noelle, it's me. Please call me back. I don't know what the hell is going on, but Ten just called, and I can't believe this shit. Sheridan, she . . . Just call me, babe, please."

Nick ended the call after leaving yet another message for Noelle. He'd tried calling and texting several times ever since his sister called, snapping.

"Ten, I swear—" Nick tried to get a word in edgewise, but Tenille was so livid that she kept cutting him off. She'd called while he was in his office, focused while going over team evaluations.

His sister's voice pierced through the phone, filled with a mix of anger and frustration that instantly put him on edge. "I don't need you to swear anything, Nick. I told you to leave her alone. I knew this shit was gonna happen. It's always some bullshit with you when it comes to females, and now you've brought it to my doorstep. My place of business is not your personal drama stage."

"I know that—"

"I can't tell. Not the way that homegirl rolled up here acting a damn fool." Tenille interrupted him again. "Oh, wait. She came to warn Noelle that she was still fucking you."

"What? She's lying, Ten." Nick finally managed to get out a full sentence, but his words didn't matter because his sister continued her rant.

"It doesn't matter if she was lying or not. You're lucky as hell I didn't have a client in the studio, and even though I didn't, it was still embarrassing for me and Noelle."

The anger Nick had for Sheridan was quickly replaced by concern for Noelle. He couldn't imagine what she was thinking or feeling, and he needed to see her. While Tenille chastised him like he was a high school kid who'd gotten caught skipping school, he quickly stood up and packed his briefcase, preparing to leave for the day. Damn the evaluations. He needed to get to his woman.

"Ten, you've gotta know that Sheridan is on some kinda bullshit. I don't even know how she found out about Noelle. I've never even mentioned her."

"Well, your boy Eric damn sure did."

Nick stood in the middle of his office, letting the revelation that Tenille had mentioned sink in, almost as if it were an afterthought. As the realization hit him, his eyes widened in disbelief.

"Wait, what did you just say? Eric told Sheridan?"

"He damn sure did," she confirmed.

It was damn near too much to process. Eric was one of his closest friends, someone he'd shared countless conversations with and confided in. Hearing that Eric had betrayed him like this was a blow that he wasn't prepared for. His mind raced, recalling their recent conversation about Sheridan, Noelle, and the understanding that he thought they had about the situation.

"I need to talk to him," Nick stated.

"You do that. But the damage has already been done, and this is one mess that's been created because of you, not Eric, and I'm the one who has to deal with the aftermath of all."

"You don't." It was Nick's turn to interrupt. "I'm gonna deal with it."

Ending the call abruptly wasn't intentional, but Nick was too caught in his own thoughts and emotions to even care. He stormed into Eric's office, his face a mix of anger and hurt. Eric looked up from his desk, his expression shifting from surprise to concern.

"Nick, what's going on, man?" Eric asked.

"Don't play dumb, Eric," Nick said, his voice tight. "I know that you told Sheridan about Noelle and me. What the hell?"

Eric's eyes widened slightly. "Look, man, I didn't mean for it to turn into this."

Nick's jaw clenched. "Well, it did. And now everything's a mess. My life is fucked. Why would you even say anything to her?"

Eric sighed, leaning back in his chair. "Nick, I only brought it up because you told me you were going to be honest with Sheridan. I thought she knew until she mentioned transferring to our office to be closer to you. I didn't want her to do that and end up hurt."

Nick's face flushed with frustration. "But you didn't have to say anything at all. I already told her I was seeing someone else. I just didn't tell her who because it was none of her business, and it wasn't yours to tell. Honestly, this feels like a betrayal. I considered you more than just a coworker. I thought you were my friend."

Eric shook his head. "I get that, but I was coming from a place of integrity. Unlike you, who kept quiet about your promotion, I thought I was being up-front. It wasn't meant to hurt you. I thought it would be better to clear the air."

Hearing Eric mention the promotion Nick was working toward came as a surprise, but Nick was too angry to respond to explain. "This ain't about the promotion, Eric. It's about trust."

"Exactly," Eric said.

Nick's silence was his only response as he walked out of the office, his mind racing with thoughts of what he needed to do next.

For hours, Nick rode around trying to clear his head. He knew that Noelle wouldn't answer, but he tried calling anyway and left voicemails and sent texts. He contemplated going to her house but didn't want to seem like a stalker. He didn't know what to do. For once in his life, he'd done the right thing and been completely honest with a woman, and it still resulted in becoming a clusterfuck. It seemed like the right time to reach out for some female advice, and since Tenille wasn't talking to him, he opted to call Sabrina.

"What do you want, Nick?" she answered, her tone letting him know that she knew the trouble that he'd unknowingly caused.

"Brina, you've gotta believe me, this isn't my fault," he said. "I already know Ten told you about what went down at her studio today."

Sabrina said slowly, "Listen, I'm not gonna pick sides. What you did behind Tenille's back, though, was foul, especially when she specifically told you to stay away from Noelle. This is the same thing that happened with Ivy."

"No, it's not," Nick insisted. "I didn't give a damn about Ivy. I care about Noelle, a lot."

"I hear you, Nick," Sabrina told him. "Either way, you're going to have to make things right with Tenille. There's no way around it."

Nick sighed, his frustration evident. "I know. I'm going to fix it. But right now, Noelle's my priority. I don't want to lose her."

"I get that," Sabrina said, her voice softening. "Honestly, I'm the last person who should be giving love advice right now. I'm tangled up in my own situation and some things I wasn't expecting."

"My bad, Brina. I didn't mean to add to your problems. I just needed to talk it out with someone."

"I get it," Sabrina reassured him. "We all have our own messes to deal with. Just remember, you've got to handle people with care. Fix what needs fixing and be honest with everyone involved."

"I will," Nick said, grateful for her understanding. "Thanks for listening, Sabrina. I appreciate it."

"And, Nick?"

"Yeah?"

"Try to extend Ten some grace right now. She's dealing with a lot. Bye."

Nick stared at his phone, contemplating Sabrina's words. His head hurt and his heart ached.

I've gotta make things right with my sister and Noelle. They both are too important to me, and I don't want to cause either one of them any kind of pain. At that moment, he realized he was in love.

Chapter 33

Sabrina

"Okay, you want my opinion, or did you just need to vent?"

Sabrina slumped onto her bed, clutching her cell phone as she listened to Emily, whom she called as soon as she got home from Tenille's. "I want your opinion."

Emily's tone grew more serious. "I know Tenille loves you, but I think she's wrong this time. I see the way you light up when you're with Jarrett. It's not just that you're happy. You're genuinely joyful. I've never seen you so . . . alive."

Sabrina sighed. "I agree. Jarrett brings out a side of me that people usually don't get to see. With him I'm fun, flirty—something I haven't felt in a long time. But maybe I rushed things. I haven't even been single for three months."

Emily was quick to reassure her. "But you're single, Sabrina. Timelines don't matter when it comes to love. It's about how you feel and what makes you happy. If Jarrett makes you feel this way, then it's worth exploring."

Sabrina appreciated Emily's support but felt conflicted. "Thanks, Em. I know you're right, but I'm still wrestling with whether I should've waited before getting involved with him."

"Don't act like you don't see that there's a spark between you. Everyone can see it. Tenille would too if she were around the two of you. For God's sake, you took the day off to spend with this man. You never take off. Hell, Mason had appendicitis and you didn't even miss work, remember?"

"Yeah." Sabrina smiled as she thought about telling Mason that her office was right across the street from the main hospital where he was admitted and she was only a phone call away. He wasn't pleased, and neither was his mom, but she left him anyway. Her patients were her priority. But when Jarrett asked, she had no problem calling and having her schedule cleared for the day.

"Listen, you wanna go grab some drinks? Or I can come over and we can drink there," Emily offered.

"Nah, I know you and Brady have plans tonight. Jarrett told me."

Emily chuckled. "Brady and I are meeting up later, but if you need me, I'm here. And honestly, you and Jarrett talking about me and Brady? That's cute."

Sabrina smiled at the thought, feeling a bit lighter. "Thanks for the perspective. It means a lot."

As they ended the call, Sabrina was grateful for her best friend's support. But a nagging doubt lingered in her mind, whispering that maybe Tenille's concerns were valid. Just as she was about to set her phone aside, a text from Mason popped up: Sabrina, I need you. It's an emergency.

Sabrina rolled her eyes as she ignored the message, focusing instead on the encouraging words from Emily. She knew she needed time to process everything before making any decisions about Jarrett. Her thoughts swirled around Tenille's words from earlier that day.

"You're moving on too fast, Sabrina. You shouldn't be dating anybody right now. You aren't in love. Being someone's fiancée just makes you feel less guilty about fucking the guy you're with."

As she replayed the conversation in her mind, her phone rang, jolting her from her thoughts. It was Jarrett, calling during his break.

"Hey, Jarrett," Sabrina answered, her voice betraying her inner turmoil.

"Hey, you. How was the rest of your day?" Jarrett's tone was light and jovial. Just the sound of his voice put a smile on her face and made her feel better.

"It was okay," she said, the fleeting moment of joy quickly fading as she thought about the words she'd exchanged with her sister earlier.

"That's good. So listen, I was thinking about our dinner date, and there's this new Korean barbecue spot I heard about that my sergeant was talking about. It sounds fun. You down to try it out?" Jarrett asked, oblivious to the conflict brewing inside her.

Sabrina hesitated, struggling to find the right words. "Jarrett, I . . . I don't think I can see you anymore."

There was a brief silence on the other end of the line. "What? Why? Did I do something wrong?"

"No, it's not you," Sabrina said, her voice trembling. "It's just . . . everything feels like it's moving too fast. I'm still figuring things out after my recent broken engagement. It's too much too soon."

"But, Sabrina, we have something special," Jarrett argued. "I really like you."

Sabrina took a deep breath, trying to steady her voice. "You're an amazing guy, Jarrett. You deserve someone who's sure about what they want, and right now, I'm not. I need to take a step back and figure things out for myself."

"I understand that you're scared, especially after your past relationships. I get that," Jarrett said, his voice softening, "but we can work through this together."

Sabrina shook her head even though he couldn't see her. "I don't think that's possible right now. I'm sorry, Jarrett. It's best for both of us if we just quit while we're ahead before things get too complicated."

"There's nothing complicated about it. I'm feeling you, and I know that you feel the same way. I'm not questioning that."

She hadn't questioned her growing feelings for Jarrett either until now. It wasn't as if she planned to fall for him. Hell, truth be told, based on the way they met, he would be the last person she expected to be cool with, let alone share a connection with. But she did. Or did she?

Is the spark because I started sleeping with him? Is it too much too soon?

"Goodbye, Jarrett," Sabrina said quietly. "You are a good guy and a decent human being. I hope you find what you're looking for. You deserve to be happy."

"Sabrina, you—"

"Goodbye," Sabrina repeated, her heart breaking as she ended the call. She sat there, tears welling. The weight of her decision pressed heavily on her chest as the drops fell from her eyes, streaming down her face.

The crying continued as she made her way to bed. The pain of ending things with Jarrett and the disagreement with her sister overwhelmed her.

As if her life weren't complicated enough, her phone rang again. She picked it up, expecting to see Jarrett's name, but it wasn't him. It was Mason. Sabrina ignored the call and did something she should've done a long time ago. She blocked him, then cried herself to sleep, feeling the ache of her broken heart and uncertainty of her future.

Chapter 34

Tenille

"Mom, this was great," Marquise said as they walked out of the Brazilian steakhouse. "You need to get more big contracts so we can celebrate here more often."

Tenille laughed at her son. Initially, she had planned on spending the evening moping at home, but after picking Marquise up from practice and sharing her good news, he suggested that they go to dinner and celebrate. She was so glad that they did.

"I'm glad you had fun, Mookie. And that is definitely the motivation I need to keep going."

"Like you always tell me, every step we take to reach our goals gets us one step closer, even the tiny ones. This contract is one step closer to you becoming the world-class photographer you always wanted to be." He put his arm around her.

"That's what I used to wanna be. Now my goal is to be the best mom in the world to my son." Tenille hugged him.

"You're already that."

Marquise's grin melted her heart. He was certainly her greatest achievement in life.

"You're just saying that because I agreed to let you attend Frazier. Don't even try it." She playfully pushed him away.

"No, I'm not. I really am happy for you, Mom. You work hard, and now the big companies are taking notice," Marquise insisted. "But since you got this new big contract that's gonna bring in the big bucks, you think I can get a new gaming computer?"

Tenille tossed her head back and laughed. "What?"

"I'm just saying. You're the one who said you wanted to be the best mother in the world, right?"

"Get your tail in this truck so we can get home." Tenille unlocked the doors. "It's already close to your bedtime."

They got into the truck, and as they headed home, Sparkle called.

"How was dinner?" she asked.

"It was so good. We went to Fogo De Chao, and it was amazing. Marquise loved it." Tenille glanced over at her son, who was already asleep. "He's currently in a food coma."

"I'm sorry I couldn't join y'all because of my worrisome-ass sister, but I'm glad your day ended on a positive note," Sparkle told her. "Did you talk to Nick?"

"Not since I cussed him out earlier. I can't believe him," Tenille told her. "He even called Marquise while we were at dinner to go through him to get to me."

Sparkle laughed. "That's funny."

"I'm glad someone thinks so," Tenille murmured. "Mookie handed me that phone, and I immediately hit the end call button."

"I guess you haven't talked to Sabrina either."

"Hell no. I don't have nothing to say to either one of my siblings," Tenille announced.

"You know your parents aren't going to go for that. They are going to make you talk to them, Ten," Sparkle insisted.

"Which is why I haven't talked to them either. Didn't even tell 'em about the Windstar contract." Tenille knew that mentioning her good news to her parents would lead to her mentioning the incidents with her siblings, and she didn't even have the energy or capacity to deal with their reactions or instructions to resolve their issues.

"And Brandon?"

At the mention of her husband's name, Tenille tensed and wanted to end the update conversation with her bestie. As much as she didn't want to deal with her siblings, she had even less of a desire to deal with her husband. They were definitely not seeing eye to eye on anything, and she wasn't sure if they would. At that moment, she turned onto their street, and as she pulled up to their house, she saw Brandon's truck in the driveway.

"Hey, girl, I just got to the crib. I'll call you tomorrow when I'm on my way to work," Tenille told her.

"Okay. Congratulations again, Ten. We'll celebrate this weekend," Sparkle told her.

"For sure. Let's make it happen," Tenille said as she parked beside Brandon. "Mook, wake up. We're home."

"Huh?" Mookie's eyes fluttered open, and he looked around. For a moment, he frowned and said, "Brandon's home? Shouldn't he be at work?"

"I guess he didn't go." Tenille shrugged. "Come on, get out."

As Tenille walked past Brandon's truck, she glanced in the back seat and spotted a leather oversized weekender bag that she'd never seen before. She thought about his mom's doctor's appointment earlier and wondered if whatever was wrong meant she'd be staying at the house overnight, or longer. Either way, Tenille wasn't too thrilled, especially since he hadn't mentioned anything about it.

"Good night, Mom." Marquise hugged her after they entered through the front door.

The house was dark and quiet, a clear indication that no one other than Brandon was home. Had his mother been there, the television in the den would've been on.

"Good night, Mook," she said. "Take a shower and brush your teeth before going to bed. And don't turn that game on."

"Yes, ma'am," he said, then hopped the stairs two at a time until he reached the top.

Tenille skipped the glass of wine she'd planned to have as a nightcap and instead went upstairs to her bedroom. She'd barely stepped into the master suite when she stopped and stared at Brandon.

"What are you doing?" she asked, confused by the open suitcase on the bed that he was packing. "Are you going somewhere?"

"Yep." Brandon barely looked up from the shirts he was folding and placing into the bag.

Confused, she stepped closer, her arms folded. "Where are you going?"

"I'm leaving, Tenille. This is over," Brandon replied.

"What do you mean '*this*'?"

Brandon turned and took a deep breath before pointing his finger back and forth. "This, whatever you want to call you and me, because it damn sure ain't a marriage, and it hasn't been for a long time. I kept trying to figure out why, and now I know, so I'm getting the fuck up outta here."

"What the hell are you talking about, Brandon?"

"I'm going to save both of us the time we'd waste going back and forth about how we got here and keep it simple. I know about everything, including you and Xavier."

Tenille stood in silence, stunned by Brandon's revelation. Her mind raced, trying to process his words. She hadn't expected this confrontation, not here and not like this.

Brandon continued, his voice tinged with hurt and frustration, "You saw him in Jamaica, had lunch, and you went to dinner after Marquise's game on your birthday."

Her heart sank. It was all true. They had spent time together, but in her mind, it had always been innocent, friendly. She struggled to find the right words to explain herself.

"Brandon, we're just friends," Tenille finally managed to say, her voice pleading. "Nothing more."

Brandon shook his head, his expression clouded with disbelief. "He's your fucking *ex,* Tenille."

"We were catching up, mainly about Marquise," Tenille insisted, her voice rising slightly in defense. "We talk about business, life . . . it's nothing more."

"Wow, nothing more, but he's helping you secure the location for the same expansion for your business that you just told me about earlier?"

"Yes," Tenille said, her voice lowered.

"Did you fuck him?"

"No!" Tenille insisted. "We're friends, that's all."

"You're lying to yourself, Tenille," Brandon said quietly, his tone heavy with disappointment. "And to me."

Tears welled up in her eyes as the weight of his words settled in. She knew she had crossed a line, even if it was just in perception. Brandon turned away, grabbing his keys and the suitcase from the bed. Then he walked out, leaving Tenille standing alone in the bedroom, grappling with the aftermath of their conversation and the realization that her friendship with Xavier had indeed blurred lines that she had tried to ignore.

Shit, Brandon left me. He really left me. More importantly, how the fuck did he find out about everything?

A loud chirp came from somewhere in the bedroom. She looked on the dresser and saw Brandon's cell phone, which he'd forgotten. She picked it up, planning to rush and take it to him. Against her better judgment, she looked down at the screen and read the text message.

Babe, is she home? Did you tell her? Does she know you're leaving her? Did you tell her about the divorce? What did she say?

"What the fuck?" Tenille whispered.

Another text message came across the screen. Brandon, answer me. Are you coming to pick me up and take me with you to the hotel? I love you. Now we can finally be together.

Tenille put the phone back on the dresser and sat on her side of the bed. She didn't even look at Brandon when he walked in a few minutes later and grabbed his phone.

"I'll get the rest of my things later," he told her. "I'm putting this house on the market tomorrow. Goodbye, Tenille."

Tenille didn't answer and remained silent until she heard the engine of his truck fade into the distance as he drove away. It all made sense. The mystery of how Brandon learned about her and Xavier was solved within minutes. It was a lot to deal with, and her heart ached from the betrayal. She tried to comprehend the fact that her home was being sold, her marriage was over, and her husband was having an affair with her best friend's sister.

Chapter 35

Sabrina

The sound of bells chiming drew Sabrina out of her sleep, and her eyes opened. The sun was already peeking through the blinds of her bedroom window. She reached for her phone to turn off her alarm when she looked at the time and saw that she still had ten minutes of sleep remaining. The chimes echoed again, and she realized that it wasn't her alarm but her doorbell.

"Who the hell is at my fucking door?" she snapped, sitting up and opening the security app to look at the camera on her doorbell. She expected to see Mason, and her heart skipped a beat when she saw that it was Jarrett, still dressed in his uniform. "He must've come straight from work."

As if he could sense her staring, Jarrett looked right into the camera and smiled, holding up a venti Starbucks cup. "Don't be mad. I come bearing gifts."

Sabrina hopped out of bed, did a quick check of her reflection in thc mirror, then hurried down the steps to greet him.

"Good morning, beautiful." Jarrett smiled when she opened the door.

"You know, I should really call the police and have your ass arrested for trespassing," she told him.

"You won't," he said. "Not when I have a nice white chocolate mocha with no foam, no classic, and six added Stevia for you."

The fact that he knew her favorite coffee order in such a short time was impressive enough for her to allow him to step inside. There was also the fact that he looked just as delicious as the beverage he hand delivered to her.

"Thanks," she said, taking the cup. "What are you doing here, Officer?"

"Wow, it's Officer? We're not even on a first-name basis anymore?" he said. "Don't be like that, Sabrina. I came so we could talk in person."

"I appreciate the effort, but talking face-to-face doesn't change what I said on the phone, Jarrett." Sabrina put the coffee on the small table in the hallway. Her mind was racing, and the tension between them was uncomfortable. "Listen, when we first started hanging out, I thought that it was going to be a casual thing. But now . . . it's just gotten complicated."

"Sabrina, if it were casual, I wouldn't have had you over to my place or spent so much time with you. I'm serious about us. That's what I was trying to tell you last night."

Her heart pounded as she processed his words. The reality of Jarrett's feelings hit her like a wave. "I didn't expect you to feel this way, I guess. I wasn't prepared for . . . I don't know."

Jarrett took a deep breath as he reached for her hand. "I get it. But if I'm being honest, that's what I expected too. But then as we began to spend time together, I realized how much I care about you—it's all more than just casual to me. I thought you'd know that by now."

"I care about you, Jarrett. But I'm fresh off a broken engagement. I wasn't expecting to dive into something serious so quickly."

"I told you, I understand your past is still fresh, but that doesn't change how I feel about you or what I want. I'm trying to build a future with you. If you're not looking for that, you need to be honest with yourself and with me."

Sabrina looked down at their joined hands, struggling to find the right words. She had always enjoyed their time together, but this new revelation threw her off-balance.

"I know this is a lot. I just wanted to tell you face-to-face how I feel. Take all the time you need. Just know that I'm here and I'm committed if you are."

As they stood in her foyer, the air between them charged with unspoken emotions, Sabrina was even more confused than the night before. The morning had unfolded in a way she hadn't anticipated, revealing a deeper level of commitment from Jarrett that she now had to consider. The sound of the doorbell chiming saved them both from saying anything.

"Did you order breakfast with this coffee?" Sabrina asked.

"Nah, I knew you had to get to work, but I was gonna offer to send you lunch." Jarret shrugged.

Sabrina walked over to the door and opened it. Her mouth dropped open, and her eyes widened in disbelief.

"Mason." Her voice was barely above a whisper. "What are you doing here?"

"Sabrina, please," he begged and took a step toward her. She could see that he'd been crying. "I need you."

"Mason, now's not a good time," she told him.

"My mother died," Mason sobbed, grabbing her and pulling her close.

Although she couldn't see him, Sabrina could feel Jarrett's eyes staring at the emotional chaos that was happening in real time. She didn't know what to do other than put her arm around Mason and hold him tight as he continued to cry.

Chapter 36

Nick

Nick drove up to his parents' house, the morning sun creating long shadows across the driveway. He had hoped to seek some fatherly advice about Noelle, but when he saw Tenille's SUV parked outside, he paused. He debated turning around but was stopped by his father, who had spotted him from the front porch.

"Nick!" his father called out, waving him in. "What a surprise. Come on in."

Nick hesitated, but he knew he couldn't avoid it. Reluctantly, he parked the car and walked up the driveway. He thought about what he was about to walk into as he entered the house. As soon as he entered the den, he was immediately met by Tenille's cold stare.

"Great, just what I needed," Tenille muttered under her breath.

Nick's patience was thin. "So I guess you came over here to tattle on me, Tenille?"

"Tattle? Boy, please. Mom and Dad know how you operate, especially when it comes to women. They are well aware of your constant whoring. I don't have to tell them anything."

Nick balked. "Whoring? Really, Ten? That's not who I am or what I do."

"Honestly, I don't care what you do, Nick. Screw whoever you want, whenever you want. Just stay away from

Noelle and keep your drama away from me," Tenille snapped.

"All right, enough," yelled their mom, who'd been sitting quietly on the sofa.

Nick immediately felt bad and walked over, kissing her forehead. "Sorry, Mom. I didn't mean to be disrespectful. You gotta know that I didn't mean for any of that to happen yesterday, and I apologized to Tenille immediately and tried to again last night."

"You really think everyone's life revolves around you, don't you?" Tenille sat back and shook her head.

"No, not at all. And just so you know, I'm not staying away from Noelle," Nick told her.

"See? It's always what you want, isn't it?" Tenille jumped up, stood in front of him, and they squared off. Although he was taller than his older sister, she was slightly larger. Despite knowing that things weren't going to get physical, he couldn't help but measure her and weigh whether he could take her down.

"Not usually, but this time I'm fighting for what I want, and that's Noelle," Nick yelled, refusing to back down.

"Like hell. You're not getting anywhere near her. She deserves someone a hell of a lot better than you, that's for sure." Tenille scowled, her hurtful words causing him to flinch slightly. "I know that for a fact."

"You don't know shit, Ten. I love her."

Before Tenille could respond, their parents intervened.

"Now, hold on a second," their father said, stepping between them. "Everyone just calm down."

"Nick, Tenille, sit!" their mother instructed.

Neither one moved. Instead, their attention turned to Sabrina walking into the den, looking confused and asking, "What's going on?"

Their father took a deep breath. "Well, since you're here, you should know. Tenille came over to tell us that

Brandon asked for a divorce and is cheating with Ivy. And Nick just told us that he's in love with Noelle."

Sabrina's eyes widened. "What? Oh God, Ten, I'm so sorry to hear about Brandon and Ivy. That's messed up."

Nick, shocked by the news about his sister and her marriage, immediately turned and said, "Ten, why didn't you tell me?"

Tenille didn't answer him. Instead, her attention remained on Sabrina. "Wait, why are you here?"

Sabrina's gaze softened. "Mason's mom passed away."

The room fell silent as everyone absorbed the news. The severity of the situation left a heavy weight in the air, making the personal conflicts that had sparked the argument seem minimal.

Their father sighed, trying to restore some sense of order. "All right, let's all take a deep breath. There's a lot going on, but it seems that we need to support each other right now."

"And we will." Their mother nodded.

Nick looked around at his family, realizing that despite the tension and unresolved issues, they needed to find a way to come together.

"I'm sorry, Ten." Nick hugged his sister, then grabbed Sabrina's hand. "I'm sorry for you too, Brina. I know this has to be hard for Mason, and you."

"How about everyone sit down?" their dad said.

The siblings all took their normal seats in the den: Tenille on the sofa beside their mother, Sabrina on the far end, and Nick on the arm of the recliner where his father sat. For a moment, it was as if they were teens about to be given ground rules about chores, school, and curfews. Instead, they were adults, still trying to navigate life's problems and seeking guidance from the two most important people in their lives.

"Brina, what I said to you yesterday about Jarrett was wrong, and I shouldn't have projected my problems on you. If you like him, dating him should be your decision, not mine." Tenille offered her apology. "I know how it feels to have someone on the outside of your relationship telling you what to do, and that's not fair or right."

"It's okay, Ten. I know it came from a place of both love and hurt," Sabrina said.

"Hurt is an understatement. I should've never listened to Sparkle. I wouldn't even be with Brandon. I'd be . . ." Tenille's words faded, and then she spoke up. "She's my best friend, and I thought she was right."

"Honey, there's a difference between a supporter and a spectator. Sparkle had a front-row seat," her mother stated.

"And obviously she has been telling her sister everything she saw." Tenille shook her head. "I can't believe I've been stupid all this time."

"No, Ten. You weren't stupid," Nick told her. "You were a good friend. She wasn't."

"Thanks, Nick," Tenille told him.

"You're also a good sister, and I love you," Nick replied.

"I always hated Ivy," Sabrina sneered.

"Same." Nick shrugged, then asked Sabrina, "So, you and Jarrett are a thing now?"

"No, I broke up with him last night and this morning." Sabrina shrugged. "I do like him, but I don't think the time is right for us."

"Time is right?" Their dad laughed.

"Yes, Daddy. I want to find true love like you and Mom that's strong, fun, enduring, and right on time," Sabrina explained.

"Our love is all of those things, but I don't know about the timing of it." Their mother laughed, reaching across to grab their father's hand. "You kids know about when and where we first met."

"At a funeral," they all said.

"Exactly. At the funeral of my abusive, hateful husband who happened to be your father's war buddy. They both served in the army, and he came to pay his respects," she said.

"I sure did. Your mama was sitting right there on the front row, looking like the most beautiful woman I'd ever laid eyes on in that black suit and hat with the veil. I was in love."

"And I was five months pregnant with you." She looked over at Tenille. "Can you imagine how everyone talked when your daddy began courting me? Believe me, they had plenty to say."

"I didn't give a damn about any of it. I knew that your mother was the one, and I promised to marry her if she let me. Thank God that she did, and thank God for that bus that hit him while he was drunk and crossing the street that night."

"Johnny!" their mother scolded him.

"What I'm saying is that the timing wasn't perfect, but the love was, Frances, that's all," he told her. "And I wouldn't have it any other way."

"Me either." She beamed at him.

Hearing his parents' love story brought Nick to tears. The way they still looked at each other after nearly forty years of marriage was inspiring and something he knew he wanted.

"You really love Noelle?" Sabrina asked.

"I do." Nick nodded.

"How do you know that, Nick?" Tenille questioned.

"Because she's the first person I think of when I wake up, and her voice is the last one I want to hear at night. We met over a decade ago, and I've never forgotten about her. It's like I've been waiting to find her again."

"Well, ain't that something?" Their dad smirked.

"I mean it, Dad. She reminds me of Mom in so many ways," Nick told him. "She's not just beautiful, but she's warm and funny and just makes me happy every time I see her. When I look at her, it's the same way you look at Mom—like she's your everything," Nick explained.

"Damn, you really do love her," Sabrina said, then quickly corrected herself. "I mean, dang."

"I'm praying that she forgives me and gives me another chance." Nick shook his head. "She won't even talk to me."

"She will, son. Don't worry," his mom said.

"You think so?" Nick asked, wiping the tears that had formed in his eyes.

"I know so. When the time is right." She stood and gave him a hug.

As they embraced, they were joined by the rest of the family. Despite all their troubles, they did exactly what their father said they would do: they came together to support each other.

Epilogue

One Year Later

The parking lot of Macedonia Baptist Church was filled to capacity, and so was the sanctuary. The sound of the organist playing softly could be heard in the choir room where the bridesmaids had gathered to wait for the ceremony to start.

"Are you okay? How are you feeling?" Sabrina asked Tenille, who stood near the window, fanning herself.

"Hot and nervous," Tenille answered. "What about you?"

"Same." Sabrina laughed. "Who picked these dresses anyway?"

"You did," Tenille reminded her.

"Oh, yeah, these were my choice."

Both dresses were strikingly elegant yet uniquely tailored to their individual styles, a deep, rich shade of burgundy, cascading to the floor in flowing, sophisticated lines. They had been the perfect choice six months ago, but now she wasn't sure. She regretted not choosing something lighter, cooler, and loose fitting. Despite feeling so constricted and uncomfortable, Sabrina was also happy, and so were the people she loved.

She recalled the family conversation they'd had in the living room a year earlier—a turning point for everyone. It was the day they had resolved to follow their hearts and embrace the reality that love is messy, unpredictable, and timeless. More importantly, they had learned that while love can be flawed and complicated, with the right person, it is undeniably perfect. It was a lifelong lesson learned from their parents that they'd witnessed firsthand.

"Well, duty calls." Tenille picked up her camera and aimed it at Sabrina.

"No, Ten," Sabrina whined, shielding her face with her hand.

"Fine, at least let me get a shot of that rock on your finger." She instructed, "Hold it up and say, 'Got him.'"

"I'm not saying that." Sabrina held her hand up and smiled so that her sister could get a decent photo of the gorgeous five-carat diamond.

"You're so boring." Tenille shook her head.

"Clearly, I'm not, considering I got him." Sabrina laughed.

"Yeah, well, so did I." Tenille held up her own ring that was just as fabulous.

"Checkmate," Sabrina agreed.

"Is Tenille in here?" Khalil's voice came from the other side of the room.

They looked over and saw him standing in the doorway looking quite dapper in his gray tuxedo.

"What do you want, Khalil?" Sabrina groaned. "Why are you in here? Shouldn't you be ushering in guests? That's what ushers do."

"Typically that's what they do, unless they are sent to find the photographer who's supposed to be taking pictures of the groomsmen before they get drunk while waiting for the wedding to start," Khalil said. Then he added, "Those were your mother's words, not mine."

"I'm on my way right now. Jeez." Tenille shook her head. "Does that woman not know that I've done this professionally for nearly ten years, not to mention that I'm not getting paid for this gig?"

"I'm sure she knows all of that," Sabrina told her.

"Oh, and, Brina, your baby daddy told me to make sure you had this." Khalil handed her a bottle of ginger ale.

Sabrina quickly snatched it and hissed, "First of all, that's my husband. And second, lower your damn tone. We haven't announced anything to anybody yet."

“Obviously Ten knew,” Khalil pointed out.

“Wait, how do you even know?” Tenille asked.

“I suspected when he asked me to bring you the soda, but your reaction just confirmed it.” Khalil laughed.

“Get out,” Tenille told him. “Tell the groomsmen that I’m coming in five minutes and they’d better be camera ready.”

“See, this is why I can’t do my job as an usher. I’m too busy running around delivering messages,” Khalil mumbled as he exited the room.

“Awww, that was sweet of him.” Tenille pointed to the soda Sabrina was holding. “He’s going to make a terrific dad, Sabrina. I’m happy for you.”

“He is amazing,” Sabrina agreed, grateful that he’d sensed that she’d been fighting nausea and needed some relief. “I couldn’t ask for a better husband. Jarrett is everything I wanted and more.”

After the conversation with their parents, it hadn’t taken long for Sabrina to realize that Jarrett was the man she wanted to share her life with. Especially when he supported her through the guilt she dealt with after Mason’s mom passed away. He navigated her feelings about her ex, who was grieving.

“You’re the only woman I have now that’s she’s gone,” Mason had cried to her one night when she called to check on him. “Please come back to me, Brina. I can’t be alone.”

“You’re not alone, Mason,” Sabrina told him. “You have family and friends there. You just have to let them support you the same way I am.”

“I don’t want their support. I only want you. It’s what Ma wanted. That’s what she was trying to tell you before she left here.”

“You can’t have me, Mason. I’m not yours.” Sabrina remained calm and was sincere in what she was telling him. “I’m sorry about your mom, and I’m sorry that I didn’t take the time to talk with her. That doesn’t mean that we’re getting back together.”

"Is this because of that police dude who was at your house? Is that who you're fucking now?" Mason demanded.

Sabrina took a deep breath and simply said, "Yes, I am. Goodbye, Mason."

That was the last conversation they had. Even after that exchange, Jarrett encouraged her to attend the funeral and pay her respects. She and Mason had hugged, but they didn't talk.

Jarrett gave her the time and space to deal with it all, but they remained close, talking daily and going on dates occasionally. He was so understanding and kind. He listened without judgment and allowed her to be herself even though their physical relationship was on pause.

"I love you, Jarrett," she told him one night when he walked her to the door.

Without hesitation, he said, "I love you too, Sabrina."

The kiss they shared was long, passionate, and gave her butterflies.

"Wait, does this mean you're ready to pick up where we left off?" he asked.

"I am." Sabrina nodded.

"Well, in that case . . ." Jarrett reached into his pocket and got down on one knee. Sabrina gasped as he looked up into her eyes and asked, "Will you marry me?"

Sabrina stared at the ring he was holding and laughed. "Yes."

He jumped up and kissed her again, this time lifting her into the air and swinging her around.

"Wait, so you carry an engagement ring around just for kicks?" Sabrina asked when he put her down.

"I've been carrying that ring in my pocket since the day I bought it, the day after we went axe throwing. I knew that night that I wanted to marry you. I was just waiting for the perfect time to ask," Jarrett answered.

They married three months later, Sabrina letting go of her dreams of a big church wedding and opting for a small, intimate ceremony with family and friends, planned by Tenille, her mother, and soon-to-be sister-in-law, Noelle.

"And to think you tried to break up with him." Tenille smirked.

"Good thing I didn't listen to your advice, huh?"

"You're right about that. When are y'all gonna make the announcement?"

"We're waiting until after the wedding. I'm only fourteen weeks, so we have time. We didn't want to distract anyone from today. This wedding is the event we never thought would happen." Sabrina laughed.

"I still can't believe our baby brother is getting married." Tenille shook her head in disbelief. "And to such an amazing woman."

"I can," Sabrina said, opening her soda and taking a sip. "The moment Nick stood in that den and told us how he felt about Noelle, I knew he'd found his forever. Lord knows it took him long enough."

"Tenille, the bride is asking for you," one of the bridesmaids yelled. "She just got here."

"Damn." Tenille looked down at her camera.

"You go get the pics of the groomsmen. I'll check on the bride." Sabrina put the top on her drink, and they both headed out.

Sabrina stepped into the church's waiting room and was momentarily caught off guard by the sight before her. Noelle stood there, radiant and poised in her wedding gown, which draped flawlessly over her curves. The gown was a masterpiece of intricate lace and delicate beading that made Noelle seem to glow. Her hair was styled in soft waves, perfectly framing her face, and her makeup highlighted her features with a subtle elegance.

"Noelle!" Sabrina gasped.

"Do I look okay?" Noelle asked nervously. "Where's Ten? I need her."

"She's taking pictures of the guys, but she'll be right here." Sabrina took her hand and gave her a reassuring squeeze. "And you look flawlessly gorgeous."

"Did you see the inside of the church? Is everything—"

"Noelle, everything is absolutely perfect. You did a great job with the flowers, candles, and all the other details. Now, calm down, because in about"—Sabrina looked at her watch—"ten minutes, you'll be walking down the aisle to become Mrs. Nicholas Chambers."

"Mrs. Nicholas Chambers. I love the sound of that." Noelle relaxed and smiled. "Thank you, Brina. One of the best things about marrying Nick is becoming a part of the family and gaining you and Ten as sisters."

"We're happy to gain you as a sister," Sabrina told her.

"Oh, and also getting Jarrett and Xavier as brothers and Mookie and Fabian as my nephew and niece. Oh, and your parents—"

"I get it." Sabrina laughed.

There was a knock on the door, and before they could give permission, Tenille entered. "Is she ready?"

"She is." Sabrina moved so Tenille could see.

"You look gorgeous." Tenille's voice cracked and tears filled her eyes.

"Don't make me cry, Ten," Noelle whined.

"Both of y'all better hold it together and get these pictures done. We're on a tight schedule, and I do not want to hear Mom's mouth."

"You're right," Tenille said and quickly began taking photos of Noelle. After she'd snapped a few shots, there was another knock at the door. This time the person on the other side waited patiently until Sabrina opened it.

"Is the bride ready?" Xavier asked as he stepped inside, looking extremely handsome in his tuxedo, a slightly darker gray than the one Khalil wore. He stared at Noelle and looked as if he were about to cry.

"Which one?" Sabrina teased.

"The one getting married today," he answered. "But I'll definitely take the other one if she's ready too."

Seeing them finally together brought Sabrina so much joy. Her sister's divorce didn't take long, and they celebrated with a huge party where Xavier did what he should've done years before: he proposed.

Tenille slid over and gave him a kiss. "I'm ready when you are."

"No, you can't have her today," Noelle commented. "You can have her at your own wedding in Jamaica in three months, sir."

"Then I guess you'll be the only one I'll be walking down the aisle and giving away." He smiled and reached for Noelle. "My bride-to-be will just have to wait."

"The two of you are going to have to wait too. I need to get these shots of you," Tenille told them and proceeded to snap away with the camera.

"Uh, I hate to interrupt, but it's time to start," Emily, who was serving as hostess, came in and told them. She handed all three ladies their bouquets and said, "Chop-chop, people."

Sabrina took one final look at Noelle on Xavier's arm and said, "I love you. You're a beautiful bride."

"Thank you." Noelle nodded.

"Let's go." Emily pulled her by the arm and out the door.

They rushed down the hallway to the vestibule of the church where Nick and the guys were assembled, pacing as they waited to enter the crowded sanctuary. The ceremony had already begun, the parents escorted inside and seated. Sabrina smiled at Marquise and Thaddeus, who were both Nick's best men, along with the other handsome groomsman, her husband. There was a slight tinge of sadness that Eric wasn't a part of the bridal party. As close as he and Nick had been, their friendship wasn't the same after the Sheridan fiasco.

"Babe, you good?" Jarrett walked over and hugged her. "You look gorgeous."

"I'm fine, boo," she said. "But not as fine as you in that tux."

The sound of Eric Benét's "Spend My Life with You" began playing from inside, causing Emily to clap her hands and whisper loudly, "That's your cue. Places, everyone."

Nick stood in front of the line, and directly behind him was Tenille, her arms linked with Marquise and Thad on each side of her. They were followed by Jarrett, who put his arm into Sabrina's. The doors opened, and they rhythmically, gracefully made their way down the aisle and took their places at the altar. The doors closed, and everyone waited for the bride to enter.

The soloist hired for the occasion began singing a beautiful rendition of "Inseperable," the same song their parents had danced to the day they got married. The doors opened, and the attendees stood as Noelle entered. Sabrina glanced at her parents, both crying. Then she looked at Nick, who was barely holding it together.

Sensing Jarrett's eyes on her, she looked across the aisle and smiled.

He mouthed the words, "I love you."

"I love you too," she returned to him, dabbing the tears that had formed.

Sabrina's heart swelled with joy as her attention went back to Noelle, the epitome of a perfect bride, now standing before Nick. She couldn't help but feel a surge of excitement, knowing with absolute certainty that Noelle was the ideal match for her brother. The genuine smiles as they looked at one another filled Sabrina with an overwhelming sense of happiness. Today was a day of celebration, and as Sabrina watched them exchange vows, surrounded by the people she loved, she felt an immense pride and a deep satisfaction that everything had fallen into place as it should, and love conquered all.

The End